ALSO BY ROB NETO

Fiction

Beyond the Grate
Into the Darkness Beyond
Beyond Hope

Adventure series

Beneath the Jungle of Cozumel: Connecting the Crowns
The Hidden Rivers of Florida: Discoveries

Non-fiction

Sidemount Diving The Almost *Comprehensive Guide 2ⁿᵈ edition*
Available in English, Dutch, German, and Spanish

BEYOND THE END OF THE LINE

ROB NETO

Published by Chipola Publishing, LLC,
Greenwood, Florida 32443, U.S.A.
www.chipolapublishing.com

Cover photography, artwork, & design by Rob Neto

Author photography by Jen Neto

PUBLISHER'S NOTE

This is a work of fiction. Names, characters, places, and incidents either are the product of the author's imagination or are used fictitiously, and any resemblance to actual persons, living or dead, business establishments, events, or locales is entirely coincidental. While the names of certain locales, such as Blue Spring Recreational Area and Jackson Blue Spring, are used to add depth and reality to the story, they are in no way meant to disparage such locales or past or present ownership of such establishments.

ISBN: 9781961612150

BEYOND THE END OF THE LINE

ROB NETO

Published by Chipola Publishing, LLC,
Greenwood, Florida 32443, U.S.A.
www.chipolapublishing.com

PUBLISHER'S NOTE

This is a work of fiction. Names, characters, places, and incidents either are the product of the author's imagination or are used fictitiously, and any resemblance to actual persons, living or dead, business establishments, events, or locales is entirely coincidental. While the names of certain locales, such as Blue Spring Recreational Area and Jackson Blue Spring, are used to add depth and reality to the story, they are in no way meant to disparage such locales or past or present ownership of such establishments.

ISBN: 9781961612150

DEDICATION

This book is dedicated to the memory of Marius Frei, a true explorer.

ACKNOWLEDGMENTS

First, I'd like to thank my readers. My books have been a success because of you. I especially thank those who have left reviews. The reviews help me learn what I'm doing right and what I'm doing wrong. They help me improve my writing and make my books better than the previous ones. Don't feel obligated to leave a review. but know that I do appreciate it when you take time out of your busy schedule to do so.

I would like to acknowledge Marius Frei. He died much too young while climbing a mountain in Switzerland. We never had a chance to dive with each other, but we did communicate often, and I learned a lot from him. His exploration projects in north Florida were amazing. He extended the end of the line in many passages that others didn't bother looking at. He pushed farther into caves than most. He had no fear. It is because of him that caves such as Jackson Blue and Hole in the Wall in Marianna, Florida, as well as Devil's Spring in High Springs, Florida are so much longer since their original explorations. His discoveries resulted in a lot of new guidelines being added to them.

Finally, I would like to thank my wife for supporting me throughout the writing of all of my books. I embarked on this writing journey many years ago. It has become a passion which has placed me in front of my computer for many hours writing, editing, and recording. She has not only had to be a sounding board to ideas I've had, but she's also been my first and last editor for each book that I've written. That means she's read each book at least twice. Her suggestions and advice have been invaluable to me. My stories are better because of her.

FOREWORD

The idea for *Beyond the End of the Line* was inspired by the explorations of Marius Frei, a cave diver from Switzerland that visited Florida often to search the underwater caves for unexplored, virgin passages. Marius was in Florida so frequently that he had an entire set of cave diving equipment stored here, including dive propulsion vehicles and a full-size van to carry it all during his adventures.

Marius and I never got to dive together unfortunately. His last trip to the United States was not long after I had moved to Florida. While our paths had crossed and we communicated with each other in private messages frequently, he had injured his back in a motorcycle accident and hadn't recovered enough to return to diving before his untimely death while mountain climbing in Switzerland. Just prior to his passing, we had been discussing his return trip to Florida so we could explore the caves together. Our last messages to each other happened only two days before he died.

Marius openly shared his exploration experiences with me and gave me advice on how to approach passages he had found and where he had laid line. He encouraged me to reach the ends of his lines and continue pushing the passages beyond. He wasn't possessive about his projects. He enjoyed underwater cave exploration and wanted to share his experiences with the world.

We planned on diving together and visiting many of his discoveries at some point. He had rehabilitated from his injuries enough to become active again. He was making preliminary plans to return to Florida. Sadly, he died before that trip happened. I was in shock when I heard the news. His loss was a tragedy to cave diving as much as it was to his family and friends.

In his memory, I named one of the passages that led to a very large section of a cave that Marius found the Freiway. Unfortunately, he was never able to see just how much cave passage had been lined after his discovery of this passage.

Some of Marius' discoveries were claimed by others to be their own. Because he didn't live in Florida full-time, Marius wasn't able to dispute these claims. Truthfully, Marius didn't care and wouldn't have bothered to dispute them if he had lived in Florida. He wasn't after the notoriety. He just enjoyed underwater cave exploration and had the desire to find new places where no one had ever been.

The idea for this story came from these false claims to Marius' discoveries. That's the extent of the similarities between the story and reality. Joey gets upset over being scooped. It didn't bother Marius at all. Not being bothered doesn't make for a good story, though. Getting upset and possessive brings a lot of drama to the situation. And that makes for a great story.

* * *

Parts of this book contain spoilers for *Into the Darkness Beyond*. You can read this book without having read the other first, but you are forewarned that it may alter your experience when you decide to

FOREWORD

The idea for *Beyond the End of the Line* was inspired by the explorations of Marius Frei, a cave diver from Switzerland that visited Florida often to search the underwater caves for unexplored, virgin passages. Marius was in Florida so frequently that he had an entire set of cave diving equipment stored here, including dive propulsion vehicles and a full-size van to carry it all during his adventures.

Marius and I never got to dive together unfortunately. His last trip to the United States was not long after I had moved to Florida. While our paths had crossed and we communicated with each other in private messages frequently, he had injured his back in a motorcycle accident and hadn't recovered enough to return to diving before his untimely death while mountain climbing in Switzerland. Just prior to his passing, we had been discussing his return trip to Florida so we could explore the caves together. Our last messages to each other happened only two days before he died.

Marius openly shared his exploration experiences with me and gave me advice on how to approach passages he had found and where he had laid line. He encouraged me to reach the ends of his lines and continue pushing the passages beyond. He wasn't possessive about his projects. He enjoyed underwater cave exploration and wanted to share his experiences with the world.

We planned on diving together and visiting many of his discoveries at some point. He had rehabilitated from his injuries enough to become active again. He was making preliminary plans to return to Florida. Sadly, he died before that trip happened. I was in shock when I heard the news. His loss was a tragedy to cave diving as much as it was to his family and friends.

In his memory, I named one of the passages that led to a very large section of a cave that Marius found the Freiway. Unfortunately, he was never able to see just how much cave passage had been lined after his discovery of this passage.

Some of Marius' discoveries were claimed by others to be their own. Because he didn't live in Florida full-time, Marius wasn't able to dispute these claims. Truthfully, Marius didn't care and wouldn't have bothered to dispute them if he had lived in Florida. He wasn't after the notoriety. He just enjoyed underwater cave exploration and had the desire to find new places where no one had ever been.

The idea for this story came from these false claims to Marius' discoveries. That's the extent of the similarities between the story and reality. Joey gets upset over being scooped. It didn't bother Marius at all. Not being bothered doesn't make for a good story, though. Getting upset and possessive brings a lot of drama to the situation. And that makes for a great story.

* * *

Parts of this book contain spoilers for *Into the Darkness Beyond.* You can read this book without having read the other first, but you are forewarned that it may alter your experience when you decide to read the second book in the *Beyond* series.

There is a diver mentioned in this book by the name of Doron Nof. Doron was real and did as described in this book. He was a good friend, and I was able to enjoy some dives with him before he passed in 2022 from natural causes at the age of seventy-eight. I miss my talks with Doron. He was a good person.

Other than parts describing the inside of the Jackson Blue cave system, the details presented in the following pages are products of the author's imagination. The unexplored cave passages are made up. However, the rest of the cave is described accurately, including the details about the ceiling collapse which occurred in 2014.

The characters are not real and not intended to represent any persons living or dead. There are incidents in this book which are true. Included are references to other incidents that have happened to cave divers. This is all done to add a realistic element to the story.

In no way is this story or any of the scenes included in it intended to disparage the reputation of any living or dead person. The story is fictional from beginning to end with only parts of real events inserted to add a sense of reality. The actual divers involved in the incidents are not a part of this story and nothing in this story is meant to be applied to them or how they handled their own situations.

* * *

This book is a work of fiction. The characters, incidents, and dialogue are drawn from the author's imagination and are not to be construed as real. Any resemblance to actual events or persons, living or dead, is entirely coincidental. This story is simply one in which the author creates a story based on his imagination of what could have happened. The snippets of fact embedded in the story are included to give it more depth and reality. They are by no means implicated in any wrongdoing by anyone.

There is no Joey Simmons. There is no Lindsey Carter. The other characters in the story do not exist. These characters are imaginative creations. This work of fiction simply takes an element of reality and creates a tale of fictional events to tell a story.

Every explorer I have met has been driven—not coincidentally but quintessentially—by curiosity, by a single-minded, insatiable, and even jubilant need to know.

— Jacques-Yves Cousteau, 6/11/1910 – 6/25/1997
The Human, the Orchid, and the Octopus: Exploring and Conserving Our Natural World

1

Joey

"I can't believe someone scooped my lead! That's not cool! I've been working that area for months. I've surveyed and mapped it. I've spent more than twenty hours exploring that section of the cave."

"Babe, calm down."

"I don't wanna fuckin' calm down! That was my lead! That was my cave to explore. Whoever it was didn't just extend the end of my line by a couple of hundred feet. There are hundreds of feet of lined passages back there now, maybe thousands, beyond the end of *my* line!"

"We'll get back there and survey it and add it to your map and then continue to explore it."

"We don't have time for that. We have to get to the end of the line and keep pushing. The survey will have to come later. If we try to survey the new line we found today, whoever placed it there will keep pushing the end of the line farther and farther and we'll never get caught up. We'll never get to put in more line."

"Yeah, you have a point. So we'll go back there next weekend and find the new end of the line. Whoever did this probably left a line arrow with his initials or his name on it. We'll know who it is then. But I don't know what difference that will make."

"It'll make a difference because I'm going to find that asshole and set him straight. That's my find! That's my exploration! He has no right being back there!"

"What are you going to do? What can you do? You can't kick

someone's ass because they don't give a shit about cave diving etiquette."

"Why not?"

"Well, maybe because that could get you arrested for assault."

"He stole my lead!"

"That's not a crime, babe."

"But…FUCK!"

That wasn't what I wanted to hear. I wanted Lindsey to be supportive and back me on this. I didn't want her to talk sensibly. I stomped around the room looking for a way to get rid of the feelings I was having, a way to deal with my anger. I turned toward Lindsey, "Dammit! It's just so frustrating!"

"I know it is. We've worked hard on this. Especially you. You've put a lot of hours into this project."

Lindsey got up from her place on the couch. I started to move around the room again looking for something to hit. I was that mad. She was probably coming over to comfort me, but I was too upset. I had to release the tension. I didn't want to break anything, especially my hand. It wasn't worth it. But I had to get my frustration out somehow.

"Aaaaaaaaahhhhhhhhhhh!!!!!"

"Feel better now?" Lindsey said as she backed away.

It was pissing me off that Lindsey was being so calm and rational. She had put almost as much work as I had into this project. With the exception of the weekends she had to teach, we were both in the back of Jackson Blue exploring the new section we had found. Why wasn't she as angry as I was?

"No, I don't. I won't feel better until I have the end of the line to claim as my own again. And I don't want to wait until next weekend to get it back. By then it might be too late."

"What are you going to do? We can't go back there tonight. We already did a three-hour dive today. And you're way too upset to be able to dive safely."

"I can control it. I just need to get back there and look around. I

need to see how much passage has been lined. I need to see how far the asshole that did this has gotten."

"We'll find out in due time."

"But what if he goes back there during the week? What if while we're stuck at work, he's in the cave pushing more virgin passage? What if he's in the cave extending the end of the line hundreds or even thousands of feet more?"

"What if he is doing that? You can't just stop going to work to go cave diving every day. Yeah, that would be nice, but it's not realistic. We're not rich and can't afford that. We have rent to pay and food to buy. Besides, our light and scooter batteries aren't even charged."

"Dammit! I didn't think about that!" I continued to pace around the room. "Who could it be? Who could have known we were working that area of the cave? I haven't told anyone. I haven't posted anything about it on social media. I've been careful not to go back there if anyone else was in the area."

"It wouldn't be too difficult to figure it out. We have safety tanks in the cave. Sure, they're tucked away, but they can still be seen from the line if you're looking. And you've been leaving your line markers all over the place marking the lines that you've surveyed. All someone would have to do is come across some of those and they'd quickly figure out you were doing something back there."

"Dammit! That was stupid! I should have figured out another way to mark those lines." I dropped onto the couch next to Lindsey.

"Well, hindsight babe. We can't change the past."

"I can change the future though. I'm going to find out who did this and I'm calling him out on it."

"Let's cross that bridge when we get to it. Let's find out who this is first."

I grabbed the pillow that was on the couch next to me and punched it. I punched it again. And again and again. It wasn't helping. I needed something more substantial. I needed to break something. Just then Lindsey took the last swig from her beer and set the bottle on the table. I quickly snatched it up, stood, and looked around. Seeing nothing I could throw it against without causing major damage, I walked toward the door to our balcony.

"Where are you going? Why do you have my beer bottle?"

I yanked the door open and stepped outside, slamming the door shut behind me. I wished it was a swinging door instead of a sliding door. Sliding doors didn't have the same effect when slammed. I looked around the apartment complex. I couldn't see anyone in the parking lot. I flung the beer bottle over the banister toward the sidewalk below with all of the force I could muster. It crashed on the edge of the sidewalk and broke into hundreds of little pieces, most of them flying onto the mulch landscape. It wasn't as satisfying as I had hoped. I should have gone out the front door, down the steps, and gotten closer to the sidewalk. Or better yet, I should have walked out to the dumpster across the parking lot and slammed the bottle against its side.

I turned around and stormed back into our apartment. Lindsey was sipping beer from a newly opened bottle.

"Do you feel better?"

"No!" She must have seen me through the door. I grabbed her bottle and gulped the beer down in one long swallow.

"Hey! That was my beer!"

I ignored Lindsey, turned around, and stormed back out of the room. This time I went out of the front door and slammed it. That was much more satisfying than the sliding door had been. I walked down the steps, through the breezeway, and across the parking lot. When I was only five feet from the dumpster, I flung the bottle as hard as I could against its side. The bottle shattered into thousands of pieces. I felt small bits of glass hitting my face and my bare arms and legs as they ricocheted back toward me.

Now I felt better.

2

5 hours earlier

What the fuck!?!?! I couldn't believe what I was seeing. I had just laid the line I was following farther into the cave the day before. This was virgin passage before that. Unexplored and unoccupied by a human and never exposed to light prior to me swimming through it as I extended the previous end of my line. This was where I had stopped and turned around because I had breathed the air in my scuba tanks down to our agreed turn pressure. I hadn't been ready to turn around and exit the cave. I still had knotted line on my reel. I had hoped to surface with all of the line left behind in previously uncharted tunnels in the cave.

The problem was that I had breathed one-fourth of the air in my sidemounted scuba tanks. That left me with one-fourth to make my way to the stage tank I had left a couple thousand feet back and the remaining half reserved for any potential emergencies. Usually, we allowed ourselves one-third for the penetration, one-third for the exit, and one-third for emergency reserves. Except we were using dive propulsion vehicles, also known as underwater scooters, to get us through the mile plus of cave from the entrance to this point much faster. The scooters cut our penetration time down to about a third of what it would be if we had to swim that distance. If the scooters broke and we had to swim out, one third of the air in our tanks wouldn't be enough to get us back to the surface. I shuddered as I thought back to that time I had gotten stuck in this very cave near the traffic light that marked the beginning of the Trash Room.

I couldn't continue to push into the virgin passage safely at this point. I couldn't keep going even though I had more knotted line on my explorer reel and the cave passage in front of me was still large and inviting me to continue pushing forward. I didn't know what was beyond the end of the line. I didn't know what waited for me around the next corner. As much as I wanted to find out, I couldn't guarantee that my dive equipment wouldn't have a malfunction on the way out. If something happened that delayed my exit, I might need every bit of the emergency air reserves in my scuba tanks.

I learned the lesson of the importance of sticking to the plan the hard way a few months earlier in Mexico. I kept swimming farther into the cave, looking around the next corner, ignoring the pressure gauges on my tanks. I pushed it a little too far. I was lucky I got out of that cave alive. Lindsey was lucky to have survived. I endangered both of our lives. I swore that day that I would never push the limits again. Yet here I was contemplating it and trying to justify it. Reason won out this time. I had breathed through the first fourth of the air in my sidemounted tanks and had to tie off the guideline I was laying in this tunnel, no matter how much I wanted to go a little farther and see what was around the next corner only twenty feet ahead.

But it was only twenty feet…

No, I couldn't do it. The last time I ignored the limits it didn't turn out well. So I grudgingly secured my line to a formation sticking up out of the floor and cut it, leaving a loop on the end so I could easily secure more line to it the next day. I placed a personalized line arrow onto the guideline just three inches from the end pointing back toward the exit more than a mile behind me. I formed another loop on the end of the line on my explorer reel, took in the slack, and secured the loop to the lock screw. I then clipped the reel to one of the D-rings on the back of my harness. I turned around, shoulders slumped, and began to survey the line I had laid. It was always bittersweet. I was happy to have found more virgin cave passage and to have been able to place line in it. But I was sad that I had to turn around and leave the cave. It might not have been so bad if I didn't have such a long distance to travel through the cave to get to the area each time. We were pushing a mile and a half with the line I had left the day before.

The marker personalized with my initials would serve as my claim to the guideline and the exploration being done in that area of the cave. That and the loop showing that I intended to come back and continue my exploration. It was a trick I learned from a more experienced underwater cave explorer. I had found some of his old leads that were left like that, recognized the name on the line arrows, and reached out to him. He hadn't been back in those areas in years and gave me his blessing to continue pushing the passages. I did, but most of the tunnels ended only a few hundred feet later.

The loops weren't completely unknown. Anyone who had the experience to be this far back in the cave should know they meant exploration was still ongoing and should respect that. At least that was my thought on the matter. Apparently, that wasn't universal. Someone had come into the cave, to this very spot, and scooped my lead. He had tied his own line into my loop and continued to line my lead. My passage. It wasn't right!

My personalized line marker and the loop were clear indicators that I was planning on returning to keep pushing the passage. The line was obviously newly placed in the tunnel. It was still as bright as if it had been bleached the day before. Cave diving etiquette dictated that it should have been left alone. My line should not have been extended by anyone but me. Yet, here I was, looking at my line, and seeing someone else's line extending into the darkness and around the corner into the virgin cave tunnel I had found. This was bullshit!

I turned toward Lindsey and pointed to the atrocity I was looking at. She shrugged her shoulders like it was no big deal. Like it didn't bother her that someone had come into the cave and stolen a lead that we had worked hard to find. It didn't seem to faze her one bit. I turned away and continued to follow the line. I had to see how far the tunnel had been pushed. I had to see what was around that next corner. I should have pushed that last twenty feet the day before! Hopefully, whoever had done this hadn't put very much line in. How far could he have gotten? Especially without being familiar with this area of the cave.

We were almost eight thousand feet from the cave entrance. More than a mile! It took us a little more than an hour to get there using our scooters. If we were able to leave our jump lines in place overnight, it would take us less than an hour. But we didn't dare leave our jump lines. We didn't want someone to see them, follow them, and find the area where we had been working. Apparently, it didn't matter. Someone found it anyway. We might as well have left the jump lines.

I thought back to the first time my cave diving instructor taught us about jumps and gaps and how to deal with them inside of a submerged cave.

"I don't understand. Why aren't the lines all connected to each other? Why bother leaving gaps in them?" I asked Adam, my instructor.

"Think back to the dives you've been doing at the intro cave diver level and what your limitations have been," Adam replied.

"I could only breathe one-sixth of the air in my tanks before having to turn and exit the cave. I couldn't go deeper than one hundred feet. I had to stay on the main line in the cave. No navigational decisions."

"Exactly! And how many lines going off to side tunnels have you seen just here in Jackson Blue?"

I thought about it for a moment. The Horseshoe Circuit, Young's Siphon, Parallel Line, the Squirrel Tunnel. Those were all loops that started and ended on the main line. That was eight jumps just in the first four hundred feet.

"Okay, I get your point. If the lines were left connected to the main line, intro cave divers would have to turn around long before they reached their turn pressure. But what about farther back in the cave? Beyond where intro cave divers might go? Why are there gaps back there?"

"Well, part of that is force of habit. We're so used to having gaps in the front of the cave that we continue to have them throughout. Although, once you start heading farther into the cave, you'll notice there are a lot more intersecting lines. There are even some gold line Ts where white cave lines tie into the main passage gold line." Adam said referring to the places where the lines in the offshoot tunnels

were tied to the line in the main tunnel. "As you get off the main tunnel and into the smaller side tunnels, you'll see even more intersecting lines. You'll still see some jumps along the main tunnel simply because the rules state you have to mark all navigational decisions. A line intersection is a navigational decision and requires you to stop and place a personalized line marker on the guideline leading out of the cave. Usually, if you're that far back, you're on a scooter and stopping isn't as convenient as when you're swimming."

"That makes sense."

"Another thing is exploration. Anyone doing exploration in a cave isn't going to want to mark the way to where they're exploring. Explorers will typically leave longer gaps to try to keep others from finding the path to the area where they're exploring."

That had been my first lesson in underwater cave exploration. Having these gaps in place, especially the longer ones, kept some divers out of the less traveled offshoot areas. They either didn't know about them, or they were too lazy to bother placing longer jump lines. Except this time. This time, someone found the area I had been exploring. And that someone stole my lead.

Cave diving etiquette dictated that if someone was working on an exploration project in a cave, that area was off limits to other cave divers as long as the exploration was ongoing. I'd been working in this area for months and diving it every weekend with few exceptions, so there was no reason to think my exploration wasn't ongoing.

But I wasn't talking about it. I was worried about someone hearing about my find and ignoring cave diving etiquette. That kept me from saying anything about it. So did this person technically scoop my lead? If it wasn't common knowledge that I was exploring this cave, could it be considered bad form? I didn't know and, at that moment, I didn't care. All I cared about was that my lead had been scooped, and I had to find out how much line had been laid beyond the end of my line. I went around the corner twenty feet past the end of my line and the cave passage opened up even bigger. The tunnel must have tripled in size!

Not only was this going to be a fight to keep the end of the line, but now I had walls in a dark cave that were at least forty feet apart from each other. Finding new leads off of this main tunnel was going to be a lot more difficult. I wished I hadn't left my scooter behind. It was slow going swimming farther into the cave. I wanted to zoom over the line to get to the end of it so I could tie in the line from my own reel and take back the end of the line for myself. I continued swimming as quickly as I could, looking around occasionally to see if any leads off of this tunnel jumped out at me. I was more concerned about where this line went, though. How far had the thief gotten?

I looked at my dive computer display. I had already swum ten minutes beyond the end of my line. Ten minutes! At my usual swim pace of fifty feet per minute, that meant five hundred feet. I was moving a bit faster than that though. Maybe sixty to seventy feet per minute. My end of line had been extended six to seven hundred feet. So far. I wasn't at the end of this new line yet. And I didn't see the end in sight.

As I swept my light beam around the tunnel, I noticed a line heading to the right. The tunnel looked like it kept going straight beyond that. Had the thief decided to turn right for some reason? I kicked harder and sped up even more. A few seconds later I saw that the line continued straight and the line I had seen was tied into it heading to the right. Whoever did this not only extended the end of my line but had also explored tunnels shooting off from this one.

How was I going to get all of this surveyed and continue my exploration? Fuck the survey! I just needed to find the end of the line and reclaim it as my own.

I noticed another light behind me. It was slowly moving side to side, the light signal used to get another diver's attention. I looked back. It was Lindsey. I had forgotten she was with me. I reluctantly stopped and turned around, frustrated that she was preventing me from continuing and getting to the end of this line. Lindsey pointed her index finger up and circled it around, the hand signal for turning around. What the hell? I shook my head no. She circled her finger again and then pointed at the pressure gauge on one of her tanks. I reflexively looked at my own pressure gauge. The needle was pointing at twenty-seven hundred psi. That was our turn pressure. I had breathed through one fourth of the air in my sidemount tanks. Fuck!

3

Lindsey

I slowly walked toward Joey. He was standing in the parking lot among pieces of broken glass in front of the apartment complex dumpster. I looked around but didn't see anyone else. Thankfully, no one had witnessed his outburst. I had never seen him like this. He was normally quiet and reserved. Joey wasn't one to make a scene. It was very out of character for him. I approached cautiously.

"Joe? You okay?"

He turned around to face me and raised his arms. I instinctively jumped back. I didn't know why but I was afraid he was going to hit me. He had never touched me in a bad way so there wasn't a reason for me to feel like he would do such a thing. Except I had also never witnessed him behaving this way. When I stood up inside the apartment he walked away from me. I wasn't quite sure what was going on or what might happen next.

"Yeah, I guess."

He reached out for me, and I flinched again.

"What's up with that? Why are you jumping away from me?"

"I don't know, Joe. I'm not meaning to do it. I've just never seen you behave this way. It's a reflex."

"I'm not going to hurt you. I would never do that! I'm sorry I lost it. I don't know what came over me. I'm just so angry at what happened."

"I know, babe. I'm upset about it, too. We'll deal with it. We'll find out who did this and confront him. That much I promise."

I reached out to Joey and pulled him into my arms. As I held him, I could feel his body trembling. This thing really had him upset. More than upset. It was affecting him physically. We stood in the parking lot surrounded by little brown bits of broken beer bottle until the headlights of a car came around the corner. I pulled back from Joey before the lights swept around and flooded us. I started sweeping as much of the glass to the side as I could, trying to be careful not to cut my feet in the process. I was wearing flip-flops. Joey had hit the side of the dumpster with so much force that there weren't any pieces large enough to cause a flat tire, but I didn't want to take any chances. Joey started sweeping pieces to the side with his flip-flopped feet as well.

Fortunately, the car pulled into an empty space on the other end of the lot and never reached us. We continued to sweep the glass aside.

"Stop that before you cut your feet. I'll go get a broom," Joey said as he turned to run to the apartment.

I followed him to the curb just as the driver of the car shut the engine off and stepped out. She briefly looked our way. That's when I recognized Kelly, one of our new neighbors. She moved in about a month earlier. We had all hung out together a few times already. Joey wasn't fond of her and always complained about her drinking our beer. I thought she was nice. A little awkward, but nice. And she was fun. She worked as an ER nurse and had a lot of great stories about her experiences. Sometimes she seemed to share too much, though. I always thought patient interactions were supposed to be private. Maybe it was just the beer loosening up her tongue.

As I waited for Joey to return, I watched Kelly pull out shopping bag after shopping bag of groceries. A lot of groceries for just one person. Maybe she liked to get all of her shopping done once a month. The bags kept coming. She was holding at least ten so far. It looked like she was going to attempt the one trip shopping bag carry or die trying. I was about to walk over to offer a hand when I heard Joey's flip flops smacking the pavement as he ran through the breezeway.

"Here. I even brought a dustpan to pick up the pieces."

"Do you think breaking that bottle was worth all of this extra trouble?"

"Definitely! When that bottle smashed against the side of the dumpster it was like a vise had released its grip on me. All of this pressure just blew out. I would definitely do it again." Joey said with a shit-eating grin on his face.

Boys! Why does everything have to be physical with them?

"Hey, don't forget to gather up as much of the glass from around the sidewalk as you can, too."

I walked over to the sidewalk below our balcony and picked up the larger pieces, trying to be careful to not cut myself, while Joey swept up the glass near the dumpster. The balcony bottle hadn't broken into pieces as small as the one slammed against the side of the dumpster. I tossed the larger pieces I had gathered into the trash as Joey was finishing his task. I grabbed the broom from him, walked back to the sidewalk and did my best to sweep the broken bits from the mulch onto the sidewalk where it would be easier to get into the dustpan. Joey walked up next to me and held the dustpan while I swept the pile into it. As he walked back to the dumpster to dispose of the incriminating evidence, I swung the broom back and forth over the mulch to try to get the remaining bits buried. I really hoped Joey had gotten relief from his outburst.

I glanced back at Kelly to see how she was doing with the one trip shopping bag endeavor and watched her struggle across the parking lot with what looked like at least a dozen shopping bags swinging from each arm.

"How do you suppose she's going to get her door open with all of those bags?" Joey asked as he walked up beside me.

Kelly glanced at us, tilted her head to the side, and the corners of her mouth turned up in a crooked smile.

"I have no clue. I'm not even sure how she's going to get upstairs with that mess. The elevator is broken again. We should walk over and offer to help."

"It's more entertaining to watch her struggle."

I lightly punched Joey in the arm.

"Yeah, but is it the neighborly thing to do?"

Just then one of the bags Kelly was holding burst at the bottom seam and the contents dropped to the asphalt in a crash. By the sound of it, among the contents were glass bottles.

"We already have the broom and dustpan out. Might as well help her now."

We ran toward Kelly.

"Let us help you with those bags," Joey called out as he handed the broom to me. I was a little surprised he said anything.

Joey grabbed the entire lot of bags from her and set them down on the ground a few feet away from the broken bottles that I could now identify as what used to be a six-pack of Bud Light. Not a single bottle survived the impact. At least her tastebuds would survive for one more night.

"Before I pick these bags up again, is there anything else breakable in them?"

"No, that was all that was breakable. I told the bagboy to double bag that one. I guess he ignored me. And that was my beer," Kelly whined. "Why do things like this always happen to me?"

"Maybe you should have made a couple of trips up the steps instead of trying to carry everything all at once," Joey said with a laugh. I smacked his arm again.

"That's not nice, Joseph!" I chastised him.

"No, it's okay. I deserved that. I guess I over did it a little. I shouldn't have tried to bring everything in at once. I just hate those stairs. I wish I could have gotten a ground floor unit. I didn't realize the elevator would always be broken."

Kelly was a shorter than me and sported straight dark brown hair with a slight reddish tint that ended just below her shoulders. Her most distinguishing feature was her high forehead. She kind of reminded me of Dooneese from that Kristin Wiig SNL skit years ago. Except Dooneese wouldn't have been able to carry all those shopping bags because of… Well…

"We'll help you get this cleaned up and get your groceries into your apartment. We were just out sweeping up some glass in front of the dumpster." I held up the broom and dustpan.

Dooneese, I mean Kelly, grabbed the broom and started to sweep the broken glass into a pile. Damn Joey for always referring to her as Dooneese when we were alone. One of these days I was going to slip and call her that to her face.

"I'll get these bags to the door while you two clean up the mess out here. Is the door open?" Joey asked Kelly.

"Ugh, no! I guess I should have gone up and opened it before attempting this. I didn't even think about trying to get the door unlocked while carrying all of these bags! It's just those steps."

"Well, at least you're not on the third floor. That would be really bad, especially since the elevator is never working."

"I'm not so sure. It would almost be worth it to be on the top floor. My upstairs neighbors are really loud. They walk around all night long like they've strapped bricks to their feet. I've complained to management, but they said they can't do anything about heavy footsteps. I guess I'll just have to go up there myself and say something."

"You can always go up on the roof above their apartment and stomp around for a few hours." Joey said. I couldn't tell if he was joking or being serious.

"Let's get this mess cleaned up before a car comes through and gets a piece of glass in a tire," I knelt down and held the dustpan in front of the pile Kelly had made.

"Oh yeah, right!" Kelly swept the pile into the dustpan a little too enthusiastically and flung some pieces over the back edge onto my hand. "Oh my gosh! I'm so sorry! I'm such a klutz!"

"That's okay." I moved the dustpan back behind the new pile. "Try a little more slowly this time."

When Kelly had swept the remaining glass into the dustpan, I stood up.

"Why don't you let Joey into your apartment with your groceries while I go deposit this into the dumpster?"

"Oh, right!"

We had only known Kelly for a month, but I already felt like there was something off with her. She was nice enough, but she seemed a little awkward. A little needy. She was super friendly. And she was willing to sit in our living room listening to Joey go on and on about his cave exploration. I sometimes wondered if she had a crush on him. If she did, I didn't think she would act on it. She didn't seem to hold any animosity toward me. It was strange. Joey was indifferent toward her. I was the one always reaching out to her. Maybe she sensed that Joey didn't like her very much and was just trying to bring him around. Regardless of what it was, I couldn't shake off that feeling about her.

4

Joey

Kelly fumbled with her keys trying to get the right one into the lock.

"So, how is the job going? Are you liking it at the hospital in Destin?"

"It's not bad. It's all pretty much the same everywhere. Just different people. The other nurses are nice. I'm not too happy with the person who does the scheduling, though. She hasn't put me on the schedule two nights in a row since I started. I feel like a hermit working every other night. I'm having to stay up on my nights off, so I keep the same sleep schedule. That's really throwing my social life for a loop. I'm not getting any time to go hang out on the beach because I'm sleeping during the day. This is my first travel contract. I didn't know it was going to be this way."

Wow! That was a lot to dump on me. That'll teach me to make small talk. Damn Lindsey for making us rush over to help! Dooneese had already come knocking on our door a few times in the past month since moving in. Not wanting to borrow anything or ask for help. She was just lonely and wanted to hang out. I blame that mostly on Lindsey inviting her over at least once a week. It had started as a friendly invitation the first week she moved in. Then Dooneese kind of forced herself on us the following week. During the past two weeks she had been over five times already!

It had gotten bad enough that whenever I pulled into the parking lot in the evening, I searched for her car. If I saw it, I parked on the other side of the complex and tried to sneak into my own apartment without her seeing me. After today, she would probably be knocking on our door every day asking for help with one thing or another or wanting to hang out. The only thing that was cool about her was that she didn't mind listening to me talk about cave diving. She seemed enthralled by it. Or maybe she was enthralled by me. I shuddered at that last thought.

"Well, maybe it will get better." *Keep it short and simple.*

"I hope so. I love the beach and I'm looking forward to spending as much time as I can there. I'm going to have to figure out how to do it, though. I've tried sleeping from about three in the morning until eleven so I can at least spend the afternoon on the beach. I drove around this afternoon, but I couldn't find a single parking spot anywhere near it. I even went to Grayton Beach State Park, but they had shut it down claiming they were at max occupancy, whatever that means. I didn't know this area was so crowded. I thought with it being in the panhandle, it would be less populated than somewhere like south Florida. I went on vacation there last year and there were so many people. The beaches were so crowded I could never find a spot to lay out my towel. It almost seems worse here!"

When Dooneese got started on something, she didn't shut up about it.

"Well, the areas away from the coast are less populated. You can probably head north and find some springs to hang out at. The beach is pretty crowded, though, especially in the summer. We get so many tourists that it's bumper to bumper traffic on the weekends. Even the weekdays are getting bad. Unfortunately, they didn't plan very well for this kind of congestion." *Why Joey? Why? Why was I talking so much now? What happened to short and simple?*

All this time Dooneese was fumbling with the lock as my arms were getting tired from holding all of her groceries. I was just about to set the bags on the walkway to snatch the keys from her when she finally got the key in the lock and turned it. The door swung open, and I hoisted the shopping bags up so I could turn sideways to fit through the door.

"Where do you want these?"

"Oh, over there on the counter if there's room. I got a furnished apartment, but there's not much furniture in it. They just give you the basics. A bed, a couch, a coffee table. It didn't even include a TV. I had to go out and buy one myself. And they have the breakfast counter but no stools to sit on."

I nudged my way past Dooneese and walked across the small studio apartment, setting half the bags on the counter and the other half on the floor just below them. For only having been here less than a month, the apartment was completely disorganized. I caught a glimpse of the sleeping area and saw three suitcases spread around the bed on the floor, all open with piles of clothing that appeared to be growing out of them. None of the clothes were folded or in any kind of order. She had a comforter thrown on the floor in the corner of the room. There was something I couldn't identify piled beneath it. I glanced at the dresser. There were duffel bags stacked on top of it. I wondered if Dooneese had opened the dresser drawers or even thought of using them. Her place was a mess.

"Hey guys! Anyone in there? I hope you're decent." Lindsey yelled out and laughed as she approached the open door.

"Yeah, c'mon in," Dooneese called out then turned toward me and yelled even louder. "Quick! Pull your pants back up, Joey."

I looked at her in disbelief. What the hell! Why would she say that?

Lindsey stepped inside and eyed us both suspiciously. Damn Dooneese! Damn them both for joking that way. I didn't quite understand the look on Lindsey's face. She started it with the 'hope you're decent' comment. If she thought I was doing anything inappropriate with Dooneese, she didn't know me very well.

Dooneese was already coming across as way too needy for my liking. Even if I was single and she was the most beautiful and sexy woman on this earth, I wouldn't consider being with her. There was no way I could tolerate being around her for very long. I barely managed on the nights she came over to hang out with us. If it wasn't for her being willing to listen to me talk about cave diving, I wouldn't have tolerated her at all.

"The glass is disposed of. Looks like Joey got your groceries inside for you. Are you all set?" Lindsey looked at me with one eyebrow cocked.

"Um, yeah, I guess I should put away my food so I can get back out to the store to get another six pack before they close."

"We've got some beer in our apartment. You're welcome to join us if you want."

What the hell, Lindsey?? Why would she invite her over again? Dooneese had been over three nights earlier! I just wanted to get back to our apartment, pop open another beer, and start planning how we were going to deal with this guy that scooped my lead.

"Umm, yeah, okay. If you're sure it's no imposition."

"Well…"

"None at all!" Lindsey cut me off before I could get us out of this situation.

"No, sure, c'mon over," I surrendered.

Lindsey unpacked the groceries from their bags while Dooneese found places in the fridge and the cabinets for everything. I sat on the couch scrolling through the cave diving groups on Facebook trying to find any mention of exploration happening in Jackson Blue. Maybe whoever had scooped us would be stupid enough to post about it.

As I was scrolling, I heard a lot of indecision about where to store the new groceries. I think if Lindsey hadn't jumped in and started unpacking the bags, Dooneese would have left them on the counter and the floor, fridge and freezer items included. Ten minutes later, with the groceries put away and me having no luck with my search of the cave diving groups, the three of us headed back to our apartment.

5

Two Saturdays prior

"Did you see that Simmons kid coming out of the cave with an empty reel?"

"Yeah, I saw it. Y'think he went in with it full of line? Or y'think he was just doing some line repair?"

"No tellin'. I mean, it's Simmons. It was probably just line repair. The reel probably wasn't even full when he went in. He's not the explorer type. You remember what happened with him a couple of years back and Jack Johnson had to rescue him. If it hadn't been for Jack, Simmons would have died in there. Besides, this is Jackson Blue. There's nothin' left to explore here."

"Or is there?"

"Whaddaya mean?"

"I don't know. Some guy just found a whole new section over at Ginnie Springs in the Devil's cave system. Apparently, it was beyond a sidemount restriction. It's got everyone all worked up over there. Even the backmounters are getting' back there and trying to get through. Some of 'em are pulling off their tanks and pushin' 'em through ahead of them, then puttin' 'em back on th'other side of the restriction. Crazy shit, man."

"That's nuts! What happens if they get into it beyond the restriction? Then they gotta pull their tanks off again to get back out? Not for me, dude!"

"Me neither! But some people are crazy."

"Yeah, they should just get themselves a sidemount rig. It would be so much simpler."

"Well, I heard there's at least one guy that's been back there with a sledgehammer trying to break the restriction open so he could fit through in his backmounted tanks."

"What the fuck?!?!?"

"I dunno. I might do that myself if I wasn't already diving sidemount. I mean, if money is tight and all, it's cheaper and quicker to buy a sledgehammer than it is to buy a sidemount kit and learn how to dive it."

"But that's destroying the cave. That's not right!"

"Ya do what ya gotta do."

"Whatever, man. Not me. I have my limits."

"You do you. So, ya think Simmons'll be back here tomorra ta lay more line, if that's what he's doin'?"

"I've seen him out here almost every weekend I've been here. Chances are, he'll be here. I don't know about layin' line though."

"Maybe we should plan on bein' here, too. We can time ourselves so we start our dive right before him. Then we'll duck back into the Parallel Line tunnel and wait for him to scoot by. Should be easy enough to follow him from there and see what he's up to."

"Won't he notice our lights behind him?"

"Nah, we'll cut our lights and just follow'm. We know this cave well enough, and we should be able to follow close enough to use his light to avoid hittin' anything."

"I don't know. That doesn't sound like a good idea."

"It'll be fine. And if it ends up being too much, we can stop and do our own thing. He'll never even know."

"I guess."

"Alright, let's get our shit loaded up so we can beat the rush at Cave Masters. I hear a beer calling my name over at the Mexican restaurant."

6

Joey

Present day

"Finally! I can't believe Dooneese stayed so long. She drank all of our beer!"

"We did help. And at least now you have a bunch of bottles to throw at the dumpster if you get mad again." Lindsey laughed hysterically.

"Haha. Very funny. I know that was a stupid thing to do, but it made me feel better."

"Well, at least there's that."

"So, why did you have to go and invite Dooneese up here?"

"I don't know. I guess I felt sorry for her. She's new to the area. Doesn't know anyone. And she seemed helpless. I kind of like her. I don't have all that many girlfriends. At least not ones that want to do anything except lounge on the beach or do a spa day. Doo…Kelly seems different. And you need to stop calling her Dooneese. You have me doing it now. I'm going to slip up and call her that to her face one day. I don't want to hurt her feelings."

"I'll make you a deal. I'll stop calling her Dooneese if you stop inviting her over so often. She's already been coming over too much this past month. First, because of your invitations to hang out. Then it turned into her knocking on the door every other day asking for help with one thing or another. I hope she doesn't think this means she now has an open invitation to visit and drink our beer anytime she wants. She put away an entire six pack! And then she couldn't even hold her liquor. Have you checked the bathroom yet? I hope she at least had good aim and was able to puke in the toilet and not all over it."

"Yeah, I glanced at it when I helped her out of there. It didn't look bad. I should go and throw some toilet cleaner in though." Lindsey jumped up and ran into the bathroom. A few seconds later the cabinet door slammed shut and she reappeared at the door. "I hope Kelly will be okay tonight. She's going to have one helluva hangover tomorrow. Hopefully, she recovers by the time she has to go to work. Her sleep schedule is probably going to be a little off."

"Yeah, well, that's not our problem. I warned her to slow down. Although I was more concerned about our diminishing beer supply than I was about her hangover."

"You're so compassionate, Joe…"

"Well, you know me." I smiled sheepishly, or at least tried to make it look that way. "Anyway, enough about Doo… I mean Kelly and her drunk self. I'm just happy she didn't try to throw herself at me and puke all over me. I think she's into me."

"In your dreams. You think every girl that talks to you is into you. Don't flatter yourself. Just because you got me doesn't mean you can get anyone."

We both laughed. I knew some people wondered why Lindsey was with someone like me. I wasn't ugly by any means, but Lindsey was definitely a few steps above my league. Not that it mattered. I loved her for who she was not what she looked like. It did boost my ego a bit that she fell in love with me, though.

"Anyway, I need to figure out how I'm going to get to Jackson Blue before whoever scooped my lead gets back there. Damn! I hate that I have to work!"

"Ya gotta pay the bills somehow. Which reminds me, rent is due tomorrow. Where's your half?"

"It's in my sock drawer. I'll leave it on the dresser tomorrow before I leave for work."

"Alright. That way I can drop it off at the office on my way to the shop."

"When are you going to get a decent high paying job so I can quit my job and be a kept man?"

Lindsey laughed hysterically again.

"Even if I was making more than you, you'd still have to pull your own weight, mister! Don't think I'm gonna support you even if I have more money than Carter's got little pills."

"What's that supposed to mean? Who's Carter? Your grandfather?"

"No. I don't know. It's just something my nana used to say. Maybe she was talking about one of grandpa's kin."

"Yeah, well, if you ever get more money than Carter, I'm planning on becoming a house husband. That's all I'm saying!

"We're not even married!"

"If you're rich, we will be! And no prenup!"

7

Lindsey

I hit the snooze button on the alarm as I woke up laughing about Joey thinking I'd be his sugar mama one day. Bless his heart. That boy was funny as all get out. I guess it was okay to have dreams. The problem was that his dreams involved me supporting him for the rest of his life! Never gonna happen.

I looked at the clock – 8:30. Well, I was awake so might as well turn the alarm off and get up. I threw the blanket to the side and sat up on the edge of the bed. I saw a stack of twenties sitting on the dresser. At least he remembered to leave his share of the rent out. After splashing water on my face, I walked out to the kitchen to get a cup of coffee. As I passed through the living room, I noticed something different. I stopped and looked around but couldn't quite figure out what it was. I shrugged my shoulders and continued toward the kitchen, around the peninsula to get the coffee pot started.

I pulled out the filter basket, ready to dump out Joey's used grounds from earlier, but was surprised to see fresh coffee grounds already in it. I noticed that there wasn't the expected old, room temperature coffee still sitting in the pot. That was strange. Joey didn't usually clean up after himself, let alone set up the pot for me. I looked at the water reservoir and noticed he had even filled it. Had he forgotten to make himself coffee this morning? No, that boy wouldn't leave without at least one cup of coffee in him. I stood there in disbelief wondering what it was he wanted from me. Other than for me to make more money so I could be his sugar mama.

I started to turn away when I realized I hadn't pushed the button to get the brew going. As I faced the coffee maker, it came to life. Lights popped on and it began making noises, apparently heating the elements in preparation for brewing the coffee. I jumped back wondering what had possessed it. I waited a minute to watch what it was going to do next, a little scared that it might blow up. When the coffee began dripping out of the filter basket about a minute later, I jumped again. It didn't blow up. All that happened was the carafe started to fill with the wonderful dark caffeine concoction, and I was smelling the glorious aroma of freshly brewed coffee.

I leaned in and took a closer look at the buttons on the side of the coffee maker. That's when I noticed there was a timer function on it. Hmmm. I had no idea this coffee maker could do that. And we've owned it for more than a year. Leave it to Joey to know about these things. He must have set everything up and set the timer to come on when my alarm went off. If I had snoozed a couple of times like I usually did, I would have woken up to the smell of fresh coffee permeating the apartment.

Now, I was really suspicious. Joey definitely wanted something. I had no clue what it could be. Maybe after I had some coffee and got the blood flowing to my brain again, I could figure it out. I grabbed a glass out of the cabinet and walked to the fridge to get the orange juice. I pulled the door open and on the top shelf sat a full glass. Okay! This was now too much. I loved Joey and he was thoughtful in many ways, but this was over the top for him. Something was definitely going on.

I drank my orange juice as I watched the coffee dripping into the pot. When the carafe was a third full, I pulled it out and filled the mug Joey had conveniently left on the counter next to the coffee maker. I didn't know about the timer function on the machine, but I knew it would stop dripping when I removed the carafe from it.

Joey was being awfully sweet this morning. I wondered whether he had done something wrong or if this was in anticipation of a new piece of scuba equipment he wanted to buy. He could buy anything he wanted with his money. But we were saving up for our next dive trip so any additional expenses only meant it would be longer before we could go on that trip. Sometimes Joey got so caught up in all of this new gear that was coming out that he didn't stop long enough to think about things.

Or maybe he didn't end up having enough money for his share of the rent! I placed the coffee mug on the counter and ran into the bedroom, briefly noticing something was still amiss in the living room. Once in the bedroom, I grabbed the stack of money Joey had left on the dresser and began to count it. I neatly set out stacks of five $20 bills side by side until there were seven stacks with three bills left over. It was all there so that wasn't it. Placing the bills together in one stack again, I slipped them into the bank envelope that contained my share of the rent and placed the envelope in my purse. If that wasn't the reason Joey was being so thoughtful, then what was it?

As I walked back into the living room, I finally figured out what had been bothering me every time I walked through it. Living in a small apartment, we didn't have much space. The living room contained one couch, a coffee table, and a television set. There was no room for any other furniture because we had to store our dive equipment somewhere, and the living room was the only space we had for that.

I looked at the corner where we kept our scuba tanks and dive equipment duffel bags and saw what had been bothering me. Joey's tanks and bag were gone. And so were both of our scooters!

8

Joey

Three and a half hours earlier

I was so thankful Lindsey didn't wake up when my alarm went off at five o'clock that morning. As soon as I heard it, I slammed my hand on the snooze button, then found the switch to turn it off. I usually didn't get up until six, but I had plans other than work this morning. I carefully slipped out of bed and out of the bedroom, gently closing the door behind me, careful not to make any noise. I stepped into the bathroom and relieved my bladder of the pressure that had built up overnight. It seemed like I was standing there forever. I guess the beers I drank the night before were finally ready to be recycled. I washed my hands and splashed water on my face.

With an empty bladder and a little more awake from the cold water hitting my face, I exited the bathroom. I had already laid out my clothing in the living room the night before. Fortunately, Lindsey was a late sleeper. I would be, too, if I had the choice, but I had to be at work at seven so that wasn't an option. Except this morning. I wasn't planning on going to work.

I put on a pot of coffee and poured myself a glass of orange juice. As I sipped my juice, I walked to the couch. I placed the glass on one of the coasters on the coffee table and quickly changed. I usually showered in the evening. After spending the entire day around dogs and cats, I had to get the fur off of me when I got home. I did miss having animals around us at home. Unfortunately, Lindsey had to leave Kona with her parents when we moved into this apartment. We couldn't find a place that would allow an eighty-pound dog. The place where we were living permitted pets, but they had a seventy-five-pound limit. Kona missed it by five pounds. She was all muscle and looked every bit of eighty pounds, so it wasn't like we could lie about her weight or put her on a diet.

We were always on the lookout for a different place where we could have Kona with us, ready to break our lease if we found something affordable. Nothing had turned up yet. In the meantime, Lindsey made sure to visit Kona every morning before work and then again, every evening after work. It was rare that she missed going over there to walk her. I usually joined them in the evenings and on the weekends. We also brought Kona along whenever we went hiking or to the beach.

I had wanted to bring Zoe, my cat, with me. I figured it would be easier to sneak a cat into the apartment without anyone knowing, but my mother wouldn't allow it unless I showed her a rental agreement that stated cats were allowed. Leave it to her to be a stickler for the rules! The apartment complex allowed dogs but not cats. I guess they were afraid of cats clawing everything up. I couldn't blame them. Zoe had almost clawed through one of the pieces of door trim to my bedroom at my parents.

I finished getting dressed, grabbed my orange juice, gulped down the remainder in one swallow, and headed back to the kitchen. I pulled a travel mug out of the cabinet and filled it with coffee. I found our thermos in a bottom cabinet and poured the rest of the coffee into it. I wasn't planning on hanging around the apartment for very long this morning. I had a tight schedule to keep if I was going to get back into town on time.

I took a sip of the coffee, almost burning my lip. As hot as it was, it was invigorating. There was nothing like that very first sip of coffee in the morning. Well, except that first sip of coffee after lunch, and the first sip of coffee after dinner. Yeah, I was a little addicted to coffee. There could be worse things to be addicted to.

I grabbed a couple of packs of pop tarts from the cabinet, grabbed the mug and thermos, and set them all on the coffee table ready to go. After brushing my teeth, I went back into the kitchen to clean the coffee pot and set it up for when Lindsey woke up. I didn't usually do this but figured it would be a nice gesture and maybe get her to not be so mad at me when she found out what I was about to do. With the coffee pot timer set to turn the pot on five minutes after Lindsey's alarm was set to go off, I started to walk out of the kitchen. Then a thought came to me. I turned around and grabbed a clean glass out of the cabinet, filled it with orange juice, and set it on the top shelf in the fridge. I stood back and admired my thoughtfulness. That should really please Lindsey. She would be so happy she couldn't possibly be upset with me.

Everything was set. I went back into the living room, grabbed the duffel bag containing my dive gear, and heaved the strap over my shoulder. I grabbed the pop tarts and coffee and quietly opened the door. I felt the humidity immediately. It was practically suffocating me. I couldn't believe the difference in temperature between the apartment and outside. It wasn't even five thirty and it was already that hot. It probably hadn't cooled down overnight. Slowly closing the door, careful not to make any noise, I was thankful Kona didn't live with us. She would have been barking her head off to come outside with me. I made my way to the top of the steps and began my descent to the courtyard. I really wished we had been able to find a ground level apartment, or at least a complex with a working elevator. Carrying all of this gear up and down the steps every weekend was getting old. At least we weren't on the third floor.

Once I was at the car, I placed my breakfast on the roof so I could fish out my keys. Dammit! I forgot to grab the keys from the hook inside the apartment. I wondered if I had inadvertently locked the door when I stepped out. I didn't think I had. But if I had, that would ruin my plans for the day. I set my duffel bag on the closed trunk lid and ran back to the apartment. Hopefully, the bag would still be there when I got back. It was early enough. Or late enough. The thieves should all be in bed by now.

Fortunately, I hadn't locked the door. Carefully opening it, I reached inside and grabbed the keys from the hook next to it. I decided I might as well take another load down to the parking lot rather than go empty-handed. I slipped inside, leaving the door open slightly so it would be easier to get the scuba tanks outside. I walked over to the tanks, grabbed one in each hand by the valve, and carried them to the door, kicking it open with one foot. The door swung wildly to the side making its way toward the wall, the wall that was shared with our bedroom. If the door slammed against it, Lindsey would be certain to wake up.

I managed to block the door with my other foot, stopping it just in time. Quickly stepping through it, I walked to the top of the steps and set the tanks down next to the railing so I could go back and grab the stage tanks and decompression tank. Back in the apartment, I walked across to the sliding doors and looked out at my car. My bag was still on the trunk. I walked back to the scuba corner, grabbed a couple of stage tanks from the pile, and carried them outside, careful to not swing the door open with as much force this time. I stood the tanks up next to the steel tanks.

I looked at the steel tanks, and not for the first time, wondered why the bottoms were rounded instead of flat like the aluminum stage tanks. Yeah, I could have left the boots on them so they could be stood up as well, but tank boots were frowned upon in the cave diving community. I had enough trouble with my reputation after what had happened a couple of years earlier. I didn't need to be caught using boots on my tanks.

I turned and headed back into the apartment to grab my decompression tank, the smallest of the set. I made one last sweep of the room to make sure I hadn't forgotten anything. It looked like I had everything. Then I noticed there were two scooters standing in the scuba corner next to the wall. I wouldn't get very far in the cave without those. I set the decompression tank just outside the door and walked to the corner to get the scooters. I grabbed one by the handle on the nose in each hand and carried them to the door. They were a bit heavier than the scuba tanks, by about ten pounds each. At least they could also be stood upright unlike the steel round-bottom tanks.

I set the scooters on the walkway just outside the door next to the decompression tank and poked my head back inside the apartment, doing another final sweep. This time it looked like I had gotten everything. I patted my pocket to make sure the keys were there, then flipped off the light and locked the door. I turned around and looked at the pile of gear near the top of the steps. Five tanks and two scooters. My legs were going to get a workout this morning. I gently pulled the door closed and grabbed one of the scooters. Four more trips down the steps with about three hundred pounds of equipment. I was working up a sweat just thinking about it.

I got to the car, unlocked the doors, and opened the driver's side rear door. I placed the scooter in the back seat with the seatbelt wrapped around it, securing it in place. I grabbed the duffel bag off of the trunk, popped the lid open, and tossed the bag to one side. I headed back to the top of the steps to grab the next scooter. I got that one down to the car, placed it in the back behind the passenger seat, and strapped it in. Back up to the top of the stairs to get the next load. My legs were already protesting. Good thing I was scootering and not swimming.

At the top of the steps, I grabbed the steel tanks and set them on their rounded bottoms leaning against the railing. I hoisted one onto my left shoulder. Once it was settled in place, I grabbed the other with my right hand and began heading down the steps. As I approached the last step, I heard one of the apartment doors open.

"Hey Joey!" Doo… Kelly, I corrected myself, yelled out as she waved frantically from in front of her apartment door.

Great! That was the last thing I needed this morning. It wasn't enough that she spent a couple of hours in our apartment last night drinking all of our beer. Why was she awake so early? She should be in bed nursing a hangover.

"Oh, hey, uhhh, D…Kelly." I called out, unable to wave back

because I was carrying almost one hundred pounds of steel. I walked through the breezeway to my car and set the tank carried by my right hand down on the ground leaning against the rear bumper so I could place the tank that was on my shoulder inside the trunk. Just as I set the tank down, Kelly appeared to my left.

"Hi!"

I hadn't seen her coming because the large, heavy tank on my left shoulder had been blocking my view. She surprised me and I almost dropped the tank on top of her giant forehead.

"Hey again."

"Whatcha doin'?"

"I'm loading up my car," I grumbled.

"Well, I can see that, silly! I mean, what are you doing with all of that stuff?"

Why do people always do this? She can see I'm standing here holding a heavy tank on my shoulder. Why is she trying to engage me in conversation? Why was she so bright and chipper? I expected her to have a full-blown hangover after the way she drank the night before and puked up everything all over our bathroom. She was not normal.

"I'm heading to one of the springs to go diving."

"Oh!" Kelly looked perplexed. "The one you've been telling me about? Jackson Hole?"

"Jackson Blue."

"Oh, right. On a Monday? Don't you have to work today? Are you still working on that exploration project you've been telling me about? I remember you saying something about it last night, but I guess the beer got to my head and made me forget. Oh hey, is Lindsey awake?"

I started to panic. If Kelly went and knocked on our apartment door, she would wake up Lindsey and I'd be busted.

"No, no! Lindsey's still in bed. She doesn't have to be at work until ten, so she doesn't wake up until around eight thirty."

A big pout appeared on Kelly's face. She genuinely looked upset at the news I had just given her. I finally stepped to my right so I had room to swing the steel tank without it coming down on top of Kelly's head. I set it inside of the trunk.

"You're heading out really early. I guess you're a morning person, too."

"Not really, but I like to get going early whenever I'm going diving."

I grabbed the tank that was leaning on the bumper and placed it inside the trunk next to the first tank.

"Shouldn't you be going to work today? Did I ask you that already? Didn't you say you worked as a vet tech?"

I turned to head back to get my stage tanks.

"I have the day off."

Kelly immediately smiled. "Wanna get brekkie together? With all those groceries I got yesterday, I forgot to get something for breakfast. And I really need coffee in the mornings. I'm not a nice person if I don't have my coffee."

Right about this time I was thinking she wasn't a nice person for bothering me so early in the morning. The last thing I wanted to see was Kelly hyped up on coffee. She was already too bubbly for me no matter what time of the day, never mind it being five thirty in the morning. And I hate it when people do that to words. Brekkie! What the hell is that? Breakfast is also two syllables! It's not any quicker to say brekkie. Just say the damn word!

"I wish I could, but I'm already running kinda late. I'm meeting a buddy at the spring this morning." I lied.

Another pout appeared on Kelly's face. I started walking back toward the breezeway.

"I have to get the rest of my tanks down here and loaded."

"Oh, can I help you?"

She wasn't getting the hint. Might as well save myself a trip and have her carry a tank down.

"Sure, you can carry the small tank down for me. Are you okay with carrying a tank full of oxygen?"

"Of course, silly! I'm a nurse, remember?" Kelly laughed. "But why do you have oxygen? Do you have COPD or something?"

What was she talking about? Why would she think I had COPD? Even as a vet tech I knew enough about that to know someone my age that doesn't smoke wasn't likely to have lung disease. Especially someone who was a diver.

"The oxygen is for my decompression stop at the end of my dive.":

Kelly followed me through the breezeway and up the steps. I handed the small decompression tank to her, then grabbed a stage tank in each hand.

"What does oxygen do during the decompression stop? Isn't it dangerous to be bringing oxygen with you underwater? What if it blows up?"

I started to walk down the steps hoping Kelly would shut up. But I knew that wasn't going to happen. Instead, I decided to give her a long explanation hoping that would keep her from talking so much.

"It helps divers off gas the nitrogen that builds up in our blood and soft tissues when we're diving. By breathing pure oxygen, we eliminate any additional nitrogen from getting into our blood so we can decompress more quickly and surface sooner. The only danger to it is if we breathe it deeper than twenty feet. We can have an oxygen toxicity seizure if we do that. And no, it won't blow up. Any more questions?" Dammit! Now I was inviting her to talk more.

We arrived at the car, and I set one of the stage tanks on the ground and hoisted the other one up and into the trunk leaving a small space between it and the steel tanks. I took the decompression tank from Kelly and placed it in the small space I had left for it. The last tank went on the end of the line up. I shifted the duffel bag over so it was on top of the stage tanks. There wasn't much of a weight difference, but I wanted to try to distribute it as evenly as possible.

"Hmmmm, that sounds really interesting. You sure know a lot about that stuff. Why don't you teach people how to scuba dive? Or do you? Have I asked you that before?" Kelly paused for a breath with a pensive look on her face. "I don't have any more questions right now. But maybe I'll think of some during brekkie."

There she goes inviting herself to breakfast with me again. I walked back through the breezeway so I could look up at the balcony to make sure I had everything. Kelly following me around like a lost puppy dog and trying to help was breaking my routine.

"Oooo, need more help?"

"I think I got it all, thanks."

I looked back at Kelly. She was staring at me. "Are you sure you don't have time for brekkie? I don't know anyone else in the area and I hate to eat in a restaurant alone."

"Why don't you go through a drive through or something?"

"I hate fast food. And I figured since you were up and about… Besides, if you're going diving you need a better brekkie than pop tarts." Kelly pointed at the packages sitting on top of my car.

I considered declining her invitation again, but I worried that she might head to our apartment and wake up Lindsey. Best to keep her busy this morning and away from Lindsey.

"Fine, just a quick brekkie, I mean breakfast." Dammit! She had me saying brekkie now!

9

Lindsey

Present time

What the hell was that boy doing today? Was he playing hooky from work? I looked at the time – almost nine. I hit the call Joey widget on my phone. The phone app popped up on the screen and I hit the speaker button. One ring, two rings, three rings. *He better answer.* Four rings. Voicemail. He can't already be diving. Even if he left the house at six thirty, he still had to stop at Cave Masters to sign in, drive to Jackson Blue, and set up his equipment. Maybe he was already in the water. It would be close.

I suddenly felt nauseous. Ugh. That coffee wasn't sitting well in my stomach. I walked into the kitchen to make some toast. Maybe having something in my stomach would make it feel better. I grabbed the loaf of bread to get a slice to place in the toaster. Just as I was dropping it into the slot, I felt my stomach contract and tasted bile in the back of my mouth. I turned toward the sink and threw up my coffee and orange juice. I flipped the faucet handle and splashed cold water on my face, then cupped my hands so I could rinse my mouth. I stood near the sink waiting for the nausea to pass. I was afraid to get too far from it in case I got the urge to vomit again.

A few minutes later, the nausea passed. I looked at the coffee pot and decided not to tempt fate. My thoughts turned back to Joey. An idea came to me. I hurried into the bedroom and checked Joey's alarm clock. His alarm was set for five. He never got up that early. He had been planning this since last night. Getting his lead scooped had really gotten to him.

I went back out to the kitchen, grabbed my mug, and took a sip before I remembered the nausea. Fortunately, I didn't feel sick again. I took another sip. The coffee had cooled just enough to make it perfect. I walked to the couch and sat down, wrapping myself in a blanket until the coffee warmed me. Why did Joey have the AC so cold? I wrapped my hands around the mug and breathed in the aroma from the steam. It smelled so good! I took another sip. And then the nausea hit again.

That bout didn't result in vomiting. Not that there was anything in my stomach to throw up other than a few sips of coffee. I heard the ding of the toaster while I was waiting for the nausea to pass. I got up, walked into the kitchen, and poured the coffee in my mug down the drain. I didn't want to make that mistake again. Maybe the orange juice made me sick.

I opened the fridge and checked the date on the carton. It was still good for another month. And we had only opened the carton a couple of days ago. I unscrewed the lid and sniffed the contents. Another wave of nausea came over me, but the juice smelled fine. Not that I knew what bad juice would smell like. It didn't smell off though. I placed the carton back in the fridge and grabbed a paper towel and my toast. I would only nibble for now. I stayed in the kitchen near the sink just in case.

How was I going to handle this situation with Joey? This wasn't the first time he had gone off and done something like this. A couple of years earlier he went to Jackson Blue to dive alone while I was at Eddy Spring divemastering an open water class. It was his first time diving alone in a cave. I was so pissed at him for that! We had discussed it several times and he knew I didn't approve. He ended up confessing. Well, after Danny, the tank monkey at Cave Masters, failed to keep his mouth shut about me calling there looking for Joey.

Being a tank monkey, a dive shop employee that spent most of the day filling scuba tanks, often put you in the right place at the right time. Tank monkeys were able to hear all of the gossip going on in the area of North Florida called cave country where most of the underwater caves were located. Because of this, it was nearly impossible to fart in a drysuit without everyone in the cave diving community finding out about it within hours.

Danny didn't spread gossip to be mean. He didn't even realize he was spreading gossip most of the time. He just wanted to be accepted by cave divers because he wanted to be one so badly himself. He was only halfway through his training. He thought passing along information got him in their good graces and by the time he finished his training he would have a variety of cave divers to dive with. If he only knew…

I slowly nibbled on the toast, letting it settle in my stomach and absorb the acid that was churning around in there. I could smell the odor of coffee coming from the coffee maker. I really wanted some caffeine. I needed it to make its way throughout my body, especially into my brain cells. I didn't know how Joey got up so early every day. I didn't think I could do it. I didn't think I could ever hold a regular nine to five job. Getting to work at ten was sometimes a challenge.

I started scrolling through Facebook as I finished my toast. Mindless activity was about all I could handle this early in the morning, especially without the benefit of caffeine. I'd see what was going on in the virtual world and plug the shop wherever I found the opportunity. I made a mental note to talk to Joanne about getting a raise. I did a lot for the dive shop, including during my time off. And the shop was doing well finally. Joanne no longer had to pay my wages out of her own pocket during the winter months. I liked to think I was at least somewhat responsible for that. Hopefully Joanne saw it that way too.

My phone vibrated and dinged, surprising me and causing me to drop it on the kitchen floor. I almost dropped my toast as well. I picked my phone up off of the floor and looked at the notifications, noticing the screen protector had a new crack in it. I'd have to get Joey to replace it for me. I hated doing those things. The message was mom asking if I was stopping by to walk Kona. I tapped the suggested "Yes" response and ate the last bite of toast. Mom knew I stopped by every morning. I didn't know why she insisted on messaging me every day to ask. Actually, she was making sure to remind me, like I would forget. Just mom being mom.

Time for a shower so I could head over to see my big girl. Maybe the water flowing over my body would make me feel better. I walked out of the kitchen and looked back at the scuba corner. My sidemount tanks, stage tanks, and decompression tank were all there as well as my duffle bag of equipment. Joey had taken my scooter though. So he was going back to the area he's been exploring. I started to get worried. Joey had been cave diving alone several more times since that first time he snuck off. As far as I knew, those were fairly easy, laid-back dives. He just scootered back to the Trash Room or Middle Grounds and swam around. The area where he was going today was twice the distance and required that he pass through a small restriction. Two restrictions. He would be in the water for close to four hours. Alone. Damn him!

I felt another wave of nausea beginning and ran to the bathroom.

10

Joey

After deciding on a place to eat, and by that I mean telling Kelly to follow me because she still didn't know any of the restaurants, I got in my car. Kelly tried to worm her way into riding with me, but I told her I didn't have time to come back to the apartment complex to drop her off. She grudgingly moped off to her car. I couldn't figure her out. Was she trying to hit on me? She knew Lindsey. The first time we all met, Lindsey was the one that had initiated contact. I got roped into going along.

Kelly had spent plenty of evenings hanging out with us in our apartment over the past month. She was knocking on our door asking for one favor or another on the days she wasn't working and sleeping. She had latched onto us. And now she was latching onto me. Was she that dense? Or was she just a clingy person? I pushed the thoughts aside. I had enough going on without having to worry about some clingy, helpless neighbor. We'd have a quick breakfast and I'd be on my way to Marianna and Jackson Blue.

Kelly had to run back to her apartment to grab her purse and keys. I didn't know why she hadn't brought them with her in the first place. It seemed like it was taking forever. I considered taking off and leaving her to fend for her own breakfast. On second thought, that wasn't a good idea. She might knock on our door and wake Lindsey. Lindsey would call me and there would be a whole thing. I decided to call work while I was waiting for Kelly and leave them a message on voicemail. I hadn't called out sick in almost a year. I deserved a mental health day, especially after what I discovered during our dive the day before. I called and left a message. Just as I finished speaking, Kelly appeared next to my car, her shadow causing me to jump. Why wasn't she already in her car? I rolled down the window.

"Ya ready?"

"I'm ready!" Kelly said at the same time.

Then she just stood there. Doing nothing.

"Umm, are you going to get in your car?"

"Oh, I was hoping you had changed your mind about us riding over together."

"Nope. Haven't changed my mind."

"Oh, okay. I'll follow you then."

Kelly was way too energetic and bubbly in the morning. I wished Lindsey was more of a morning person, especially on the weekends when we were going diving. But I definitely didn't want her to be this much of a morning person. Kelly still hadn't moved so I brought up the window and put the car in reverse. She finally got the message and skipped off toward her car. I pulled out of my parking space and started toward the exit. I wanted to get this over and get on the road to Marianna. I reached over to grab my coffee, but it wasn't there. I looked around the car but didn't see my travel mug, thermos, or my pop tarts.

Dammit! I left them on the roof of the car. Kelly had me so distracted I forgot to grab them. I slowly stopped the car, hoping the coffee was still on the roof, and brought the window back down. I reached up and felt around, quickly finding my travel mug near the edge, still standing upright. I pulled it inside of the car, set it in the cup holder and reached back above me to feel for the thermos. It was also within reach. Kelly had been standing right beside my car with my mug and thermos directly in front of her face. How had she not noticed them and handed them to me? Or at least told me they were there?

The pop tarts were also within reach, thankfully. I didn't want to get out of the car and have Kelly skipping over from her car wondering what I was doing. That would only delay things. With everything safely in the car, I took a sip of coffee from the travel mug. It was still scalding. Damn, these mugs were good! It had been at least twenty-five minutes since I filled it with coffee, and it was still as hot as it had been when it was first brewed. I popped the lid off to allow it to cool faster.

I looked into the rearview mirror and saw a car pull up behind me. I scanned the windshield and confirmed it was Kelly just as she stuck her arm out of the window and waved it frantically back and forth. Yeah, yeah, I know you're there.

About ten minutes away was a small diner style restaurant that Lindsey and I went to every now and then. The food was decent, but best of all, the service was fast. I could probably get in and out of there in less than thirty minutes. That was if Kelly didn't try to talk my ear off and ate her food. We arrived and I found a parking space in between a couple of trucks in the small lot. There were two spaces side by side, but I avoided those so I wouldn't be stuck talking to Kelly even longer after breakfast. Kelly parked in one of the empty side by side spaces. The diner didn't look busy. That meant we should be able to get a table right away so I could get on my way soon.

I took another sip of coffee. The lid had been off long enough to make it drinkable. I took another couple of swallows. I would order a coffee with breakfast, but I needed the additional boost before being subjected to Kelly's overbearing bubbliness. I replaced the lid to keep the coffee hot while I was inside the restaurant and exited my car. Kelly was standing right there waiting for me. I almost stood up into her. What was with this girl?

"Why didn't you park in the space next to where I parked? It's closer to the door."

"Oh, I-I guess I didn't see it," I lied. "Let's go in. I can't be here long. Like I said, I have to meet someone this morning."

"Just call him and let him know you'll be a little late."

"I already did while you were getting your stuff from your apartment. He wasn't too happy about it. I told him I'd only be half an hour late, so we need to make this quick."

A frown appeared on Kelly's face. Why did I allow myself to be talked into this? I doubted I would be getting out of here in thirty minutes. I'd be lucky if I got out of the restaurant in an hour. I looked at the time on my phone – six. She had forty-five minutes max. That would still get me to Blue Spring Park by eight thirty, and I could call Cave Masters to sign in when I turned off of the interstate.

Just as we started walking toward the door a truck came rolling into the parking lot, a truck I hadn't seen in a couple of years. Not since the cave collapse in Jackson Blue.

It was Jack Johnson.

11

Two Sundays prior

"Shouldn't he be here by now? Maybe he had something else going on and isn't gonna show."

"He'll be here. He's been here every weekend as far back as I can remember. Maybe his girl is coming along today. Whenever she's with him, they usually get here late."

"Damn! I hope so! She's frickin' hot! I'd follow her anywhere."

"Keep it in your pants. I hear they've been together for years. Besides, even if she was single or one to stray, she'd never be interested in the likes of you."

"What's that supposed to mean?"

"I'm just saying. Have you looked in a mirror recently?"

"Screw you!"

"Ouch! What the crap, man! I was just giving you shit. You didn't have to hit me so hard."

"You deserved it."

"There he is."

"Dammit! Looks like he's alone. No eye candy to look at today. I was kind a hoping to follow her through the cave."

"It's best that she's not here. She's a little more observant than Simmons. She'd likely see us following them."

"You have a point. I wonder why she's only here every other weekend."

"I heard Simmons telling someone that she teaches scuba classes when she's not here. He's usually diving with those homos when she's teaching, but I haven't seen them in a few weeks."

"Yeah, that's strange. They're usually here every weekend, too."

"They're probably busy diving into their own deep dark holes."

"Dude, that's nasty! Now I'm going to have that image in my head the entire dive."

They both laughed.

"Let's start moving our shit over to the water. By the time he's set up, we can start our dive and go find a place to hide until he scooters by. Then we'll go into stealth mode and follow him."

"I still think he's gonna see us."

"If he does, we just head off somewhere else. No big deal. It's not like we're trespassing. Anyone can dive the cave."

* * *

Three hours later.

"Why did you stop us from following him? All he did was turn off of the gold line."

"Yeah, but now we know what area of the cave he's going to. We didn't know that before today."

"Yeah, maybe. I still think we should have kept following him. Here. Look at this. That area doesn't look too bad on the map. There's only one main passage. And the name Source Nouveau is interesting."

"There're a lot more tunnels back there than what's on that map. The map doesn't even begin to show how complex it is in that area. Remember we did that jump last year. Remember how we didn't bother to put any personalized markers on the lines and almost got lost?"

"Oh, shit! That was there?"

"Yeah, right off of the thirty-three-hundred-foot marker."

"Well, damn! That's not going to be easy. That was stupid of us to not use our markers. We almost didn't make it out of there."

"That's why I grabbed you and stopped. It was fine to follow him with our lights out along the main passage, but I didn't want to go in there without any lights. It was bad enough with our lights that one time."

"Yeah, but that was freaky. It was hazy and really silty. Who would have thought there would be some unexplored lead back there?"

"I wish we had gone back there some more now. It would have been good to learn that area of the cave. Hell, we might have been the ones to find whatever passage Simmons found."

"So what are we gonna do now?"

"Let's pack up before he surfaces. I think those are his exhalation bubbles coming out of the cave. We'll come back tomorrow when Simmons isn't around and go check out that area. Maybe we'll stumble across something."

12

Joey

We went into the restaurant and were seated in an empty booth near the back. I didn't pick up a menu. I knew what I was going to order. It was the same thing I always ordered. Kelly picked up her menu and began flipping through the pages. Then she flipped back to the front. Then again to the back. During this process, she let out a few *hmphhs* and sighs.

"Is there a problem?"

"There's just so much to choose from. I'm not sure what I want."

"It's all good. Just choose something. Remember, I don't have very long."

"Y'all ready to order?" The server was standing at the end of the booth.

"I'll take the Seaside special, eggs over medium with white toast."

Kelly dropped her menu on the table and let out another *hmphh*.

"Is there a problem?"

"Isn't it customary for the lady to order first?"

"Are you ready to order?"

"Well…"

"Just order anything. It's all good."

"Hmphh!" Kelly faced the server. "I'll take a stack of pancakes with bacon. Make sure it's crispy."

"I'll have your order up in a few minutes."

The server walked away, stopping at another table to ask how they were doing. As I watched the server, a shadow fell over us.

"Well, lookie here! Haven't seen you a while." Jack stood at the end of the booth Kelly and I were seated in.

"What do you want?" I sneered.

Jack placed his hands over his heart and feigned a hurt expression. I noticed a lot of scars on his left arm from the surgeries he must have had to have over the past couple of years.

"Just saying howdy. Seeing how you're doin'"

"I'm doing just fine." I looked at Jack's left arm again and examined the scars. I recognized the markings of rods and screws. They were similar to the animals who were hit by cars and broke their legs. Only Jack had a lot more. He must have had more than a dozen surgeries following the collapse of the cave ceiling that crushed his arm. I could only imagine how painful that must have been. Must still be. "How's your arm?"

I didn't really care. But I knew that was a sore subject with Jack. I wanted to stick the knife in and twist it a little.

"Oh, it's just fine. The docs fixed it up almost good as new." He held his arm out and moved it around in all directions while closing his hand into a fist several times. It was barely perceptible, but I noticed him wincing. "In fact, I was cleared to dive again a couple a months ago. It's been nice being back in the water. Back to explorin' the caves. Hopefully, we didn't lose too many cave divers during my absence."

I almost laughed out loud. He was still on that story. Still trying to be the hero who was rescuing everyone. The urge to laugh instantly faded as I thought about what Jack had just said about exploring the caves. I wondered where he had been diving. Before his accident, you could find him at Jackson Blue several times a week. I hadn't seen him there in more than two years. Then a realization hit me. Was Jack the one that scooped my lead? Was he the one going back there and pushing my passages? That would be something Jack would do. It had to be him. I thought about calling him out on it, but I couldn't accuse him outright. I had no proof, and he would deny it emphatically. If he wasn't the one, then I'd be letting him know I had found unexplored passage in Jackson Blue and putting him on the scent. I'd have two people back there pushing the ends of my lines. I had to figure out another way to confront him on this and try to get a confession. I also had to find out when Gary and Jim were supposed to be back in town. I could really use their help.

"I haven't seen you on the Mill Pond. And I've been there every weekend."

"I'm there mostly during the week. I prefer diving the river caves on the weekends. Keeps me away from the weekend crowds. It's quieter at the river caves. Just have ta deal with kayakers on occasion. Ya haven't introduced me to your new girlfriend. What happened to you and that spunky blonde gal? She decide to move onto greener pastures?" Jack laughed.

"I'm still with Lindsey." I growled at Jack. "This is our neighbor, Kelly."

"Ahhh, getting a little side action." Jack winked at me.

"That's not at all what this is!" I almost stood up to push Jack away from the booth. I thought better of it. I couldn't let him get under my skin. I couldn't let him push my buttons. There was no point in making a scene.

Just then the server arrived with our food. Jack stepped aside to let her set the plates on the table.

"Ya'll need anything else?"

"No thank you," replied Kelly. I had been so focused on Jack that I forgot Kelly was sitting across from me.

"I'm good."

When the server left, I looked back up at Jack. "Look, you said hello. Now why don't you go find a table and leave us alone? Or better yet, go find another restaurant. I'm kind of in a hurry this morning anyway and need to eat so I can get going."

"Aw, I was hopin' to join ya'll."

"Well..." Kelly started until I held up my hand. I glared at Jack until he got the message.

"I see. Maybe there is more to this little rendezvous I caught you in. Well, enjoy your breakfast. I'm sure I'll see you around." Jack snatched a piece of bacon from Kelly's plate, turned on his heel and walked to the other end of the dining room where there was an empty booth waiting for him.

"Hey!" Kelly started to get up to chase after Jack and her bacon.

"Sit down. He's not worth it."

"Who was that?" Kelly asked wide-eyed.

"No one important. Just an old acquaintance from a couple of years ago. Not someone I'm friends with or even want to be friends with. He's actually an asshole."

"Well, he seemed nice. Other than stealing my bacon."

"Trust me, he's not nice. He can come across as your best friend, but deep down inside, he's a conniving asshole who's always looking for ways to make himself look better, even at the expense of others."

"Do you want me to go over and tell him we aren't doing anything? We're just having brekkie together."

"No!" I practically screamed out. I glanced in the direction of Jack and noticed he had his nose in the menu. But the look on his face revealed he heard my outburst. I turned back toward Kelly and said in almost a whisper. "That will only make him think the opposite. It's best to just ignore him."

I picked up my utensils and unwrapped them from the napkin. I found the fork and began eating my eggs. I had eaten four bites when I noticed Kelly hadn't touched her food.

"Look, I do have to meet someone and have to leave as soon as I'm done eating. I hate to leave you here finishing your breakfast alone so you should start eating."

"Oh, sorry, I was just thinking about that guy, Jack, and what you said about him. He seems like a nice guy, but you obviously don't like him. What did he do to you?"

"He's also a cave diver, and… Look, I don't want to talk about it. He's not important. Eat!"

Kelly was quiet for two whole minutes while she nibbled on her bacon. Then she started talking again.

"So tell me more about this thing you're doing, umm, in Marietta, is it? Why is it so important that you're going there when you should be going to work?"

"It's Marianna. And I told you. I have the day off from work. It's the exploration Lindsey and I have been telling you about while you've been over hanging out with us. Remember we told you there are a bunch of underwater caves in Marianna. I found a tunnel in one of them a couple of months ago that hadn't ever been found before back about five thousand feet from the entrance. I've been going there and exploring the area and laying line in it."

"Laying line?"

"Yeah, when we go into caves, we always run a guideline so if the visibility gets bad, we can still get out by touching the line and following it to the opening of the cave. When we explore the caves, we lay line in them for that purpose and also so we can survey the tunnels."

"What do you mean survey?"

"We take compass headings, record that and the depth, and then get the distance between stations, places where the line changes direction, and we create maps from that. You remember the map I showed you last week and again last night?"

"Oh yeah! I remember that. That was pretty cool. I can't believe those caves go that far from the park and under that big farm field." Kelly paused to take a bite of her hashbrown. Then with food still in her mouth. "Is it hard to do that underwater? You know, to do that survey stuff. Does the visibility get bad every time you're in the cave?"

"Man, I hope not! No, the visibility is usually good. At least, it's good when the tunnel is big enough that we don't stir up the sediment on the floor. But there's always a chance that someone else might screw it up."

Kelly reached over with her fork and stabbed a piece of one of my eggs and brought it to her mouth.

"What are you doing??"

"Huh? Eating. What does it look like?"

"Those were my eggs!"

"Oh, don't you share? You're welcome to help yourself to my pancakes. I don't mind." She snatched a piece of toast from my plate.

"No, I do not share. Please stop eating from my plate! You didn't like it when Jack stole your bacon."

"That was different." Kelly took a bite of the toast she had grabbed from my plate. "So what are you doing there today? Aren't you supposed to be at work?"

I pulled my plate closer to me and moved my coffee cup so that it was blocking Kelly's reach.

"I am, but I called out from work." Dammit! She made me slip. I might as well continue. It wasn't like she could do anything with the information anyway. "Yesterday, I got to the end of one of the lines I put in there on Saturday and found that someone had gone in and put his own line after mine. That's not cool. I've been exploring that area and whoever did that should respect that I laid claim to it first. He should have turned and left the area."

"How do you know it's a guy?"

"Huh?"

"You keep saying he. Aren't there women cave divers? I thought Lindsey was a cave diver, too."

"Well, yeah, I suppose it could be a woman, but it's doubtful. There aren't very many women cave divers. I'd say nine out of every ten cave divers are guys. And I don't know of any women cave divers in Florida who do these types of dives other than Lindsey. At least not anymore. There have been some here and there, but it's rare."

"Who do you think did this to you?"

"I thought it was this guy I've seen lurking around the park. Well, not really lurking. Just behaving strangely. I haven't actually seen him. It could be a couple of guys. I've seen their truck, but they pulled in and turned around to leave almost right away. I think when they saw me, they decided to go do something else until I was done diving. But now that I've seen Jack and know that he's cave diving again, I think it might be him. This sounds like something he would do. Besides, he has a beef with me. I wouldn't put it past him to do this just to get back at me for embarrassing him a couple of years ago."

Kelly turned and looked toward Jack. She stared at him for about half a minute. Jack eventually noticed and looked up. Kelly quickly turned away.

"Now that I look at him closer, he doesn't seem like such a nice guy after all."

"Trust me, he's not."

"I hope he gets whatever he has coming to him. Do you think he's going to Mari… umm…"

"Marianna."

"Do you think he's going to Marianna today? Do you think you'll see him at whatever cave you're diving today?"

"Jackson Blue. He might be. I thought he lived in that area, but I used to see him down this way a bit before his accident. He might live down here."

"His accident?"

"There was a ceiling collapse in Jackson Blue and Jack got pinned beneath it. Lindsey and I were in the cave when it happened. We actually saw Jack right before it happened. He was directly beneath the pieces that fell. We didn't know it was him when we saw it happening. The silt took over the passage too fast for us to recognize who it was. After we found a way around the collapse, we went back in to look for the diver we had seen and found Jack pinned beneath a large chunk of the ceiling. I'm not sure how we did it, but we got him free and saved his life."

"Wow! That's incredible! Why would you go back in that cave after the ceiling collapsed? Aren't you worried it will do it again? Aren't you scared of getting crushed to death?"

"I'm not so sure how incredible it was now. I kinda wish we hadn't gone back in to look for him. And I'm not too worried about another cave collapse. It's a rare event. I've been diving Jackson Blue for about four years and that's the only collapse I've heard of. Anyway, I have to get going. If Jack is going to Jackson Blue today, I want to make sure I'm in the water and long gone before he gets there. If he's the one that scooped my lead, maybe he'll go somewhere else."

I pushed my plate near the edge of the table. Kelly glanced at it, probably hoping to get another bite of my breakfast, but I had cleaned the plate. The server walked over a few seconds later to clear the table.

"Will this be on one or two checks?"

"Two."

"One." Kelly told the server, then turned to me. "This is my treat. I really appreciate the help you and Lindsey have given me over the past few weeks. And inviting me over last night to hang out and drink your beer was awfully sweet. It's the least I can do."

Well, now I felt bad. Here I was being kind of an asshole to Kelly, and she goes and pays for brekkie – Dammit! Breakfast! – and thanks me for helping her.

"Thanks. Sorry I've been kind of a dick. I'm just not much of a people person and…"

"No apology necessary! And you haven't been a dick. At least, not that bad. I know I can come across as a bit much. I've been told that by my friends. I've been working on it, but when I get stressed, it comes right out. And being in a new place, new apartment, new job, with no friends around. Well, that's been a little stressful."

Kelly paused for a moment, reached out, and grabbed my hand in hers. It felt awkward. I wanted to pull away, but I didn't want to make her feel worse than she already did.

"I was lucky to meet you, and Lindsey, when I moved into the apartment down the way," Kelly continued. "And you were both so helpful yesterday evening. You've been so helpful since I moved in. And your cave diving stories are so interesting. I love hearing about your discoveries!"

Kelly stopped talking briefly and looked down at her lap. "I'm sorry if I pushed myself on you when I saw you again this morning. Sometimes I just can't help myself."

"It's okay. I'll try to be a little more understanding as well." I glanced at Jack and noticed he was staring right at us. I pulled my hand away from Kelly's and looked at the time on my phone. "Look…"

"I know. I've already made you late. Thanks for agreeing to go to breakfast with me. Like I said, I hate eating alone in restaurants. I have to head out anyway. I'm going to see if I can finally find somewhere close to the beach to park this morning. Maybe I'll see you and Lindsey later on."

We both slid out from the booth and stood up. Then Kelly moved in and put her arms around me in an awkward hug. I looked over her shoulder and saw Jack still staring at us with a huge smile on his face.

Dammit!

13

Lindsey

The nausea finally passed, but not before the piece of toast made its way into the toilet. Ugh! I hated throwing up! I ate another piece of toast and even tempted fate with some coffee. This time I kept everything down. I filled a travel cup and headed out to mom and dad's house. I tried calling Joey again on my way over to take Kona for a walk. He still wasn't answering. Not that I expected him to. If he was diving, and I was fairly certain he was, he wouldn't be answering his phone. But at least this way, he would see a couple of missed phone calls from me. It was going to be interesting to see if he tried to play it off and claim he was too busy at work. It *was* Monday, his busiest day at the vet's office. That wouldn't explain the missing scuba equipment.

Unless he was planning on going diving after work. He'd have to tell me about it beforehand, though. I only worked until seven tonight. If he left work at four, he wouldn't get to Jackson Blue until close to six. With a four-hour dive and a couple of hours to set up and break down, that would put him getting home long after midnight. That wouldn't leave him with much time to sleep before having to be at work the next day. He had to be diving right now.

After taking Kona for a walk, I brought her back to my parents, made sure she had fresh water and a snack, as well as her favorite toys, and headed to work. So far, the nausea was being kept at bay. So strange. I wondered again if the orange juice had gone bad. I would pick up a new carton on my way home from work and dump the rest of the old one down the drain. Better to be safe than sorry.

I arrived at the dive shop and parked right in front of the door. We didn't get many customers until after four when most people got off work. Everyone started coming in to drop off rental equipment and tanks in the evenings. I'd move my car during lunch to free up the space for customers. I unlocked the shop door, opened it, and quickly stepped inside the cool air-conditioned showroom. I entered my code into the alarm keypad to disarm it. I walked through the shop, set my purse and coffee on the counter, and flipped the light switches on. As I was flipping the last switch, I heard the door chime ring. That was strange. We usually didn't get any customers this early. I couldn't remember the last time we had a customer right at opening. I turned around to greet whoever had just triggered the sensor.

It was Jack Johnson.

I could feel the hairs on the back of my neck stand up along with heat rising from my shoulders. What the hell was *he* doing here? Jack hadn't been around since the incident at Jackson Blue. I thought he was done diving. I thought the injuries he sustained would have been enough to keep him from diving ever again. I considered throwing him out of the store. I wanted to yell at him to get out, to leave the store. He wasn't welcome. I stopped myself. I should be better than that.

I was surprised at the feelings that had resurfaced. I had just about forgotten Jack and what he had done to me. What he had done to Joey. The feelings were as strong at this moment as I stared at Jack as they had been that day two years earlier at Eddy Spring. I tried to push them aside. I would be the better person.

The last time I saw Jack, he wasn't so big and bad and tough. He tried to act like he was, but everyone knew he wasn't. Even the jackasses, his collection of fanboys, had stopped discussing him in the social media cave diving groups about a week after he had been taken away to the hospital.

"How can I help you this morning?" My voice squeaked a little. I hated that it did that.

"Well, well, well. Lookie who we have here. Lindsey, ain't it?"

It seemed Jack hadn't changed a bit since the incident. Still the same smug, egotistical prick he always was. Joey and I should have left him in the cave trapped beneath that boulder.

"Look, Jack, it's no secret that I don't like you. But this is a place of business, and I do represent it. Tell me what you need, and I'll sell it to you so you can leave. There's no sense in small talk."

Jack placed his hands over his heart as a hurt expression appeared on his face. The scars on his left arm were easy to see. I hoped they caused him horrible pain.

"That hurts."

I ignored his comment. "Do you need anything in particular? We don't sell a lot of cave diving equipment, so you're better off heading to Marianna to Cave Masters for that. I'm sure Danny would love to help you. If you need your tanks filled to dive around here, you'll have to come back this afternoon. I just got in and haven't had a chance to top off the banks from the weekend."

"I just need a new mask, darlin'. My old one got some rubber rot from sittin' in storage the past couple a years."

"You know they're made of silicone, not rubber." I said with a deadpan look on my face.

"Yeah, well, this was an old mask."

"Masks are over there." I pointed at the mask display to my right. "Look them over and bring whichever one you decide on to the counter. I'm sure you know how to pick out a mask that fits."

I turned away from him and headed behind the counter. I grabbed my purse and placed it on the shelf below, out of view of the customers. I had a concealed carry permit and kept a small handgun in it. I liked to keep it close by just in case. Not that anyone would try to rob a dive shop. At least I'd never heard of that happening. But with all the strange stuff happening these days, I felt safer having it at hand.

Jack stood in front of the display looking over the variety of masks we offered. Most of them had clear skirts and colorful frames. That's what the recreational divers we primarily catered to liked. We did have some black masks, mainly because Joanne knew Joey and I liked those. They were the desired color for most cave and technical divers because they kept the glare from penetrating through the mask skirts.

Out of the corner of my eye I watched Jack grab one of the black masks and put it on his face. It was the brand and model I used, and I knew it would be too small for him. I watched as he sucked in through his nose to test the skirt seal over his face. As I expected, it must not have felt good on his face because he placed it back on the display rack and grabbed another one. I made a mental note of which one it was so I could wipe it down when Jack left.

He tried on all three black masks that we had in stock, but none of them seemed to work for him. Next, he began trying on the masks with clear skirts. That would be hilarious to see big, bad Jack Johnson in a cave wearing a clear mask with pink or yellow trim. He went for the blue framed masks first. He tried on several masks. I gave up trying to remember which ones. I would wipe them all down after he left.

I continued watching Jack as I stood behind the counter bringing the computer online and getting ready for the day. Jack finally found a mask he settled on. He slowly walked over while looking around the shop as if he was trying to decide whether he needed anything else. A few seconds later, he appeared in front of me and placed the mask on the counter.

"Do you need some mask defogger with that?"

"Oh, ya know, I might as well. Mine was dried up."

I grabbed a bottle of mask defogger from the display tower next to the counter.

"Anything else?"

"I think that'll do it, darlin'."

I started to enter the items into the computer so I could get his total.

"Oh, I saw your boy this mornin' at breakfast with some brunette. They looked pretty chumsy, if you know what I mean. I hope things are alright on the home front." A shit-eating grin appeared on Jack's face.

I tried not to look shocked at this news. What was Joey doing at breakfast with someone else? Was that why he had left the house so early? Was the missing dive equipment just an excuse for missing work when he was really spending the day with another woman? What the fuck was going on?

14

Joey

It was eight thirty when I pulled off interstate 10 at exit 136 and headed into the small town of Marianna, Florida. I drove past the old Dozier School for Boys and thought about the reports of what had happened there. Dozier was a state operated facility that housed troubled boys. A reform school. It had opened at the beginning of the previous century and remained open until only a few years ago after reports of abuse. Apparently, the staff used to beat and torture the boys. There were even reports of rape and murder. The latest report said a team from the University of South Florida had found fifty-five bodies buried on the one hundred-and-fifty-nine-acre campus. Records at the facility only claimed thirty-one graves. What a horrible thing to have happened. It was too late for those boys, but it was a good thing it was finally being investigated. Maybe their families could get some closure unlike the family of the diver whose body I found at Eddy Spring. They still had no clue what happened to him.

I pushed those thoughts out of my head and a couple of minutes later, I turned onto Lafayette, the main street in Marianna. Traffic was a bit heavier during the week in the small town. Still nothing like it was in Destin, or even Santa Rosa Beach, but definitely busier than I was used to experiencing on the weekends. I arrived at a red light and checked the time on my phone. Eight thirty-seven. Danny should be settled in by now. I hit the speed dial icon for Cave Masters and heard the ringing through the car speakers.

"Gooood morning! Cave Masters. This is Danny. How can I help you this fine morning?"

Geez! Another bubbly morning person. Maybe I could set up Danny and Kelly. They were two peas in a pod, as Lindsey would say. No! Never mind! Lindsey would want to go on a double date, and I couldn't handle a double dose of that type of personality. I would probably end up stabbing my eardrums with ice picks after only five minutes of sitting across from them.

"Hey Danny, it's Joey Simmons. Can you check me into JB, please?"

"Sure Joey! Is Miss Lindsey with you?" Danny giggled.

Danny had a crush on Lindsey. It had been a few years since he started working at Cave Masters. He was just a young kid at the time, barely seventeen. He was about to turn twenty-one this year. He was sure to remind us of this every time we went to the shop. He had hinted at us all going to Beef O'Brady's to hang out at the bar and drink. Lindsey felt sorry for the kid and was actually considering it. That was all we needed, for Danny to get drunk and throw himself all over Lindsey. That would be awkward. I thought by now the infatuation would have worn off. Apparently not. It was still strong and evident. I didn't know if it hadn't occurred to Danny how obvious it was or if he didn't care. Maybe Kelly would be a good thing for him. I would just have to figure out a way to get out of any type of double date.

The light turned green. I lifted my foot off the brake and started moving through the intersection.

"No, just me this morning."

"Hey, wait a minute! It's Monday. You usually only dive on the weekends. Don't you have work today?"

Man, this kid was nosey. And talkative. And if Lindsey called Cave Masters like she had the last time…

"I took the day off. But hey, do me a favor. If Lindsey calls, don't mention that you talked to me or that I'm diving. I didn't tell her I was taking a mental health day from work."

"Ooooooo! Sneaking around behind the missus! You're gonna get busted!"

"I'm not sneaking around." I said, not bothering to hide my annoyance. "I just didn't mention it. I only decided this morning, and she was asleep when I left the apartment. Lindsey's not much of a morning person and I didn't want to wake her." Dammit! Why was I explaining myself to him? I didn't owe Danny any explanations and it only made me sound guilty of something.

"Alrighty, I won't say anything. Your secret is safe with me. I've got ya all signed in. How far back ya planning on going today?"

There he goes again. Danny was always interested in how far back everyone was going. It was his dream to one day be able to scooter far into the cave and see all of the sites back there. Danny had been a tank monkey for Cave Masters for as long as I could remember. The kid got the job there because he thought it would be the fast track to getting his cave diving certification and doing the big dives he dreamed of doing. Almost five years later Danny was still an intro cave diver. Only halfway to a goal that should have taken no more than two years. So much for the fast track.

Despite Danny being a royal pain in my butt, I felt bad for him. His boss had promised him a discount on dive equipment and free cave diving classes when he hired on. He got a discount alright, ten percent off. That was the same discount the shop owner offered to pretty much anyone who shopped there frequently. And it wasn't that great of a discount. He had offered it to Lindsey and me a few times.

Fortunately, with Lindsey's job at a dive shop, she was able to get us dive equipment at cost, which was close to a fifty percent discount. Lindsey was even nice enough to offer it to Danny because she felt bad for him and his situation. He declined. He didn't want to get his boss mad at him for buying dive equipment from somewhere else. He was still hopeful he would someday get his full cave diving certification from him. The even sadder part was that the free classes didn't happen quite as Danny had hoped for. I walked into the shop one day shortly after I had gotten certified and heard Danny in the back office talking to the owner.

"Do you think I'll be able to jump into this next cavern class you're teaching?"

"I wish I could Danny, but I need someone here in the shop to attend to customers. You know that. And right now I can't afford to hire someone else."

"Well, maybe we can plan on some dives in the evenings after the shop closes. I've already done the classroom and land drills during all those other classes you taught."

"Did you?"

"Yeah, sure, don't you remember? I sat in on a few different classes when there were no customers. It took me a few classes, but I finally got everything done. I even took the written exam."

"Oh. Yeah. I don't know. We'll see. I'm usually pretty wiped by the end of the day. Not sure I want to get back in the water in the evening."

A couple of minutes later, Danny walked out into the showroom with a dejected look on his face and his shoulders slumped. I actually felt sorry for him and the situation he was in.

"Oh hey, Joey."

He even sounded sad.

That was the only time I had seen Danny look depressed. Every other time he was overbearingly happy. Danny would have done better to get a good paying job and pay full price for his cave diving equipment and training. It would have been quicker, and he would probably have more money left over than he did at the moment. He eventually managed to get his cavern dives done and received his certification card for that level. I'm not sure how he finally convinced his boss to do the dives with him.

It was one of the happiest times of Danny's life. Lindsey and I happened to be there the next day. I thought he was bad the other times. He was really bubbly that day. He was practically walking on the ceiling. And he kept asking us over and over if we wanted to go do a cavern dive with him. I didn't want to waste time in the cavern, but Lindsey reminded me how I felt after I received my cavern diving certification.

Danny worked every weekend, and I worked during the week, so we had to plan on staying late one Saturday to meet Danny at Jackson Blue after he got off from work to go dive with him. He was so happy we agreed to stay. It was like all of his dreams had come true. I felt bad for being irritated at him all of the time.

Danny finally got his intro cave diver certification three years after that. It took that long for him to convince the dive shop owner to schedule the four required dives. I didn't know why Danny tolerated that place for so long. When he asked Lindsey and me to go on an intro cave dive with him, I didn't even fight it. It was kind of fun to see his excitement and relive my own early days of cave diving.

I wondered how much longer it would take him to get his full cave diver certification. That required a minimum of eight cave dives, and they were all much longer than the cavern and intro cave dives. He also had to complete his decompression diving classes before that. I doubted his boss would work those into the schedule. I had secretly been pushing Danny into scheduling his remaining classes with my cave diving instructor on his days off. I think he finally came around and was saving money for it.

"Joey? Ya still there?" Danny's voice broke into my thoughts.

"Oh, yeah, sorry. Not sure, Danny, just heading back for a nice, leisurely dive. Nothing in particular planned."

"Oh," Danny said, the disappointment in his voice evident. He loved to live vicariously through our dives. I felt sorry for him again. I wished I could help him get his classes done more quickly, but I could barely afford my own cave diving habit. "Well, don't forget to come by to fill your tanks after your dive. I'll sign you out then."

I was sure that meant come by and tell me all about your dive and answer the never-ending barrage of questions I'm going to have for you about your dive because my boss is too much of an asshole to live up to his word and let me take the classes he promised me years ago.

"Sure thing. See ya later."

Unfortunately, I would have to get my tanks filled at Cave Masters afterwards because I didn't want to fill them at Lindsey's shop and have to explain why they needed to be filled again. That meant I would have to endure all of the questions Danny had and to try to provide some kind of answer that would satisfy his need to experience dives he wasn't trained to do yet. I was a little surprised Danny hadn't started to push the limits of his training. I wouldn't be surprised if he eventually did now that he had his intro cave diver certification. Hopefully, he wouldn't get himself killed.

The call to Cave Masters took much longer than I expected. By the time I ended it, I had already driven through town and turned onto highway 71. I drove past Cave Masters and saw Danny outside checking on the fill whips. He saw me driving by and waved frantically. I was thankful the call had ended before I passed the shop. Otherwise Danny would have gone on about seeing me and asking me to stop in and one thing after another. After my encounter with Kelly this morning, I could only take a small dose of Danny, and only over the phone.

I turned onto Blue Spring Road and continued toward Blue Spring Recreation Area. The park was operated by the county in the summer months as a local swimming hole. It was quite busy on the weekends and made it a little difficult to get scuba equipment set and to the water efficiently. Everyone was interested in what we were doing. Everyone had questions. I felt especially bad for the divers still using backmounted tanks. They always got stopped while walking from the pavilion to the water and had to answer a bunch of questions while standing there with a hundred pounds of steel hanging from their backs. People didn't seem to notice, or didn't care.

A couple of minutes later I pulled up to the gate at Blue Spring Recreation Area. I shifted into park and exited my car to enter the code into the keypad and open the gate. It was mid-September, so the park was closed for the season. There would be no crowds to deal with. I pulled through the open gate and shifted into park again so I could close and lock it. I wished they had an automatic gate. Just enter the code and have it open and close on its own. It couldn't have been that much more expensive to get one of those gates.

Once the gate was secured behind me, I drove along the gravel road between the pines toward the parking areas. It was only a couple of hundred feet and I was at the turn off before the restrooms that led to the lower parking area. I stopped for a moment to take in the scenery. The building where the restrooms and a concession stand were located blocked part of the view of the spring basin. I eased the car onto the road to my right, stopping before I lost too much elevation. Once the entire spring basin was in view, I stopped the car again.

What a beautiful view! I looked at the blue-hued spring basin that opened onto Merritt's Mill Pond to the south. Immediately outside of the basin on the opposite bank stood several cypress trees growing out of the water. It never failed to amaze me how they were able to have their roots and the bottoms of their trunks submerged in several feet of water and not fall over. The root systems must have been extensive.

I peered down the pond and just made out the dock near Twin Caves. I couldn't wait to get a boat so I could visit the other caves on the Mill Pond more often. But first I would need to get a truck to tow the boat. Rental boats were available on the pond, but that got expensive. I could barely afford to go diving every weekend without the added expense of a boat rental.

I snapped out of my daydreaming and eased my foot off of the brake. The car began to roll forward down the hill toward the parking area. It was large enough to accommodate about a dozen cars. I backed my car near the pavilion closest to the water. There were no other cars in the lot. It was nice to be diving during the off-season when the park was closed. In the summer, it was packed with people. If we didn't arrive early, we had to park on the other side of the lot. We were never early. No matter how hard I tried, I couldn't get Lindsey up and going before eight. That meant we didn't get to the park until after ten. Ten was when they opened the gates to the non-divers during the summer.

I exited the car and quickly unloaded my duffel bag and tanks from the trunk and placed them on a table under the pavilion. I grabbed the scooters from the back seat and set them on the ground. I still had to connect the motors to the batteries before putting them in the water.

Half an hour later I had the two scooters in the water and all of my tanks lined up on top of the concrete retaining wall next to the water near the diving board platform. The platform was located directly over the opening of the cave. That was the deepest part of the spring basin. In the summer there was usually a line of kids waiting their turn to jump from the diving board into the clear sixty-nine-degree water below. Whenever we exited the cave, we had to make sure we didn't get pounced on by someone dropping into the water from six feet above. I didn't know how they tolerated the cold water in swim trunks and bikinis. I couldn't tolerate it without my drysuit. Speaking of.

Time to get into my drysuit. It was already in the low nineties, and I was not looking forward to that. I kicked off my shoes and pulled my shorts off so I could put on my undergarment. Normally, I would head into the restroom to do this, but since there was no one else around, I didn't see a point. I whipped around as I heard a vehicle driving over the gravel at the top of the hill. I scrambled for my undergarment before someone drove down and caught me standing there in my briefs. I really should start wearing boxers, at least when diving.

The vehicle stopped at the top of the hill. It looked a lot like Jack's truck, but I couldn't be sure. It was the same make and model and color, but there were lots of trucks that looked like that in the Florida panhandle. I had seen the truck here previously doing the same thing. The thought of it being Jack's truck hadn't occurred to me the last time. After the encounter at the diner, that was my first thought.

I waited to see if the truck would head down to the parking area, but it remained parked at the top of the hill for a few minutes just like the last time. This all seemed like a big déjà vu moment. I had felt that sense of familiarity the last time, too. But that had been relative to the first time I had seen Gary and Jim sitting in their truck talking. I didn't think this was going to turn into a friendship like it had with those guys.

I couldn't wait for Gary and Jim to get back from their trip. They headed to south Florida to go on a cruise right before I made my discovery. They had planned to stay down there for a few days to visit with Jim's parents after the cruise. During their stay, Jim's dad had a heart attack. He survived but ended up having to have open heart surgery. Since Jim and Gary both worked from home, they stayed to help out. They hadn't seen the new section where I was laying line. Gary was going to be so jealous when he got back and I took him there.

The truck finally turned onto the road leading down the hill, but instead of driving down, it stopped and backed up, so it was facing back toward the gate. It then took off, tossing up gravel behind it. I threw my undergarment aside, slipped my feet into my flip flops, and started running up the hill. Someone was going to have to get out of the truck to open the gate. As I was running, one of the flip flops flew off of my foot. My bare foot hit the gravel and pain shot across the sole. I stopped to retrieve my flip flop and continued to run up the hill a little more cautiously, careful not to lose my flip flop again. Unfortunately, by the time I reached the top of the hill and could see the gate, all I saw was the back of the truck as it sped away on Blue Spring Road. I still didn't know if Jack or someone else was driving it.

15

"Hey, isn't that Simmons?"

"It looks like him. I wonder what he's doing here on a weekday."

"I have no clue, but that screws up our plans for today's dive."

"I know it."

"Well, whaddaya wanna do?"

"What can we do?"

"We can just plan a different dive. Or we can head over to Cavern's Park and rent a couple of canoes and go dive Bozel."

"I kind of wanted to get back over to the Source Nouveau area and continue what we were doing the other day."

"Yeah, me too. Why don't we head back into town and find something to do for a few hours? It looks like he's about to start his dive in a couple of minutes. I don't imagine he'll be on his dive more than a couple three hours. We'll come back and start our dive while he's on his way out. I'm kinda curious what he plans on doing today."

"How're we gonna know where he's been? It's not like he's gonna leave a trail of markers for us to follow."

"No, he won't, but he might leave some signs wherever he goes. We might find some sediment hangin' in the water in the passages he's been in. If we go to the area where we found his markers on the lines before we're bound to see some evidence of where he went."

"So whaddya wanna do?"

"Let's go to the Waffle House and hang out there. We'll come back in a few hours and see if we can't figure out where all he went."

"Alright, well, let's get out of here before he decides to come up here and talk to us."

"Get ready to jump out and open the gate. And think about what you want to do for the next three to four hours. We can't be in the Waffle House all that time."

"Why not? They have bottomless coffee!"

16

Joey

That was strange. Why would someone pull into the park, then turn around and leave? The possibility of it being Jack gnawed at me. Who else could it be? Who else would do something like that? On second thought, Jack wouldn't do something like that. He would have come right down the hill and walked around like a peacock strutting its feathers. He wasn't one to hide in the background. It had to be someone else.

The more I thought about it, I had doubts about it being the same truck I had seen at the diner that morning. This truck had more chrome on it. Jack's truck was all one color with no chrome. Maybe Jack was riding with a buddy of his. Couldn't be that. Jack didn't have many friends, especially after what happened the last time I saw him at Jackson Blue. The news of his last dive a few years ago quickly made its way around the cave diving community. Besides, no one was with him at breakfast this morning.

Well, whether it was Jack or someone else, they were gone now. I couldn't help but think that whoever it was had to be the one that scooped my lead. I wished I had been able to see who was driving the truck. I pushed the thoughts out of my head. I had to have a clear mind for this dive. I couldn't let my thoughts be wandering and wondering about these things. It was going to be difficult enough to stay focused after what I found the day before. Scootering more than five thousand feet into the cave made for a long time to think about things. I needed to stay on top of my game.

I sat on one of the benches, pulled my drysuit on over my undergarment up to my waist. I stripped off my T-shirt. It was already soaked from sweat. The run up the hill hadn't helped. I grabbed a towel dried the sweat off of my upper body then tossed the towel into the trunk. I slipped a moisture wicking shirt over my head and pulled the undergarment that was hanging from my waist up and over my shoulders. The warmth was almost unbearable, but this would be necessary for me to tolerate being in sixty-nine-degree water for four hours. I wasn't sure I could tolerate one hour in that water without the undergarment and a drysuit.

I reached down and pulled the drysuit up, squeezing my head through the neck seal, making sure it was situated properly so no water would get into the suit. I pulled the zipper closed and bent down, hugging myself to squeeze the excess air out. When I stood, I felt the suit squeeze against my body now that most of the air was expelled from inside. I glanced around the area beneath the pavilion and confirmed that everything I wasn't taking with me was stowed away in the trunk of the car. Nothing extra was laying around, so I stuck my valet key into my drysuit pocket, clipping it onto a small D-ring, and slammed the trunk shut. I hurried to the water, anxious to jump in and cool off. The rest of my equipment was already by the water on top of my tanks. I didn't usually do that because it was so busy in the summer. Being the only one at the park, I changed my routine.

With that change, I decided I would enter the water by using the diving board that was usually crowded with local swimmers. I stepped onto the board and walked out to the edge. Bending my knees, I started the board bouncing until it was pushing me up into the air. After three bounces, I tucked my legs in and tried to spin my body so I could dive into the water headfirst. It didn't feel as graceful as I had hoped it would. It probably looked even worse.

The cold water felt good on my head and face. A few seconds later I felt the coolness penetrating through the thick material of my drysuit and undergarments. It wasn't quite as cold as the water directly in contact with my head, but it did feel good. It would stop the sweating.

I tried to hold myself underwater for as long as I could, but the positive buoyancy of the drysuit was fighting me and forced my body to rise toward the surface. As I ascended, I felt cold water come rushing onto my back through the neck seal. I started kicking frantically to get to the surface faster. I didn't know if my neck seal had torn or if the seal around my neck had been compromised. What I did know was that sixty-nine-degree water was pouring into my suit, and it felt really cold. It hadn't been a good idea to dive headfirst into the water! What had I been thinking?

17

Lindsey

Jack paid for his items and left the store. He caught me off guard saying he saw Joey with some girl this morning. I didn't know if it was true or not. I wouldn't put it past Jack to make something like that up to try to get under my skin. Either way, things weren't looking good for Joey. I already caught him in a lie. Or at least an omission. He should have told me he was going diving today. He should have told me his plans. Then to hear Jack say he saw him at breakfast with some floozy. I tried to suppress any reaction, but I'm sure something showed on my face. Jack was acting too smug and proud of himself after telling me he saw Joey. It took every bit of restraint I had to keep from going around that counter, putting my hands around his neck, and squeezing the life out of him.

I couldn't believe Jack was back. Not only back, but up to his old ways. It seemed he hadn't changed a bit. I thought after having his arm crushed and almost dying, he might have changed. I thought the time away might have helped him to reflect on things and see what an asshole he had always been. I also thought that after not seeing him for so long, we were done with the man. I thought he had left the area, gone back to wherever he had come from, and we would never see him again. I guess that was just wishful thinking. After a couple of years, I had become too comfortable with Jack Johnson being gone.

I wondered how Joey reacted to seeing Jack this morning. I wondered if he even saw him. Of course he did. Jack wouldn't have been able to keep himself from walking over and making sure Joey knew he was back. Just like he purposely came here to make sure I knew he was back and to try to stir some shit by telling me he saw Joey with another woman. I doubted he really needed a new mask.

If it was true that he had seen Joey with some woman, it had to be Kelly. Who else would Joey be at breakfast with? Kelly was probably up early and saw Joey loading the dive equipment into his car and invited herself to breakfast. That would totally be a Kelly move.

On second thought, Kelly was pretty drunk when I walked her back to her apartment the night before. I had to practically carry her. Could it have been someone else? Joey set his alarm for five this morning. That meant he would have left before six. Would Kelly have been up that early after she drank so much beer and then threw up in our bathroom? She should be home nursing a hangover, not up and in the parking lot only six hours later. She probably wasn't even awake yet. If it wasn't Kelly, who was the floozy Joey was with?

What was Jack up to? Coming in here to buy a mask wasn't purely by chance. Jack planned it once he saw Joey. I just know it. Jack could hardly pull the rescue thing again. After what happened, news got out to the cave diving community quickly. And with Jack in the hospital getting multiple surgeries to fix his arm, there wasn't much he could do to dispute any of it. Besides, most of it was happening on the social media sites and Jack never had a big presence on those. He was up to something though. For him to come in here all cocky like he had. Too big for his britches for sure. We would definitely need to keep an eye on him.

What I couldn't figure out was why Joey was at breakfast with some girl. Who would he be at breakfast with? It wasn't like he had time to cheat on me. He spent his weekdays at work and came by the shop straight from the vet's office to be with me most days. On the weekends, we were always diving together. Most weekends anyway. I did have to teach one or two weekends a month and Joey no longer spent those days hanging out in Eddy Spring. He went to Marianna to cave dive instead. He could also be involved with some girl from work. That didn't explain why he took his dive equipment today, though.

Unless she was going with him.

What other woman do we know that's a cave diver and lives in this area? Well, maybe it wasn't a coworker. Maybe it was another cave diver that was in the panhandle diving the caves in the area. Or maybe it was someone from out of the area. None of it made any sense.

I called Joey once more. Still no answer. Not that I expected him to answer. Then I thought about my bout of nausea earlier that morning. Had Joey tried to poison me?

18

Joey

After climbing out of the water, I stripped my drysuit off and inspected the neck seal. It wasn't torn. It was just my stupid Ninja Turtle dive into the water that compromised the seal around my neck. I turned the suit inside out and draped it over the back of the bench closest to the water. There were a few rubber coated metal benches anchored into the ground around the spring basin. It shouldn't take long for the suit to dry in the Florida heat. I pulled the top half of my undergarment off and squeezed the water out of it while my suit was getting some ultraviolet rays. Fortunately, the water had only penetrated down to my chest before I got to the surface. That should dry quickly as well. That move was really idiotic of me. That was what I got for trying to show off. Not that anyone was around to see me. Thankfully.

I sat sideways on the bench next to my drysuit and draped the top half of my undergarment behind me on the seat, allowing it to dry out. I was going to be in the water for three and a half to four hours, the last forty-five minutes or so motionless in the Deco Room letting the nitrogen slowly release from my body. I didn't want to start the dive cold and wet.

After about half an hour, my drysuit was dry and my undergarments were only damp. I'd sweat more dampness into the suit than that. Plus, the sun on it made it warm. I turned the drysuit right side out and stepped inside of it, pulling it up my legs. I pulled the top half of my undergarment on. I then pulled my dry suit up and carefully slid my head through the neck seal, making sure it was folded properly. I didn't need more water intrusion. I zipped the suit closed and knelt down, feeling the air in the suit rising toward my neck. I hugged myself again, trying to squeeze the air out and felt it slowly escaping between my neck and the seal. All appeared to be in working order.

I walked to the water and this time jumped in from the retaining wall where my tanks were. That was only a three-foot drop to the bottom of the basin. The water came up to my waist. I didn't want to chance things by jumping in from the diving board again. Once was more than enough. Ten minutes later I had my tanks clipped on and my scooters ready to go.

I dropped below the surface and situated everything properly, so I was trimmed out and balanced. I reached back, felt the oxygen tank clipped onto the rail of my butt plate, and situated Lindsey's scooter between my legs where it would trail behind me as I used my own scooter for propulsion. Everything was where it should be. I turned toward the diving platform and watched the current coming out of the cave below it, hitting the eel grass that had rooted itself just outside of the opening. The tunnels in Jackson Blue were situated beneath some farm fields and the water coming out of the cave was rich in nitrates. The eel grass loved nitrates. Just in the few years I had been diving at Jackson Blue, I noticed an increase in the amount of eel grass in the basin. It was taking over.

I hit the trigger on my scooter. The motor came to life and the propeller began to spin. I felt a rush of water pushing against my chest as the propeller sucked the water through and back toward me. The force pulled me forward and I began moving toward the cave opening. When I arrived in front of the entrance, I felt the rush of water coming out of the cave grab me and push me to the right. I rotated the scooter to the left and shoved the shroud to my right, turning the nose of the scooter into the current. The scooter overpowered the current and my body followed behind. A moment later, I was enveloped by the darkness of the cave. I reached over and pressed the power button on my dive light, illuminating the dark passage ahead.

* * *

An hour and fifteen minutes later I arrived at the end of the guideline that I had placed in the cave only two days earlier. It hadn't been easy. I usually clipped my scooter to the line a thousand feet before that location. The restrictions between there and the area I was in were small. Pushing the scooter and stage tank through had taken time. Once I was past them, I got back on the trigger and flew through the cave. It would have taken another twenty minutes if I had swum that last thousand feet. The scooter cut that time in half.

I unclipped my remaining stage tank, closed the valve, and secured it to the line. I would retrieve it on the way back. I repositioned the scooter in front of me, squeezed the trigger, and continued through the passage. I had only been through this part of the cave once the day before. I shouldn't have brought the scooter beyond the end of my line, but I didn't want to waste time trying to swim. The air in my scuba tanks limited how long I could spend in the cave. While scootering allowed me to go farther into the cave than swimming, it also meant I couldn't use as much air to penetrate the cave. The rule of thirds no longer applied. I didn't breathe quite as much when being pulled by the scooter as when I was swimming and expending more energy.

Planning a dive when swimming was fairly easy. I could use one third of the air in my tanks to penetrate the cave and one third to exit. The last third was held in reserve in case of an emergency. We never breathed a full third of the air before turning around though. That was pushing the limits a little too close, especially since the gauges were as accurate as a news story about politics no matter which side you support. They couldn't be trusted. The gauges and the reporters, but I was referring to the gauges here.

I had proven that to myself a few years earlier when I noticed the gauges on my sidemount tank regulators were always one hundred psi different from each other. I swapped the regulators on the tanks, and they were still different, only the readings were opposite what they had been. In other words, they still had the same pressures, but on different tanks. Being a little obsessive, I decided to test all of my gauges and Lindsey's, as well. There was one gauge that was five hundred psi lower than the gauge with the highest pressure. I had no clue if either one was accurate, or which one was closest to being accurate. Shaving a couple hundred psi from the penetration part of a dive was a small price to pay for the peace of mind that I would have enough air to surface from the cave even if I had issues that required me to start breathing my reserve air.

When we took scooters into the caves, it was different. The scooters allowed us to travel three to four times faster than when we were swimming. We also breathed less since we weren't exerting ourselves by having to move our legs. Even if we did breathe the same, there wouldn't be enough air in our tanks to swim out if the scooter malfunctioned. If I used one thousand psi to scooter into the cave and had to swim out, I would need three thousand psi if my breathing rate remained the same. My sidemount tanks were only filled to thirty-five hundred psi.

That meant air management had to be planned backwards. I had to determine how much air I would need to swim out from the farthest penetration I planned to make into the cave, multiply that by one and a half to give me an added buffer, and reserve that amount for the exit. If I needed eighteen hundred psi to swim out, I had to reserve twenty-seven hundred psi for the exit. That meant I could breathe eight hundred psi scootering into the cave. It doesn't sound like much, but when I was scootering, I breathed about a third less air than I did when swimming. I also moved through the cave much faster. And I always brought additional scuba tanks with me. These were the stage tanks that contained about three-fifths the volume of air that each of my sidemount tanks contained.

All of this planning was especially important when I only had one scooter, which was usually the case. Lindsey was using her scooter when we were diving together. Or Gary and Jim had their scooters. Sure, if one of us had a scooter failure, we could tow each other out. Our pace through the cave would still be faster than if we were swimming, but it would be slower than if we were not towing each other because of the additional resistance created by two divers being pulled by one scooter. I had been wanting to buy another scooter to have as a backup so if there was a scooter failure, we wouldn't have to tow each other. We had redundancy in everything else. We should have redundancy with our scooters.

Lindsey wasn't going for it, though. New scooters cost upwards of five thousand dollars. The one I wanted, anyway. Lindsey wanted us to save for another dive trip. I kind of did, too. I wanted to go back to Cozumel to do some more cave diving in Aerolito. Lindsey was more interested in going somewhere else. She wanted to go on a recreational scuba diving trip. After what happened in Aerolito when we were there six months earlier, she wasn't too anxious to go back. I couldn't blame her. But I told her she needed to face her fears.

As I scootered along the line I thought about my previous dive in this location the day before. That was when I discovered someone had scooped my lead. I went about six hundred feet beyond the end of my line. That placed me about sixty-five hundred feet from the cave opening, more than a mile. I planned on going at least fifteen hundred feet beyond that. That was if the line went that far. I was hoping it didn't. I had to reserve all of the air in my sidemount tanks to exit but could use all of the air in my stage tanks to get back to that point in the cave. I didn't do it that way, though. I divided the air more evenly among the scuba tanks. Instead of breathing the stage tanks empty, I breathed a little less than half of the air in them before clipping them to the line along the way. They would still be there on the way back. That also meant I could leave one stage tank clipped to the line before the restriction and it meant I had less to drag with me as I left the stage tanks along my path.

Because Lindsey wasn't with me, I brought her scooter to have full redundancy on this dive. Even so, I still had to plan for a complete failure requiring me to swim back out. Mechanical devices can and do fail. I could end up grabbing Lindsey's scooter to use only to find that the battery wasn't fully charged or had been drained somehow. It wasn't likely that both scooters would fail, but it was possible. I wasn't bringing the second scooter to be able to stay longer. I was bringing it so that if my scooter failed, I might have a backup that would prevent me from having to do double or triple the amount of time on my decompression stops. I had already planned for an hour of decompression stops. I certainly didn't want to do two or three hours. I left Lindsey's scooter secured to the line with the stage tank I had breathed coming into the cave. If my scooter failed, I would still have to swim part of the way, but I'd have her scooter for the last forty-eight hundred feet.

I moved along quickly, following the new line, breathing from my full sidemount tank. When I was diving with Lindsey, I usually had to switch to my sidemount tank much sooner. She moved a little more slowly through the cave than I did. It wasn't that she couldn't go faster. She could. She just didn't want to. She intentionally went slower. I didn't understand that girl sometimes. She was a very skilled diver. Better than me. But she didn't seem to want to employ that skill all the time. I didn't get it. I didn't understand why she held herself back. I tried talking to her about it, but all she said was that she liked to take it slow. She liked to watch the cave. I loved diving with Lindsey, but it was nice to be able to go at my own, much faster pace. I almost looked more forward to cave diving when she was busy teaching. I had more options. I also had plenty of air to stay back in this section for a while. I might even survey some of the new line on the way out.

I arrived at the intersection I had seen the day before. I stopped and placed a personalized non-directional marker on the line leading back out of the cave. There were no other markers on the lines. Typically, there would be. I suppose if I were stealing someone's lead, I probably wouldn't have left a marker with my name or initials on it either. I looked along both lines, trying to decide which way I wanted to go. The passage heading straight was bigger and made more sense, but there was a reason there was a guideline going to the right. Maybe whoever had done this had gone straight and run into a dead-end. On the way out, he saw this lead to the side and went that way. Maybe that was the path where the cave continued.

I hovered motionless trying to discern any water current from either passage. Where the water flow came from was usually the path to follow. This was a high flow cave, one of thirty-three first magnitude springs in Florida. This meant at least sixty-four million gallons of water came pouring out of the opening each day. That would fill almost one hundred Olympic sized swimming pools. That was when the flow was low. It usually wasn't that low.

Even with the water flow being average, I couldn't feel any significant current. The problem was that the tunnel was large. It was about twenty to twenty-five feet from floor to ceiling and thirty to forty feet from wall to wall. The current wasn't strong enough in such a large passage to make me drift one way or the other. I had to guess based on appearance. Unfortunately, that wasn't the best way to determine which path the cave kept going.

I decided to go straight. I had a feeling it might come to a dead-end. That was the only way I could explain the intersecting line. Whoever had put these lines here had walled out the passage ahead and came back to find the lead where the other line went. Even though I believed the passage straight ahead wouldn't go much farther, at least I would quickly find that out and be able to mark that off as I continued to explore the other tunnel. I knew it would bug me if I didn't check it first. I hit the trigger and took off straight in front of me.

∗ ∗ ∗

I surfaced from my dive almost four hours later. The dive lasted longer than I had expected it to. Nothing went wrong. At least not with the dive. I even turned around when I hit my turn pressure. It just took longer than I planned. I always planned my dives using conservative breathing rates, so I had a bit more air than I anticipated. Because I was so far back, more than a mile and a half, I decided to adjust my plan and stay until I reached my turn pressure rather than turning based on the time I had calculated. Lindsey would never have agreed to do that. But Lindsey wasn't on the dive with me.

I couldn't believe what I found beyond the end of my line. I wish I could have stayed longer, but I had to start making my way out. I had pushed it longer than originally planned. Fortunately, the water current in the main passage of the cave was pretty strong once I got back to the smaller area and my exit only took an hour from where I had left my second stage tank.

My decompression stops were another thing. I absorbed so much nitrogen from being at depth for almost three hours that I had to stay at my ten-foot-deep stop for almost forty minutes. That was after being at twenty feet of depth for eighteen minutes. My first decompression stop was at forty feet of depth. I couldn't believe it! I had never done a decompression stop that deep before. And because I had stayed a little longer than planned, I hadn't accounted for the forty- and thirty-foot-deep stops my dive computer told me I had to do.

I was glad Lindsey wasn't with me. She would have been upset with me for incurring a stop I hadn't planned. Actually, I wouldn't have had a forty-foot stop if she had been with me because I wouldn't have stayed in the cave as long as I did. She was definitely a stickler for the rules.

I wondered if Lindsey had figured out that I skipped out of work yet. Probably. I shouldn't have left the coffee maker set up and a glass of orange juice in the fridge for her. I thought I was being slick, but I had second thoughts about that as I was driving to Marianna. Doing all of that probably only made her suspicious.

I took my time placing my scuba tanks on the ledge over the retaining wall at the edge of the spring basin. I didn't want to overexert myself after such a long decompression obligation. I clipped the tow ropes from the scooters to one of the tanks. I pulled myself up on top of the wall next to the tanks and looked around the park. There was that truck from earlier. Only this time, it was in the parking area next to the pavilions not too far from my car. That explained the oxygen tanks I saw in the cavern. There were two tanks left on the floor in the Deco Room. That confirmed there were two divers. I wished I had thought to look for names or initials when I was in the cavern doing my decompression stops for almost an hour. At that point, I just wanted to get through the mandatory stops and get out of the cave. I was wiped from such a long dive.

Where had the divers from the truck gone? I didn't like the fact that they left earlier, probably because they saw me. They were up to something. They had to be the ones who scooped my lead. At least, they had to be one of the divers who were back there. After this dive, I had a feeling I had been scooped by more than one person, and they weren't working together.

Why didn't I see the divers from the truck on my way out? There was only one way back there. I should have seen them heading in as I was exiting. I didn't see any jump spools on the line or markers at the line intersections, so they didn't go into an offshoot unless they didn't run a line or mark their turn. That would be stupid and dangerous, but not that uncommon.

I walked over to the truck and looked in the windows. I could see two cave diving park passes on the dashboard, but the names were covered by the sunshade. That was convenient. I wondered if it was intentional. I tried to peek under the sunshade but couldn't see either name. I didn't see anything else in or on the truck that told me who these guys were. Maybe they would surface while I was still here. Maybe I'd stay until they surfaced.

I grabbed my clothes, shoes, and a towel from the trunk of my car and changed under the pavilion, wiping the sweat off of my body from having the undergarment and drysuit on. The undergarment held more dampness than it had from my mishap before the dive, just as I had expected it would. I gathered my tanks and scooter and set them on the picnic table so everything could dry while I pulled the regulators off. I moved slowly, waiting to see if I would see bubbles on the surface of the water just outside of the cave opening.

I had no idea when these guys came back and when they started their dive. Maybe they left earlier because they had forgotten something and ran back to Cave Masters to buy or borrow some piece of equipment. If that was the case, they should be heading out soon. I was in the water for almost four hours. That was a long dive by most standards. Certainly, they wouldn't be diving that long.

I pulled the regulators off of my tanks and placed them in my bag. Still no bubbles coming from inside of the cave. I looked back at the truck. I walked over to it again, looking over my shoulder at the spring basin to make sure their bubbles hadn't suddenly appeared on the surface. It remained flat except for the boil about twenty feet out from the opening created by the water flowing from the cave. I reached the truck and placed my hand on the hood. It felt warm, but I couldn't tell if that was heat from the engine recently running or from it being a hot Florida day. I walked to my car and felt my hood. It didn't feel quite as warm. They hadn't just gone to Cave Masters to get a piece of equipment.

These had to be the guys that scooped my lead. They came back and saw me and took off so I wouldn't see them. But where were they? Why hadn't I seen them on my way out? Maybe they ducked off to the side when they saw my light. I did the same thing when I saw Jack Johnson coming into Jackson Blue that one time. He hadn't slowed down, so I know he didn't see me. If these guys did the same thing, I probably wouldn't have seen them either. Especially with my mind being occupied thinking about what I had found. At least one of the guidelines I saw back there had to be placed by them. Dammit! They were heading back to put more line in the cave!

19

Lindsey

I called Joey several more times throughout the day. He didn't answer. If he was at work, he would have responded by now. He would have at least sent me a message to let me know he was busy. By noon I started to get worried. He got up at five thirty this morning. He should have been out of the water. If he was diving. Granted, there was that time he forgot his phone in the trunk of the car. He had met Gary and Jim for the first time and got to talking and never thought to get his phone from its hiding place. Gary and Jim weren't back from south Florida yet. Maybe Joey met someone else. Or maybe he was still with that woman Jack mentioned.

I thought about calling Kelly. I wanted to feel her out and see if she might be the one that Jack saw with Joey. I pulled up her contact information on my phone and sat there staring at it trying to decide whether to tap call or not. I decided against it. I didn't want to get Kelly involved if it wasn't her. And if it was her, would she tell me the truth? I had to figure out a better way to find out what was going on.

I snapped myself out of my thoughts. Why was I acting like such a jealous bitch? Joey wouldn't cheat on me. Sure, he hadn't always been truthful with me, but those incidents were about diving and pushing the limits more than I felt he should. He never lied to me about anything else.

That I was aware of.

When I hadn't heard from Joey by three, I decided to call Kelly and check in with her. Joey should have called by now. He was either dead in the cave or he was with another woman, in which case he would be dead when I saw him. I pulled up Kelly's number and tapped dial. She had been really drunk the night before. I could use that as an excuse for the call.

"Hello."

"Hey, Kelly, how are you feeling today? How's the hangover? You got pretty wasted last night."

"Oh, hey, Linds! I'm fine." She drew out the fine. Said it like fiiiiiine. It almost sounded seductive. Like she'd been up to no good. "I don't get hangovers. Never have. Don't know why, but I'm not complaining."

"Wow! I wish I was like that. I've had some doozies. After all you drank last night, and then throwing up, I thought for sure you'd be hungover this morning. Or rather this afternoon. I'm sure you slept in."

"That's funny. I don't even remember throwing up. Actually, I was up bright and early. Me and Joey went to breakfast together. He's such a nice guy. And pretty cute, too. You're a lucky girl, Linds! If you weren't in the picture, I would definitely snatch him up."

She put an emphasis on the words you and definitely. I was starting not to like Kelly so much. It was confirmed that it was Kelly who Jack saw Joey with this morning. Why would Joey get up early to go to breakfast with her? He acted like he couldn't stand her. Something was not right.

"Yeah, he is a nice guy. Oh, hey, I gotta go. I just had a customer walk into the shop. I'm glad you're feeling okay. Talk to you later."

I quickly ended the call before Kelly could get another word in. If I stayed on for another second, I would probably say something I ended up regretting. Maybe even call her a few choice names, like whore and slut. How could she do that to me? She sat in our living room drinking our beer on several occasions. She knew Joey and I had been together for almost four years. I thought we were friends. How could Joey do that to me?

My phone rang. I looked at the screen. It was Joey. Probably calling because he was lying next to Kelly when I called her, and he was worried I was onto them. He was calling to feel me out. Well, I wouldn't give him the satisfaction. Let him sweat it out. He could move in with her if he wanted to step out on me. I rejected the call. A minute later, it rang again. I rejected the call again. He would get the message. Just hang out with your new girlfriend and don't worry about me, mister. The phone rang a third time. This time, after rejecting the call, I turned it off. He was going to keep calling until I answered. And I wasn't going to answer. He didn't deserve a response.

Oooo, I was so mad! He might as well start packing his stuff and move to her place. I didn't want to spend another moment with him. There was no way I could forgive him for this.

No, that was too good for him. I'd pack my belongings and move back with my parents. Then he would be stuck with the lease on the apartment and have to pay the rent himself every month. The lease was in his name anyway. I was glad I never signed it. Let's see how he feels having to come up with the rent all by himself. He would have to cut back on his diving. He might not even be able to afford to dive at all. That would serve him right. Damn! I wish I hadn't paid the rent this morning before coming to work. That would have really left him in a jam. Just then the chime on the door sounded. I looked up.

"Hey, Roger!" I hated having to sound happy and cheerful when I wasn't feeling that way. I knew people that did that and could never understand how they could be upset one minute and happy-go-lucky the next. Joey's mother was like that. She never wanted to give anyone the impression that there was something wrong in her life.

"Hey, Linds! Just dropping off the tanks I rented this weekend. I also have the final payment for my dive gear. I can finally bring it all home with me!"

"Wow! Congratulations, Roger!" I forced a smile. "I'm sure that's a huge relief to have that paid off. Next, you'll have to buy your own tanks, so you just have to come in here to get them filled. We got a new shipment in last week. All different colors."

"No thank you! I'll keep renting tanks. I've thought about buying my own, but with the cost of the annual inspection and the pressure testing every five years, it doesn't make sense. Besides, I live on the third floor in the same apartment complex as you. And you know our elevator is broken more often than it's working. I'd hate to carry tanks up and down those steps every time I want to go diving!"

I couldn't hide it anymore. At the mention of living in the apartment complex, the dam broke and the tears came. I couldn't help myself. Roger ran around the counter to console me.

"Oh, hey Lindsey, if it means that much to you, I'll buy a tank. I didn't know that would upset you so much."

I laughed through the tears.

"No, Rog, it's not that. I'm sorry. I've just been emotional lately. That was unprofessional of me. It's just, well, Joey and I are in the middle of something. I'm moving back in with my parents temporarily. When you mentioned the apartments, I guess it just got to me."

"Oh no! I'm sorry to hear that. I thought you and Joey would be together forever. You always seemed happy with each other."

"I thought so, too. I don't know what happened. I never saw it coming."

I couldn't believe I was telling Roger all of this. Granted, I've known Roger for longer than I've known Joey. Roger has been coming into the shop for longer than I've been working for Joanne. He was the first customer I ever waited on. And he's been a faithful customer, coming in at least twice a month for the past six years. Other than that one dive trip to Cozumel before I was dating Joey, I've never seen Roger outside the shop except when our paths occasionally crossed at the apartment complex after Joey and I moved in a year earlier. That was rare, though, because we kept different hours.

"Well, whatever it is, you'll get through this. You're a strong person." Roger paused for a moment. "Look, if you need any help with moving, or anything else, let me know. Even if the elevator is out of order. I'll do what I can for you."

"That's so sweet! Thank you, Roger. I'll let you know. I'm still trying to process everything. For now, I'm just going to grab some clothes and head to my parents. When I go to get some of the bigger stuff, I might give you a call."

"Alright, hon, I'll be waiting for it." Roger started walking toward the door.

"Bye, Roger."

"Bye, Linds."

I didn't know what was happening. I didn't know why I lost control like that. That wasn't normal. I wasn't quite like Mrs. Simmons, but I could at least put on a good act when the situation dictated it. Except today. The emotions felt overpowering. I loved Joey and I thought we were going to be together forever, but I never thought he could illicit emotions like this from me. I didn't think anyone could.

I pushed the feelings aside and checked the time. I had three hours left before I could close the shop for the night. I almost started to cry again, but another customer pulled into the parking lot. I ran to the restroom and splashed cold water on my face. I could do this. I had to do this. I couldn't be a blubbering idiot in front of every customer that walked through that door.

It was bad enough that I lost it in front of Roger. He was a nice guy, but he's had a crush on me for years. He was always a little flirtatious. Not enough to be creepy, but it was there. I had a feeling his offer to help might have meant more than that. Not that I thought he'd take advantage of me so soon after a breakup. He was too nice for that. He might be setting himself up for a future opportunity though. After giving it some thought I decided I wouldn't be calling him for help.

The customer I saw pull into the parking lot stepped through the door as I walked back into the showroom.

"Hey, Julie! How were your dives this weekend?" I bit my tongue to distract myself. I didn't want to break down in tears again.

20

Joey

I took my time disassembling my equipment and loading it into my car. I waited to see if whoever belonged with the truck would surface so I could try to identify them. I walked to the truck to look inside again. Maybe I had missed something. There was nothing. Before I got a valet key to keep in my drysuit pocket, I used to hide my car keys inside the gas door. Pretty stupid because that seemed to be where most divers hid their keys. Fortunately, I never had them or my car stolen. I looked back at the water. Still no bubbles. I flipped open the door to the gas cap. No key. Damn!

I walked back to the pavilion and sat on the picnic table. As I waited for bubbles to hit the surface of the water, I reached for my phone to see what time it was. My pocket was empty. I had forgotten to get my phone from its hiding place in the trunk. I ran to the car to retrieve it. If nothing else, I could pass the time by scrolling through Facebook and Instagram. I hadn't been on either one yet that day. I got up too early, then Kelly inserted herself into my schedule, making me get here later than I had planned.

I pulled my phone out and pressed the power button, waking up the display. I had a missed call from Lindsey. No big deal. She usually called me around lunchtime to see how my day was going. If it was busy, I didn't answer. She knew to expect that. I unlocked the phone and swiped down to look at the other notifications. Holy crap! Lindsey called me eleven times! I wondered what was wrong. I checked my text messages, but there was nothing from her. Just the missed phone calls. I tapped the call back icon and waited as the phone rang. After four rings, it went to voicemail. She must be with a customer. I hung up and called again. Four rings, then voicemail again. That was strange. She usually answered the second time, even if she was with a customer. I called a third time. This time it didn't even ring. It went straight to voicemail. That was strange. Maybe Lindsey was trying to call me at the same time.

I looked at the time. Holy crap! Where had the day gone? I knew I had been moving slowly and sitting and waiting for a while, but almost two hours had passed since I got out of the water. Had I really been at the park that long?

I tried calling Lindsey a fourth time. Straight to voicemail again. What were the chances we were trying to call each other at exactly the same time twice in a row? Something was wrong. Her phone wasn't even ringing anymore. I slammed the trunk shut and ran to the driver's door. I glanced back at the water. I thought I saw bubbles popping up to the surface. I looked back at the time on my phone. I didn't know what time those guys had gone into the water, but I had already been on the surface for more than two hours. Even if they had started their dive right before I got back to the cavern and started doing my decompression stops, that was a really long dive. Their decompression stop obligation would be a lot longer than mine had been. I couldn't wait around another hour. I had to start driving back to Destin to find out what was going on with Lindsey. I slid into the car and took off up the hill.

After securing the gate, I got back in my car and turned onto the road. A few minutes later, as I was approaching Cave Masters, I saw Danny outside filling someone's tanks. He waved. He was expecting me to stop. I didn't have time. I still had more than an hour and a half drive back to Destin. The truck backed up against the scuba tank fill station looked familiar. As I passed the shop, Jack Johnson stepped out of the front door. That confirmed that he wasn't one of the guys in the cave. What was he doing in Marianna so late? Was he going back into Jackson Blue to lay more line in my section of the cave?

There was so much line back in that area. After today, I already suspected that there was more than one diver pushing my passages. Maybe both Jack and the guys from this morning were laying line all over the place. There was too much line there for just one person to have done it all in only five days.

Dammit! Why weren't Gary and Jim back from south Florida? I needed help. If there was more than one person scooping my leads, I'd never be able to reclaim the end of the line and stay ahead of them. I decided to call Gary later in the evening to see what their plans were. I needed those guys to get back so they could help me. The only way I was going to stay ahead of anyone was if I had Gary and Jim on the dives with me. We needed to get back there, split up, and line the crap out of those passages.

The traffic light at the intersection after Cave Masters turned red and I stopped just before entering the intersection. I grabbed my phone and checked my messages again. Still nothing from Lindsey. Just those missed calls. Wait! I could call the dive shop. I pulled up the contact information for the shop and tapped the call icon. I heard it ringing over the speakers. Lindsey should answer that phone. Or if she wasn't there, Joanne or one of the instructors or divemasters would answer. It rang four times then the shop voicemail message came on. That was strange. I hung up before the beep. I didn't want to leave a message.

I started to get really worried. Jack was back in town. What if he went to the shop and set Lindsey off? What if he told Lindsey he saw Kelly and me at breakfast? Would she be pissed off at him or at me? Would she think something was going on with Kelly and me? I certainly hoped not. I didn't do anything wrong. Well, except calling in sick and going diving without telling her. Yeah, she'd be pissed at me for doing that.

I called the dive shop again. Still no answer. She was pissed. Unless something happened and she had to close the shop and leave early. I didn't know what would cause her to do that. Lindsey took her job seriously. She wouldn't leave unless she couldn't help it. On second thought, it was Monday. It was one of their busiest days with everyone returning rental equipment and tanks from the weekend diving activities. She could be really busy and not able to get to the phone. That wasn't like Lindsey, though. She would have at least answered it and told me she'd call back.

I heard a horn blowing behind me and looked up at the rearview mirror. There was a guy in a dark blue Dodge Ram shaking his fist and flipping me off. I looked at the traffic light just as it was changing from green to yellow. I had completely missed it changing to green. I stepped on the gas and moved through the intersection just before it changed back to red. The asshole in the Ram laid on the horn. He started to chase after me but slammed on his brakes as another car entered the intersection from the other direction. He got stuck at the light waiting for it to cycle through again. Usually, karma like that made me happy, but I was too worried about Lindsey to enjoy the moment. I returned my attention to the road in front of me and saw a sheriff's car driving in the opposite direction. That must have been why the Ram stopped at the light rather than cutting off the other guy and chasing after me.

My stomach grumbled. I hadn't eaten anything since breakfast with Kelly. That was more than nine hours earlier. I looked at the Burger King and Taco Bell as I turned the corner onto Lafayette Street in Marianna. More grumbling. I didn't have time to stop. Not even for five minutes to go through a drive-thru. I wished I had brought snacks. I usually had something to eat with me when I went diving on the weekends, but I was too focused on sneaking out quietly this morning and hadn't thought about it. The day was not turning out well. It was one disappointment after another.

The traffic on Lafayette was still busier than usual. There were a lot more cars on the road, and everyone was driving like they had nowhere to go. I zigzagged from lane to lane, trying to pass the slower drivers, but it did me no good. I was just exchanging one slow driver for another. Why was all this traffic out on the road? Then I remembered. It was Monday afternoon. These must be people on the way home from work. I was used to being in Marianna on Saturdays and Sundays when traffic was lighter. I resigned myself to being stuck in traffic and remained in the left lane.

I slowly made my way through town, passing a Hungry Howie's in the Winn Dixie shopping center and a Subway on the other side of the street. I swallowed back the extra saliva that formed in my mouth. Screw you, Pavlov! I drove up the hill and got a red light at Madison Street. I looked over at the steak house set back from the road. My stomach grumbled again. The light turned green, and we slowly moved forward. Then came to another stop. The light a block away had turned red. Just my luck! Why didn't they have timed lights in this city? I was in the heart of the town and there was a traffic light every block. It looked like I was going to hit every red light. At least there weren't any restaurants at this intersection.

After what seemed like the longest time, I finally got through all of the lights along the downtown area of Marianna. I decided to turn onto Caledonia and take South Street to get to the interstate. It brought me through a residential area of town, but I would avoid a couple of traffic lights and, more importantly, all of the restaurants on the west end of Lafayette. Sonic onion rings sounded really good. I pushed the thought out of my head. I picked up my speed once I was on South, trying my hardest to keep it reasonable. I had taken this alternate route a few times before and always saw a cop along the way.

I couldn't get on the interstate soon enough. I tried calling Lindsey's phone again. It was still going directly to voicemail. I tried the dive shop. It rang four times before going to voicemail. I almost left a message this time but thought better of it. I had screwed up by going diving and not telling Lindsey about it. I couldn't confess that and apologize in a voicemail. Especially not on the dive shop voicemail.

A few minutes later, I was finally speeding down I-10 toward Defuniak Springs. I had ninety minutes before I got to Destin. Why wasn't Lindsey answering her phone or the dive shop phone?

21

Meanwhile, back at Jackson Blue

"How are you boys doing?" Jack asked the two guys that had just surfaced from their dive as he set his scuba tanks on the ledge near the water. "Y'all have a good dive?"

"Great dive! But you know what they say, a bad day diving is still better than a good day at work. Hey, you're Jack Johnson, aren't you?" One of the divers asked as he pulled his mask from his face.

"Yeah, that's me."

The other diver pulled his hood off of his head. "Haven't seen you around in a while. I heard you got injured pretty bad a couple years back. How are you doing?"

"Much better. Had a bunch of surgeries. Almost back to normal. Still a little stiffness in my arm." Jack flexed his left forearm and hand and rotated his wrist around in a circle, suppressing a grimace from the pain it was causing. He wasn't about to let these pansies see any vulnerabilities in him. "It's good enough to go divin' again. The hyperbaric treatment I'm gettin' during my decompression stops seems to be helping it heal faster."

The two divers in the water placed their stage tanks on the retaining wall next to Jack's and clipped the tow lines on their scooters to the hardware on the tanks.

"It's great to see you back in the game, man. I couldn't believe the lies they were spreading about you back then. Not cool to kick a guy in the nuts like that when he's down."

Jack couldn't suppress the grimace that came with that remark. The things that were said about him after that incident were worse than any physical pain he had.

"Well, that's the nature of cave divers. Ya do somethin' good, and they can't stand it wasn't them, so they talk crap about ya."

"We never believed any of the stuff that was going around. I mean, how's an inexperienced kid whose only been diving a couple a years gonna rescue the great Jack Johnson? I don't think most people believed it."

Jack wondered if they really meant it, or if they were just blowing smoke up his ass and trying to grease him for information. This wouldn't be the first time he'd been stroked by another cave diver. Fortunately, most of the grovelers were sincere, but ever since that incident, Jack couldn't be sure.

The divers pulled their sidemount tanks off and placed them next to their stage tanks.

"It don't matter none to me. I know what the truth is. And so do my friends. That's all that matters."

The divers didn't believe Jack meant that. While they liked Jack and looked up to him, they also knew he had a big ego. And people with big egos didn't like it when shit talk was happening about them.

With their sidemount tanks unclipped and on the ledge, the divers hopped out of the water and onto the grass.

"I'm Steve." The first diver said as he held out his hand to shake Jack's hand.

"I'm Brad." Brad held out his hand and shook Jack's.

"Nice to meet you, Steve and Brad." Jack shook each of their hands. "Where all did y'all go on your dive? Looks like y'all were in there a good while."

"We were in for almost four hours." Steve answered.

Jack noticed Brad trying to discreetly nudge Steve. He wondered what these boys were up to? Steve was the talkative one. Other than his comment about Jack's injury, Brad hadn't said anything else. And now it looked like he was trying to get Steve to shut his mouth about their dive. That was interesting. Jack might have to poke around the cave to look for signs of where they had been diving.

"Woooo-eeeeee! Four hours! That's a pretty long dive. I imagine more than an hour of that was on decompression."

"Yeah, we had about an hour and ten minutes of deco." Steve said.

"We were just putzing around, scootering around the Middle Grounds and Crinoid Glory area. You know how it's a maze back there. Then we did the loop back to the main passage and took our time heading out. Where are you planning on going?" Brad asked, trying to change the subject.

"Uh huh," replied Jack. "It's been a while since I've been in that area. I've been back diving here for a couple weeks now, but I've been working on an old project of mine from a couple a years ago. Somethin' I found right before my, um, accident, but then got sidetracked with all the surgeries."

"Oh cool! I wonder if it's…" Brad bumped Steve, this time not bothering to hide it.

"Hey, look at the time." Brad said as he looked at his dive computer. "It was nice running into you, Jack. Maybe we can get together some time and do a dive." Brad turned towards Steve. "You ready to load our stuff up and go eat? I'm starving."

"Huh? Oh, yeah, sure. Nice meeting you, Jack. Yeah, like Steve said, maybe we can go dive together some time. I'd really like that."

"Sounds good, gentlemen, I'll see you around." Jack turned and walked back to his truck to get his stage tanks.

That was strange, Jack thought. Those guys were hiding something. He hadn't seen any evidence of them doing any exploration in the cave, but it was a big cave. There were a few miles of tunnels in it. That one section was more than a mile in from the entrance. Jack slowly carried his stage tanks from his truck to the water. He planned on taking his time. Steve was the talkative one. Maybe Brad would head to the restroom and give Jack a minute to grill Steve about what they were doing.

Jack had his own secrets and wanted to know if he had to be more discreet. He was already taking precautions and diving at Jackson Blue in the afternoons when most people were done diving for the day. He was going to start avoiding the place on Saturdays after his last encounter. On Sundays, he didn't show up until the evening after everyone was gone.

The Saturday before, Jack had a close encounter when he was doing his decompression stop in the cavern. It was already eleven at night when he saw another diver come zooming in on a scooter. That one was all alone. Jack didn't think the diver saw him. Jack was tucked in at the side of the cavern with his light turned off enjoying the quiet and darkness that was only disturbed by a hint of moonlight seeping in. Then a bright light broke into the cave. He saw the diver scooter through the cavern toward the Rock Garden room. Jack hadn't seen the usual markings of a name or initials on the scooter, so he couldn't tell who the diver was. That was a strange hour for someone to be starting his dive.

Jack set his stage tanks down next to his sidemount tanks on the other side of Steve and Brad's. He looked in the water at the scooters that the guys had left clipped to their tanks. Maybe Brad was sneaking back at night without Steve. He seemed like the type of person who might do that. One of the scooters had three-inch-tall reflective letters on the side. BL. It wasn't that Brad fellow. The other scooter looked like it had initials on it as well, only the scooter was turned so Jack couldn't see them. Probably S something. That diver on Saturday night hadn't been either of these guys. Was there someone else sneaking around in the cave? Or was that just someone who preferred to be diving later in the day to avoid the hot sun? No telling.

Back at his truck, Jack grabbed his scooters and set them on the tailgate. He had already connected the motors to the batteries, but he pretended he was doing that now to kill some time and see if he could get Steve alone. He pulled the body off of the motor assembly, careful to remain positioned between the scooters and his new friends so they wouldn't see that the connectors were already joined. He looked over his shoulder. They were busy stripping their drysuits off and not paying attention. If Brad was going to walk off to the restroom, it should happen soon. Jack jiggled the connection around for a few seconds, then replaced the body of the scooter back over the batteries and clipped it to the motor assembly, making sure there wasn't any debris on the o ring that might prevent a good seal and allow water to leak in. He hoisted the scooter onto his shoulder and carried it to the water, lowering it in by the tow rope, and clipping it to one of his tanks.

Watching Steve and Brad out of the corner of his eye, Jack walked back to his truck and went through the same routine with his other scooter. He was going to have to buy a new battery for this scooter soon. The batteries only lasted for so long, whether they were being used or not. Jack wasn't hurting for money, but it still bothered him to spend almost two thousand dollars for a set of batteries that he hadn't used over the past two years. Jack finished his battery connecting act and carried the second scooter to the water. Steve and Brad were in their street clothes, but neither made a move for the restrooms. They were probably the kind of guys that went to the bathroom together, Jack thought. They had to hold each other's peckers while they pissed.

With his tanks near the water and the scooters floating at the surface, Jack had nothing else to do but change into his drysuit. He walked to the restroom to hold his own pecker and drain his bladder one last time before changing. He had a pee valve on his drysuit that allowed him to do his business while diving, but he liked to start with an empty bladder. Sometimes the tubing got kinked and caused the condom catheter to have a blowout. That was never fun. As Jack was standing at the urinal, the door opened. Steve walked in. Jack smiled. Here was his chance. Before the door shut completely, Brad yanked it open and followed Steve in. So much for cornering Steve. They were that type.

22

Later at Cave Masters

"Hey guys! How was y'all's dive? How far back did y'all get?" Danny called out to Brad and Steve as they entered the dive shop. "Y'all were gone a really long time! Seems everyone's doing long dives today."

"We scootered about ten miles in. I think we ended up past Greenwood and almost in Malone!" Brad replied knowing that Danny was half inclined to believe him. Brad wondered who Danny was referring to when he said everyone was doing long dives. He knew the Simmons kid was there most of the day. Had anyone else gone in there while they were diving? Or maybe there were other cave divers out on Merritt's Mill Pond diving Hole in the Wall or Twin caves.

"Really? Ten miles?" Danny replied wide-eyed, then realized his leg was being pulled and started laughing. "Nah! Jackson Blue doesn't go that far back!"

Steve laughed with Danny. Brad maintained a stoic expression. He didn't like Danny. Danny talked too much. He was always getting into everyone's business and passing along the information to other cave divers. Brad didn't like his business broadcast, especially in a community that loved to spread rumors and talk about others behind their backs.

"We just went back about eight thousand feet or so." Steve told Danny. Brad smacked him in the arm.

Danny's eyes got wide.

"Oooo! Were you back in that section called Jackson Blue Two? I've heard about that place. I didn't know if it really existed or not. No one will say anything about it."

"Steve doesn't know what he's talking about. We were back near the end of the line by the Terminal Room and then we stopped over in the Stratosphere for a little while. Nothing new."

Danny's expression turned to a frown. Brad hated to ask the next question, but he had no choice.

"Ya got any cave line for sale?"

"Cave line!" Danny's frown disappeared and his eyes got big again. "What do you need cave line for? Did you find any new passage? Are you laying line in virgin passages? Man I wish I had my full cave certification already! This is killing me." Danny practically yelled out.

"No, nothing like that. The line on my primary reel is just wearing out and I need to replace it. Gonna go through all of my spools, too, and replace everything that's getting old."

Another frown from Danny, disappointed that Brad and Steve weren't laying line in Jackson Blue. He thought for sure they were diving in the Jackson Blue Two section, if it existed.

"Oh, yeah, we keep it in the back. I'll get you a spool." Danny turned to walk into the stockroom.

"Make that three spools."

Danny started to turn back toward Brad to make another comment until he saw Brad glaring at him and thought better of it.

"Three it is."

23

Joey

The drive was taking forever. I didn't even make my usual stop in Chipley to grab a salted caramel frappe from my favorite coffee shop. Chipley, Florida had less than half of the population of Marianna, but it seemed to have a lot more to offer its residents. It had the usual Walmart and Lowe's and most of the other chains that Marianna had. The typical fast-food restaurants were also there, but so were a few local places. And it had a coffee shop. Not a chain like Starbucks, but a locally owned non-franchise place. Stopping there on the way home from diving in Marianna had become one of my few guilty pleasures. I justified the extra calories with the fact that I had burned them off in the cave. I even allowed myself a cinnamon roll every now and then when they still had one left over from the morning.

My stomach grumbled in protest with the thought of what I was passing up as I drove past the exit to Highway 77. I'd have to wait until the weekend to indulge. Or maybe the next day. I didn't know if I could wait five more days to come back.

The drive went a little faster on the interstate, but then I got stuck behind a line of slow drivers on 331. There were two slow cars side by side leading the pack, and everyone was bunched up behind them. I hated it when drivers did that. It was like they were doing it on purpose to exert control over those of us unfortunate enough to have gotten stuck following them. And I was stuck behind them driving only forty-five miles per hour. I tried to call Lindsey and the dive shop a few more times, but there was no answer at either number. I no longer believed Lindsey wasn't answering because it was too busy at work. She couldn't be that busy for the entire past hour. She was avoiding me. What had I done?

I shouldn't have called in sick and gone diving without telling Lindsey. I should have told her the truth. She would have been upset. No, she would have been pissed, but at least I would know it. I'd rather her be pissed at me and yell at me than give me the silent treatment. I couldn't stand her avoiding my calls. I had to figure out what to do next. I didn't want to go to the shop and cause a scene. It was one of the busiest nights of the week. There would be lots of divers coming in throughout the evening to return rental equipment. We wouldn't have time to talk. And I wasn't prepared for the look Lindsey would give me. If looks could kill…

No, it was probably best that I went to the apartment and waited until she got home from work. The conversation that was going to follow would be best done in the privacy of our own home. Dammit! I should have thought this through. This was how I always ended up in trouble. I didn't think things through.

We were down to forty miles per hour. This was killing me. At this rate, Lindsey was going to get home before I did. Why was it always like this when I was in a hurry? I could no longer see the line of cars around a large van in front of me. I inched out onto the shoulder to try to see around it. I quickly swerved back into the lane just in time to avoid hitting a car that had been abandoned on the shoulder, a large orange sticker adorning its window warning of an impending tow and storage fee. Damn! That was close! I inched back over, slower this time. I leaned toward the passenger seat to try to get a better angle on my view ahead. Why did I have to get stuck behind this van? I hated being stuck behind someone I couldn't see around. I was about halfway onto the shoulder when I saw another vehicle stopped on the crest of the hill ahead.

I swerved back into my lane, but not before I got a glance of the line of cars driving south. There were a lot of cars in front of me. They were all lined up close to each other. I also got a peek at one of the offending vehicles in the front of the line. The original car that had been there was no longer in the lead. Now it was an old, converted school bus with the top removed so that it could be used to haul watermelons. Great! No wonder this lane was moving so slow. I couldn't see the culprit in the left lane because it was blocked by the converted bus. That was the asshole, though. As loaded down as the bus was, it wasn't able to move any faster.

I resigned myself to being stuck in the slow progression south. I should have taken 231 to 20 instead. It normally took about fifteen minutes longer going that way, but maybe the traffic wouldn't have been so bad. I would have also had more options on how to get to Destin. At the speed we were going on 331, this was going to take me half an hour longer than it should. I slammed my fist on the steering wheel. This was so frustrating! I really wanted to smash another beer bottle. I hated slow drivers!

This issue with the exploration project was really getting to me. It was stressing me out. I couldn't remember ever feeling this much anxiety. I didn't feel like this even when Earl Hewitt was forcing me to get rid of a dead body.

I started thinking about the dive I had done earlier to try to keep my mind off of the traffic. If I could focus on it analytically, maybe something would pop out that I hadn't thought of before. I went straight at the line intersection thinking it would dead-end soon after. I couldn't see a reason for there being an intersection otherwise. Boy was I wrong. The passage kept going and going. I finally reached the end of the line. The tunnel just ended at a wall. There was an arrow near the end of the line. I looked at it and read the initials JS. My initials, but it wasn't one of my personalized line arrows. Someone was mocking me. Someone had marked their line arrows with my initials and placed one of them there. It had become personal.

I wanted to look around the passage to try to find a lead that would keep going beyond the end of the line, but I was too curious about the other line. The line at the intersection. If I was going to have time to check out the passage it led into, I had to turn around. I hadn't expected there to be so much line, not with the intersection as well.

I had briefly considered surveying the line on the way out, but that would have taken too long. I didn't have the time or the air in my scuba tanks to do that and check out the other passage. The air I did have went quickly. I was too upset, too angry, and I was breathing through it faster than I normally did.

On second thought, maybe thinking about the dive wasn't such a good idea. It was making me more anxious and upset than dealing with the traffic and thinking about Lindsey being mad at me. I needed to occupy my mind with something. What was up with Kelly? Clingy Kelly. I laughed out loud at that. It was appropriate. She had only moved in a month earlier and had latched onto Lindsey and me. Lindsey encouraged it. She should never have invited her over that first night when we met her in the parking lot. Now I had to be stealthy to get into my apartment when I got home after work. Apparently in the morning as well.

Had I known she was going to be awake when I was leaving this morning, I would have tried to avoid her. Who would have thought she would be up so early as if nothing had happened after drinking so much and throwing up in our bathroom. Maybe throwing up had helped her avoid a hangover. I filed that in the back of my mind for future reference.

I didn't get Clingy Kelly. I was never super friendly with her. I tolerated her at best. I was almost mean to her. Yet, she ignored that and kept coming over anyway. It would be one thing if it was all about hanging out with Lindsey, but she seemed to be more interested in me. Even though she wasn't a scuba diver, she seemed so interested in the cave diving we were doing.

Granted, a lot of people showed interest. It seemed different with Kelly. I never thought she was being flirtatious, but I wasn't sure anymore. Maybe that was her end goal. Maybe the interest in cave diving was her way of trying to get closer to me. And I played right into it this morning. It wasn't cool of her to do that to Lindsey. Kelly genuinely seemed to like Lindsey. I didn't get it, and I certainly wasn't interested in Kelly that way. I wasn't interested in her at all.

The watermelon bus finally turned off onto a dirt road a few miles back, but the car that was behind it in the right lane didn't move any faster. It might have even been going slower. I considered taking the car onto the shoulder and passing everyone, but with my luck, there would be another broken down car blocking my path and I'd never get back into the lane. The car in the left lane turned off of 331 at the light in Freeport. As soon as the light changed to green, the line of cars in the left lane took off through the intersection. I found an opening, swerved into the left lane, and sped up. The car in the left lane that ended up behind me laid on the horn. There was plenty of room. The driver was just being an ass. There was sufficient space between us and if she didn't speed up, someone else would have done the same thing.

It took me more than an hour to get to this point. I still had another forty-five minutes to go. That was if I didn't get stuck behind more slow drivers. Fortunately, the rest of the drive went faster. By the time I got to Destin, my stomach was really angry at me. I hadn't put any food into it in almost twelve hours. I couldn't remember the last time I had gone that long without eating. I tried to ignore it.

I drove to the dive shop and turned into the parking lot before I noticed Lindsey's car wasn't parked under the tree in its usual spot. I moved my phone to wake up the screen and saw it was only a little after five. That was strange. Lindsey should still be at work. The shop didn't close until seven on Mondays.

I cruised through the lot. Maybe there had been another car in her usual spot when she got here this morning. I scanned all of the cars until I saw Joanne's SUV. That was also strange. Joanne was never at the shop on Mondays. She hated all the activity and usually left that to Lindsey. I turned at the end of the line of parked cars and started coming back toward the shop in the lane closest to the front of the shopping center. I stopped in front of the shop and looked in through the glass door. I saw Joanne behind the counter helping a line of customers. She looked frazzled, her hair was up in a messy bun, strands sticking out everywhere. No wonder the phone wasn't being answered. Lindsey had to be in the back putting returned rental equipment away or pulling some new equipment out of storage for one of the customers. I watched for a few minutes, expecting to see Lindsey walk out from the back room any minute.

I heard a horn sound. I looked in the rearview mirror. There was a dark blue Dodge Ram behind me. Was that the same one from Marianna? I tried to get a look at the driver, but the sun was reflecting off of the windshield and I couldn't see through the glare. I eased off the brake and inched up, glancing one last time into the shop hoping to see Lindsey. She never made an appearance.

Lindsey wasn't at work. She couldn't be. I wondered if she had come in at all. I considered parking and going in to talk to Joanne, but there were too many customers in there for her to attend to me. She would probably put me to work helping her. I had never worked there, but I spent enough time in the shop hanging out with Lindsey that I had started helping her whenever it got busy. I was probably more familiar with the stockroom and computer system than Joanne. There was no way I could stay and help. I had to find Lindsey, and I had to get something to eat.

I decided to head to our apartment instead. Maybe Lindsey felt sick this morning. But if she had, why hadn't she left a message? She called a bunch of times. How difficult would it have been to leave a message that she wasn't feeling well and took the day off from work? She hadn't sent a text message either.

The irony of my thoughts hit me. I had no room to talk.

I started to get really worried. This wasn't like Lindsey. I turned toward the parking lot exit and almost drove head on into the Ram. There was no glare on the windshield this time. How had he gotten from behind me to in front of me?

The driver started shaking his fist at me, one of his fingers was pointed straight up. It was the same guy from Marianna. This time, looking at him straight on rather than through my rearview mirror, I recognized him. I didn't know his name, but I knew he was a cave diver. I had seen him at Jackson Blue several times. I wondered if he had followed me to Destin, still mad at me for leaving him stuck at the red light back in Marianna. That would be road rage on a different level. No one was that crazy.

Just as I thought that, I saw the driver's door to the Ram fly open and the man started to step out. He looked angry and was staring right at me. Was he really going to come over and try to kick my ass for holding him up at a red light two hours earlier? I stepped on the gas and swerved around the door almost clipping him. He managed to step back before I could hit him with my car. He also managed to punch the back door window of my car as I drove by. He punched it hard. I was surprised the glass didn't break. If he had hit the body, I'd almost certainly have a large dent.

I slowed to turn and then sped up once my front tires were pointing forward. I saw a car ahead starting to back out. I quickly glanced in the rearview mirror and saw the guy in the Ram running toward me. His truck remained in the middle of the parking lot with the driver's door open. What a maniac!

I hit the horn to warn off the driver ahead and swerved to the left to avoid hitting his right rear quarter panel. He stopped just in time, and we barely missed each other. Fortunately, there was no one at the exit waiting to merge into the traffic on 98. The traffic was heavy though. As I waited for my opportunity to escape into the afterwork rush hour traffic slowly moving along 98, I glanced to my right and saw Dodge Man running back to his truck. He had given up on the idea of a foot chase. I looked back at the traffic and saw an opportunity for me to turn right out of the parking lot. It wasn't the way I wanted to go, but I decided it would be best to get out of that parking lot and get lost in traffic before the maniac that was after me caught up and pulled a gun out. I didn't want to be featured on the next Florida Man episode as the victim.

I found my chance and stepped on the gas, spinning my tires before they found their grip on the asphalt and pushed me out into the flow of traffic. More horns blasting. That time it was close, and I deserved it. I did kind of cut someone off. But that was a lower risk than what I had facing me back in the parking lot with Maniac Man. As I sped off westbound on 98, I looked to my right and saw the Ram guy slamming his fists on his steering wheel as he waited for the same driver that almost blocked my exit. At least I thought he was hitting the steering wheel. All I saw were his arms flailing up and down from my viewpoint in my car. His truck was jacked up too high for me to see below his shoulders. A product of inadequacy.

I hoped he hadn't recognized me, but that was unlikely. I was going to have to keep an eye out for this guy whenever I went diving at Jackson Blue. He was a little unbalanced. Okay a lot. There was no telling what he would do the next time he saw me if he recognized my car. I still wasn't sure if he had followed me to Destin because of the traffic light incident or if it was coincidence that I saw him twice in the same day.

I drove to the light right before the Destin Bridge and got into the left turn lane going toward the Destin Harbor Boardwalk. I kept an eye on the rearview mirror to make sure Maniac Manny hadn't caught up to me yet. That was my nickname for him. The green left turn arrow lit up and I flipped a U-turn and started heading east. A minute later, I saw the Ram heading in the opposite direction. I found an opening in the right lane, swerved over, and eased up so I was partially hidden by the car to my left.

Before I lost sight of him, I saw Manny in his truck looking straight ahead. He was apparently trying to locate me in the traffic congestion in front of him. I ducked down just in case he turned to look to his left. As we passed each other, I relaxed. Even if he had seen me and turned around, he would never catch up to me in this traffic. I would be turned off of Highway 98 before that happened. Just in case, I kept looking back to watch him. It was easy to spot the jacked-up Ram above all of the traffic on 98. When I saw him drive past the next break in the median, I relaxed even more. He wasn't flipping a U-turn. He hadn't seen me.

Being chased by a crazy Florida Man had given me a respite from worrying about Lindsey, but now with that no longer an issue, the worry came back tenfold. A few minutes earlier, I had been thankful for the heavy traffic. Now I wanted everyone to get out of my way so I could get home. Traffic in the left lane seemed to be moving a little faster, so I swerved over when I found an opening. As soon as I did that, the traffic in the right lane began moving faster. Figures! That always happened. Lindsey was always telling me to pick a lane and stay in it. We weren't going to get there any faster by constantly changing lanes. I knew she was right, but I couldn't help myself. I hated to be stuck in a slow-moving lane as faster traffic moved by next to me. I resisted the urge to switch lanes again. A few seconds later the left lane was moving faster again. I was thankful for my ability to not follow my impulse that time.

Fifteen long minutes later I pulled into the parking lot to our apartment complex. It should have taken less than ten minutes. I turned to the left to go toward our building. As I rounded the corner near the dumpster, I saw tiny shards of glass reflecting off of the asphalt. We hadn't gotten all of it swept up the night before. They weren't big enough to cause any issues unless someone was walking around barefoot. If they did that, then they got what they deserved.

I looked for Lindsey's car, but it wasn't in its usual spot. We didn't have reserved spaces unless we were willing to pay for covered parking, which we weren't. Everyone in the complex, at least on this side of it, tended to park in the same spot every time. I looked at the other cars in the parking log just in case someone else had been parked in Lindsey's usual spot when she got home. That sometimes happened when people had guests visiting. Her car wasn't anywhere to be found.

I parked my car and ran toward our apartment. Maybe she left me a note. I didn't try the elevator. It probably still wasn't working. I ran to the steps instead and took them two at a time to the second floor. I flew down the walkway and jammed my key into the lock when I reached the door. I pushed open the door and rushed inside. Lindsey wasn't in her usual spot on the couch. I ran into the bedroom. No sign of her there either. What the hell? Where could she be?

I scanned all of the surfaces for any notes that she might have left. Just then I noticed the closet door was open. That was strange. Lindsey never left the closet door open. I walked toward it, reached in, and flipped the light switch on. Nothing looked out of order. But then again, I usually only looked at the small area in the back corner that was relegated for my use. As I looked around the perimeter of the closet, I noticed something different. The bag Lindsey used whenever we headed off for a long weekend was missing. And some of her clothes might have been missing, too. At least, from what I could tell by the empty hangers. Where had she gone, and why hadn't she told me she was leaving? I tried calling her again. Still no answer.

24

Lindsey

A couple of hours earlier

I was thankful Joanne had rushed in to relieve me. While I had been feeling queasy, it wasn't bad enough that I needed to take something. It had to be my nerves after seeing Jack this morning and hearing him say he saw Joey and Kelly at breakfast. I knew I wasn't going to be able to deal with customer after customer coming into the shop that evening. When Joey began calling the shop phone, it was too much. It was easy enough to turn my phone off to avoid his calls, but I couldn't turn off the ringer on the shop's landline. And it didn't look professional to ignore the phone with customers standing right in front of me. I had to make up the excuse that it was one of our suppliers a couple of times and that I'd get back with them when I wasn't so busy. I got tired of making excuses.

I left the shop and drove to the apartment. I wanted to get in and out before Joey got home. His first call happened an hour earlier, and if he was just leaving Jackson Blue, I had about an hour before he got home. He could have first called me once he was on the interstate, though, which only gave me about half an hour until he got home. That might be cutting it close. I grabbed my weekend duffel bag and stuffed it full of clothes and shoes. It was too full to zip it closed. I glanced around the bedroom but didn't see anything else I thought I might need tonight. I ran out and down to my car. I wanted to be gone when Joey got home. I wasn't ready to face him yet.

I got into my car and backed out of the space. Just as I was shifting into drive, Kelly pulled into the parking lot and started hitting her horn. Ugh! She was the last person I wanted to see. Well, second to last. Kelly pulled up next to me with her window down. She was waving at me. I had no choice but to acknowledge her and open my window. *Keep it together, Linds.*

"Hey, Lindsey! I didn't expect to see you here so early. Aren't you usually at work at this time?"

She conveniently knew my schedule. I wondered if she was heading home from being with Joey or to spend an hour with him before I was supposed to get home.

"Oh, I wasn't feeling well so I took off early." I didn't want to say too much. I certainly didn't want to tell her I was going to my parents' house. She might mention it to Joey, and he might show up. "I'm just going to get some milk of magnesia for my belly. I've been feeling queasy all day."

"Aww, I'm so sorry. I hope it's nothing major. Anyway…"

"Look, I have to go. I need to get this done and get some rest. I'll talk to you later."

I stepped on the gas and sped away. I heard Kelly start to say something as I was pulling away but couldn't make out what it was over the sound of the engine. I quickly pulled out of the parking lot and turned left, away from 98. It wasn't the most direct route, but it would insure that I didn't pass Joey on the road. I hadn't wanted to run into anyone, especially Kelly. Although, I'd be okay with running *over* Kelly.

I drove to the beach. I needed to go for a long walk and clear my head before going home. I hadn't even called mom yet to tell her I was moving back into my old room. I wasn't ready to talk to anyone about it. It was bad enough I had to tell Roger earlier after breaking down in front of him. I wasn't sure I wanted to tell mom. I might just get a hotel room for the night and think things over.

I pulled into the small parking lot for the public beach access. I parked the car, kicked off my flip flops, and ran toward the water. I instantly felt a little less stressed just hearing the sound of the waves and feeling the sand between my toes. I loved living near the beach. It was my escape from the stressors of life. Not that I had much stress in my life. At least not until Joey showed up.

I had never thought about it before, but the big stressors only started after I met Joey, and they all had to do with him. First there was Earl. Then there was Jack. Then that incident with Gary in Mexico. And now this. Never mind all the little events like him sneaking off to go diving alone. I worried about him every time he went cave diving without me. Jim was a little more reserved and tended to keep Joey and Gary in line. But they weren't in town at the moment, so Joey was left to his own devices on the weekends I had to work.

I didn't have any other stress in my life. I had a job I loved. It would be nice to earn more money, but I knew Joanne paid me better than most dive shops paid their employees. I saw the revenue the shop took in. There had been some months when Joanne had to pay me out of her own pocket because there wasn't enough revenue streaming in to cover the payroll. I felt a little bad about it, but I couldn't afford to not get paid. Joanne knew that and didn't take advantage of our friendship. Fortunately, I had been able to change some things so that the shop was bringing in enough money during the winter months and that hadn't been an issue this past year.

Not that it mattered much. Joanne didn't need the money. She was well off. She had a retirement check coming in from a previous career. The dive shop was just a way for her to travel around the world scuba diving and writing it off on her taxes. I wasn't sure if she made any money from the business.

I enjoyed the work and the people. I loved the atmosphere. And I really loved scuba diving. Even if the money wasn't the best, the life I had because of it was worth it. The only real stress was not having Kona living with me. I hated not having her at home to snuggle up with in the mornings while I drank my coffee and in the evening while I streamed Netflix. That was partly my fault. I didn't earn enough for us to live in any of the places we had found that allowed pets. I still got to see her every day, though. I made sure of that. But not having her living with me was the only stress in my life other than Joey.

I couldn't believe he was cheating on me. And with someone he claimed to not like. Was it all just an act? Did he say those things to try to throw me off? His dislike of Kelly almost seemed over the top. How had I let myself be fooled like that? How had I not seen it? All of these questions flew through my head as I walked ankle deep in the surf along the beach. The answers weren't coming to me, though. I never thought this was possible. I never thought Joey would cheat on me. I thought he loved me. I thought we were forever. Boy was I wrong!

I didn't know why I was getting so emotional. I loved Joey and it hurt for this to be happening, but it wasn't like me to react this way. I usually had better control over my emotions. I could at least control them at work in front of customers. I still couldn't get over how I had lost it in front of Roger. That was unprofessional. And Roger was the last person I wanted to seem vulnerable to. He was a nice guy, but now he was probably going to get more flirtatious.

I remembered the times Roger had asked me out before Joey and I started dating. How could I have forgotten about that? It was disgusting. Roger was eight years older than me, and I was only seventeen at the time. It wasn't much of an age difference now that I was twenty-three and Roger was thirty-one. But for some reason seventeen to twenty-five seemed wrong. I kept giving him excuses, but he still asked at least once a month. He wasn't overbearing, just persistent.

I finally told Roger I wasn't interested because of the age difference. Unfortunately, that didn't slow him down. With the knowledge of why I was rebuking his advances, he tried to find ways to minimize the age difference. I still knew he was twenty-five. It wasn't until Joey and I were dating that Roger finally backed off. But only a little. Roger was still mildly flirtatious. He just didn't ask me out anymore. That was sure to change.

Why was I thinking about Roger? I should be thinking about the situation between Joey and me. I should be thinking about what I was going to do next. Besides moving out. I would have to go back to the apartment to get the rest of my belongings at some point. That would be easy. I could get them while Joey was at work. Or at least while he was supposed to be at work. I wasn't sure he had gone to work today.

First, he got up super early, even for him. His dive equipment was gone and so was my scooter. Then Jack came in and told me he saw Joey at breakfast with another woman, which Kelly confirmed it was her. And he didn't answer his phone all day. Did he go diving? Or did he take the equipment so he could use it as an excuse when he was really spending the day with Kelly? How long had this been going on? I broke down in tears again.

Maybe I didn't need to think about any of this. Maybe I just needed to walk along the beach, enjoy the sunset, and listen to the waves gently breaking at my feet. I stopped walking and squished my toes into the wet sand. That felt so good! I pulled my phone and keys out of my pocket and sat down on the sand right where I was. A small wave came at me and broke over my legs, soaking my shorts. I didn't care. There were towels in the car. I squished my toes into the sand and enjoyed the feeling of the wetness oozing between them and the warm water dripping off of my legs. I laid back, not caring how wet I got. I wished I had remembered to grab the drybag from the car so I wouldn't have to hold the phone and keys up out of the water. No matter. They would be fine as long as I didn't submerge them.

My phone rang. I held it above my face to see who was calling. Joey. I wondered if he had gotten home yet. It was almost six. He was probably there. This was about the time he usually got home from work. Had he gone by the dive shop and seen Joanne there instead of me? Probably. He usually stopped in. The phone stopped ringing. It must have gone to voicemail. Well, I wasn't ready to talk to him yet. Let him suffer for once. If he even cared that I wasn't there.

The phone rang again. I should never have turned it back on. There was no notification alerting me that I had a new voicemail. He must have disconnected and redialed. Good. He knew something was wrong. I wondered how many times he would call before he finally gave up. Why was he bothering? Why didn't he just go over to Kelly's so she could console him. Did he even need to be consoled? I started crying. Maybe I should talk to Joey. Maybe I should answer the call and tell him where I think he should go. It stopped ringing again. Maybe he would leave a message this time.

No message. Instead, the phone rang for the third time since I had gotten to the beach. My finger hovered over the green icon while I contemplated whether I wanted to talk to him or not. I wasn't ready to think about this, but if I didn't answer he would keep calling over and over. I held my finger over the screen trying to decide what to do.

I finally swiped down, rejecting the call, and turned my phone off. I tossed it toward the dry sand behind me. It was too late for him to apologize. I wanted him to leave me alone so I could relax on the beach and clear my mind. I twisted my head and looked back at my phone to make sure it made it beyond the reach of the surf. I tossed my keys and watched them land just beyond the phone. Joey would have been proud of that. I started crying harder just thinking about him. Why was I so emotional? I hugged myself and lay there listening to the surf and watching the sun slowly setting below the horizon to my right.

* * *

I was dreaming that I was drowning. Water was splashing onto my face, into my mouth, and down my throat. I couldn't breathe. I started coughing and woke up. I continued coughing, trying to clear the salty water out of my throat. What was going on? I raised my head, confused and unsure of where I was. Why was I wet? I rubbed the sleep out of my eyes and pushed myself up into a sitting position. I was still on the beach. I must have fallen asleep while the tide was coming in. I started shivering. The temperature had also dropped with the sun. The water was warm, but once it receded and left me exposed to the chilled air, I felt the cold. Being soaked through didn't help matters. I remembered my phone and my keys. I whipped my head around and saw them lying on the sand several feet behind me. The surf had reached them, but only sporadically. The sand beneath them was wet, but they weren't submerged.

I scooted back on my bottom until I could reach them and snatched them up from the wet sand just as another surge of water washed over me reaching beyond where the phone and keys had been. The screen on my phone lit up when I pressed the power button. At least that was okay. It was supposed to be water resistant, but I didn't trust that claim. I wouldn't dunk it in the water. Although after this I might have to in order to rinse the saltwater residue off of it. I hoped my key fob had fared as well as the phone. My hand trembled from the cold as I felt the protective cover. It didn't feel wet, but it was difficult to tell because my hands were wet and shriveled from being in the water while I slept. How long had I been asleep?

With my hand shaking from being cold, I pressed the tip of my finger against the fingerprint sensor on the phone. It didn't recognize it. I tried again. Still nothing. Maybe I was shaking too much. I tried the other finger I had programmed into it. Still nothing. I looked at my trembling hands and saw the prune-like appearance of my palms and fingertips. Even at the best of times, the sensor only worked about half the time. There was no way it would work with my fingers looking like that. I wondered how I had not woken up when the water had soaked me.

I tapped the power button on the side of the phone, almost dropping it into the water because I was shaking so much. A pattern of nine dots appeared on the screen and I quickly swiped the shape of an L over them, except it was more of an E than an L because I was shaking even more. I tried a few more times and finally got the correct pattern the fourth time. The phone screen came to life. It was eight o'clock! I had been asleep for two hours.

The trembling in my hands suddenly moved up my arms and, before I knew it, my entire body was shaking uncontrollably. I had to get out of these wet clothes and warm myself up. I struggled to stand, having difficulty because of the shakiness in my limbs. It took about a minute, but I finally managed to get upright. I wrapped my arms around myself to try to get some heat into my core. I looked around trying to remember where I was in relation to my car. I was having trouble thinking straight and remembering what had happened once I parked. I looked at the sand, but my footprints had been washed away by the surf. I was pretty sure I had walked to the east when I got here. Yes, I had. I had started going west, but that put the sun in my eyes, so I turned around and walked to the east with the sun on my back. Remembering that, I turned to the west and began walking. I couldn't remember how far I had walked before throwing myself down onto the wet sand.

That was so stupid, Lindsey! What were you thinking?

I chastised myself for getting into this situation. I picked up the pace and tried to run. My legs were too weak and shaky to run very fast, but maybe the movement would help me warm up. I moved away from the water toward the houses to my right. I still couldn't remember how far I had walked, and I didn't want to walk past the public parking lot where I left my car.

As I stepped from the wet sand onto the dry sand out of reach of the surf, I felt the warmth left over from the heat of the sun. I thought about lying down and covering myself with the warm sand. That would feel so good! I decided against it. I was afraid I would get too comfortable and fall asleep again. It would be better to get to my car, strip off my wet clothes, and use the towels I kept in the backseat to dry my skin and wrap around myself. I could also get in the car and blast the heat.

My legs started to feel a little stronger and I jogged faster, looking up every path leading out of the beach back toward the road. I had parked my car right next to the sand. I would be able to see it from where I was jogging. A few minutes later I finally came to the lot where I had left it. I turned onto the path and ran toward the car, trying to make the key fob work and unlock the doors. I hoped it still worked.

I knew there was a way to unlock the door manually, but I didn't know how. And I really needed the key fob to work so I could start the car and turn the heater on.

Nothing happened during the first couple of attempts at unlocking the doors. I was afraid the fob had gotten wet and wasn't going to work. I kept pressing the buttons, hoping for something to happen. Finally, the lights on the car flashed on as the doors unlocked. Thank goodness! A few seconds later I tossed my phone and keys on the roof of the car and pulled the back door open so I could grab the towels from the backseat. I glanced around to make sure I was alone. There was light traffic on scenic 98, but no foot traffic. I pulled my shirt up over my head and wrapped a towel around my torso, rubbing vigorously to dry off and try to get some heat back into my core.

Once I was mostly dry from the waist up, I draped the towel over my shoulders and grabbed the other towel. I pushed my shorts off and wrapped the second towel around my waist and rubbed my legs dry. I was still shivering but not nearly as bad as I had been. I chastised myself again for falling asleep in the surf during high tide. *That was so stupid!*

I finally finished drying myself off. Well, everything except where my bra and panties were, but that would have to do. I wasn't about to strip down completely naked in public. It was dark. I could pass my underwear off as a bikini if anyone pulled into the lot. I was going to have to put my wet clothes back on before checking into a hotel, though.

I began to close the rear door of my car when I noticed my duffel bag on the seat farthest from me. *I had clothing with me!!!* I had forgotten about that. As tears began to well up, I grabbed it, pulled it toward me, and reached inside to sort through the clothes. I pulled out a pair of yoga pants and a sweatshirt. I used the sweatshirt to wipe my eyes. I had no idea why I was crying again. I was happy that I had packed some warm clothing! I felt around until I found a pair of panties and a bra. So much for not stripping down in public. I wasn't about to put dry clothes on top of my wet underclothes. I scanned the area around me. Still no pedestrians, just the occasional car on the road, and my car was blocking anyone's view of me from the shoulders down.

I kept the towel around my shoulders and tugged my wet bra off. After drying myself, I pulled the sweatshirt on, relishing its warmth. The sun shining in through the car windows earlier had heated up the clothes in my duffel bag. I tossed the dry bra onto the front seat. I would deal with that once I was completely dry and sitting in the car. Thankfully, the sweatshirt was long enough to reach down to my thighs. It could almost be worn as a dress. One more glance around and I dropped the wet panties and dried myself off. I slipped into my dry panties followed by my yoga pants. I finally stopped shivering. The warm, dry clothes felt so good! The tears started back up.

I wiped them away and tossed the wet towels on the floor of the back seat, grabbed my phone and keys off of the roof of the car, and shut the door. I opened the driver's door, picked up the bra from the seat and tossed it in the back as I crawled inside. I started the car immediately. The air conditioner came on blasting frigid air on me. I quickly rotated the temperature setting to hot. Thankfully, the heat of the day meant hot air was blowing out of the vents almost instantly. It felt wonderful! I sat there hugging myself, trying to get my body temperature back up. *That was so stupid, Linds!* I almost got hypothermia all because of some stupid guy. With that thought, the tears were back.

25

Joey

I searched the apartment for any clues as to why Lindsey had left work early. Maybe she left me a note. There was nothing on the kitchen counter or the coffee table. Nothing on the dresser. I pulled the couch and the bed away from the walls. I pulled the cover and sheet off of the bed. There was no note. It was foolish of me to think there might be one. I didn't think we even had any writing paper in the house. We did everything on our phones. She would have sent me a text message.

I checked my phone. There was still no message from Lindsey. I called her again, but it went directly to voicemail. I thought about calling her mom, but I didn't want to worry her. Actually, I didn't want to have to answer to her mom. She would not only be upset about Lindsey being off somewhere alone, but she would ask me question after question, and I wouldn't have any answers. Where the hell had Lindsey gone? Why wasn't she answering my calls or text messages?

I checked the time. If she had been at work, she would be heading to her parents' house in about thirty minutes to take Kona for a walk. That gave me enough time to bring my dive equipment up to the apartment and head over to try to catch her there. I ran down to the car and started to unload everything. I grabbed the scooters from the back seat, put one on my right shoulder and carried the other by the handle on the nose. I started to walk toward the steps. I should have checked the elevator before grabbing the scooters. It was Monday and it might be working. Then again, probably not. I'd walk the scooters up the steps and check the elevator before hauling the scuba tanks up.

As it was, the elevator was still out of order. So much for that idea. I headed back to the car and made three more trips back up to the apartment. One good thing about living in this apartment complex was that I didn't ever have to work out my legs. They got plenty of exercise on those damn stairs, especially on the weekends when I moved the dive equipment back and forth.

I should have hung up the wet gear and drysuit in the bathroom, but I was running out of time, so I dumped it all in the bottom of the tub. Lindsey would kill me if she saw that. She should be on her way to her parents' by now. I didn't even have time to jump in the shower and rinse off. She'd have to deal with my musky odor from being in the drysuit for four hours.

I stepped out of the apartment, locking the door behind me, and started down the steps. I glanced over at Kelly's apartment just as her door was opening. Dammit! I didn't want to get stuck talking to her. I quickly ran down the steps, jumping down the last five steps and ducking around the corner. That was a mistake. I landed with my ankle in a weird position, twisted it, and instantly felt a sharp pain. Great! I ducked into the alcove of one of the apartment units, but not before I noticed Kelly was carrying a large duffel bag. I wondered where she was going. When I was in her apartment the evening before I had only noticed suitcases spread around the bedroom area. That must have been shoved beneath something. Maybe she was going away for a few nights. That would be a relief to not have to hide from her every time I stepped outside.

I rubbed my ankle as I watched Kelly from my hiding spot in the shadows. She reached the bottom of the steps and started walking toward the parking lot with the duffel bag hanging from her shoulder. Whatever she had in it looked heavy. There was no form to the bag. It had to be packed with clothes. That was a lot of clothes for just a few nights. Maybe she was heading to the laundromat. I started to follow behind her so I could run to my car as soon as she got into hers. Only she didn't get in her car. She opened the back door, tossed the duffel bag inside, closed the door, and started toward her apartment. I ducked into the shadows again and crept back to my hiding place to wait for her to go up the steps and into her apartment. The pain in my ankle flared from the quick movement to hide. Kelly was acting odd. At least, it was odd for her. I couldn't quite place a finger on it. She just didn't seem like her usual awkward self.

I watched her reach the top of the stairs and heard her footsteps on the walkway above my head. When I heard a door open, I half ran, half hopped from my hiding spot to my car. I had to get out of there before she came back down and saw me. She might try to stop me and invite herself out to din-din. I didn't have time for her nonsense tonight.

I managed to get in the car and back out of the parking space just in time. I saw Kelly step into the parking lot from my rearview mirror as I was driving away. She didn't appear to recognize that it was me pulling away. At least, she didn't act like she recognized me. I wasn't sure she even noticed my car. That had been close.

Ten minutes later, I turned onto Lindsey's parents' street from the opposite end of where Lindsey normally approached it coming from the dive shop. I pulled to the side and parked behind a minivan so my car was shielded from view. I would be able to see any cars approaching the house. I awkwardly felt like Dwayne Morrow, that wannabe P.I. from Ohio, on a stake-out. He was always in the national news about some murder he stumbled onto and somehow managed to solve. Some people were starting to wonder if he was the killer rather than the people that got blamed for it. He wasn't even a real investigator.

I continued watching the road, waiting for Lindsey. I didn't know why I was hiding. I should have just gone to the house and parked in front of it. Except I had a feeling something was wrong and if Lindsey saw my car there, she might keep going. It was better to lie in wait and catch her when she was walking Kona.

Thirty minutes passed and there was still no sign of Lindsey. I checked the time. It was ten minutes to eight. She should have been here long ago. I thought about knocking on the door and talking to her mom. On occasion, Lindsey was too tired to stop by and she would call to let her know she wasn't coming. Maybe today was one of those days. I didn't feel like getting into a whole thing with her mom, though. And I really didn't feel like having to explain anything to her father. Her parents liked me enough, but they were still her parents. If Lindsey decided not to walk Kona tonight, she would be heading home. I started the car, pulled out of my hiding spot, and drove past the house. Nothing looked amiss at the Carters. I would detour by the dive shop to see if Lindsey was there. Maybe she was stuck working later. With the distraction of Maniac Manny, I could have missed her car earlier.

Ten minutes later I pulled into the empty parking lot of the shopping center where the dive shop was located. No one was in the shop. It was locked up for the night with only the security lights on inside. I circled the parking lot and pulled back out onto highway 98 headed to the apartment. Eight minutes later, I was driving through the apartment parking lot. There was no sign of Lindsey's car. Thankfully, there was no sign of Kelly's car either, so I wouldn't have to sneak around. I parked and limped upstairs. I checked the apartment, but everything was as I had left it. Lindsey hadn't been there while I was gone. Where could she be?

It occurred to me that maybe she went to the beach. She often did that whenever there was something she needed to think about. Maybe she noticed my dive equipment and the scooters gone, got upset with me, and was sorting that out. No. This wouldn't be the first time I did something to upset her. Something like that wouldn't cause her to leave work early.

What if Jack had gone to the dive shop and mentioned seeing me at breakfast with another woman? *Crap!* That might upset her enough. She should have known me better than that, but there was no telling. If she did go to the beach, I knew where she would park. She always went to the same place.

Fifteen minutes later I was driving along scenic 98. I was a few blocks from the small beach access parking lot when I saw a car pull out. At least, it looked like it was pulling out of the lot. I was too far away to tell for certain where it came from. It was also too dark for me to tell whether it was Lindsey or not. It could have been. I started to speed up but thought better of it. It wasn't unusual to see cops on this road. The car that had pulled out onto the road turned off after a couple of blocks.

About a minute and a half later I pulled into the small lot. There were no cars in it. I turned around and headed back out to try to find the car I had seen coming out of the lot. It was too late, though. By the time I got to the main Highway 98, there were too many cars. If it was Lindsey, I had missed her.

26

Lindsey

There were plenty of inexpensive hotels along Highway 98 in Destin. It was a popular tourist destination after all. I looked on my phone at the ones nearby and settled on one of the local, non-chain hotels that wasn't too far away and had reasonable rates. I called and they had a vacancy. I asked if they had a discount for locals, and they said they would give me one as long as I could provide proof of local residency. That helped. I pulled out of the parking lot, turned onto scenic 98, and made my way toward the main highway. Ten minutes later I turned into the parking lot and stopped in front of the lobby doors. I pulled down the sun visor, flipped up the mirror cover, and looked at my face. I looked horrible. My eyes were red and puffy from crying so much. My nose was red. It was obvious what was going on. I was embarrassed, but there was nothing I could do about it. I had to sleep somewhere, and I didn't want to sleep in my car.

I grabbed one of the damp towels from the floorboard behind me and rubbed my face with it. It didn't help. Oh well, it was worth a try. I threw the towel over the seat, unclipped my seatbelt, and opened my door. Might as well get this over with. Hopefully, the woman working the desk wouldn't say anything about my appearance or take pity on me. That was the last thing I needed. I grabbed my purse and pulled myself out of the car.

Ten minutes later, I was walking back to my car with a key card. The woman behind the desk had stared at me and looked as if she was going to comment a few times, but I gave her a look that made her understand I wasn't in the mood to hear it. I was sure she had seen this type of thing before. I couldn't be the first person to have a fight and get a hotel room for the night. Well, I guess there was no fight. That would have been better. I would have rather had a fight with Joey than to have him sneaking around behind my back. The thought of Joey brought tears to my eyes just as I was getting back in my car. Why was I so emotional?

I drove around to the side of the hotel and found my room number on the door about halfway back. There happened to be an open parking space right in front of the door. I parked, grabbed my duffel bag, along with my wet clothes and towels, and headed toward the room. I was standing in front of the door trying to get the key card to unlock it and grant me access when I heard the door to the room next to mine open. I fumbled with the card some more. I hated these things. I could never figure out which way they were supposed to go into the slot. I dropped the card as I was trying to flip it over with my hands full. I let out a scream and dropped everything I had been holding. The man that was leaving the room next door paused as if he was considering coming to my aid. I glared at him, and he quickly dropped his head and hurried toward his vehicle. I did not need any man to help me.

I bent down to pick up the key card and try again, only it wasn't there. I started flinging my clothes and towels behind me as I dug beneath everything searching for it. All I wanted was to open the door, get inside the room, and crawl into bed. Why was everything so difficult? I finally found the key card beneath the duffel bag. The last thing I pulled up in my search. Figures. I stood up and tried the key card again, finally getting it in the slot the proper way on the third try. The lock clicked open. It might as well have been a USB port. I never got those seated in the right way until the third time either.

I pushed the door in and held it open with my foot while I reached back for my duffel bag. I dropped the bag between the door and the door jamb, not wanting to deal with unlocking it again. I turned around and saw my clothes and towels scattered all over the sidewalk.

I broke down in tears once more. I didn't know why I had brought them from the car. I had this idea that I would rinse them in the tub and hang them to dry, but I didn't even want to rinse myself off.

After a few seconds of crying, I gathered everything in my arms, pushed the door open with my shoulder, and kicked the duffel bag inside, stepping in behind it. The stale smell of cigarette smoke immediately hit me. I glanced at the no smoking sign on the door. I was pretty sure the hotel manager was quick to charge a smoking fee to whoever had smoked in the room, but they didn't bother to spend it to get rid of the odor. I was too exhausted to care. I wasn't about to go back to the office to ask for another room. They probably didn't even have any other rooms. I threw my wet clothes and towels on the floor near the bathroom and thought about showering but quickly pushed that thought aside. I turned to the bed, pulled back the covers, and crawled in between the sheets.

* * *

I was startled awake. I was nauseated again. I threw the covers back and ran to the bathroom. I wasn't going to make it to the toilet, so I ran for the sink just outside of the bathroom. There wasn't much that came up. It had been a while since I last ate. I was surprised that there was anything in my stomach. I continued to dry heave into the sink wishing I had eaten. I'd much rather throw up than dry heave.

After a couple of minutes the heaves stopped. I still felt queasy but no longer felt like I was going to vomit. I turned on the cold water and splashed my face. I cupped my hands and filled them so I could rinse my mouth. Once the water was in my mouth, the thirst came. I rinsed and gargled with the water, then cupped my hands under the faucet and drank. And I drank and I drank. I finally stopped myself, afraid it would come back up. At least this time there would be something in my stomach to throw up. I splashed water around the sink in a meager attempt to clean the partially digested pieces of food, but there were larger bits that wouldn't fit through the holes of the strainer. I turned and started to go back to the bed when I noticed all of the lights were still on. I hadn't shut them off last night.

I had no idea what time it was. I found my purse on the floor next to my duffel bag and reached inside for my phone. It wasn't there. I felt around in all of the pockets and compartments. I dumped all of the contents onto the ugly hotel carpeting without considering how filthy it might be. I didn't care. I just wanted my phone.

It seemed I had everything in my purse except a phone. I must have left it in the car. Or did I leave it on the beach? No, it had to be in the car. I called the hotel from the beach parking lot. Wow. Now my memory was affected. I had to be sick. Great. That was the last thing I needed.

I found my keys in the middle of all of the purse contents and headed toward the door so I could retrieve my phone. Just as I stepped outside, I realized I didn't have my key card. I quickly turned around and shot my arm toward the door to keep it from closing. The heavy door slammed onto my hand, pinning it against the door jamb. I screamed out in pain as I kicked the door open. Scratch that. *This* was the last thing I needed. My hand was throbbing. I slowly wiggled my fingers. They all moved. Nothing appeared to be broken. They still hurt and would probably swell up.

I turned my attention to the room and saw the key card on the dresser just inside the door. I grabbed it with my other hand, which was also holding my car keys, and started to go back outside. I rethought that. I flipped the security bar out so it would stop the door from shutting. I didn't want to mess with the key card again.

I was back in my room after retrieving my phone from where I had left it on the passenger seat. My hand was throbbing. I was nauseous. I was thirsty. I was hungry. And I wasn't thinking all that clearly. My life seemed to be spiraling out of control. This wasn't like me. I prided myself on maintaining control, most of the time. There was that time in Jackson Blue with Jack Johnson. And there were the tears again. It seemed like the smallest things brought them on.

I steeled myself against the feelings I was having. I couldn't let this have control over me. I always had a plan and knew how to handle things. I couldn't let it be any different now. Except right now, I was having trouble controlling my feelings. Right now, I didn't know what to do. I dropped my car keys onto the pile of purse contents on the floor and sat on the bed to look at my phone.

I still didn't know the time. My phone was powered off. I hoped the battery hadn't drained. I didn't even know if I had my charger with me. *Oh lord! Why me?* Then I remembered I had turned the phone off after calling the hotel. I didn't want to deal with Joey's incessant calls. I pressed the power button and waited for the phone to cycle on.

While my phone was powering on, I examined my hand. It was throbbing and looked like it was starting to swell. I looked around the room and saw an ice bucket on top of the mini fridge. It would probably do me good to ice my hand. I could also chew on some cubes. That might help with the nausea. I put my phone down on the bed and grabbed the ice bucket. I had to find the ice machine.

I walked back out, leaving the door propped open with the security bar again, and listened for the hum of the ice machine. I thought I heard something to my right. I looked and saw a breezeway a few doors down that crossed to the other side of the hotel. I headed in that direction. A minute later I found the ice machine and filled the bucket. I took a handful of ice, dropped a couple of small cubes in my mouth and held the rest. It helped the throbbing calm down almost immediately.

Back in my room, I put the ice bucket on the nightstand next to the bed and grabbed my phone with my good hand. It had finally powered on. It was still buzzing with all of the notifications coming through. I unlocked the screen and watched the notifications pop up. I swiped down and saw that most of them were from Joey calling and texting. Then I noticed mom had also called and texted. *Crap!* I forgot about going to the house to walk Kona! Mom was probably worried out of her mind. The last call from her was just before midnight. I looked at the time. It was 3:22 in the morning. I had slept more than six hours. I tapped on the text messages from mom.

7:27 Hi hon are you coming over to walk Kong tonight?

7:28 Kona. Stupid autocorrect!

8:04 Hey just checking to see what's going on. I know Monday nights are usually busy, but this is late even for a Monday. Is everything ok?

8:58 I'm starting to get worried now. I've tried calling but it keeps going straight to voicemail. I also called Joey but he's not answering either. Please call me

9:42 Lindsey this isn't funky. I need to hear from you soon

9:43 Funny

10:33 I've called the hospital but they haven't had anyone that fits your description but you probably already know that

10:34 Unless you're lying dead on the side of the road somewhere.

10:35 Sorry about that. I didn't mean it. I'm just really worried about you hon

11:05 Your father is driving around looking for your car. Please call!!!

11:47 Lindsey you have us really worried about you. This isn't at all like you. Please call when you see this. I don't care what time it is

I tossed the phone on the bed. I should have sent mom a text last night to tell her I didn't have time to stop by and walk Kona. It wasn't often I did that, but it wouldn't have been that unusual. Now I was going to have to come up with a reason for why I hadn't answered my phone. I debated whether I should call her at three thirty in the morning or wait until a more reasonable hour. Knowing mom, she was probably not getting very good sleep, if any sleep at all. I decided to call her and deal with the consequences. But first I needed to throw up again. The nausea was back even worse than before.

27

The same evening at Jackson Blue

The vehicle eased into the park. Fortunately, the county didn't change the code to the lock…ever. It had been easy to get the code. Almost too easy. As far as could be determined, the sheriff's deputies didn't bother to patrol the park at night. They must have figured that as long as there was a locked gate, driving in to check on things wasn't necessary. It was easy to sneak into the park at night without anyone knowing.

Having pulled through the gate, the driver stepped out to swing the gate closed and resecure it. At the same moment, headlights appeared up the road along with the sound of a car traveling at a high rate of speed. *Shit!* The driver ran back to the vehicle and flipped the headlights off, then ran back to the gate and swung it closed, crouching down behind the post holding the gate. None of it would make any difference if the vehicle was coming to the park, but it was better to be safe.

A truck sped by without slowing down. Fortunately, there were no lights over the gate, so the car wasn't easy to see parked on the opposite side from the road. Even if there had been a light, as fast as that truck was moving, it wasn't likely anyone inside would have noticed a vehicle parked beyond the gate in the dark.

With the truck gone, there were no other sounds except for the frogs that tended to make their presence known every evening in this soggy state of Florida. The frogs were everywhere. They were especially bad after it rained. When it rained, they came out in droves and croaked all night long. Hundreds of them. Maybe even thousands. They were small. The fact that they could be so loud was amazing. They also somehow managed to get indoors. No clue how they did it with the windows and doors shut, but they did. It was inevitable that one would be found hopping across the floor after a good rain. Maybe it had hitched a ride on the scuba equipment.

Standing up from behind the post, the car's owner walked to where the gates met and secured the latch, making sure the lock was activated. A quick shake of the gates and the driver turned and walked back to the vehicle, sliding into the seat. Headlights weren't necessary. There was no point. The moon was bright enough and the gravel road was familiar. It was easy to follow down the hill to the parking area by the pavilions, out of sight from the road.

Hopefully, there wouldn't be any other vehicles this evening. The driver eased the car to the turn off a couple of hundred feet from the gate and looked down the hill to the parking area. Empty. No one else around tonight. That was good.

There were too many other cave divers during the day. Too many prying eyes. The late-night visitor was doing dives that were best done when no one else was around. Scooping someone else's project wouldn't win anyone a popularity contest. And that was exactly what this diver was doing. It would have been great to see the look on Simmons' face when he saw the additional lines beyond the end of his line.

Putting those other lines in had been an afterthought in hopes of providing a distraction for Simmons. There was no current coming from those passages. They led to dead-ends. The real lead was hidden away, not connected to Simmons' line. Not even close to Simmons' line. And no one knew about these late-night dives. Well, except maybe the diver that had also been in the cave the other night. That had been unexpected.

The only time another vehicle had been in the park this late was a couple of nights earlier, on Saturday. Upon seeing the truck at the bottom of the hill that night, the late-night diver almost turned around and left. After driving a couple of hours to get there, though, it was decided the risk was worth it. There was the potential of being caught. Not just being seen diving Jackson Blue at such odd hours but also being caught trespassing. The county charged a land access fee to cave divers to be able to use the park to get to the cave opening. Why pay a fee when it was so easy to get the gate code and sneak in?

Two nights prior, the late-night trespasser walked over to the truck that was already there and felt the hood. It was cold. It felt like it had been parked for a while. Maybe whoever it belonged to hadn't been able to get it started and left it for the night. Even if there was a diver inside the cave, the chances of being recognized were low. With everyone wearing black and having masks on, it was nearly impossible to recognize each other. The trespasser took a chance and decided to stay and dive.

The trespasser set up the dive equipment quickly and got in the water in record time. Just as the diver stepped into the water, bubbles appeared on the surface outside of the cave opening. No time was wasted. Grabbing the scuba tanks and the scooter, the diver moved about twenty feet away into the eel grass. It was a pain to get set up with the eel grass getting tangled in the equipment, but the area was hidden enough that if the source of the bubbles exited the cave nothing could be seen.

Strangely, there hadn't been anyone else in the cave. The source of the bubbles was never found. Maybe the bubbles were just the cumulation of the daytime cave divers' exhaust bubbles finally making it out to the opening. The cave was burping. They were too steady though. There must have been someone hiding in the dark. That was disconcerting, and a little distracting.

The truck was gone after the dive. So whoever it belonged to had to have been diving. The other diver must have been tucked away into a crevice in the Deco Room with lights out. The trespasser had done that a few times. It didn't matter. It wasn't like anyone around would recognize the vehicle in the parking lot. They wouldn't even know it belonged to a cave diver. The trespasser wasn't known in this area of

Florida.

Up until recently, the trespasser had only been diving in the High Springs, Florida area. There hadn't been any intention of starting to sneak dive the caves in Marianna. Then news of Simmons' exploration in the back of Jackson Blue hit the rumor mill. Word had gotten out that Simmons was surfacing from his dives with an empty explorer reel. The temptation was too great.

That was when the decision was made that it might be best to keep this little trip to the Florida panhandle and these late-night dives secretive for the time being. It was better that way. It had been easy to find the area where Simmons was laying line. It had been easier to find a lead he had missed. A lead that turned out to be the main artery of the cave.

Up until Saturday, it had gone well. Nothing changed other than seeing that truck in the lot before the dive and then not seeing it after the dive. It had been a risk. Probably one that shouldn't have been taken, even if it meant the drive would have been time wasted. The dive had been worth it, though.

Simmons hadn't made much progress during his dive earlier in the day. There was concern that he might stumble upon the other lines in the area. The decision was made to mess with Simmons and put in decoy lines to throw him off rather than continue to push the main artery. It was a risk. Up until that point, there hadn't been any signs of anyone else diving back there. Two weeks of visits into the area without Simmons finding out. More than two thousand feet of newly lined passage that Simmons was oblivious to.

Even if he found it, he would have a difficult time seeing it all in one dive. It wouldn't be difficult to stay ahead of him, especially considering that Simmons was only diving there on the weekends. The decoy line wasn't necessary. Was the intention behind putting the new line in plain sight really to throw him off? Or was it to rub it in his face that someone else was back there? Truth be told, it was the latter. Simmons had become cocky about what he was doing. He had to be put in his place.

Extending the end of Simmons' line meant forgoing further exploration along the main artery for a dive and instead dedicating the time to the decoy line. It also required that a couple of spools of line be sacrificed. It was still previously unexplored, virgin cave passage. It just wasn't the main path the cave was taking.

It was worth it, especially after finding out how pissed Simmons was after he saw it. If he ever stumbled upon the hidden passages, he would really lose his shit. None of them were surveyed. There wasn't time for that. Why survey when there was so much virgin cave passage to put line in?

Five spools of line had been placed in the hidden passages. That was about four thousand feet of newly lined cave, which was in addition to the two spools used for the decoy. Tonight's dive would push the hidden passages beyond the one-mile mark. It was a shame that this information couldn't be shared with anyone. At least, not yet. That time would come.

28

Joey

With nowhere else to check, I headed back to the apartment. Maybe our paths had crossed, and Lindsey got home after I left. I called her again. It went straight to voicemail. I was really worried. What if she got into an accident? I passed the turn off to the apartments and continued to head east toward the hospital. I would stop and check in at the emergency room to make sure no one matching her description was there. I told Siri to search the local news for traffic accidents. Nothing came up. That didn't mean there hadn't been any. Maybe the news hadn't posted anything yet. Hopefully, if there had been an accident, Lindsey wasn't involved. Not hearing from Lindsey was driving me crazy!

Thirty minutes later I pulled into the apartment complex parking lot. The emergency room didn't have any patients matching Lindsey's description. That was a bit of a relief, but I still didn't know what was going on. I parked my car. Lindsey's usual space was vacant. I didn't see her car anywhere else in the area. I noticed that Kelly's car was also gone. Good. Maybe she had managed to get a few days in a row off from work and went back to central Florida to visit family. It would be nice not having to avoid her every time I left or returned to the apartment.

I jogged across the parking lot and ducked into the breezeway leading to the stairs. My ankle was still tender, but I was anxious to check the apartment again. I took the steps up two at a time. Even though I hadn't seen Lindsey's car in the parking lot, I was hopeful that she might have parked somewhere else, and I'd find her sitting on the couch pissed at me for being gone all day and most of the evening. I reached the top of the stairs and noted the window was dark. I doubted she was in there.

The phone rang as I searched the apartment for that elusive note that I hadn't found earlier. I didn't think there was a note, but it kept me busy. It kept my mind focused on something. I ran from the bedroom to the kitchen where I had left my phone on the counter and snatched it up. It was Lindsey's mom. Why would she be calling? I contemplated whether to answer it or not. Just as I made the decision to answer, the call disappeared from the screen.

I waited to see if Mrs. Carter would leave a voicemail or send me a text message. A couple of minutes later, with no new notifications on my phone, I placed it back on the counter. I probably should have called her back, but I didn't know what I would say.

Two hours later I was driving around Destin again looking for Lindsey's car. She still wasn't answering her phone. I was beyond worry. Lindsey had never done something like this before. This was even worse than several months earlier in Cozumel when we couldn't find Gary. At least then, we knew that Gary was somewhere in the cave. I had no clue where Lindsey was. I had no clue where she might be. I had no clue what might have happened. It was driving me crazy.

She had been behaving strangely over the past week. She was quick to snap at me, even concerning little things. Things that shouldn't have been a big deal. Things I did regularly that might annoy her but never made her lose her temper. I stripped off my scrubs when I got home from a particularly long, hard day at work last week. I tossed them on the bathroom floor and got in the shower. Usually, after my shower, I scooped them up and threw them in the laundry basket in our bedroom. I was so mentally drained I forgot about them, and they remained on the bathroom floor. After dinner, Lindsey walked into the bathroom and screamed at me.

"Joseph! What the hell is wrong with you? Why can't you clean up after yourself?"

"Umm, what do you mean?"

"You left your nasty work clothes on the floor in the bathroom! There's dog hair all over the bathmat! That's not where they belong!"

"Sorry, I guess…"

"I don't want to hear any excuses or apologies. Just come pick them up and put them where they belong before I throw them out! And shake out the mat!"

I ran into the bathroom and scooped them up as Lindsey glared at me. I thought about asking her what was wrong. I thought about asking her if something had happened at work. I stopped myself. If I asked her anything she'd probably accuse me of thinking she was having an unreasonable emotional response to the clothes being on the floor because she was PMSing. Well…maybe she was. If that was the case, it was best to just agree with her and do as she said. We had lived together long enough that I knew better than to poke that bear. That probably sounded bad, but physiological and biological changes in a person could cause out of the ordinary responses. It was just the way life was. I didn't make the rules.

I drove around Destin for more than an hour and hadn't seen any sign of Lindsey. I stopped at the hospital again to check in with them. The same person was sitting at the intake desk and gave me a strange look. When I asked her once again if she had seen a short, petite, woman with long blond hair, she told me she still hadn't. Then she asked, "Are you sure she didn't go spend the night with a friend or with her parents, hon?" I knew what she was implying. I should have felt insulted by it, but I didn't. It was very possible Lindsey had somehow figured out I skipped out of work to go diving. The way she got mad at me over a set of scrubs left on the floor, she might run off to spend the night at her parents' house over that. I should have called her mom back. I looked at the time. It was past ten. Too late to call. I decided to head to her parents' house to see if Lindsey's car was there.

Fifteen minutes later, I slowly drove past their house. No car, but I did see a light on inside. That was strange. Lindsey's parents usually didn't stay up much past ten and it was almost eleven. Why would they be awake this late? I thought about stopping in and knocking on the door. Even though her car wasn't there, maybe they had heard from her. I wasn't sure I wanted to deal with Mrs. Carter, especially this late at night. It wasn't that we didn't get along. Both of Lindsey's parents liked me well enough. While they weren't happy with us moving in together, they didn't try to stop us from doing it. They tolerated it. And they didn't blame me. At least not completely. They knew Lindsey was independent…and stubborn.

I decided to stop after all. If I didn't, it would bug me the rest of the night. I turned into their driveway and shut off the car. As I was pulling off my seatbelt, I saw the front door to the house open. The storm door opened next, and I watched Mrs. Carter stick her head out to see who was in the driveway. She must have recognized my car because she ran toward me. That made me even more concerned.

"Joey! Have you heard from Lindsey? She never showed up to walk Kona and she's not answering her phone!"

Crap! Something happened to Lindsey.

29

Meanwhile eight thousand feet inside Jackson Blue cave

The area that Simmons had been exploring was located about two weeks earlier. It was easy to find the end of his line. He had pushed the passage a good distance, a couple of thousand feet. But he had missed the big lead to the right. The main artery that now had almost one mile of new line in it. In just four dives, there was more line in that area than what Simmons had put in. It hadn't taken long. Using the scooter to move through the passage as line was spooled off of the explorer reel made it go much faster. The reel was certainly getting a workout at those speeds.

Not bothering to survey any of the new line in the cave made it even less time-consuming. It allowed more time to put additional line in the cave. Simmons had been surveying his line. Surveying took a lot of time, more time than it took to put the line in. Time wasn't plentiful with the rapidly decreasing air supply in the scuba tanks. As it was, limits were being pushed. Sometimes they were even broken.

No one else had found the main artery. That wasn't by chance. The line was tucked away out of view far from Simmons' line. Then, just in case, and to keep things interesting, a diversion was created Saturday night. The end of Simmons' line was extended about twelve hundred feet. On the way back, another line going to a different part of the cave was placed. It intersected the main line beyond the end of the line Simmons had put there. Those two lines would be enough to keep Simmons distracted for a while. They should keep him from finding the real continuation of the cave. The current was coming from this other area. How Simmons missed the current was beyond belief, but he had.

There were signs that Simmons had been in the diversionary area where the intersection was. There were a couple of additional personalized line arrows placed on the line. There was even a line cookie on the floor of the cave where it had fallen unnoticed. None of those had been there Saturday night. Simmons had done two dives in Jackson Blue over the past two days, but it didn't look like he had found anything of consequence. He had been too focused on the decoy lines. He was probably too busy surveying them to bother to look around. For some reason, he was determined to survey and create a map.

It was disappointing that an entire dive and a couple of spools of line had to be dedicated to creating the decoy. It would keep Simmons distracted enough to stay away from the real exploration. Unlike Simmons, the focus wasn't to lay *more* line, but rather to push the cave as far in as possible and own the end of the line. That was the ego boost. The section of the cave where the real end of the line was, the one that kept going farther from the opening, was hidden from the view of anyone swimming along the line Simmons had placed. Not only was it hidden, but there was a lot of distance between Simmons' line and the beginning of the line in the hidden passages. About three hundred feet.

When the passage was first discovered about a week earlier, the line intersection was left in place. There was little risk of anyone finding it for several days. The discovery happened on a Monday and Simmons would be at work all week. The intersection remained that way until Wednesday when it was cut back three hundred feet to keep anyone else from finding it. There were probably others diving Jackson Blue that were looking for Simmons' passage. They must have seen him coming out of the cave with empty explorer reels. The fool had even posted pictures of his empty reels on all of his social media accounts. That was what gave him away. He hadn't mentioned a location, but everyone knew that he spent most of his time diving Jackson Blue. If he wanted to keep things a secret, he would have kept those to himself. It was too much for his ego to allow that.

Eventually, someone else would find this area of the cave. They might have already found it. The section was so big and had so many tunnels, it was hard to tell. It was too much for one diver to explore everything in such a short period of time. Simmons had been consistent in placing line arrows on the lines. There were a few sections of line that weren't connected to his line that didn't have any line markers. Those might be someone else's doing. It was either that or Simmons had run out of arrows to mark the lines. Most likely, someone else was also exploring the area. There was Jack Johnson. He would do something like that. Not that any judgement was being passed.

If there were others, that meant extra precautions had to be taken. It might not be enough to keep the lines hidden. Someone would eventually notice the water flow and find the tunnel leading from the main passage. It would only be a matter of time for them to find the lines tucked behind the corner more than three hundred feet away.

It was a pain to have to run a line that far during every dive, but it was necessary to maintain the secrecy. It meant bringing an additional reel which held four hundred feet of line more than six thousand feet inside of the cave. It also meant slowing down progression into the cave while setting that additional three hundred feet of line to maintain a continuous guideline out of the cave.

It would have been much faster to scooter those three hundred feet. That would only take a couple of minutes. It took almost four times that to run a line every night. Maybe tonight the reel could be left in place, or mostly in place. A one-hundred-foot gap should be long enough. At least until the weekend rolled around again. There didn't seem to be many divers during the week.

The concern of someone finding the main artery was getting greater, especially if there were others exploring the area. It was always a little surprising to find that there wasn't a new line in that gap. With Simmons diving back there every weekend and at least one other diver or group of divers also there, it was getting more difficult to keep the dives below the radar.

Trespassing into the park and diving late at night helped. Except that other night when that truck was there before the dive and gone afterwards. That was strange. The risk shouldn't have been taken. The dive should have been aborted before it began. Now someone knew there was another person diving Jackson Blue late at night and might even recognize the vehicle at some point.

Maintaining secrecy presented other risks. Diving so far back made the use of safety tanks necessary. Fortunately, Simmons and Carter had at least two in place. They had hidden them out of the way, probably to try to keep their own activity a secret. The tanks weren't that well camouflaged. They could be seen from the right angle. They were probably set in those locations intentionally to make them easier to find. It also made it easier for others to find. Simmons and Carter weren't being as inconspicuous as they thought. But two safety scuba tanks weren't enough for a solo diver doing such a long penetration. There really should be a couple more safety tanks in the cave.

Those thoughts were pushed aside. It was time to grab the explorer reel and tie it into the end of the line. It was nice to get back to the real exploration. Saturday night had been necessary, but it was difficult to concentrate knowing the main artery was only a couple of thousand feet away. The decoy was needed to buy some time, though.

The line from the explorer reel was secured and ready to go. Ahead in the darkness a tall, wide tunnel with no line in it waited to be explored. No one had ever been in that tunnel. No person had ever seen it. That was about to change. It had been difficult to stop at this point in the middle of this huge tunnel five days earlier. It was never easy to turn around, especially when the threat of others finding it and taking over exploration was increasing.

Turning around had been necessary. Limits were being pushed too far. The possibility of having to *borrow* one of Simmons' safety tanks to make it out of the cave was increasing as the time passed without turning to exit. That would have been a dead giveaway. Simmons and

Carter were certainly checking on the safety tanks each time they went by them.

As it turned out, the safety tank wasn't needed. The exit went more quickly than expected because of the water current. A heavy rain the week before had increased the amount of water flowing out of the cave. That meant it took longer to get into the cave, but it also went much faster getting out. Even so, pushing the limits hadn't been a good thing. It had been too close. There was only a couple of hundred psi of air in each tank once back at the surface. One of the regulators had become hard to breathe from. That tank had nearly been drained of air.

The safety tank should have been retrieved from its hiding place and used. The problem was that it happened on Wednesday night and the tank wouldn't be able to be replaced until Saturday night. By then, Simmons and Carter would have noticed it missing during their dive. Not that it mattered. The decision to place the decoy lines was made that night anyway, so they would know by Sunday that someone was scooping their leads. And that was exactly what happened. They finally knew someone else was back there laying line.

The diversion would only work for so long. Simmons would survey it in a couple of dives and realize the lines led nowhere. He would discover that the passage heading straight eventually ended and that would cause him to start looking in other areas of the cave. There was no telling how much time it would take for him to find the real main passage, but eventually he would. The only way to guarantee that wouldn't happen was to somehow keep them out of the cave. There might be a way to do that. It would have to be confirmed on the way out of the cave. It would take some planning and preparation. And it might be a little dangerous.

30

Lindsey

I woke up shivering and sore on the floor of the bathroom with my head resting on the edge of the toilet seat. I hoped they did a good job cleaning these things. I started to examine the toilet but thought better of it. I had already used it as a pillow, so it didn't matter.

The last bout of nausea had been worse than the first one. I brought my hand to my forehead to see if I felt warm. I did, compared to the temperature of my hand. But I was cold so unsure of whether I had a fever or not. I pushed myself off of the floor, stepped out of the bathroom, and turned toward the sink. I splashed my face with cold water to try to wake up. I was so cold my whole body was trembling. I had to be sick. I dried my hands and face and crawled into bed in between the sheets and scrunched myself into a fetal position. I pulled the covers in around me tightly as I continued to shiver. I should have turned on the heater. I was too cold and too tired to get out of bed and turn it on. I pulled the covers more tightly around me, forming a cocoon in an attempt to warm up. I would get up in a few minutes.

* * *

I must have dozed off and never turned the heat on. That was a good thing because when I woke up I was sweating. I was actually drenched. I tossed the blanket aside and stretched out on the bed and assessed my status. I wasn't feeling any nausea at the moment, but I hadn't sat up yet. I pulled at my shirt to unstick it from my skin. I needed a shower. I also had to brush my teeth. The aftertaste of the food that had come back up last night was still in my mouth.

I swung my legs over the edge of the bed and slowly pushed myself into a seated position. Dizziness overtook me and I immediately felt nauseous again. I sat on the edge of the bed for a minute, trying to push back the nausea and let the dizziness pass. My whole body was sore. It felt like I had run a marathon the day before.

The dizziness resolved after a couple of minutes. I was probably dehydrated. I stood up and slowly walked toward the bathroom. I emptied my bladder, splashed cold water on my face, rinsed my mouth, and drank several handfuls of water. I wanted to brush my teeth, but I forgot to pack my toothbrush and toothpaste. *Crap!*

I grabbed the towel I had tossed in the corner of the countertop earlier and noticed a tray of items beneath it. I was happy to see a small tube of toothpaste among the small soap and plastic cups provided by the hotel. I picked up the tube, squeezed a little paste onto my finger, and rubbed it vigorously on the surface of my teeth and mouth. This would have to do for now. It was minty and eliminated the nasty taste of bile. It also helped settle the nausea.

I reached in and turned on the shower faucet before stripping out of my sweat-soaked clothing. I was amassing a decent pile of laundry. When steam started rolling out from behind the shower curtain, I pulled it aside and stepped under the stream of water. The heat felt so good against my sore muscles. I stood there and let the hot water cascade over my body. I immediately started feeling better. I must have had a 24-hour bug, or more like a 12-hour bug. Or maybe it was just the stress of what was going on with Joey.

At the thought of Joey, I began to cry. *No! Stop it, Linds!* I turned to let the hot water hit my face and wash the tears away. A wave of nausea came over me and, before I knew it, the water I drank came rushing back out. Somehow, I also had chunks of my lunch from the day before splattered all over my feet. How was that still in my stomach?

So much for brushing my teeth! At least with that bout, the nausea seemed to have passed. I pushed all thoughts out of my mind and looked around the tub for a bar of soap. When I didn't see anything, I pulled the shower curtain back and noticed a bar sitting on top of the towels on the towel rack over the toilet.

A few minutes later I was sitting on the edge of the bed wrapped in a towel and feeling a lot better. Physically, anyway. Mentally was a different story. I grabbed my phone to look at the time. It was a few minutes past eight. That meant I had slept for more than twelve hours including the nap on the beach. There were a bunch of missed calls and text messages. I still hadn't returned any of mom's. There were a few new ones this morning. It didn't appear that she knew what was going on. They were just more messages asking why I wasn't responding to her and asking if I was going to come by this morning to walk Kona. She also mentioned that Joey had stopped by last night. She knew something was going on.

I responded to mom. She was bound to be worried out of her head by now. I sent her a quick text message telling her I wasn't feeling well the evening before, had left work early, and fell asleep. That was all true. I told her I was planning on walking Kona this morning. That was also true. That would hopefully keep her off of my back for the rest of the day. At least until she left work. I would tell her about Joey when I saw her then.

I was teaching for the dive shop all weekend, so I had the next two days off. That was a relief. I didn't have it in me to go into work and deal with people. I also didn't want to impose on Joanne again after having to call her the day before. Thankfully it had been too busy for her to question me about what was going on. I would deal with that on Thursday. Today would be dedicated to going to the apartment to gather the rest of my stuff, or most of it anyway, and cramming it into the car. I would sneak it into my room at my parents' house while they were at work. I doubted mom would notice. And dad definitely wouldn't.

There were several missed calls from Joey. He had left a few voicemails this time. And even more text messages. He was worried. Good! I glanced at the beginning of the text messages. No apologies for lying to me or going to breakfast with Kelly. I would have thought that he would address at least one of those things after I never showed up at the apartment. All I saw were *Where are you?* and *Why aren't you responding?*

I didn't feel like dealing with him at the moment. I swiped the text messages away without opening them. They would appear unread to him. I also swiped away the voicemail notifications. I would deal with all of that later. All I wanted to do was get dressed, get something bland to put in my stomach, and get my stuff out of the apartment. Hopefully Joey had gone to work or diving again. Or maybe he was hanging out with Kelly. *The bastard!*

Thirty minutes later, I pulled into the apartment complex parking lot. I had decided to stay at the hotel one more night and stopped at the front desk to extend my stay. I didn't want to deal with my parents quite yet. I wasn't emotionally ready for it. I didn't want to hear the *I told you so* and the *you were too young to make such a commitment* speeches. I might even extend my stay until Thursday morning so I could relax at the hotel during my days off.

I drove through the apartment complex parking lot and didn't see Joey's car. I should have driven by the veterinary office to see if it was there. He could have called in and just ran out for a few minutes. I thought about heading over but decided against it. It would be too stalkish. I didn't want to be that girl. Besides, if he had gone diving, his car wouldn't be there.

I parked the car and started walking across the parking lot. I noticed the small bits of broken glass from Joey's tantrum two days earlier. I remembered being scared by his outrage and his reaction. It was odd. I had never been scared of him. He hadn't ever given me any reason to be scared. But that evening I was. I didn't know why. I must have sensed something was off, something was different about him. It was better to figure it out sooner rather than later.

I looked around the parking lot and saw Kelly's car parked in its usual space. She was probably asleep. Her every other night schedule at work made her a day sleeper pretty much all of the time. Served her right. That would make for an interesting time trying to schedule things with Joey with him working during the week and diving on the weekends. I couldn't figure out what he saw in her.

By the time I got to the top of the stairs, the nausea had returned. What was up with me? The shower had made me feel better. I still felt okay except for the nausea. Was it stress? Or did I have a stomach bug? I leaned over for a minute until the wave of nausea passed. Once I felt better, I straightened up and walked to the apartment. I unlocked the door and opened it slowly. I hadn't seen Joey's car, but I was being cautious in case he had parked it on the other side of the complex. I was ready to make a quick getaway if he was home. I was afraid I would toss him over the balcony like he had done with that beer bottle. It would be better to avoid any encounters while I felt that way.

Fortunately, he wasn't home. His dive equipment and both of the scooters were back in their corner. He must have decided to go to work. That meant I had time to get things gathered. The first things I grabbed were my toothbrush and a tube of toothpaste. I brushed my teeth before packing up the rest of my toiletries.

An hour and a half later and several trips up and down the stairs, everything that belonged to me was out of the apartment except for my dive equipment. That would have to wait. I didn't have room in my car for all of the tanks and the scooter. I also wasn't up to carrying the heavy stuff down the stairs. The nausea had passed, but I was feeling tired and weak.

I drove to my parents' house and unloaded my belongings into my old room, hiding most of it in the dresser, the closet, and under the bed. Kona was excited to see me. She followed me back and forth as I unloaded the car into my old bedroom. She seemed to sense that something was different. She was more excited than she usually got when we went for walks. Maybe she figured out that my things were being brought back into the house. Maybe she knew I was moving back in.

It was obvious Kona had missed her walk the evening before. She jumped up and put her front paws on my shoulders almost knocking me over. She usually jumped like that, but I was pretty good at deflecting it. She caught me by surprise that morning. I was also still feeling weak. I almost decided not to walk her. I was afraid I might not have the strength to control her. I changed my mind. She was good about listening to me as long as we didn't see any squirrels along the way.

The walk around the neighborhood was uneventful. No squirrels. No other people out. It gave me time to enjoy being with Kona and to think about my situation. The more I thought about it, the more I convinced myself that I couldn't live with what Joey was doing. I wasn't the type of person to *stand by her man* when she'd been wronged. I might be southern, but I wasn't a fool.

I couldn't believe Joey would do such a thing to me. I never in a million years would have guessed this could happen. I found myself getting angrier and angrier. The tears were done. I no longer felt sad. I was mad. And mark my words, Joey was going to regret what he did.

31

Tuesday afternoon at Jackson Blue

"Don't you boys have jobs?" Jack asked Brad and Steve as their heads broke the surface of the water.

Brad looked up and glared at Jack.

"We took a little time off work because…" Steve began to reply with a smile until Brad smacked him in the arm again.

"Hey!" Steve turned toward Brad and yelled. "I was just going to say because we wanted to dive all week."

Brad sneered at Steve. Jack didn't like that fellow. He wasn't the friendly type. Neither was Jack, but at least Jack could fake it with the best of them. He had faked it for many years. He had lots of cave divers believing he was a great all-around guy despite what happened almost two years earlier with that Carter girl and the Simmons boy. That still irked Jack.

Even though many of his admirers had stuck with him, there were some people who didn't like him and no longer trusted him after what those two had done. Jack hadn't figured out what he was going to do to get his reputation restored. He was guessing that Brad was one of those people. Either that or Brad was just an asshole. There were those types of cave divers as well.

"Didn't mean to start anything up between the two of y'all." Jack said as he held his hands up and backed away a few steps. The grimace on his face from the pain caused by moving his arm that way was apparent to Brad.

"You didn't start nothing," Brad replied. "Steve just likes to talk too much." Brad gave Steve a menacing look.

"Well, look, y'all don't have to worry none about me. I'm just tryin' to get my gills wet again after bein' out of the water for a couple a years. If y'all have some exploration goin' on in here, I won't get in your way. I'm just tryin' to be neighborly."

As Jack was busy trying to relax Brad and gain his trust, he was also busy looking over their equipment. They had a lot of scuba tanks with them. They also had explorer reels that were not quite as full as they should have been. That didn't mean much. The reels were about half full of line. They could have started out that way. Jack didn't know of any self-respecting cave explorer who would begin a dive with a reel that wasn't full of line. He also didn't know if these boys were really explorers, or if they were just putzing around in the cave wanting to be explorers.

"Sorry, man. It's just, well, ya never know who ya can trust these days. Too many people interested in scooping other people's exploration projects. I realize you're Jack Johnson, but, well…" Brad's voice trailed off. Jack knew he was referring to what had happened a couple of years earlier. Might as well try to restore his reputation. At least Steve would probably back him up on this and work Brad from that side. Jack would try the dismissive approach first.

"Nah, I get it. Some ugly things were said about me a couple a years ago. Most people know the truth of the matter, but I know there are some, like you, that have their doubts. I wasn't tryin' to get into your business. Like I said, just being neighborly. I'll let you get back to it."

Jack turned and walked back to his truck to get his stage tanks and bring them to the water's edge. He dragged his hand truck behind him. He really hated using that thing. Before his accident, he recalled talking shit about cave divers who used them. Not openly to just anyone. Only among those he trusted. Those who he knew would talk him up, both in person and on those social media sites he so hated. He missed the good old days when cave diving was only done by the toughest of men, and the occasional woman that managed to sneak into the ranks every now and then. He missed the days when rumors were spread in person and not hidden behind a keyboard using an anonymous screenname. The days when you talked shit and had to be prepared to stand behind your claims. The days when cave divers like good old George Irvine posted on the message boards and called people strokes and got away with it. George, or GI3 as he was better known, was one of a kind, for sure. None of that was possible these days. People were too sensitive. It seemed Brad was one of those sensitive types.

Unfortunately, Jack's arm hadn't fully recovered since the accident. He wasn't able to handle carrying two scuba tanks or at the same time. He had tried a couple of times, the day before included, but he always ended up paying for it later in the evening. He was still feeling it after forgoing the hand truck the day before. So he was stuck using the very thing that he called people pansies for using. The irony hurt more than his arm. He loaded both of his stage tanks onto the hand truck and turned to head back to the water, almost walking into Brad.

"Hey, I mean it. Sorry about that back there. I'm just a little bit on edge lately. There have been people asking around about what we've been doing, and it's got me on the defensive." Brad held his hand out to Jack. "Truce?"

Jack leaned the hand truck against his tailgate and grabbed Brad's hand.

"Sure. No hard feelin's." Jack looked into Brad's eyes and noticed dark circles beneath them. The boy looked tired. Jack once again wondered if it had been Brad he saw on Saturday night. Maybe Brad was keeping secrets from his buddy, Steve.

"So, are you back to doing any exploration in here? Or are you just getting used to being back in the water?"

There it was. Brad wasn't interested in a truce or being friends. He wanted information. Brad wanted to know where Jack had been going. Maybe that wasn't Brad Saturday night after all. Maybe Brad wasn't a real explorer. Maybe he had gone into the cave with a half-filled explorer reel. Jack looked toward Brad's truck and saw Steve pulling a hand truck out of the bed. Brad was a pansy.

32

Joey

"When are you guys coming back home? I really need your help. Not just with my exploration project but also with Lindsey. I don't know what's going on with her. She won't answer any of my calls or respond to any of my messages. She left work a couple of days ago and I haven't seen or heard from her since. Neither have her parents."

"We're on the road right now. We finally got Jim's parents settled and found someone to check in on them every day to make sure they don't need anything. We should be pulling into Tallahassee tonight. We can meet you halfway tomorrow after you get off work if you want to get dinner at the Mexican restaurant in Marianna." Gary responded.

I was thrilled to hear Gary and Jim were finally coming back to the Florida panhandle. Well, technically, the Big Bend area, but back in the area rather than nine hours away in south Florida. I missed diving with those guys and hanging out with them on the weekends. I could also use their help on the dives. I couldn't wait to show them the new area.

I had to find Lindsey first. I wondered whether her mom really hadn't heard from her or if she was just telling me that. When her mom ran out to my car the other night, she was worried and surprised that I didn't know what was going on. When I called her again today, she didn't sound like a mother should sound if she hadn't heard from her daughter in two days, and her daughter's boyfriend hadn't either. Something was up.

Lindsey had a temper. I found this out early in our relationship. If someone upset her, she didn't hold back. She wasn't afraid to stand up for herself or someone she liked. A few times I thought that might be to her detriment. She often reacted without thinking about the consequences. Fortunately, nothing had ever come back on her. She somehow avoided the consequences.

Maybe she was pissed at me for not telling her I was calling out from work to go diving. She'd been upset at me before, but it was always for much more minor things. Maybe I had pushed her over the edge this time. Or maybe it was Jack. I could see Jack making a special trip to the dive shop and casually mentioning he saw me and another woman at breakfast. That would really piss Lindsey off. But it should have made her pissed off at Jack, not me. She didn't even bother to confront me with it. That was not like Lindsey at all. That was what concerned me so much more.

Things would be resolved tomorrow one way or another. As long as Lindsey went to work as scheduled. Of course, all of this had to go down right before her midweek days off making it impossible for me to find her. The situation was taking a toll on me. I was distracted at work and screwing things up. I wasn't getting good sleep at night alone in the apartment. I couldn't afford to take any more days off.

I had planned on heading to Jackson Blue after work to get another dive in. I wanted to get to the end of the line where the arrow with my initials was located to look around and see if I could find a lead. Although, if I found one, there might already be line in it. Whoever put that line there probably left a gap to throw me off.

I thought back to the last dive I did in Jackson Blue. I had turned around and scootered back to the intersecting lines, looking for other possible leads along the way. There were none, at least that I could see while scootering through the tunnel. I wouldn't be certain until I was able to get back there and swim slowly through the passage. That would go faster with Gary and Jim there to help.

Once at the intersection, I turned to follow the other line. That area was a maze. There were so many lines, I didn't know where to go first. I found a few line arrows with the initials JS written on them. Someone was definitely fucking with me. It had to be Jack. This was his way of getting back at me for calling him out on his lies two years ago. It was working. He had pushed the right buttons.

Most of the lines only extended a hundred feet or so before ending in dead-ends. I wasn't sure why they were left in place. One of the lines I followed looped back onto the main passage. Jack, or whoever had done this, didn't tie it back into the main line. The end of that line was far enough from the main passage that it couldn't be seen. And there wasn't a marker on the main line to indicate it was there. It didn't make sense why one line was left connected, and the other was hidden.

I never reached the end of what appeared to be the main passage in that section. I didn't have enough time or air in my scuba tanks. I spent way too long looking at all of the intersecting lines, most of which were apparently decoys designed to waste my time. It worked. I wasted two dives to see where the new additions led and didn't get much out of it. Eight hours of my time. Actually more. Add another eight hours of driving plus four hours of setting up and disassembling equipment. Twenty hours. When I found out who was doing this…

It was probably best that I hadn't gone to Jackson Blue after work. That would have taken ten hours. Assuming I left right at five, I wouldn't be home until three. I would have gotten very little sleep. Not that sleep was coming easy since Lindsey disappeared. That should be resolved the next day. I might finally be able to get some sleep tomorrow night. That would be good, because I was hoping to drive to Marianna right after work to go dive Jackson Blue in the evening. I might even get lucky and run into whoever it was that was back there scooping my project.

In the meantime, I had to ask if I could leave work a few hours early the next day. Not only did I have to go to the dive shop to try to sort things out with Lindsey, but I also had to make it up to Cave Masters to get my tanks filled before they closed at six. I didn't want to count on Lindsey filling them. It probably wouldn't be smart to walk into the shop carrying my tanks when I was supposed to be trying to figure out what was going on. She certainly wouldn't be happy with that.

I pulled into the apartment complex parking lot and saw Kelly walking toward her car. I looked at the time. It was just after five, a little early for her to be leaving for work. Unfortunately, she saw me and ran my way. She got to my car just as I pulled into my parking space. She stood directly behind my car. The thought of shifting into reverse and pushing the gas pedal to the floor flashed through my mind.

Kelly wasn't that bad. I didn't like her, but I didn't want to kill her. If it was Jack, that would be a different story. When I shut off the engine, Kelly ran around to the driver's side and stood there not so patiently waiting for me to open the door and get out.

"Hey, Joey! How are you doing? I haven't seen you and Lindsey in a couple of days. Well, I briefly saw Lindsey on Monday. She was in a big hurry to go somewhere. I barely got a few words in before she said she had to go and took off out of the parking lot. What have you been up to? I haven't seen you since brekkie on Monday."

I reached up and put my hand over Kelly's mouth to stop her from saying things. It was too much. It was too much to hear her talking. It was too much to hear her mention she had seen Lindsey on Monday. That had to have been after we went our separate ways from breakfast.

"When exactly did you see Lindsey on Monday? Was it in the morning after breakfast? Or was it later in the day?"

"Well, first she called me earlier in the day. I think that was sometime in the afternoon. I had just woken up from my nap. You know, because I always take a nap on my days off to try to stay on my night shift schedule. Then…"

"Why did she call you? What did she want?" I interrupted her.

"Oh, she called to ask me how I was doing. She thought I would have a hangover. I told her I never got hangovers. Never had. I don't know why. It just doesn't ha-"

"Stop! Did you mention seeing me and going to breakfast?"

"Of course, silly! Why wouldn't I? I told her I ran into you in the parking lot and started to tell her about breakfast and that man, but then she said a customer just came in and she had to go."

"And then you saw her later in the day?"

"Yeah, she was in her car pulling out as I was getting home from the store. I honked my horn and stopped to talk to her. She said something about going to the store to get some stomach medicine. I was about to tell her about that man at breakfast again, but she said she had to go and took off without saying goodbye. Why are you asking all of these questions?"

"What time did you see her?"

"Oh, four, maybe five. I'm not sure."

That was interesting. Lindsey left work early, came by here to pack a bag, and took off somewhere. I doubted she was really going to get any medicine. Lindsey never got sick.

"Never mind. Thanks for the information. I have to run, Cl- err Kelly. I'll talk to you later."

I had broken myself of calling her Dooneese only to start calling her Clingy. I would have to watch myself more closely. I got back in the car and pulled out of the parking space, spinning the tires. I didn't have to go anywhere, but if I started walking to my apartment, Kelly would follow me and keep talking. And right now, I needed to think about all of the new information I received. Something was going on. I had to find Lindsey and talk to her.

33

Lindsey

I made sure to stop in at my parents and walk Kona a couple of times a day while mom and dad were at work. The tears were done, but I wasn't ready to sit down and talk to them about what was going on. I had the hotel room until Thursday morning anyway. I would go home Thursday after work and sit down with mom. I would tell her everything that had happened.

The nausea came and went. I eventually ended up going to the store to get some medicine to try to counteract it. Nothing helped. If this kept up, I was going to have to go into Patients First urgent care and get a prescription. I couldn't deal with this for much longer. The thought of it being a little stomach bug had come and gone.

I spent time on the beach reading a book. It was nice to get lost in an imaginary world and not think about everything that was going on in my life. In between chapters, I took short naps. I had grabbed the beach umbrella from the apartment, so I didn't have to worry about getting a sunburn. I doubted Joey even noticed. He probably hadn't noticed that any of my stuff was gone. As long as the scuba equipment was there, he wouldn't care about anything else. He hadn't even sent me a text or tried to call me since earlier that morning, probably when he was on his way to work. The day before I was getting text messages from him almost every hour on the hour.

By Wednesday night I was ready to return to work. I had enough of the time off trying to distract myself so I wouldn't think about the situation Joey had put me in. The only problem was that he would know where I was and might stop by. Or maybe he wouldn't. Maybe he didn't care anymore. After all, he hadn't tried to get in touch with me all day. The tears almost came back, but I pushed them away. I couldn't let myself fall into that depression again. I had to remain strong. I had to remain angry.

On Thursday morning, I got to work a little before ten. I woke up earlier than usual and had a good run with Kona. I worked up a good sweat. I wasn't sure we would get to run because I woke up nauseated again. Thankfully, I didn't throw up. Maybe whatever stomach bug I had was getting better. At least I felt well enough to go for a jog. After dropping Kona off at mom and dad's, I drove to the hotel, took a shower, and checked out. I'd be going back to mom and dad's after work and spending the night there. I finally had to talk to them.

I had spoken to mom and told her there were some things that I wanted to tell her. She was making sure dad was out of the way so we could have a woman to woman conversation. I wasn't ready to bring dad into it. Mom could fill him in after I went to bed. I would talk to him over the weekend after he had a couple of days to calm down. I almost pitied Joey if he and dad encountered each other over the next few days.

Work was slow. This was typical for a Thursday. Friday would be busier with everyone coming in to prepare for a weekend of diving. I tried to keep myself busy and my mind occupied. I was in the stock room doing inventory when I heard the door chime sound. I ran out to the showroom and saw Joey walking in. Fuck!

"You need to leave! This is not the place for this."

"Linds! Please! I've been calling and messaging you for the past three days! You haven't answered the phone or responded to me. This is the only way I know to talk to you."

"I'm not ready to talk. I don't know if I ever will be. I can't believe a thing you say, so what's the point? Just leave!"

"But Lindsey…"

"LEAVE!!!"

The door chime sounded again. Another customer walked in.

Dammit! I had to put on an act to deal with the customer. I watched Joey turn around. He didn't leave. Instead, he walked to the display of BCs and started looking through them. I knew he was just killing time until the customer left. He had no use for a recreational scuba diving BC.

"Good afternoon. Is there anything I can help you with?" I said with a smile, as much as it pained me to smile.

About twenty minutes later, the customer left with a new set of mask, snorkel, and fins. She wasn't interested in scuba diving, just snorkeling. While I was showing her what we had, she kept glancing at Joey. I'm sure she thought it was rude of me to help her first when Joey had been in the store when she came in. I didn't address it. I just wanted to assist her and get her out of the store so I could tell Joey to leave or I would call the cops.

"Please. Just. Leave." I said, enunciating each word slowly.

"Look, Linds, all I want is a few minutes to talk. I don't even know what I did. I have no idea what you're mad about." He put his hands up as I was about to yell at him again. "I know. I probably should know why you're mad, but I don't. Can you give me fifteen minutes? That's all I ask."

I stood there glaring at Joey. I didn't want to give him fifteen seconds, never mind fifteen minutes, but if that was the only way I was going to get him to leave.

"Fine. Tomorrow night after the shop closes. Meet me at the public beach access at seven fifteen. Don't be late. I'm leaving at seven thirty no matter what."

"Tomorrow? You can't talk to me tonight?"

"I already have plans for tonight. Tomorrow. Take it or leave it. I don't care. Now please leave."

Joey turned around and left, shoulders slumped. Good! It was his turn to feel bad. He needed to feel the way I felt. The door chime sounded as he walked out. I watched him get in his car and drive away. It was only then that I allowed myself to break down. The tears came and wouldn't stop. I ran into the restroom, locked myself in there, and cried for at least ten minutes. It could have been fifteen.

When I finally had no more tears to shed, I splashed water on my face and blew my nose. I glanced in the mirror. I looked terrible. There was nothing I could do about it. I wasn't one to wear makeup often, so I didn't have anything I could cover up the redness with. If anyone came in and asked, I would pass it off to allergies. I walked back into the showroom. No one was there. I hadn't heard the door chime while I was in the restroom, but I had been crying pretty hard.

The rest of the day went by slowly, too slowly. All I wanted to do was go home and crawl into my bed and sleep. I didn't want to talk to mom, but I knew I had to. Fortunately, it was Thursday. The shop closed at five instead of seven on Tuesdays, Wednesdays, and Thursdays because there weren't usually many customers on those days. Two more customers came in before closing time. One wanted to sign up for a weekend of diving in the gulf and the other was looking at regulators but didn't buy anything. Usually, I would have pushed a sale a little harder, but I didn't have it in me. I was thankful when he left after only ten minutes of browsing.

Everything was closed out and I was ready to get out of there. I set the burglar alarm and stepped out of the shop at exactly five. I looked around the parking lot, expecting Joey to be waiting for me. Fortunately, he wasn't. I didn't know if I was relieved or disappointed. Had he really given up that easily? I started to cry again. What was going on? I didn't know why I was upset that Joey wasn't there. I was mad at him. I didn't want him in my life anymore. This was absolutely crazy!

I got into my car and started to drive. I caught myself heading to the apartment instead of mom and dad's. I found an empty parking lot and pulled in to turn around. I started heading to their home…my home. It was strange because I usually headed to their house after work to walk Kona. I didn't know why I had started to head to the apartment. Damn Joey for making me confused. I was mad. I was done with him. Why did he have to show up at work?

After I took Kona for a walk, I entered the house, and mom was waiting for me in the living room.

"Where's dad?"

"He went out for a while. I asked him to give us a couple of hours. He wasn't too happy about it, but he agreed. He'll still get to bed in time."

I sat down on the couch next to mom.

"Oh, mom!" I turned toward her and hugged her.

"What's going on, honey?"

"I think Joey is cheating on me."

I started to cry again. Just when I thought all of the crying was done, here it was again. Mom held me and let me cry onto her shoulder. It was exactly what I needed. After a couple of minutes, I sat back and pulled up the bottom of my shirt to dry my face.

"Tell me exactly what happened."

I told mom everything, from waking up and noticing Joey's dive equipment gone, to Jack Johnson telling me he saw Joey out with someone else, to getting confirmation from Kelly that it was her. I told her about Joey not answering my phone calls, then me not answering his.

"And to make things even worse, I've been sick over the past few days. I wake up nauseous every day. I've been throwing up every morning since Monday. And I've been so emotional. I don't know how much more of this I can take."

"When was your last period, honey?"

"What does that have to do with anything?"

"Just answer my question, darling."

"I don't know. Maybe a month ago. I haven't even thought about it. Let me look at my app."

I pulled my phone out and pulled up my menstrual tracker. My jaw dropped when I saw the date of my last period. I felt mom pushing against me so she could get a look at my phone screen.

"Oh baby, you're not sick. You're pregnant."

34

Late afternoon Thursday at Jackson Blue

Jack was back at it. Tuesday was a bust. His encounter with Brad and Steve put him on edge. He didn't like it when people interfered with his projects. He had a feeling they were doing exactly that. The pansies disassembled their equipment and left within half an hour of surfacing. About fifteen minutes later, Jack began his dive. It started out okay, but when he was about three thousand feet inside of the cave, his left arm started cramping.

All he did with that hand was hold his dive light out, so he pulled it back in toward his body. That didn't help. By the time he was passing over the donut trench in the floor of the cave caused by a diver on a runaway scooter about twenty years earlier, he was in severe pain. He didn't even give much thought to the scooter trench. Jack hated to do it, but he turned around and began his exit from the cave. There was no way he would be able to concentrate on the dive with as much pain as he was experiencing.

That day really sucked, Jack thought to himself. This would be a better day. First, no one was around. He had the park all to himself. No pansies to get in his way or get him worked up. Second, he had decided to take one of his pain pills when he got to the park. He hated taking those things. He rarely took one. He could usually push through the pain. Tuesday was different, though. It was the worst pain he had experienced since his arm was crushed two years prior. He had taken the pill as soon as he got home that day. He had also decided he would approach his next dive differently.

By the time he began his dive, the pain pill should have kicked in. It would be his first time diving so soon after taking a pain pill. He usually didn't take one at all before dives. He had been warned to not drive or operate heavy machinery while under the influence of those pills. He wasn't doing either one of those things. Truth be told, the little white pills didn't make him feel loopy or impaired. He didn't see the point in the warning. He felt fine on the rare occasions when he took one. Well, maybe not so rare, but he only took them when he needed them. They numbed the pain. What would it hurt to take one before a dive? He didn't want to have to end another dive because his arm was acting up. He would be fine.

After getting his equipment set up and his drysuit on, Jack jumped into the water from the top of the retaining wall. He took his time clipping his scuba tanks onto his harness. Clipping onto the D ring on the left rear of the harness wasn't the easiest thing for him. Damn his arm. He had been doing his physical therapy exercises tirelessly. He needed his arm to be back to normal. It had been going great. He wasn't sure what caused the setback a couple of days before.

Once everything was clipped onto his harness, Jack dropped below the surface. He let the scuba tanks settle into place and pulled his scooter so it was in front of him. He did a quick mental assessment. He felt fine. No strange side effects from the pain pill. Jack squeezed the trigger on his scooter and took off into the cave.

The dive was going well. Jack felt fine. He wasn't feeling any pain in his arm. He was thinking clearly. They must put that warning on the side of the pill container because their lawyers required it. Typical legal bullshit. He moved quickly through the cave. It felt like he was moving much faster than he had ever moved on his scooter. It was like a turbo drive had been installed.

Then, it hit him. About fifteen hundred feet from the entrance, as he descended ten feet in depth just beyond a breakdown area, Jack felt the narcosis. He felt the Martini Effect, as Jacques Cousteau had phrased it. He was about eighty-five feet deep so that would be equivalent to almost five martinis. Or was it four? The math wasn't working in his head. That was strange. He shouldn't feel narcosis at eighty-five feet of depth. Jackson Blue had an average depth of eighty-five feet, and he had never felt narcosis in that cave. Yet he was.

Jack released the trigger and glided to a stop just before the Hall of the Mountain King, a large room with two mounds making it appear similar to a mountain range. He looked at the first mound in front of him. It blocked his path. He couldn't figure out where to go. He wondered if there had been another ceiling collapse. He wondered if the passage was blocked. He looked to his right and saw the gold-colored line that marked the main passage of the cave about three feet away. Best to get in contact with that line, he thought to himself.

Jack moved toward the line and grabbed it with his right hand, letting go of his scooter. The current moving through the cave passage pushed the scooter behind him. There was current so the passage couldn't be completely blocked. Jack looked at the mound again and noticed that the gold line took a path even with the top of it. There was another ten feet above that to the ceiling. Maybe if he got shallower he could move over the collapsed section. Maybe the narcosis would resolve itself. He knew he would have to descend to exit the cave, but he needed a few moments of clear thinking before he could turn and exit.

Jack tried to fin his way up to the top of the mound, but his legs didn't want to work correctly. It didn't help that the water flow was strong and working against him. Jack couldn't figure out what was going on. The passage didn't look right, but there was still current. He used the gold line to pull himself farther into the cave, as well as shallower. He had to relieve the narcosis. What seemed like several minutes later, but in reality, was probably only a minute or two, Jack made it to the top of the mound. The narcosis hadn't eased off. Maybe he needed more time at the shallower depth.

In the middle of the passage, Jack felt unstable. He started to descend so he could settle onto the top of the mound but decided against that. The mound was covered in sediment and that would certainly silt the room out and the visibility would be gone. He looked at the ceiling. He would have to let go of the line to get to it, but he'd still have a visual on the line. He turned around so he was facing the way out, opened his hand, and inhaled. A few seconds later, he began to rise in the water column.

After what seemed like several more minutes, Jack felt himself slam against the ceiling. The air in his buoyancy compensator had expanded enough to keep him pinned against it. He inflated The BC with a little more air just to be on the safe side. He didn't want to start to descend while he was getting his wits back. After settling in, Jack looked around the room. He saw the large mounds that gave the Hall of the Mountain King its name. Nothing looked disturbed. Maybe there hadn't been a ceiling collapse after all. He didn't see the gold line, though. He looked around frantically trying to locate it. The feeling was strange. Jack had never had anything less than total control over his mental and physical being when diving, or any other time for that matter. He was getting irritated.

Jack flashed his dive light around the room, scanning every bit of it. He finally saw the gold line about fifteen feet ahead. He had gotten high enough that the line was hidden behind where the ceiling dipped down to his left. That was a relief. In hindsight, Jack should have deployed a safety spool line from the gold line to himself so he could be assured that he would not lose it. Too late to do that at this point.

The narcosis didn't decrease in intensity. The change in depth hadn't helped. If anything, it was worse. Jack finally admitted to himself that it wasn't narcosis he was feeling. It had to be that damn little white pill he had taken almost an hour earlier. While it didn't have any effect on his mental faculties on the surface, the depth apparently intensified its effects and made him extremely loopy. This was not good.

At least he wasn't three thousand feet in from the opening like he had been on Tuesday. He was more than half of that distance in, though. Somehow, he had to get himself back out and to the surface. Jack wasn't sure he would be able to do it. Thousands of dives and dozens of rescues, and a little white pill was going to be the end of Jack Johnson.

35

Joey

When Lindsey suggested we talk Friday night, I almost panicked. I hadn't been to Jackson Blue since Monday. That meant whoever was scooping me had three days to continue to go back there and put more line in my section of the cave. Friday would make it four. I almost made an excuse for not being able to meet her but thought better of it. I had to fix things with Lindsey. I had to find out what was going on and either make her see that I didn't do anything wrong or apologize for whatever I did wrong. I had to find out what that was first, though.

At least, it didn't affect my plans for tonight. I left the shop and headed to Marianna. It was a little early to meet Gary and Jim, but I had to get my scuba tanks filled. I'd head to Cave Masters, get that done, and maybe head to Jackson Blue to see if anyone was diving. By that time, the guys should be arriving in town, and we could go have an early dinner with some special tableside guacamole. It was fattening, but it was so good. It was better than the guacamole in Cozumel.

A couple of hours later I pulled into the parking lot at Cave Masters. Danny came running outside to greet me. It must have been a slow day.

"Hey Joey! How've ya been? You didn't stop by Monday after your dive. Did you have a good dive then? How far back did you get?"

Again with the 'how far back' question.

"My dive lasted a little longer than expected and I had to get back to Destin. Didn't have time to stop. But I'm here now to get my tanks filled."

"Hey, wait a minute! It's Thursday! That's twice on a weekday this week."

"I took off from work early today cuz I'm meeting Gary and Jim for dinner. I figured I'd come by…"

"Gary and Jim are back in town! Wow! I haven't seen those two in, what? A month? Month and a half? Are they coming by tonight? Are they gonna be around to go diving soon? This weekend maybe? Hey! What time are you meeting them for dinner? Can I join you?"

"Whoa! Stop talking! I'm just going to dinner with them to catch up. I know nothing else right now. I'll let you know this weekend when I'm back in town. We're meeting at six. Don't you work 'til seven?"

Danny's mood instantly changed.

"Yeah, I work until seven. Dammit! I always miss out on hanging out with everyone."

"Maybe next time, bud. Now, can I get my tanks filled? I need Nitrox in the sidemount and stage tanks and oxygen in the decompression cylinder."

With slumped shoulders, Danny pulled my tanks out of the trunk and started hooking up the fill whips. I hated to not be more sympathetic to Danny, but it was too much. He and Kelly really would be perfect for each other. I wondered who would get to talk more. Or would they keep talking to each other at the same time? I might have to figure out a way to get Kelly up here to meet Danny one day. That would be hilarious to watch.

"Look, sorry about that. I've had a rough week. I didn't mean to go off on you like that, Danny."

"It's okay. I know I get a little too excited and talk too much sometimes. Well, most of the time. I've been trying to be better. It's just… I'm doing it again. Sorry."

Danny turned away to fill the tanks. Maybe he could learn.

Twenty minutes later my tanks were filled, and my tab was paid. I took off down the road toward Jackson Blue. Five minutes after that, I was parked in the small lot near the pavilions at Blue Springs Recreation Area. There was one other vehicle in the lot. It was Jack Johnson's truck. Was he the one that was scooping my leads? Was he the one that had put that line back there?

The more I thought about it, I couldn't see Jack putting arrows with my initials on them on the line to mock me. He wouldn't care if I found out it was him. He would want me to know. I thought about the initials I saw on the line arrows. I thought they were JS, but the S looked a little strange. What if it was JJ? It had been a couple of years since I saw any of Jack's line arrows or cookies in the cave. I couldn't remember what his markings looked like. Maybe it was Jack.

I wouldn't put it past him. There had been rumors that he wasn't all that great of a cave explorer and that was why he turned to staging those rescues. If he somehow figured out Lindsey and I were doing exploration in Jackson Blue, would he search for the area and try to take over the project?

The thought of keying the sides of Jack's truck crossed my mind. I stopped myself. That would be childish and immature. Besides, Jack would probably ask Danny who else had been by and Danny wouldn't be able to help himself. I'd be busted. Not that Jack would have proof. No. I wouldn't do it. But I was going to have to get evidence that it was Jack who was scooping my leads and extending the end of my line. I didn't know what I would do with it, but something had to be done.

I checked the time on my phone. It was a little after four. I had a notification. I swiped down and saw that it was a message from Gary telling me he and Jim were leaving early. They should be in town by five thirty. That was great! I hadn't expected to see them until six. I only had an hour to kill. I wished I had brought my dive equipment with me. All I had were the scuba tanks. It was probably for the best. I wouldn't have made it to the restaurant in time to meet the guys. I decided to go for a walk in the woods to the east of the park. I heard a rumor that there was a spring somewhere in there, but I never checked it out.

I walked around the spring basin toward the edge of the trees. The brush was thick. I looked at my bare legs peeking out below the hem of my shorts and the flip-flops on my feet. Probably not the best attire to go trampling through the woods. I thought back to hiking through the jungle in Cozumel a few months earlier in the same footwear.

Gary and I had found a small path in the trees next to Aerolito and we decided to check it out one day. That was interesting. Especially when we almost encountered the chupacabra. Okay, maybe it wasn't a chupacabra, but it was disconcerting. I wondered if there was anything similar in the woods of the Florida panhandle. I heard stories about the skunk ape. There was even a house on the edge of Merritt's Mill Pond that had a plywood cutout of a skunk ape painted black and secured to a tree. I didn't think skunk apes were real. I was more concerned about encountering an alligator than anything else, especially if the spring was more than just a sinkhole.

I walked along the edge of the trees surrounding the Jackson Blue spring basin and eventually came to a trail that looked decent, even for flip-flops. I walked onto the trail and followed it into the woods. I wondered if it would lead to the spring or if I would have to go off of the trail to find it. I couldn't be so lucky. If it was visible from the trail, it would be more than a rumor. Other cave divers would probably be diving it regularly, too.

I followed the trail and came to a faded kiosk with a map of the trails on it. I pulled out my phone and snapped a photo of the map. There was no spring denoted on it, but that didn't mean there wasn't one somewhere in the area. At least with the map, I'd be able to do a more organized search for it.

I went to the right first. I could walk the outer perimeter trail and come back to the kiosk. If I still had time, I would walk the inner trails as well. Lindsey would laugh at me for my organized approach. She would have wandered aimlessly along the trails, gotten lost, and not be able to find her way out.

The thought of Lindsey brought a sad feeling over me. I thought she was overreacting to this whole thing. I had taken the day off to go diving. Did that justify moving out and not speaking to me? We had been together for almost four years. Didn't that kind of commitment mean something? Didn't I deserve an explanation? There had to be more to it. It couldn't just be the fact that I called out of work sick and went diving without telling her.

Maybe it was breakfast with Kelly. But Lindsey knew how I felt about Kelly. She knew I could barely tolerate her being around. I never showed interest in Kelly. I'll admit, other than a slightly large forehead, Kelly wasn't unattractive, physically. If I wasn't with Lindsey and I saw Kelly out, I might have looked at her more than casually. But as soon as she started talking, that would be it. There was no way I could deal with her personality and her incessant talking.

Before I knew it, I was back at the kiosk. I hadn't looked for the spring as I followed the trail. I had been so lost in my thoughts that I forgot all about it. Dammit! I looked at my phone. It was after five. Too late to walk around the trail again. I'd have to do that another day. I headed out of the trees toward the park. If I left as soon as I got to my car, I'd beat Gary and Jim to the restaurant by about five minutes. I could get a table for us and order a round of beer-garitas. Jackson County was semi-dry, so tequila couldn't be served in restaurants.

As I walked into the clearing, I looked down at the Jackson Blue spring basin and saw bubbles hitting the surface. That must be Jack finishing his dive. Perfect timing. I decided to wait to see if he surfaced with an explorer reel emptied of its line. It wouldn't be damning evidence, but it would be incriminating. I ran down to the spring basin, walked onto the diving platform, and out to the end of the diving board. I would sit and wait for Jack to come out. I should be able to easily see any explorer reels he might have clipped to the back of his harness.

36

About an hour earlier in the Hall of the Mountain King

Jack's loopiness and confusion weren't resolving. It had to be that damn little white pill. It never affected him like this before. He didn't understand why it was doing this to him now. Jack remained plastered to the ceiling sixteen hundred feet from the opening of the cave, seventy feet deep, watching the needle on his pressure gauge slowly drop as he breathed the air in his scuba tank. He had three more scuba tanks to breathe from that were full.

Technically, he could remain in that position for another four hours. By then the effects of the pill might be gone. Maybe. He had no clue. He knew he could take the pills every six hours. He took one when he got to the park. That was an hour earlier. It might be five hours before the effects wore off. He didn't have enough air to last that long. Never mind also needing to do decompression stops if he stayed at his current depth the entire time. He would have to start moving in three hours. That wouldn't do.

Jack decided to try to exit rather than wait. He couldn't stay where he was, plastered to the ceiling, until the effects of the little white pill subsided. If he started exiting now, he would have plenty of time to get there. He wouldn't have to rush.

His scooter floated in front of him. He hadn't noticed it before, but it must have been there. It didn't just move into that position. Or did it? Jack wasn't sure of anything at the moment. He wondered if he could control the scooter in his current condition. Probably not. Chances were good that he would smack his head into the ceiling somewhere along the way and possibly knock himself out going at those speeds.

Jack didn't wear a helmet. Helmets were for pansies. Just like those hand trucks. There were cave divers that swore by helmets. They claimed they were especially necessary when scootering because of the possibility of hitting your head on the ceiling and getting knocked out. *How about just controlling your scooter so that doesn't happen, ya damn pansy!* Even though he felt that way about helmets, Jack wished he had one for this exit. That was because of the stupid little white pill, not because he was a pansy.

There was no way Jack was going to be able to scooter out. He knew that. He grabbed the scooter and pushed it back between his legs, pulling the nose tow cord out. He fumbled with the cord as he tried to clip it to the D ring on the front of his crotch strap. He finally secured it after three attempts. He would swim out. It would be much safer.

With the scooter tucked behind him, Jack let air out of his BC so he could unglue himself from the ceiling. Not too much though! He didn't want to crash into the sediment covered mound below. That would be bad. Especially since the guideline wasn't within reach. He felt the ceiling let go of him as he started to descend into the water column.

As Jack dropped down, getting closer to the mound, he remembered to inject the BC bladder with some air so he could stop the descent. He started to feel more disoriented. The dizziness got worse. Moving wasn't helping matters. Or maybe it was the added pressure of the extra few feet of depth. Would only a few feet affect him that way? Jack didn't know. He shook his head to try to clear it, but that made it worse. It made him dizzier and loopier. Jack continued descending toward the mound. He reached out with his right hand to stop himself from crashing into it. His hand hit the top of the sediment and kept sinking.

Jack's hand disappeared into the sediment with his arm following. He finally felt a hard surface right after his wrist was engulfed by the mud. He saw a mushroom cloud of dust fly up from the surface. It was moving slowly. Jack felt like he was watching a movie in slow motion.

The mushroom cloud continued to grow and swallowed Jack. His vision went black. He could no longer see. The room had turned completely dark. Jack shook his left hand, the one holding his dive light, but nothing happened. The light must have quit working. Then he felt a hard surface beneath his knees. His light hadn't died. It was the silt. The mushroom cloud had gotten so big that it enveloped his whole body. It wasn't only his arm that disturbed the silt mound. His legs had dropped into it as well.

As the silt cloud continued to surround Jack, he tried to concentrate. His hand was still on the hard surface, but the guideline was somewhere to his left. At least, that's where he thought it was. He wasn't sure if he had rotated while he was descending or if he had continued to face out toward the exit. Jack tried to feel the movement of the water around his body. The thick drysuit and undergarments made it so that his body couldn't feel anything. His right hand was buried in silt, and his left hand had no sensation. He could move it and control it, but he couldn't feel with it. It was perpetually asleep. He didn't know if he would ever get sensation back in that hand.

During the *accident* two years earlier, the nerves in Jack's left arm had been crushed. One had been severed. The surgeons tried to repair them. The severed nerve was reconnected, but the crushed nerves had to be cut back. The surgeries weren't successful. The doctors didn't know if the sensation would ever be restored. They said it wasn't a sure thing. All Jack could do was wait and hope it returned.

Jack couldn't feel his hand, but he sure felt pain. He wouldn't be taking the pills if it wasn't for the pain. He wondered why he couldn't feel anything else. He couldn't feel pin pricks. He couldn't feel the temperature of the water on his skin. All he felt was pain.

Jack tried to shut the pain out of his mind. He tried to focus on his predicament. Maybe if he turned his head, he could feel the water current against the exposed skin of his face. He had to know which way the current was moving past him in order to know which way he was facing. Once he knew that, he could start looking for the guideline.

Jack turned his head to the right and waited for a minute. He thought it was a minute. Time was distorted. He couldn't tell what the current was doing, so he turned his head to the left. Still nothing. There had to be current. The flow was up. He had felt it when he was scootering into the cave. Why couldn't he feel it now?

The silt was still hanging in the water around Jack's head. The visibility hadn't improved. He couldn't see his dive light. He wasn't sure if he was holding his light. It had been strapped to the back of his left hand, the hand that didn't have any sensation. Jack moved his left hand so that it was positioned directly in front of his face. He thought he saw a glow. It had to be on his hand.

Jack decided to switch hands. He would stabilize himself on the hard surface below with his left hand and feel for the current with his right hand. He brought his left hand down and felt it against his right hand. Its motion was stopped. He couldn't feel the hard surface below it, but he thought his hand was there. He brought his right hand above his head and tried to feel the current.

That did the trick. Jack felt the rush of water past his hand. It was coming from behind him. That meant he was facing toward the opening of the cave. That meant the guideline should be to his left. Jack tried to picture the room he was in. He remembered the guideline was below a low ceiling on the edge of the passage. It was midwater. The only way he would be able to find it was by leaving the hard surface he was steadying himself on and swimming to his right. Or was it his left?

He thought about grabbing a safety spool of line to anchor himself. There was nothing to tie the line to on top of the mound. It was a smooth hilltop of sediment. He would have to take a chance and move in the direction where he thought the line might be. He was pretty sure that it was to his left. The current would probably push him out toward the opening once he left the mound. That might get him beyond the area where the guideline was beneath the lower part of the ceiling. There was only one way to find out. He pushed away from the top of the mound and pulled his hand into his chest.

Jack felt himself start to drift. The water flow snapped him up and pushed him forward. He brought his fins together and kicked a couple of times to help himself move out of the silt cloud faster. A dim light appeared in front of him. It had to be his dive light leaving the thickest part of the mushroom cloud. Jack finned again and felt himself move even faster. The light grew brighter. He looked to his left but still couldn't see the guideline. He glanced to the right, just in case. The sediment hanging in the water column was too thick to see very far.

It felt like he was moving forward, but he couldn't tell for certain. The visibility was diminished, and the little white pill still had an effect on his mind. Jack finned again. He felt the pressure in his ears increasing. He must be sinking. He must have cleared the mound. Jack wondered how far above the floor of this passage he was. Just as that thought entered his mind, he crashed into something below him. The light that had been getting brighter completely extinguished as another mushroom cloud formed around him.

Instant regret took over. Jack shouldn't have moved away from his perch on the ceiling. If anyone came into the cave and saw Jack Johnson lying on the floor of the cave surrounded by a silt cloud, it would certainly get talked about. Cave divers wouldn't be able to help themselves. It would be a big shitstorm. The good thing was that the silt cloud was probably so big, no one would see Jack on the floor. All they would see was the cloud of sediment.

Pushing himself off of the floor again, Jack kicked his fins to try to move out of this new silt cloud. He had to get himself into clear water. The absence of visibility was making him dizzier. If he was going to make it out of the cave alive, he needed to move. Hopefully, he wouldn't get lost. Hopefully, he would find the guideline and be able to follow it out to the surface.

Jack bounced along the bottom. He needed to get neutrally buoyant. If he kept bouncing, he would never get out of the silt clouds.

He fumbled around his chest looking for the power inflator mechanism that was supposed to be there. He found it and pressed the button on the side. He heard the air rushing through the hose and into his BC. He released the button and waited to ascend out of the silt and into clear water above him. Just in case, Jack kicked his fins again.

The fin kick moved him forward into what felt like a guideline just above the regulator in his mouth. Jack's right hand shot toward the line and tried to find it. He swept his hand around frantically and managed to loop the line in the crook of his arm. He slid his arm back along the guideline until it was in his hand. He closed his hand around it and held on tightly.

His spirits dropped. This wasn't the thicker gold line found in the main passage of the cave. This was thinner white cave line commonly found in offshoot passages. Jack had moved out of the main passage. At least, he was holding *a* guideline. Even if it wasn't the main guideline, it was something.

Jack analyzed his situation. He was in diminished visibility. He was holding onto a guideline, but it wasn't the main gold line. He thought he was on the line that led to King's Canyon. He couldn't think of any other line in the area that it could be. On second thought, the Queen's Bypass guideline was also nearby. This had to be the King's Canyon line. That guideline was secured to a protrusion on the wall of the mound about six feet below the main passage gold line. All Jack had to do was follow the line to where it was tied off and reach up for the gold line above his head.

Jack moved along the guideline. A minute later, he still hadn't come across the tie off. He was either moving the wrong way, or he wandered out of the main passage farther than he thought. The best course of action was to turn around and go the other way.

That's what Jack did. He rotated his body and swam the other way. The visibility seemed to be clearing. He couldn't see very far, but at least he could see the glow from his dive light. That was progress. A couple of minutes after he turned around, Jack felt the hard surface of a wall. He felt around and found no other line. He was at the tie off. That meant the main passage gold line was above him. He couldn't remember if it was directly overhead or if it was offset.

Jack swapped hands and held onto the thinner guideline with his left hand. He hoped he wouldn't inadvertently let go of it. He couldn't feel the line. He had to trust that he would keep his fist closed around it. He reached up with his right hand and swept it back and forth, feeling for the thicker gold line. It wasn't there. Or at least, it was out of reach. He stretched both arms as far as he could, but still nothing.

Jack backed away from the wall the line was secured to. He switched hands again. He wanted to remain in contact with the line with his right hand, the hand that could feel the line, while he swept above him with his left hand. Just as Jack was about to reach up, his scuba regulator stopped delivering air midbreath. He had breathed through all of the air in the stage tank.

Jack fumbled for the regulator hanging from a bungee cord necklace around his neck, but he couldn't feel anything. It didn't help that he was looking for it with his left hand. He released his grip on the guideline and brought his right hand up. He might lose orientation to where he was again, but better to do that than to drown with three scuba tanks full of air.

Jack needed to get a working regulator into his mouth so he could breathe. He moved his hand over his neck and found it. He pushed the regulator in his mouth out with his tongue and took the other regulator, purging it clear of water as he took a breath. He thought about switching to his other stage tank, but first he had to find the guideline again. It was no longer in his grasp.

Fortunately, Jack hadn't moved far from the line. He found it on his first attempt. With it back in his hand, and breathing from a full tank, he reached up once again to look for the gold line. As he stretched his left arm, he pulled up on the white cave line with his right hand. He tried not to put too much tension on it as he didn't want to pull it from its tie-off on the wall of the mound. That would be bad. After a couple of sweeps, Jack felt the thick gold line against his wrist.

That wasn't quite accurate. He didn't actually feel the line. The line stopped his arm. It was good enough. He pulled himself up, or rather, pulled the gold line down toward him and wrapped his arm around it. With it secured in the crook of his elbow, he released the white cave line and felt it let go like the bow string on a hand bow. He had stretched it pretty far.

Jack grabbed the gold line with his right hand, thankful he had finally found it. He confirmed that it was indeed the thicker line he was searching for. He brought his dive light up and saw the gold color. The visibility was hazy but not as diminished as it had been. He still couldn't see the mound or the walls around him. He certainly couldn't see the floor below him. He slid his hand along the gold line looking for the line arrow that he knew was there. It was a permanent line arrow marking the offshoot passage going to King's Canyon. He found it and confirmed the way out of the cave. He rotated his body so he was facing toward the opening and kicked his fins hoping the rest of the dive would be uneventful but knowing that sixteen hundred feet was a long way to travel in his current condition.

37

Lindsey

"Pregnant?!? No way, mom! I can't be pregnant. I'm on the pill. I haven't missed a single day."

"Honey, the pill isn't one hundred percent effective. If you use it perfectly, it's only ninety-nine percent effective. If you don't take it at the same scheduled time every day, that percentage drops. It can get as low as ninety-one percent."

I dropped my head. While I took the pill every day, I didn't always take it at the same time every day. There were days I woke up late, rushed out of the house, and forgot to take it. I often didn't remember to take it until several hours later. I thought hard about those days. When was the last time I forgot to take it before leaving the house?

Unfortunately, it happened at least once a week. Sometimes more often. For me to be pregnant enough to have missed a period and be sick, it would have had to happen a couple of months earlier. I could barely remember what I did a few days ago. I wish I had kept a better journal of when I took it. My menstrual period app had that function, but I never used it. It was difficult enough to remember to take them, never mind recording *when* I took them. Now, I really regretted that. Not only was I most likely pregnant, but Joey had stepped out on me. This wasn't good.

"Yeah, I can't promise I've taken it at the same time every day. At least once a week I forget to take it before I leave the house. It's not unusual for that to happen a couple of times a week."

"We need to get you a pregnancy test. And then we need to get you scheduled with an OB/GYN. There's a lot to be done if you're pregnant, which I believe you are."

I could see the hint of a smile on my mother's face.

"Are you happy that I'm pregnant, mom? I don't even know if I want to keep it. Not with everything going on with Joey."

"Oh dear. Honey, you can't have an abortion. That's a living being inside of you. How can you even think that? That's not the way we raised you."

"Mom, it's too much to think about right now. With everything that happened with Joey, I just can't."

"First, I don't think Joey is cheating on you. That's not the type of boy he is. I think your hormones are taking your emotions for a rollercoaster ride and you're not thinking straight. That's normal with a pregnancy. You should have seen me when I was pregnant with you! Your father… Well, never mind that. Let's run to the Walgreens and pick you up a pregnancy test. There's no point discussing anything more until you do that. Although, I just know you're pregnant." Mom said that last part under her breath, but I could hear her clearly.

Twenty minutes later, we were back home, and I was in the bathroom trying to coax my bladder into peeing. I knew I should wait until the morning to test my first pee of the day, but I was too anxious. We bought two test kits so I could retest in the morning. I couldn't tolerate not knowing for another twelve hours.

I sat on the toilet and tried to start the stream. I felt like I had to pee, but my bladder was having stage fright. It didn't want to perform for the impending results that it was about to face. After a few minutes, I finally squeezed out enough to get some on the test strip. I set the strip aside, wiped, and pulled my shorts up. I grabbed my phone and started the timer. I almost dropped the phone in the toilet when mom knocked loudly.

"Honey, can I come in?"

"Sure." I unlocked the door and let her in. She looked at the test strip sitting on the counter. "I just started the timer, Mom!"

We had to wait ten minutes. It would be the longest ten minutes of my life. I watched the pee move along the test strip into the area with the lines. The control line appeared. I just had to wait for the result line. I put the toilet seat down and sat on it to wait. Mom paced back and forth in front of me.

"Mom! Please stop! You're making me nervous."

"I'm sorry, dear. I guess I'm nervous, too."

A few minutes later, my phone sounded the end of the timer. I had placed a square of toilet paper over the strip so I wouldn't drive myself mad continually looking at it. I snatched the square off of the strip. I turned away from it to throw the square away. I wasn't ready to look at the result.

"Oh baby." Mom took me in her arms and hugged me. I knew what that meant.

"Are you seriously happy? How can you be with what's going on? I don't want to be a single mom. I'm not ready to be a mom in any capacity. How can I do my job if I'm pregnant? How am I going to teach this weekend?"

"Lindsey, dear, you need to talk to Joey. Give him the benefit of the doubt before you run off thinking he's cheating. Just ask your father what happened with us one day. You'll understand. You're also going to have to get someone else to teach the class for you this weekend. I don't know much about scuba diving, but I do know that it's not safe for the baby. We'll call the doctor's office tomorrow and get you an appointment. You also need to get on prenatal vitamins right away. You should have already been taking them."

"Mom! I had no intention of getting pregnant. I don't want to be pregnant. I can't be pregnant now with what's going on with Joey."

"Oh honey, listen to yourself. Don't talk like that. First, you need to talk to that young man. You need to tell him what's going on. I don't care if he was cheating on you, which I doubt. He still deserves to know. Maybe it will set him straight."

"Mom, I don't think I can take Joey back. Even if I decide to keep the baby."

"Stop talking that nonsense, Lindsey Marie!"

"Look, let's wait until I confirm things with a doctor. Please don't tell dad. I need to think about this. It's too much. With everything that's happened to me this week, this was the last thing I needed."

"Okay, I won't say anything to your father for now. But we need to get you in to see a doctor right away, tomorrow if possible."

"I have to work tomorrow. I doubt I'll be able to get an appointment before going in to work. Oh no!"

"What is it, darling?"

"I'm supposed to talk to Joey tomorrow night about what's been going on. I can't do this yet. I have to cancel with him."

I grabbed my phone and shot off a message to Joey cancelling our meeting the next night. No explanation given. I just told him I couldn't meet after all. I put the phone face down on the counter so it would be in *Do Not Disturb* mode. I was sure he would message or call, and I didn't want to discuss it any further. I picked up the test strip and threw it in the trash can along with the packaging. On second thought, dad might find it there. I wasn't ready to have the conversation with him. I hoped mom didn't tell him, but I didn't have a lot of faith in that. I pulled the box out of the trash and shoved the strip, packaging, and instructions inside. I would hide it beneath some other trash in the kitchen trashcan.

"What are you doing, dear?"

"I don't want dad to find that in there. Again, please don't tell him."

"Don't tell me what?"

I looked up and saw my father standing in the hall just outside the bathroom.

38

Leaving the Hall of the Mountain King

Jack slowly moved along the guideline, making his way out of the cave. The line sloped down toward the floor beneath a lower section of the ceiling. Fortunately, the floor in that area was bare. There was no layer of sediment there. The low ceiling had allowed the water current to blow all of the sediment out of the passage for the next several hundred feet. Jack was thankful for that because he was having trouble staying neutrally buoyant. He had a feeling that he was going to have to use the floor to crawl his way out.

As Jack followed the line, he hit his head against the low ceiling that led out of the Hall of the Mountain King. On top of the dizziness, he was seeing stars after that encounter. Things were not going well. He pushed himself down from the ceiling and continued to follow the guideline. The line was wrapped around a large boulder on the floor about five feet beneath the ceiling he had just smacked his head into. The line didn't stay that close to the floor, though. About a hundred feet ahead was a breakdown area and the guideline sloped up over it.

It was close enough that Jack was able to steady himself using the floor as he slowly made his way through the passage. He finned a little and the water flow helped move him faster. He awkwardly moved forward, bouncing along the floor and pulling himself, trying to maintain course. About three minutes later, he was at the breakdown.

Jack wasn't moving nearly as fast as he had hoped. The increased depth at the floor compared to where he had been at the ceiling was making his dizziness worse. He tried to focus on his dive computer display. He was eighty-six feet deep. The pressure around him had increased by half an atmosphere. The breakdown would allow him to get shallower, at least for a few minutes.

Jack crawled his way over the first large boulder of the breakdown area. The water flow coming from behind him felt stronger and helped push him over the top of the rock. He continued to follow the guideline, his right hand holding onto it tightly. He felt his knuckles scraping against the jagged tops of the huge boulders that had once been attached to the ceiling. His hand was going to be torn up and sore after this.

He thought about switching hands. He wouldn't feel the uneven limestone against his left hand. He wouldn't feel the guideline either. He decided against that. He tried to raise his hand with the guideline in it, but he didn't have the coordination to do that and continue out of the cave, so he continued to move along, his knuckles getting scraped to shreds.

Several minutes later, Jack arrived at an intersection of lines. The guideline split into two at this point. One line went slightly to the right and the other took a sharp turn to the left. Jack wasn't sure which way he should go. Both lines led out of the cave. They rejoined about two hundred feet later and a single line continued out toward the opening.

If he took the line going to the right, he would be in a shallower passage and maybe not as affected by the little white pill. But that passage also had several mounds or hills, and they were all covered by sediment. He wouldn't be able to bounce along the bottom without stirring up the mud and destroying the visibility.

The passage to the left had very little sediment on the floor. He could avoid the spots that were covered. The problem was that the passage was also ten to fifteen feet deeper than the one to the right. That meant the damn little white pill would be affecting him much worse than if he remained shallower.

It was a tough decision. Either way, Jack would have to eventually get deeper because that was the route the cave took. The good part was that there was very little sediment in the main passage between his location and the opening. That was if he went to the left. That decided it for Jack. If he went to the right and disturbed the sediment, the diminished visibility would follow him all the way out to the bottom of the chimney fissure. And he was likely to disturb the sediment. Jack moved his hand from the single line to the line going to the left and pulled himself forward toward the restriction between the boulders that had fallen from the ceiling and the ceiling that hadn't fallen…yet.

Jack suddenly felt anxiety about his decision. He had been back to diving for several weeks and had tried not to give any thought to his incident two years earlier. He pushed thoughts of the ceiling collapsing on him and pinning him down…again…out of his head. Now that he was staring directly at a piece of the ceiling that once held the boulder that he was steadying himself on, he had a rush of anxiety. He felt his heart beating rapidly in his chest. He felt his respirations getting faster. He felt the dizziness intensifying. He was certain if he moved forward that chunk of rock would fall on him and trap him.

Closing his eyes tightly, Jack stopped moving and held onto the boulder beneath him. He concentrated on his breathing and tried to slow it down. He knew he had plenty of air in his tanks. He had only breathed one stage tank empty and was breathing from the first sidemounted tank. He hadn't switched to his other stage tank like he had planned, but the sidemount tanks contained a lot more air. They should have enough to get him out of the cave. As long as he didn't panic.

What the hell?!? Jack Johnson panicking in a cave. Jack closed his eyes even tighter and focused on pushing the feelings he was experiencing out. It was so unnatural. He had never felt anything like it. He tried to convince himself that the cave wasn't going to collapse on him again. The chances of that happening were about as likely as a person getting struck by lightning twice. Except Jack had heard of people getting struck by lightning multiple times.

Jack slowed his breathing to a somewhat normal rate. He slowly opened his eyes and focused on the passage in front of him. He avoided looking at the ceiling. The ceiling that would soon be above him. The ceiling that could collapse on him.

STOP IT, JACK! He wanted to scream. He wanted to hit something. He just needed to start moving and get out of the cave. It was that little white pill. That was what was doing this to him. When he made it back to the surface, he was going to take those pills and toss them in the spring basin. He was never going to take another one again, no matter how bad the pain got. He would find another way to deal with it.

Jack kept his eyes on the floor as he moved through the restriction. He descended the five feet to the floor, feeling the dizziness increasing. He continued to focus on the floor in front of him and on the guideline he was holding in his hand. He kicked his fins and pulled himself along, following the guideline out. He tried to maintain as narrow of a focus as he could.

A few minutes later Jack felt a line arrow pass through his hand. He looked down at it and saw the number *1200* written on it. He had twelve hundred feet to go before he was at the surface. Normally, that would take him about six minutes being pulled by a scooter because of the force of the current. But he wasn't using his scooter. He wasn't even swimming. He was crawling. He'd be lucky to get out in thirty minutes. He couldn't let it go on for that long.

Jack tried to pick up his pace. He kicked more frequently and pulled himself along faster and more forcefully. Normal swimming pace would mean it would take twenty-four minutes, maybe a little less with the flow. Jack continued to focus on the passage in front of him. He arrived at a section where the ceiling dipped in the middle. The line was routed to the right of this formation. Most divers went past it to the left because that area was larger. Jack couldn't do that this time. He had to maintain contact with the guideline. That also meant passing over one of the few areas with sediment on the floor. Fortunately, it was mostly sand and would settle quickly. Jack felt the sand digging into the abrasions on the back of his hand.

Once he was past that section, Jack picked up his pace. There was more sediment on the floor, but he no longer cared. He just wanted to get out of the cave and back to the surface. Ahead, the passage made a sharp turn to the right and any of the sediment that was disturbed and rose up into the passage would be pushed into the small restriction at the corner. The visibility would be clear again to the right. Jack made it to the sharp turn and followed the line.

As he rounded the corner, he looked to the right and noticed a large grass carp hanging out on the edge of the room near the far wall. Jack shook his head back and forth. Was he seeing things? Was there really a giant fish fifteen feet away from him. He blinked his eyes rapidly, but the fish remained in his sight. The thing must have been at least four feet long. It was incredible. Jack was almost one thousand feet inside the cave. What would a fish that size be doing beyond the shadows this far in from the opening? There was nothing for it to eat. Was it really there? Or was that pill making him hallucinate?

Jack couldn't deal with it. He had to get out. He continued to pull and fin himself toward the opening. He went around another bend and saw the next intersection. This was where the two lines converged and became one again. Jack had only nine hundred feet to go before he was out of the cave and could surface. He tried to look at his dive computer display, but he couldn't focus on the numbers.

It didn't matter. It wouldn't matter until he got to the cavern where he would have to do a decompression stop before he could ascend. Hopefully, by the time he was that shallow, the effects of the little white pill wouldn't be so strong. Jack moved his hand from the guideline he was on to the single line leading out of the cave. At least he still had the mental capacity to note and confirm that he was on the correct line. He knew this because he felt the line arrow that was on that line and pointing toward the opening.

The current got stronger. The two cave passages converged with the guidelines and all of the water flowing through the cave joined together to push through a smaller passage. The force of it was substantial. Jack stopped pulling and rode the water flow out. He was moving more quickly than he had been. He kept a light hold of the guideline in the middle of a circle he formed with his thumb and index finger. He moved rapidly.

He felt another line arrow. He knew that would be the one marking eight hundred feet. A breakdown appeared in front of him. The next section of cave that had fallen from the ceiling. Jack momentarily let go of the line and allowed the water flow to direct him over the top of the breakdown area. He tried to grab the line again as he crested the top edge but missed. Instead, he crashed into the ceiling, hitting his head again. Seeing stars again.

39

Joey

While I was waiting for Jack to surface, I heard the sound of a diesel truck in the distance. There must be some divers coming in late. I looked at my phone. It was five thirty. It was a little late to be starting a dive. By the time they set up their equipment and got into the water, it would be close to six thirty. If they were doing a short dive, they might get out of the water by eight. The dive shop closed at seven. No way they'd be able to sign out of the park.

Come to think of it, how would I have signed out of the park if I went diving the next day after work? That hadn't occurred to me. I guess it was a good thing Lindsey said she would talk to me tomorrow. I'd have to ask Danny how late sign outs were handled. I couldn't be the only one wanting to dive late at night.

I looked at the notifications on my phone. There was a message from Gary. I tapped it to open it.

At restaurant. Where ya at?

Dammit! I got so focused on waiting for Jack that I forgot to message Gary and Jim. They probably already went in and ordered their drinks. I wanted to stick around and watch Jack surface from his dive. I hit the phone icon to call Gary.

"Where ya at, dumbass? We've been sitting in the parking lot for ten minutes waiting on you!"

"Sorry! I stopped by Cave Masters to get my tanks filled. I had about an hour to kill before y'all were supposed to be here, so I came to Jackson Blue to see who was diving. Guess whose truck was here?"

"Hmmm… No clue. Was it James Cameron? Is he directing another movie inside a cave and he wants you to star in it?"

"Yeah right. I wish! I forgot that you've been gone for the past month and have no clue what's going on up here."

"Well, if someone would keep us up to date on the things going on, maybe we would have a clue."

"Look, I've tried to chat or call, but y'all have been too busy. Y'all always blow me off."

"We've only been busy taking care of Jim's parents. Nothing too important. We should have dropped everything for the great Joey Simmons."

"Alright, alright! I get it. You've had more important things to do. Truce!"

"So are you going to tell us whose truck you saw, or what?"

"Oh yeah, right. It's Jack Johnson's truck. He's back in the area and diving again. And I think he's been scooping my leads in the back of JB."

"Holy crap! You owe me a coke! You owe me two cokes!"

"Guys! That's enough! Buy each other your cokes and get on with it!"

"Sorry." Both Gary and Jim chimed in at the same time again. Those guys spent far too much time together.

"Don't do it again!"

"Alright." They both said in unison.

"Anyway," I cut in before they could start up. "To kill some time I went into the woods to the east of the spring basin."

"Did you hear any banjos? You know how those woods around water are."

"No, I didn't hear any banjos. Will you let me finish?"

Silence. I was shocked.

"Anyway, I heard there's another spring somewhere in those woods. Well, I found a trail and followed it. Never found the spring. I think it's off the path. I got back and was about to head to the restaurant when I saw bubbles rising to the surface from inside of the cave. Had to be Jack. His truck is the only one here. I've been sitting on the diving board waiting for him to surface so I could see if he had an empty explorer reel. When I saw the bubbles, I completely forgot about y'all."

"We see how it is," Jim chimed in. "We're gone for a few weeks, and you forget about us, your lifelong pals who would give our lives for you. We mean that little to you." Laughter came through the phone.

"Screw you guys!" I laughed back. "Anyway, I've been sitting here for about fifteen minutes waiting for him to surface. I have no idea when that'll be, though. Could be in the next few minutes. Could be another forty-five minutes. I really want to see if he comes out with an empty reel."

"No problem. We'll go in and get started without you. We'll order you your usual. Maybe it will be on the table when you get here. Maybe not. Or maybe it will be cold and soggy."

"Hey! That's not cool!"

"Just kidding, man." Gary laughed. "Jim is already driving out of the parking lot. We'll be there in fifteen minutes. Gate code still the same?"

"Of course. What do you think? They never change that thing." I heard a car door slam behind me and turned around. "Shit! I gotta go. I'll see you in a few."

I ended the call and scooted back on the diving board. The diesel truck I heard came from a dark blue Dodge Ram. Maniac Manny, the road rager, was climbing out of it.

40

Somewhere in Jackson Blue

Jack finally stopped seeing stars. He still felt dizzy. He pushed himself off of the ceiling and slowly dropped to the top of the breakdown beneath him. The current pushed him forward as he descended into the heart of its path. He reached the floor just as he came to the edge of the large boulder that used to be attached to the ceiling. Jack once again looked at the edge of the ceiling in front of him. There was about a five-foot drop to the actual floor of the cave.

The anxiety was creeping back in with thoughts of the possibility of the ceiling crashing down on top of him. A forty-by-forty-foot section of ceiling about five to six feet thick had already fallen long ago and was directly below him. What was keeping the limestone that was still on the ceiling from falling on top of him? Would he ever get over the anxiety he was feeling? Would he ever be able to go into a cave again without the invading thoughts of the ceiling collapsing around him and on top of him?

Shoving the memory of the collapse back into the dark recesses of his mind, Jack pulled himself over the edge of the boulder and descended to the floor. The anxiety tried to creep back in, but he pushed it out, concentrating on the line beneath him and following it to get out of the cave. The flow of the water continued to move him through the passage. He felt another line arrow against his palm as he slid his hand along the guideline. He glanced at the arrow. It was the seven-hundred-foot marker. Usually Jack wouldn't think seven hundred feet was that much distance. He could swim that in his sleep.

But it seemed almost unattainable with the little white pill on board.

Sometime later, Jack wasn't sure how much time had passed, he saw a large phallic formation to his right. It stood tall in the passage, narrow on the shaft with a hat on the tip. *What the hell is that doing here?* Jack didn't remember seeing such a formation in Jackson Blue before. He wondered if he had taken a wrong turn along the way. He looked at the guideline he was following. It was the thicker gold-colored guideline. That confirmed he was in the main passage. So what was that formation?

Jack turned his head so he could keep his eyes on the formation as he approached it. That was when he recognized Chicken Head Rock. He couldn't figure out why he had never seen the phallic symbol during his exit before. He would have to remember to look for it the next time he was exiting the cave and not under the influence of drugs.

Jack felt another arrow hit his hand. He looked at it. It was the five-hundred-foot marker. Hadn't he just passed the seven-hundred-foot marker? Had he passed the six-hundred-foot line arrow? Or was it missing? He must have been so focused on the different angle of Chicken Head Rock that he didn't notice the other arrow. He had to pay more attention. He had to focus on exiting the cave and not get distracted.

Jack finally arrived at the edge of the first breakdown. He was slightly more than four hundred feet from the opening. He was poised over the boulder that had fallen from the ceiling in this location. He quickly pulled himself forward before the anxiety could creep back in. He didn't want to think about it. He entered the large room between the first breakdown and the chimney fissure. This is where the anxiety had been really bad on previous dives, even without the little white pill to make it worse. The chimney fissure was where Jack had gotten pinned to the floor of the cave by a giant boulder. This was where the ceiling collapsed on top of him, almost killing him. Worse yet, it had allowed Simmons and Carter to claim rescuing him. Dying would have been a better option.

Jack considered exiting through Young's Siphon or the Horseshoe

Circuit. Both passages would get him closer to the opening and avoid the chimney fissure. He had done it before. Actually, he had done it every single time except once since he started diving again. The one time he didn't take one of the bypasses, he almost lost his shit in the chimney fissure. The anxiety had been too much to handle.

Jack couldn't understand the response that moving through the chimney fissure evoked in him. He became lightheaded and dizzy. He felt weak. He wanted to bolt to the surface and be outside of the cave. He had never felt anxiety when cave diving before the incident. He always felt complete confidence. The feelings that took over his mind and body since he returned to the caves were overwhelming.

Jack believed he was the best cave diver that ever lived. He knew he was. He could move through the smallest passages without stirring a single speck of dust. He could even do that while speeding through the restrictions behind his scooter. He was that good. He found and explored passages that others couldn't dream of finding. And he had rescued all of those divers a couple of years earlier, regardless of what Simmons and Carter claimed.

Then, that fateful day came. He got trapped under a giant boulder that fell from the ceiling. Jack would have preferred to have been left to die there than have it play out the way it did. It was demeaning. It was degrading. The feelings that were elicited by going through that passage had to do more with the outcome rather than the fear of the ceiling falling on him again. Or did they? The fear was triggered earlier when moving past the breakdowns. Could that really be it? Could it not have anything to do with what Simmons and Carter did? Could Jack Johnson really be afraid of the ceiling coming down on him again?

Pushing those thoughts aside again, Jack decided he had to go up the chimney fissure. The Horseshoe Circuit would take too long. Young's Siphon got low and the restriction connecting it to the Rock Garden was on the small side. In his current condition, he wasn't certain he would be able to get through it. Not to mention that both bypasses had their floors covered in sediment. Jack steeled himself against the doubts and fears and pushed forward toward the chimney fissure. It wasn't that long of a passage. From the bottom of the fissure to the top was only forty-five feet.

Well, it was a forty-five-foot ascent. He would have to take it a little slow. Before the collapse he took two to three minutes to ascend it so he could allow the nitrogen bubbles in his bloodstream to off-gas slowly as the pressure around him dropped. He didn't know if he could go that slowly this time. He would have to try to restrain himself from darting up the fissure. Maybe stretching out the ascent over a minute would work. Maybe that would be tolerable.

Jack reached the bottom of the chimney fissure and grabbed onto the large rock that the guideline was wrapped around. The line took off from it at about a sixty-degree slope. Jack closed his eyes for a moment to steady himself and gather his courage. He could do this. He could get up this chimney fissure without incident. What were the chances that more of the ceiling would come down on top of him?

He shouldn't have asked himself that. The chances were higher given that it had happened there previously. Jack had also noticed a crack in the ceiling at that location. This crack was in the same spot that once held the pieces that were now scattered about below. He stopped to examine the crack every time in the past few weeks as he made his way into and out of the cave. It didn't appear to be getting bigger, but it was there and one day it would give way and drop more boulders into the chimney fissure.

Opening his eyes, Jack moved his hand from the rock to the guideline and began his ascent up the fissure. He forced himself to breathe slowly. He held his breath as long as he could before releasing the exhaust bubbles from his regulator so they could float toward the ceiling and make their way into the cracks, weakening the bond that held it in place. He felt the anxiety creeping in again and pushed it aside. He focused on getting to the top and out of the fissure. He concentrated on getting himself out of the danger zone.

About halfway up, he pulled in a breath and the regulator stopped working. He tried to suck in more air, but nothing happened. *What the hell was going on?* Jack thought to himself. He looked at his pressure gauge and saw the needle stuck to the pin. *Dammit!* He had breathed his tank empty.

Releasing his hold on the guideline, Jack reached up to find his other regulator. Grasping it in his hand, he spit the regulator in his mouth out and replaced it with the new regulator. He took in a breath, or rather, he tried to take in a breath. It also wasn't working. *Fuck!* He had grabbed the regulator that was connected to the empty stage tank.

Jack felt around his chest for the third regulator, the one that was attached to the sidemount tank that he hadn't breathed from and should still be full. He found a regulator and hoped it was that one and not the one he had just spit out. The anxiety he had been feeling in the chimney hadn't allowed the effects of the little white pill to ease off. He was still having trouble thinking straight.

Spitting out the other non-functional second stage regulator, Jack shoved what was hopefully the functional regulator into his mouth. He depressed the purge on its faceplate and felt the rush of air mixed with water hitting the back of his mouth. He reflexively coughed before the water entered his throat and found his trachea. He pulled in a full breath of dry air from the sidemount tank that was clipped onto the left side of his body. Jack exhaled and took another breath. He did this a third time before realizing where he was and also realizing that he was no longer holding onto the guideline and didn't know where it was. The anxiety came screaming back at him full force just as his body hit the ceiling above the chimney fissure. The ceiling that he was certain was going to collapse one day.

41

Joey

I reached the other end of the diving board and stood up. I turned to look toward the parking lot. Maniac Manny had walked around to the back of his truck and dropped the tailgate. He either hadn't noticed my car or he didn't recognize it as the target of his road rage on two separate occasions three days earlier. Maybe he hadn't followed me to Destin after all. Maybe he lived down there and just happened to be in the same parking lot. That would be a big coincidence.

I decided to walk over to the pavilion and see if I could find out Manny's real name. He could be the one that was scooping me. He might not even know it was me he had been scooping and might tell me what he was planning on doing on his dive. It was doubtful but worth a try.

As I walked across the grass toward the pavilion, I saw Jim's truck appear at the top of the hill. Good. It was always nice to have backup. Jim turned and drove down the hill, parking next to Manny's truck. I altered my course and walked toward the new arrivals. As I approached the parking lot, Manny stopped and looked at me. I thought I saw the hint of recognition on his face. I wasn't sure if he recognized me from crossing paths here before or from the road rage incidents. I raised my hand to wave at him.

"How's it goin'?"

"A'ight. You?"

"Good."

I kept walking toward Jim's truck to greet the boys. I would deal with Manny later. Gary jumped out of the truck and rushed over to me, pulling me in for a big bearhug of an embrace.

"Dude! I missed you so much! It's been way too long!"

"Careful, or Jim might get jealous." I jokingly chastised him. Jim and Gary had been together for many years and they both knew I was as hetero as one could get. There was no jealousy except when one of us found unexplored cave passages before the others.

"Let 'im get jealous! It's been hell being down in South Florida for the past month."

"I thought that would be more your scene, well, because, you know…"

"Yeah, maybe when we were single. Now, we're homebodies. That scene doesn't do anything for us."

I laughed hard at that. Gary and Jim were both my age. They were far too young to be an old fuddy-duddy couple sitting at home bickering at each other. Come to think of it, they didn't frequent the scene in Tallahassee, where they lived, either. They *were* a couple of old fuddy-duddies! Just then, Jim walked up behind me and put his arms around me from behind.

"Missed ya, man! How've you been?"

I turned around and hugged him back. "Things could be better. A lot has been going on the past week."

"Yeah, G filled me in on the things you've told him. Sorry we weren't here to help you deal with it."

"Nah, no need to be sorry. You were dealing with your dad. How is he, by the way?"

"He's doing much better. Fortunately, the surgery went well. Only one vessel was blocked. He's on a bunch of new medicines and they'll keep a close eye on him. He's even going to the golf course tomorrow to practice his putt, against my mom's wishes. But the doctor said he could get back to it. Activity, as long as it's not over doing it, is actually good for him."

"That's great to hear. I'm so glad you guys are back home."

"We are, too. You owe me a coke! You owe me another coke!"

I reached out and palmed both of their mouths to shut them up.

"You guys! Aren't you a little old for that stuff?"

"Maybe, but we're still young at heart." Gary said.

"And maturity." Jim piped in.

"So what's going on?" Gary asked.

I nodded toward Manny and pointed my chin toward a pavilion on the other side of the spring basin, "Let's go sit over there."

Once we were out of earshot, I filled Gary and Jim in on everything that had been going on. They knew some of it already because I had spoken with Gary briefly about it. The thing with Manny was new, though.

"He might be the one. We don't personally know him. Couldn't tell you his name. We've just seen him out here diving. I can't remember if he has a scooter or if he usually takes a bunch of stage tanks into the cave. But we'll find out shortly." Jim, the more analytical of the two, offered his opinion.

"Or we could go over there and beat the information out of him right now." Gary suggested.

"Nah, I'd rather save the ass whooping for after we find out for sure who's doing this."

"Good point. You…"

I palmed their mouths before they could start that mess again.

"Not to change the subject too much, but when I came out of the woods, I noticed those bubbles coming out of the cave opening. They've been pretty steady but haven't increased in quantity, so I don't think Jack is in the Deco Room yet. If he's doing a decompression stop in the Rock Garden, he must have started his dive a few hours ago. I've been here for at least twenty minutes, so he's bound to move into the Deco Room soon. Do y'all mind hanging out here for a little longer? I want to get a look at Jack's reel."

Gary and Jim hesitated and looked at each other before either responded. I thought they were about to say they were hungry and wanted to head out. Jim swept his hand toward Gary, giving him the floor. Apparently, the pause was so they wouldn't get their mouths palmed again.

"Yeah, we can hang out. Let's go over and talk to Manny while we wait."

"Okay, remember, though, his name isn't Manny. That's just a nickname I gave him because he was acting like a maniac on the road."

The guys laughed. "You and your nicknames. We'll try not to slip. You owe me a…" This time they stopped voluntarily.

42

The chimney fissure in Jackson Blue

Jack pushed himself away from the ceiling and toward the opening. He didn't bother to look back and see if the ceiling was about to detach and fall or not. He didn't care. He just didn't want to be anywhere near it if it did.

Once he was safely out of the way, he dared a glance back. Everything looked normal. The ceiling hadn't moved. That had been a bad place to empty his scuba tank. On the other hand, running out of air in that location distracted him enough to push the anxiety aside and get through it faster. Jack was so focused on switching regulators and getting air into his lungs that he managed to avoid a panic attack, at least until he hit the ceiling.

As he swam along the top of the fissure, he looked down and saw the boulder that had fallen on him two years earlier. It didn't look as big now as it had back then. Half of it was buried in sediment. A couple of years of current pushing more mud up the slope filled the spaces around the boulder. It looked like it had been in that location forever.

Jack looked around the rest of the silty slope at the bottom of the fissure. He noticed a couple of other boulders half buried in the mud. One of them looked like it might have been about one and a half times the size of the offending boulder that had pinned him. He would likely have died trapped under that one. As it was, he wasn't sure how he had gotten out from under the rock. That part of the incident was blocked out of his memory. All he could remember was a large cloud of silt enveloping him from behind and something hitting him from above, pinning his arm to the floor. Then he remembered being in the Deco Room breathing from his oxygen tank. He couldn't remember getting from the chimney fissure to the Deco Room.

Jack did remember the Simmons boy and Carter girl trying to manhandle him from the Deco Room to the surface and trying to claim they saved him. Ungrateful bastards. That was the thanks Jack got for rescuing both of them, Simmons right here in Jackson Blue, and Carter and that other girl at Eddy Spring. They should have been thankful Jack had been there when he was. They should have idolized him.

Jack looked directly below him at the largest chunk of ceiling that had fallen two years earlier. It would have been really bad if he had been beneath that. They would have had to cut his body into little pieces in order to get it out. What they would have been able to get of his body. Most of it would have been crushed flat as a pancake.

Jack shuddered at the thought as he felt his back hit the ceiling again. He looked to his left and saw the small crack across the sloped area of the ceiling. He wondered how long it would be before that let go and more of the ceiling went crashing down onto another unsuspecting diver. It could be Jack that it came crashing down on again.

Pushing himself away from the area that gave him anxiety, Jack moved below the large air pocket toward the Rock Garden. His thoughts were starting to clear now that he was only forty feet deep. He felt dizzy, but not so much that he thought he could no longer swim out of the cave. Jack adjusted his buoyancy so that he was neutral and hovering in the middle of the passage. He kicked his fins to assist the flow that was carrying him out toward the blue-tinted sunlight coming through the opening. That scene never got old. It was one of the prettiest sights.

Just then Jack remembered he might have a decompression obligation that wouldn't allow him to ascend directly to the surface without first stopping for several minutes. He might even have one deeper than the usual twenty-foot decompression stop. He looked at his dive computer display and saw the number *20* on it. That was a relief. He could go straight to the Deco Room, grab his oxygen tank, and tuck himself into the corner. Maybe by the time he ascended to twenty feet, he would be back to normal.

The flow continued to carry Jack out as he steered with his fins. Less than two minutes later he was caught in the current that was blasting through the restriction between the Rock Garden and the Deco Room. It grabbed Jack and pushed him toward the Deco Room ceiling. He felt it snatch his fins and push them up so that his feet were above him and leading the way toward the opening. Jack kicked with all of his might, trying to overpower the water current and get himself back to twenty feet of depth before he got the bends.

Jack's feet hit the edge of the ceiling just before it ended and gave way to the spring basin just beyond. He kicked and pushed himself off of the ceiling toward the floor. He kicked with all of his might as he tried to release whatever air was in his BC and his drysuit. Unfortunately, the air wasn't going anywhere. It had risen to the highest point, which was the bottom of the BC and the feet of the drysuit, neither of which had an exhaust vent near them. He continued to kick as hard as he could. He felt his right foot coming out of the foot pocket of the drysuit and the fin. He was about to lose that fin.

Jack reached back with his right arm and bent his knee so he could grab the fin before it fell off of the end of his drysuit leg. That motion caught the current just right allowing it to rotate him. He was flipped into an upright position. He raised his left arm to get the exhaust vent at the highest point on his body and felt the drysuit squeezing his legs as the air migrated to the shoulders. He tried to vent his BC as well but couldn't hold onto the cord long enough for it to do any good. He would take care of that once he was stabilized on the floor of the cave.

Finally reaching the floor of the Deco Room, Jack grabbed the heavy, solidified concrete bag that had been in that location for as long as he could remember. Once he had it in his grasp, he released the air from his BC and drysuit, feeling the drysuit squeeze around him. Jack felt his knees hit the rocky floor. He was thankful that there wasn't any mud or clay in this room. That would have made a mess.

Jack looked at his oxygen-filled decompression tank lying on the floor about twenty feet away. He pulled himself toward it, stealing a glance at his dive computer display. He had violated his decompression schedule by not stopping at twenty feet of depth. Even though he was only two feet too shallow, the depth reading was flashing red. Jack grabbed the decompression tank and moved farther from the opening where he could get twenty feet deep and allow the nitrogen bubbles to slowly release from his body.

Once he was at twenty feet of depth, Jack looked at the computer display. He had gotten to the proper depth just as his twenty-foot stop obligation was done. He only had a ten-foot obligation to complete. He had to remain there for nine minutes. Jack decided to stay right where he was. It didn't make a difference whether he was ten or twenty feet deep. The decompression obligation would be the same. It was easier to remain in place.

Jack reassessed his situation. The exertion had intensified the effects of the little white pill. He might as well have been at eighty feet considering what he was feeling again. Getting from the Deco Room to the surface was going to be interesting. The water flow was strong at the opening and was certain to blow him into the eel grass that had taken residence in front of it. He would have to figure out a way to prevent that from happening. It would really look bad if there was anyone on the surface to bear witness.

It would be best to exit on the side of the opening Jack was closest to. It wasn't the way he usually went and would put him on the opposite side of the diving board platform than he normally used, but the current would not be as strong and there was more to grab onto there so he could slow his exit. Getting out on that side would also direct him away from the area most other cave divers set up before their dives. It would shield him from the pavilions near the parking area. Jack planned a path from his current location to the opening that would provide him with the most handholds along the way. Then he looked at his dive computer display. One minute left. Time was flying by.

Jack watched the number *1* change to a *0* along with the words *Deco Clear*. He released his grip on the rocky floor beneath him and kicked his fins. The current grabbed him again and pushed his fins around his body, so they were leading the way out. His scooter was also caught in the flow and acting like a sail. He tried to grab onto the rocks below, but all that happened was that he ended up dragging them with him. They weren't big enough or heavy enough to overcome the strength of the current and stop his movement. Jack was spit out of the cave, into the eel grass, and went tumbling toward the surface of the spring basin.

43

Lindsey

That didn't go over well. Somehow dad snuck into the hallway without us being aware. Now he knew that I was pregnant. He was not happy. He was especially not happy when he found out that Joey was cheating on me. Dad was ready to go find Joey and beat the crap out of him.

"Dad, please don't! Give me a chance to talk to Joey first. I'm supposed to meet him tomorrow night to discuss what's going on. I haven't talked to him since Sunday other than to kick him out of the dive shop earlier today."

Thankfully, dad backed off. He was angry, but he retreated and said he would allow me a few days. He huffed off to his office and slammed the door shut behind him.

"Dad will come around, baby. Just give him time."

"I know, mom. It's just so much. I don't know what I'm going to do at this point. I mean, Joey and I talked about eventually getting married and having kids, but that was a long way off in our future. And now we don't have a future together."

"Are you certain he was cheating on you, dear? Could it just be a big misunderstanding?"

"I don't know what to think anymore, mom. I'm supposed to talk to him tomorrow night, but I don't think I can do that anymore. I need time to think about everything and figure out what I want to do before that happens."

"Don't you think that's a decision you should both make?"

"I don't know, mom. I don't know."

* * *

I spent the next hour trying to track down an instructor to take my weekend scuba class. Even though I was probably only a few weeks pregnant, scuba diving wasn't safe for the fetus. There wasn't enough known about the effects of the increased pressure on an unborn child. Divers Alert Network, the leading entity on scuba diving and medical concerns simply said don't dive if you're pregnant or think you might be. I wasn't sure what I wanted to do in regard to the pregnancy. I wasn't about to make a decision before the weekend.

I got in touch with a couple of instructors, but both were out of town and unable to take the class. None of the other instructors answered their phones, so I left messages on their voicemails asking them to call me back as soon as they got a chance. I wasn't concerned about finding a replacement. Most of the instructors were eager to take a class because it meant more certifications and that meant they were a little bit closer to being able to move to the next instructor level.

While I was waiting for return calls, I decided to call Joey and make sure he got my message about postponing the meeting we had planned for the next evening. He hadn't replied to it. Like I had told mom, I needed time to process this information. There was too much going on for me to think about it. I wanted to sleep on it and give myself time to reflect on the options. There was no doubt in my mind that I would keep the baby if things were going well between Joey and me. They weren't going well, though, and I wasn't sure I wanted to be a single mom. I also wasn't sure I could go through with an abortion. I wanted to decide before I talked to Joey.

Mom wanted me to work things out with Joey and make the decision with him. It was my body, though. I was the one who had to go through the pregnancy for nine months and then I'd be the one who had to raise that child for the next eighteen years if Joey and I didn't patch things up. I knew mom would help, but I didn't want to depend on her for the next eighteen years. I didn't know if I could forgive Joey enough to take him back. Joey would probably want to be there for the child. I didn't know how I felt about that.

Joey's phone rang and went to voicemail. I didn't leave a message. If he didn't call back before I went to bed, I'd call again and leave a message at that time. What the hell could he be doing? Was he with Kelly again? It seemed like he wanted to patch things up earlier in the day. Why would he do this if he wanted to fix things?

Maybe he was trying to have his cake and eat it, too. That would be like Joey to do something like that. I didn't know why I agreed to talk to him. At this point, I wanted to cancel the meeting, not postpone it. Joey wasn't worth my time. He didn't deserve to know anything.

44

Joey

As we began walking toward the parking area to talk with Manny, a burst of bubbles hit the surface in front of the cave opening. Jack was in the Deco Room. Gary, Jim, and I ran over to the diving platform and to the edge of the concrete slab to look down into the water. We watched a continuous stream of bubbles escaping the cave and hitting the surface of the water. I wondered how long of a decompression obligation Jack had to do before he was cleared to surface.

While we waited for Jack to make an appearance, I watched Manny setting up his equipment out of the corner of my eye. Manny got angry with something he was doing. Apparently, a piece of equipment wasn't doing what he wanted it to do. He cursed loudly and threw things around. The three of us turned our heads to watch the spectacle as it unfolded about eighty feet away from us. Manny was so angry with whatever it was that set him off that he didn't notice us staring at him. I was starting to understand the road rage. It wasn't limited to when he was behind the wheel of his truck. Manny was angry all of the time. He must live a miserable existence.

As we were watching the Manny show, I heard a splash behind us. I turned my head and saw Jack at the surface struggling. It looked like he was trying to get back underwater and into the Deco Room. I didn't know why he would be doing that. We all watched as Jack rotated around, fighting to get control of himself. His scooter had been clipped behind him, but the erratic motion swung it around so that it was catching the water current and pulling Jack into the tall eel grass in front of the cave opening. When Jack finally managed to get somewhat sorted and tried to swim against the flow into the cave, the scooter got caught in the eel grass and kept him from making any forward progress.

Jack gave up the struggle and let the water current coming from the cave push him into the eel grass and carry him into the middle of the spring basin. I wasn't sure if he was conscious or not. It didn't look like he was moving. I looked at Gary and Jim and saw looks of concern on their faces. They were thinking the same thing I was. Jack was in trouble.

I looked back toward Manny to see if he had pulled his drysuit on yet. He had not. He was still under the pavilion throwing dive equipment and slamming it on the table. How had he not killed himself while cave diving? Had all of his dives gone without any issues? After seeing his response to what was likely a minor issue with his equipment, I began doubting he was the diver scooping my leads. There was no way Manny would have the patience or control to go that far back in the cave, through multiple restrictions, without losing his shit and getting himself killed.

I turned back toward the basin. Jack was floating on the surface face down. There was so much eel grass around him, I couldn't tell if he had the second stage regulator in his mouth or if it had fallen out. I had to do something. I handed my phone and keys to Jim. I kicked off my flip flops, stripped off my shorts and shirt, and dove headfirst into the cold spring water. The shock of hitting the water with my bare skin almost took my breath away. It was one thing to jump into that water wearing a drysuit. It was something altogether different to jump in almost naked. The only thing I was wearing were my briefs. I reached down around my hips. Well, almost wearing! The dive had pushed them down from my waist. I was lucky they hadn't gone farther down my legs. That would have given Gary and Jim quite a show.

I pulled up the waistband, so it was properly situated and began to swim toward Jack. The strong current coming from the cave opening helped propel me along. I made it to him within a few seconds. The spring basin was shallow enough where Jack's body was floating so that I could stand on the bottom. I planted my feet on the sand among the eel grass roots and stood. I grabbed Jack's shoulders and began rotating him so that he was floating on his back instead of the front of his body. I had to get his mouth out of the water. As I was rotating him, I felt Jack stiffen. His right hand flew up and tried to push me away. I moved to my right and avoided his punch. I wasn't sure what he was trying to do, but I didn't need him pulling me underwater.

I grabbed Jack's right wrist and used it as leverage to finish rotating him onto his back. He pulled back but without much effort. He felt weak. His movements didn't have a lot of force. I finally got him rotated so that he was on his side, and I saw that the regulator was still in his mouth. That was good. I suppose I should have looked for bubbles rising up around his head. I'm not sure if I would have seen any with the current pushing them away and the eel grass just below the surface making it difficult to differentiate bubbles from the movement of the water. Either way, I was in the water, and I was going to get Jack on his back and pull him to the edge of the basin. I had to do it quickly. The cold sixty-nine-degree water was already starting to get to me. I didn't know how the people that came here to swim tolerated it.

Jack tried to drop his feet beneath him so he could stand. He continued struggling. He didn't have the strength to do it. Something bad must have happened to him during his dive. *His dive!* Dammit! I should have looked at the reels clipped to the D rings on his back. Was there any line on them? I couldn't remember. I was so focused on getting to Jack and helping him that I forgot why I was still at the park. I contemplated rotating Jack back around face down so I could look, but I was concerned that the regulator might drop out of his mouth, and he'd drown right there in front of me. As tempting as that was, I couldn't let that happen.

Instead of rotating Jack, I pulled him toward the edge of the spring basin. I looked back and saw Jim talking on the phone. His voice was too low for me to determine what he was saying or who he was on the phone with. I hoped it was 911. Jack was going to need some medical attention. Gary had run off of the diving platform to the grass above the retaining wall and was waiting for me so he could help pull Jack out. I looked toward the pavilion. Manny was in his own world focused on his own issues. He didn't seem to be aware of what was going on around him. So much for situational awareness.

Jack continued struggling with me as I pulled him closer to shore where Gary was waiting. He appeared to be getting weaker. I couldn't go directly toward Gary because that would have taken me over a section of the basin where the sandy floor dipped and was too deep for me to stand. I needed the traction to pull Jack and all of his scuba equipment against the water current. The eel grass got thicker and hindered our progress. I was starting to shiver and having trouble holding onto Jack's arm. The eel grass felt slimy and weird against the bare skin of my legs as I moved through it. I couldn't get out of the water fast enough.

I finally reached Gary and passed Jack's arm to him so I could unclip the scooter and tanks from his harness. There was no way we were getting him over the retaining wall with all of that stuff on. As I unclipped the scooter, I looked toward the gently sloped beach entrance that was about fifty feet away from us. I should have pulled Jack to that. Instead, I had focused on where Gary was standing, which was the usual spot we got in and out of the water. I handed Gary the tow rope on the scooter.

"Clip that around the ladder railing over there. I'm going to pull Jack to the beach so it's easier to get him out. I need to get my body out of this freezing water."

Without saying a word, Gary grabbed the bolt snap and took a few steps closer to the ladder as I grabbed Jack's arm and pulled him toward the beach. Jack resumed his resistance. Fortunately, his strength was waning. He wasn't putting up much of a fight. About a minute later, Jack was lying on the sandy slope as far out of the water as I could drag him, which wasn't that far. I was too cold and my own strength was depleting quickly. There was still about two inches of water surrounding Jack. He tried to fight me off, but he continued to get weaker.

I started to unclip his scuba tanks so we could pull him out of the water to dry land.

"Start working on that side while I get this tank off."

Gary stepped into the water with his flip-flopped feet and unclipped Jack's oxygen decompression tank. Jack had four additional tanks on him besides that one. He had been planning on going back far. I tried to sneak a look at his reel, but it was underneath him.

Just as we were getting the last two tanks unclipped from Jack, an ambulance pulled into the park and came to a stop on the grass about twenty feet away. The medics jumped out of the cab and ran over.

"Did he fall or injure his head or neck?" One of them asked.

"No, ma'am. Not that we know of. We just saw him fly out of the cave into the eel grass over there." I said as I pointed to the middle of the basin.

"On the count of three."

The medics stood on either side of Jack and grabbed his shoulders. One of them supported his head and they pulled him out of the water onto the sand. One of the medics ran to the ambulance to collect some equipment while the other one stayed with Jack.

"Tell me what happened."

"We're not sure. We were hanging out on the diving platform watching his bubbles. Our attention had been diverted elsewhere." I nodded my head toward Manny under the pavilion. "While we were looking away, we heard a splash and turned around to see Jack struggling underwater in the eel grass. It looked like he was trying to get back inside the cave."

Gary knelt down and grabbed Jack's left wrist. Jack let out a grunt.

"What are you doing, sir? Please don't touch him."

"He violated his decompression obligation. He still had nine minutes of decompression at ten feet."

The medic's eyes got wide.

"Contact the medical chopper! We need to fly him to a hyperbaric chamber. And bring the oxygen right away. Forget the other stuff."

"No, no, that ain't right. I saw the display change to zero. I saw it read deco clear." Jack slurred.

"Sir, your dive computer display is flashing red. I don't know what you saw, but it looks like you did something wrong."

"Nine minutes isn't all that much. The dive computer should be conservative enough that he won't get the bends." Gary offered.

"Our protocol says we need to fly him out of here if we can. It doesn't matter if he has nine minutes or nine seconds of decompression. Thank you for getting him this far. Can you please now step back and give us room to do our job? Thank you."

Gary and I stepped back. I guess they didn't want to know any more about what happened. Gary was right. Nine minutes wasn't that long, but Jack could possibly be bent. It was strange that Jack thought he had cleared his decompression obligation. Something was going on. I doubted he had any helium in his tanks, so it wasn't likely he got bent while he was underwater. Something happened to him while he was on that dive. Something bad.

45

As the car was approaching the entrance to Blue Springs Recreation Area, it became apparent to the driver that the gate was open. That was strange. It was a weekday. The gate should be closed. The driver wondered if the county had figured out that someone had been entering the code without first signing in at Cave Masters and sneaking in to go diving. The keypad appeared to be a simple mechanism that didn't have an internet connection or any manner of getting access logs from it.

The driver pulled the car to the side of the road about fifty feet from the entrance and looked up to see if the power pole had a camera on it. That was probably something that should have been checked sooner. There didn't appear to be anything there other than the power line that went to the pavilions and the building where the restrooms were located.

Easing off of the brake, the car rolled forward until it was almost even with the gate. There was no one visible inside of the park. That didn't mean much. The parking area for cave divers was down a hill and couldn't be seen from the road. Maybe there was a maintenance crew working on something. Glancing at the clock and noting it was after six, that possibility was discounted.

The car slowly rolled into the entrance and past the open gate. A minute later, it came to a stop at the top of the hill right in front of the road that led down to the parking area. The sound of a helicopter drowned out all other noise as it approached overhead. Down the hill an ambulance was parked on the grass. Its crew was kneeling down around a diver in a drysuit lying on the sand near the water. There was a diver beneath the closest pavilion setting up equipment. The activity happening less than one hundred feet away did not seem to faze him. Three guys stood next to the pavilion watching the medics and their patient. One of those three was Joey Simmons. At that moment, Simmons turned his head and looked up the hill at the car.

A sheriff's deputy ran up beside the car and knocked on the window. The driver opened it.

"You're gonna have to leave. That chopper is about to land here. We have to make sure there's no one else in the cave. As long as there ain't, you should be able to come back in about an hour."

"Yes, officer. Thank you."

That had been close! The driver turned the car around and started to head out of the park, disappointed. It was strange because Simmons was never at the park during the week. If he was about to go diving, it would be several hours before returning was safe. It was a shame because it would be a couple more days before coming back to dive was possible.

Coming up with something to do in the area to pass the time until everyone left the park was proving to be difficult. Marianna was too small to have a nightlife. There weren't many options besides hanging out at Walmart, and that could only be taken in small doses.

The last dive in Jackson Blue a few days earlier had led to what appeared to be a dead end. But it couldn't be. The water current had to be coming from somewhere. There had to be a restriction somewhere that led to the going passage. Things were getting complicated. Simmons had to be kept out of the area somehow. Either he would need to be injured and unable to dive, or the passage would need to be blocked, but only enough to deter him. Injuring him while remaining anonymous would prove to be difficult. It would be better to block the passage, but there had to be a way to get beyond the blockade. There was one possibility.

There was a tall room leading to the area that was about thirty feet from floor to ceiling. There was a shelf about twenty feet above the floor where a boulder was positioned near the edge. If that boulder could be pushed off so that it fell in front of the restriction below, it might deter Simmons but still allow passage around it.

The boulder looked like it would be big enough to block the passage. The only concern was leaving enough room to one side to pass through. The restriction also had to be small enough that Simmons would think it was not passable. That would be complicated. Another complication was pushing the boulder off of the shelf. Something would need to be used as leverage. A long crowbar would be perfect but too difficult to bring that far in. Maybe a stage tank could be used instead.

The plan might work. The diver decided to push the boulder off of the shelf on the way out from the next dive. Its presence in front of the restriction should be enough to deter anyone from going farther in. It was unlikely Simmons would be back before Saturday so there had been no point in making things difficult before then. Except there he was standing next to the water probably waiting to be able to go for a dive. He would have another day with free access to the section. That gave him another opportunity to go back to find the hidden passages.

The driver sat in the car trying to decide whether to go home and return Saturday, hoping that Simmons wouldn't find the hidden passages, or to find something closer than two hours away to kill the time. Dothan, Alabama wasn't far. It was less than an hour's drive and supposedly had a little more to do than this small town. As it was, if Simmons was about to go diving, that would require staying away for five or six hours, maybe longer. A dive was unlikely to happen. The next dive would have to happen on another day. The likelihood of Simmons finding anything was low. At least, that was the hope the driver had while turning the car around to head back home.

46

Joey

I heard a noise coming from above and looked up to see a helicopter approaching. As I swung my head around, I noticed a car at the top of the hill. It looked like another diver was coming into the park. This was a busy place for a Thursday evening. I wondered if it was always so busy. I looked back up at the helicopter, then looked at the car again.

Something about that car looked familiar. I couldn't quite place where I had seen it before. As I was trying to figure it out, the helicopter descended into the clearing at the opposite side of the basin from where we were. It gently settled onto the grassy field and two people dressed in blue coveralls exited, grabbed some medical bags, and ran down the hill toward the ambulance. They were going to fly Jack to a hyperbaric chamber.

I looked away from the helicopter and turned my attention back to the car that had pulled in. I saw the tail end of the car as it started to head out of the park. *Dammit!*

"I'll be right back."

I took off running up the hill to try to get a better look at the car and maybe see what was driving. Something was bothering me about it. The car would have to stop so the driver could open the gate. I had time to catch up.

When I got to the top of the hill, the car was gone. The gate stood wide open. The ambulance crew or the deputy must have left it open. It was probably another cave diver I had encountered while out diving.

I made a mental note to ask Danny who had signed in to dive Jackson Blue this evening.

Another car sped into the park as I turned back toward the action behind me. The medics were loading Jack into the ambulance. That was strange. Shouldn't they be loading him into the helicopter? As I walked down the hill, the car that had just arrived stopped and a man stepped out of it holding a camera with a long telephoto lens. The press had arrived. Jack was going to love seeing his name in the paper as a victim again.

The photographer snapped photos of the ambulance and helicopter. He turned toward me, and I held my hands up. I was wearing nothing but briefs and didn't feel like having my picture in the paper dressed like that. Or rather, undressed. Fortunately, the photographer decided it wouldn't make for a good image on the front page and turned away to snap a few more photos of the spring basin, the ambulance, and the helicopter. The medics shut the doors to the ambulance and took off up the hill next to me, gravel flying out from under its tires and hitting my bare skin. I had flashbacks to the beer bottle incident. I ran toward the diving platform to retrieve my clothing.

I got my keys from Jim and ran to my car to get a towel. I was already mostly dry. I disappeared into the men's room, dried myself off, and got dressed, carefully zipping my shorts since I was forced to go commando. Fortunately, the shorts in style were the long ones that went to my knees and not the shorts of the eighties like I had seen my father wearing in old photographs. I guess men liked to show off their thighs back then.

By the time I walked out of the restroom, the helicopter was lifting off with Jack in it. *Crap!* I forgot to look at his reel. I looked around the park, but Jack's equipment was gone. I watched one of the deputies taking off out of the park, lights and siren going. There was one deputy still in the park. He was talking to Gary and Jim. I walked over just as they were finishing. The deputy turned toward me.

"You must be Joey Simmons."

"Yessir."

"These gentlemen told me you were the one who heroically jumped into the water and saved Jack Johnson."

"Well, I don't know that I would put it that way."

"However you want to put it, you saved his life. I got most of the information I need from your friends. I just need to get your date of birth and home address for my report."

"Sure thing, deputy."

I gave the deputy the information he requested and as he was walking back to his car, I had a thought.

"Hey, deputy! Can I ask you something real quick?"

"Sure, what's up?"

"What happened to Jack's scuba equipment? His tanks and BC and stuff?"

"Oh, my sergeant loaded all of that stuff into his car to bring back to Cave Masters. He probably won't get to drop it off until tomorrow. They close in less than half an hour and he's responding to a call across town."

"Oh, thanks."

"Take care."

Dammit! I wish I had remembered to look over the equipment earlier. I wish I had a chance to see Jack's reel. By the time I got back into town on Saturday, Jack will have picked it up.

"Did either of you guys get a look at Jack's reel? Did it have line on it?"

Gary and Jim both shook their heads.

"Sorry, bud. I didn't think about it." Jim added.

"No problem. I meant to look, then that car coming in distracted me. I swear I've seen that car somewhere. I don't think it's been here at Jackson Blue."

"You mean that car that the sergeant turned away?"

"Yeah, did you recognize it?"

"No, neither of us have ever seen it. As you were running up the hill in your skivvies, we talked about it because we were wondering who would have you run off like that."

Suddenly, it occurred to me. I remembered where I had seen that car before.

"Holy crap! You're not going to believe who that was."

47

Jack

"What the hell!?! What are y'all doing to me? Where are we going?"

Jack was awake. How could he be anything but awake? There was a loud racket going on. It sounded like there was a helicopter right on top of him.

The person leaning over him put something on his head. It felt like earmuffs. No, that wasn't right. It was one of those old-time headsets that covered the ears. The person swung a microphone in front of his mouth.

"It's loud in here so I put a headset on you so we can talk without the noise of the rotors getting in the way."

There wasn't a helicopter on top of him. He was inside of a helicopter.

"Sir, you had a diving accident. You might be experiencing decompression sickness. We're enroute to Pensacola to get you to a hyperbaric chamber."

Diving accident. What the fuck!?! Jack tried hard to remember what had happened. Then it came to him. The dive flashed through his mind. That damn little white pill. It had fucked his head up big time. He had been taking it sparingly since his accident a couple of years earlier and it had never affected him like that. He had never gone diving after taking it, though. It must have been the pressure gradient along with the pill. That must have screwed his head up.

"Sir, how are you feeling now? Do you have any pain anywhere? How are your joints feeling? Your elbows, wrists, knees?"

"I'm fine." Jack could hear his voice coming over the headset. "Other than my left arm, which I injured a couple of years ago, nothing else hurts."

"Can you tell me what happened?"

Jack thought about that question. That was a loaded one if he ever heard one. He had diving insurance through Divers Alert Network like most scuba divers who went diving regularly. They should cover the bill for this whole fiasco. That is if they didn't find out about the little white pill. If they knew he had taken that pill right before diving, they might decline any claims made against his policy. Hell, they might drop his coverage altogether. Better to play it safe. Even if they did a drug test on him, he had a prescription and could say he hadn't taken one of those pills in a few days.

"I'm not sure exactly. I was feelin' fine today. Started on my dive. Then about ten minutes into the dive I got real dizzy. Just felt woozy. Never felt anything like it in my life."

"What happened then?"

Jack continued to tell the attendant about his dive. He didn't know if he was talking to a doctor or nurse or paramedic. He left out the parts about his anxiety. They didn't need to know those things. No one needed to know those things.

"I got to the Deco Room and settled in to do my twenty-foot decompression stop. Next thing I know it, that Simmons kid pulled me out of the weeds and to the shore. I don't know if I blacked out, passed out, or what."

"Well, it was a good thing that gentlemen was there and willing to jump into that cold water. You might have drowned if he hadn't done that. You were very fortunate he was there to rescue you."

Oh, fuck me! Again!?! What the hell? Once wasn't enough? It wasn't enough for Simmons to get him out from under that boulder two years earlier. Now he had to be there when Jack blacked out from that damn little white pill.

"Look, my arm is screaming at me. I don't know what that kid did when he pulled me out of the water, but it's really hurtin'. You got anything you can give me for it?"

Maybe they would give him something that would mask the positive drug test results they were bound to get when he arrived at the hospital. That way no one would know he had been taking any little white pills at all. If they did any digging, they'd likely find out the last time he had been prescribed those pills was more than six months ago. He had run out of the pills about that time and his doctor refused to renew the prescription. Fortunately for Jack, he found another source for them.

48

Joey

Gary, Jim, and I headed to our favorite Mexican restaurant in Marianna. After all of the excitement at the park, we were starved. We had the waiter bring out a basket of tortilla chips and a bowl of salsa for each of us. We also each ordered our own special tableside guacamole, as well as our usual meals and chowed down on the chips and salsa with a large bowl of queso. We decided we could share the queso.

"How crazy was that with Jack? What do you think happened to him on that dive?" Gary was the first to take a break from stuffing his mouth and ask the question we had all been pondering.

I finished chewing the chips I had in my mouth and swallowed. "I don't know. Like I told you the other day, when I got roped into going to breakfast Monday morning with Kelly, our neighbor, Jack showed up at exactly the same time. It's strange how he always pops up in places like that. He hasn't changed one bit since I last saw him and pulled him out of Jackson Blue a couple of years ago. Still cocky as ever."

"He didn't seem all that cocky today." Jim chimed in.

"Well, he did fight me a little in the water. He kept telling me to let him be and tried to pull his arm away from my grip. He had no strength to pull away, though. It was like he was a total weakling."

"It was strange as ever. I don't like Jack, but I have to admit that he's not that bad of a diver. Don't get me wrong. He's not the world's best diver like he thinks he is, but he's not the type of diver to let the current grab him and spit him out of the cave like that."

"I totally agree, G. He might have gotten bent while he was still underwater. Or maybe he threw a clot in his arm. We've put rods and pins in dogs with broken legs at the vet hospital and one of the concerns is a blood clot forming and dislodging. Maybe something similar happened to Jack."

"I know nothing about that stuff, but it sounds reasonable. If it can happen in dogs, it can probably happen in humans."

"So who's this Kelly you went to breakfast with? What's up with that?"

"Don't even get me started on that, Jim. She moved into an apartment a few doors down from us about three weeks ago, maybe four. She's a travelling nurse. Came to Destin to work a contract at the hospital. I told Gary a little about her, but I know you've been busy with your dad and Gary probably didn't get a chance to get you up to speed."

"Gary never tells me anything. If it wasn't for his Insta, I wouldn't know half the stuff he's into."

"Hey! That's not fair! I tell you plenty!"

"Yeah, okay. So, is there something going on with you and Kelly? Gary did tell me there was trouble between you and Lindsey and she supposedly moved out. Or did he post that on Insta for the world to see?"

"I did not!"

"Boys! Enough!" I laughed at their bickering. It was good to be hanging out with them again. It was exactly what I needed after the week I had. It was always like this with them. I couldn't figure out how they could stand to be together so much. They both worked from home.

"Sorry, dad. You owe me a…"

"Stop!" I laughed again. "You two are too much sometimes."

Gary and Jim lowered their heads like scolded puppies. Then they both started cackling loudly. Fortunately, the booth we were in had high backs on the benches and the only people that could see us were sitting at a table directly across from us. Although I felt the bench I was sitting on move as the person sitting on the opposite side probably tried to turn around to get a look over the top at what was going on in our booth.

"Kelly is kind of a pain. Lindsey invited her over to hang out a few days after she moved in, and she's been over two or three times a week since then. The last time she was over was last Sunday when she dropped a six-pack in the parking lot and busted all of the bottles. Lindsey invited her over again to hang out and drink more of our beer. Who goes to the store and only gets a six-pack? Especially after hanging with us and drinking so much of our beer? She should have restocked our fridge."

"Maybe that six-pack was meant for you." Jim offered.

"If only! No, she practically burst into tears because her beer was all over the parking lot. And it was Bud Light! That was when Lindsey invited her over…again."

"So what's so bad about her? Aside from poor taste in beer."

"Besides drinking our beer and forcing me to increase my booze budget? She's just strange. Seems very needy. Definitely too bubbly and outgoing. Too happy. She's the kind of person that you know must be sad and depressed when she's alone. She's got to be hiding something beneath that bubbliness."

"I've met those types of people. Worked with one when I still had to go into the office. You just know their home life is miserable."

"You know what, though, Jim. There's something more to it than that. There's something else that bugs me, but I can't quite put my finger on it."

"Do you think she's trying to break you and Lindsey up? Maybe she's got the hots for you. Could that be why Lindsey moved out?" Gary finally took a break from stuffing his face to join the conversation.

"I don't know. I mean, Lindsey did seem jealous, which is totally out of character for her. That's never been a problem until lately. And then she disappears without so much as a text to tell me what's going on. It's like she's on a mega PMS trip or something."

"I'm so glad we don't have to deal with that kind of stuff." Jim laughed.

"Speak for yourself! You may not have to use tampons, but you do get moody as hell at least once a month!"

"Like you're any better! Ya think maybe I might be moody in response to your moodiness."

And there it was! I guess life on the home front wasn't all fun and laughs for them either.

"Focus, boys! We're talking about me and Lindsey right now." We all broke out in laughter. More stares came our way.

"Anyway, I don't know. Lindsey and I are supposed to talk tomorrow after she leaves work. I was planning on heading back here right after work to go diving. I haven't been in my exploration area since Monday. There's no telling what's been going on back there over the past three days. Then to see both Jack and Manny, or whatever his name is, at Jackson Blue today. It's got me antsy. I have to talk to Lindsey, though. I have to find out what's going on inside her head."

"Probably best you do that. We can meet you here for a dive Saturday morning. We can all three head back there. I've been wanting to see this new area anyway. I might end up scooping your lead myself." Gary laughed.

"Do that and I'll cut your hoses and leave you back there as fish bait!"

"Jokes on you! There aren't any fish that far back in the cave."

Just then my phone rang. I looked at the screen and saw it was Lindsey. I held up the phone so Gary and Jim could see the screen as I stood and ran toward the door to get outside where there weren't a bunch of people trying to talk over each other. I swiped the icon up as I stepped outside.

"Hey, Linds."

49

Lindsey

"Hey, I guess you didn't get my text. I can't make it tomorrow evening. We're gonna have to reschedule for Sunday."

"Wait. What? C'mon Linds! Look, this isn't fair. You up and move out without a word to me. Disappear for a couple of days with no contact. I was worried out of my mind. What's going on?"

"Something came up. Just be home on Sunday around seven. I'll stop by then."

"Linds…"

I hung up before I could hear anything else Joey said. I didn't want to have a long, drawn-out conversation over the phone. I needed time to sort things out.

Kona was lying on the bed next to me. I grabbed her and gave her a big hug. She let out the cutest little squeaky noise in response. She always did that when I hugged her and it melted my heart. I got up from the bed and she jumped up and followed me. My Velcro dog.

I needed to do something. I was waiting to hear back from a couple more instructors so I could get the weekend class covered. I would hate to have to reschedule it with the students. They were all excited about finally being able to go scuba diving in a spring and in the gulf. It would be a huge disappointment if I had to postpone their checkout dives. I wished Joanne was an instructor. She would fill in for me. But she was only a divemaster. She didn't have any interest in becoming an instructor. I didn't understand how someone could own a dive shop and not be a scuba instructor. It didn't make sense to me.

My phone pinged. It was a text from Joey. I swiped it away without reading it.

"Let's go for a walk, girl."

I stepped out of my room with Kona at my heels. I grabbed her leash from the mud room and she started running around the house, excited for the walk that was about to happen. Things were so much simpler with animals. They had no expectations. They loved you unconditionally. Even animals that were neglected still loved their humans because they didn't know any better. I didn't know how anyone could neglect their dogs. Why have them if they weren't going to give them attention?

At that thought, I broke down in tears again. What was wrong with me? Why was I so emotional? I laughed at my own stupidity. I was pregnant. That's what was wrong with me. My hormones were out of whack. *Wow!* If I was this emotional now, I couldn't imagine what I was going to be like in a couple of months. Did I really want to put myself through that right now? Would I be able to handle it? Would I be a good mom?

Sure, I wanted to have kids someday. *Some* day. I hadn't planned on it for a few more years. I was still young and trying to establish my career. I was hoping to eventually buy the dive shop from Joanne. There were things she did that I didn't agree with. Some things that I thought would be better for the shop financially if they were different. I brought them up to Joanne, but she didn't want to change anything. She liked things the way they were. As long as she could continue to go on her scuba diving trips, she was happy.

The problem was that Joanne treated the dive shop as a hobby and not a business. She was hardly there. I handled the day-to-day management of the place. Joanne checked in every now and then and went on most of the dive trips. *Oh no!* I was supposed to lead a dive trip to Grand Cayman in the spring. That was one of the perks of managing the shop. Joanne gave up one trip, always to a location she'd already been, and let me go instead. She was letting Joey join the trip for free this time. In the past, he had to pay his way, but this trip attracted enough customers and Joanne secured two free spots for the shop. Since Joey recently completed his divemaster training, she was letting him go as the second staff member. I wouldn't be able to go on this one. What was the point if I couldn't dive? Not if I kept the baby.

The baby. I had to stop avoiding thoughts about that part of my future. I arrived at McCall Park where I usually walked Kona. She pulled me toward the soccer fields. There was a game in play and Kona wanted to run into the middle of the field to play with the ball. The first time I brought her to this park when there was a soccer game, she slipped out of her collar and ran directly into the group of players, tackling the ball and rolling with it through the throng of kids that had been chasing after it. Surprisingly, none of the kids seemed afraid of her. They stopped the game and all gathered around Kona to pet and hug her. She loved every minute of it. I loved watching the kids loving on her.

I moved my grip on the leash to shorten it and held Kona back as we approached the soccer field. We stopped at the edge of the field, and I told her to sit, which she did promptly right in front of me with her body in between my legs. That was a big accomplishment. She sat there, fidgeting, waiting for me to release her from the sitting position. Her hind end raised off of the grass a couple of inches before settling back down. She really wanted to get out there and play with the kids again. And I wanted to let her. But some of the parents hadn't been too happy the last time it happened.

"Is she nice? Can I pet her?" One of the kids from the sidelines walked over and stood a few feet away.

"Of course! She loves to get pet. Come closer. She won't bite."

The little girl looked over her shoulder at who I assumed was her mom. The mom nodded her head, and the little girl walked up to Kona and held her hand out for Kona to sniff. Once the introductions were over, the girl slowly moved her hand to the top of Kona's head and started scratching her behind the ears.

"What's her name?"

"Kona. It means lady in Hawaiian. I'm Lindsey. What's your name?"

She looked back at her mom then turned to me. "My name is Elsa, like the Disney princess."

"That's a beautiful name, Elsa. I guess you like dogs, hunh."

"I love them! I wish we could have one, but our aparpmen doesn't allow dogs."

"I used to live in an apartment that didn't allow big dogs like Kona. I really missed having her with me when I lived there."

"Where did she live when you lived there?"

"She stayed with my parents and I would go over every day before and after work to walk her and spend time with her."

"Is that what you're doing now?"

"Kind of. Only I live with her again, starting today anyway. I moved back in with my parents."

"You missed Kona too much to stay away, hunh?"

"That's part of it."

"Elsa, that's enough. Stop bothering the nice lady and her dog."

"I gotta go. Bye!" Elsa turned and ran toward her mother. "Mom, that dog's name is Kona. It means lady in Hawaya. She's a nice dog. So is the lady. I mean, the lady is nice, too, not that she's a dog."

I laughed at the little girl's excitement. All over a simple thing like petting a dog. It made my heart melt for the second time that evening. How could I give up this baby growing inside of me? Keeping the baby was going to be tough. Especially if Joey and I didn't patch things up. I didn't know if we could patch things up. I guess I should talk to him. What if I was overreacting? What if Joey hadn't done anything wrong? Well, other than playing hooky to go diving without telling me. What if it was the hormones that were making me interpret things the wrong way?

I shouldn't have canceled our talk tomorrow evening. I should have given myself time to think about things before calling him. Maybe I could call him back and tell him to ignore what I said before. Maybe he would still meet with me tomorrow. I thought about it.

Should I call him? Or would that only make me seem even crazier than I already felt? If this was what pregnancy was all about, this was going to be a long and rough nine months.

I pulled my phone out of my pocket and unlocked it. I stared at the image of Joey on my phone screen. I really wanted to call him and see him tomorrow. If he was up for it, I would see him tonight. But I didn't want him to think I was being wishy washy. My finger hovered over the widget. One tap and it would be calling his phone. Then I remembered the text message I hadn't read yet. I opened the app.

"Bye Lindsey! Thank you for letting me pet Kona! I love her!"

"You're welcome, Elsa. Maybe I'll see you out here again soon and you can pet her again."

"I would really really really like that!" Elsa turned and ran to follow her mother to the parking lot.

I looked around. The soccer game had ended. The kids were running off of the field to join their parents. Then it was probably off to McDonald's or pizza or maybe even ice cream. I couldn't wait to be able to do that with my own child. And I wanted to do it with Joey. I looked back at the phone, brought my finger down onto the screen, and watched the text message pop up.

50

Joey

"What did Lindsey want?" Gary asked as I returned to the table.

"She canceled on me for tomorrow night. She said something came up and she couldn't meet, then hung up. I sent her a text message, but I doubt she'll reply."

"What's going on with her? That's strange for Linds. She's usually the level-headed one in the relationship."

I heard the dig at me, but Jim was right. Lindsey was the level-headed one. She definitely didn't seem to be acting that way at the moment.

"Yeah, I don't know. She said she would be over on Sunday evening to talk. I don't have a good feeling about it."

"You think it's over for good?"

"Maybe." There was silence at the table for several seconds. "Look. I don't want to talk or think about this anymore. Let's enjoy our night and catch up with everything that's been going on in our lives. In fact, I'm gonna put my phone on Do Not Disturb. How 'bout y'all do the same?"

"Sounds good to me. You owe… Sorry!"

We all laughed. It was just the tension breaker that we needed.

* * *

About half an hour later, we were sitting back in the booth holding our bellies. We had eaten way too much. Ordering dessert probably hadn't been a good idea after all of the chips, salsa, and guacamole, plus the huge meals they served. I had trouble turning down the fried ice cream, though. Gary and Jim looked as miserable as I felt.

Somehow, I managed to fill them in on everything that had been going on with my project and the cave diving world while they were away. They were anxious to get into the cave this weekend and see the new area I found.

"I'm thinking about driving back up tomorrow after work and going diving. If I do that, I'll probably get a hotel room in town, so I don't have to do the two-hour drive home and come back Saturday morning to dive with you guys."

"Why don't you relax tomorrow night and wait to dive with us on Saturday? You'll have a lot more fun. We can even pull out the old light sabers. You know we always get here early because of the time change between here and Tallahassee."

"I don't know. Depends on how I feel. I'm not sure I want to hang at home alone. This thing with Lindsey is making me depressed. And with her canceling on me, it'll just put me into more of a slump."

"Yeah, I get it. You can always come over to the big city and hang out with us tomorrow. If I recall, you were alright with the bed in the guestroom the other times you did that."

"I'll give it some thought, G. That's a long drive from Destin after working all day."

"It's only an extra hour."

"Yeah, but it'll seem like an extra two because I lose an hour crossing into Eastern time zone. By the time I get there, it'll be close to ten and time to crash."

"You have a point. It's a shame you have to actually go into work instead of working from home like us. Otherwise you could follow us tonight."

"Not everyone can have the luxury of high paying slack jobs like y'all do."

We laughed. In reality, Jim was the moneymaker in the house. Gary did alright, but didn't make much more than I did. The problem was that I made more than Lindsey, so I was the money maker in my household. Well, my old household. Damn! I was going to have to figure things out. I couldn't afford the apartment on my wages alone. Not and continue to drive to Marianna every weekend to go cave diving. It was one or the other. And right in the middle of a big exploration project. This was really going to suck.

"It was great to finally see y'all after a month of being away slacking off even more than usual. I really should get going home. I still have a two-hour drive and, after this meal, all I want to do is chill out on the couch."

"Yeah, we better get going, too. We also have a two-hour drive."

"Wait a minute! Tallahassee is only an hour away."

"True, but we do have that time change, so it's actually two hours by the clock."

"Screw you! I'd trade places with you any day!"

The guys laughed. The hour loss hour gain joke was an ongoing thing.

The guys grabbed their phones. I grabbed mine and shoved it in my back pocket as I stood up.

"Alright, Joe, it was great catching up. Let us know if you change your mind about tomorrow night. Otherwise, we'll see you Saturday morning around ten. Will that give you enough time to get your beauty sleep and still make that two-hour drive?"

"That'll work. I'll let you know if I get on the road sooner. That'll still give you about a forty-five-minute heads up."

"Sounds good. Drive safe buddy."

"You too."

We hugged and parted ways. They headed east on I-10, and I headed west. I glanced at my phone and noticed a missed call. Lindsey had tried to call me about fifteen minutes earlier. Must have been right before we got up from the table. What did she want now? I thought about calling her back but decided against it. I was tired of these games. She was probably calling to cancel Sunday. I wasn't having it. We had to talk about what was going on.

* * *

Two hours later I pulled into the parking lot. I was exhausted. It had been a long day. I parked the car and as I started walking across the parking lot toward the building, I noticed Kelly's car a few spaces down. Holy crap!

Two minutes later I was on the second floor standing in front of Kelly's door knocking loudly. I saw the flicker of light through the blinds from whatever TV show she was watching. I could hear the muffled sounds of people talking, probably also from the TV. Good. Not only was she home, but she was awake. I knocked on the door again.

"Kelly! Hey, Kelly! It's Joey. C'mon, open up! I need to talk to you."

The sound from the TV was muted and I saw a brighter light shoot out between the slats of the blinds. I heard Kelly shuffling toward the door. A few seconds later, the door opened a crack.

"Oh hi, Joey, whassup?" Her words came out slurred. Had she actually gone out and bought her own beer tonight?

"Can I come in? I need to talk to you."

"Oh? What about?"

She opened the door wider to let me step in. She was wearing a loose blouse that barely contained her. I looked around her apartment. It hadn't gotten any more organized than it had been the other night when I was there with her groceries. It looked more disheveled, if that was possible. I walked to the couch and sat down, pushing aside a blanket. Kelly sat down next to me.

"Are you going to shay anything? Or are you jush going to shit there? Wanna beer?" The slurring was worse.

"Sure, I'll take a beer." Might as well start collecting on all those nights she was over drinking our beer.

"They're in the fridge."

Great. She was such a gracious host. I stood up and walked to the fridge to grab a beer. I opened the door and found a case sitting on the top shelf. What the hell? She had that kind of stash over here and she was drinking our beer for free? And it was imported beer this time! I grabbed a bottle and popped the top off with the bottle opener sitting on the counter next to the fridge, then returned to the couch, sitting on the opposite end from Kelly.

"Shooooo…I noticed Lindzhee hazhn't been around for a while. You two break up or shomething. Are you over here to hook up? Cause if you are, I'm game." She slurred her words even more.

"What? No! I mean, I don't know what's going on with me and Lindsey, but I'm definitely not here to hook up with you."

"It doezhn't have to be a permanent hookup. I'm okay with jush fooling around every now and then. Even if you two are shtill a thing."

I was getting a buzz sitting next to her. I stood up and put some distance between us. I was concerned she might grab me and try to…hook up…

"Listen. I'm not here to hook up or to fool around or to do anything like that. I just have one question for you. Were you in Marianna earlier today? More specifically, were you at the Blue Spring Recreation Area?"

51

Jack

The doctor wouldn't give Jack anything stronger than a couple of Tylenol. That wasn't going to cut it. Jack was jonesing for his little white pill. It had been several hours since they flew him to the hospital and put him in the chamber. The pain was too severe. It was getting unbearable. The problem was that he couldn't tell them the truth about the pain.

It was bad enough that they had flown him somewhere to get evaluated for the hyperbaric chamber. He didn't feel any pain in his other joints. His left arm was all that hurt. And that was the pain he had become accustomed to having ever since it was crushed and required multiple surgeries. It wasn't any worse than normal. He told them his arm was screaming at him and that got them all worked up. The nurse yelled for the doctor like Jack was dying or something. The doctor came running in.

"He said he's having excruciating pain in his left arm, doc. Should I draw some blood for cardiac enzymes, or should we expedite him to the chamber?"

They had already poked and prodded him a bunch since he got there. Not only did he have an IV in his arm, but they stabbed him again to get blood once he got to the hospital. At least he hadn't remembered them starting the IV. He must have been out of it.

"Look, doc, I didn't say excruciating. I told this fine young nurse here that my arm was screamin' at me. This ain't nothing out of the ordinary. I hurt my arm a couple years ago and I've had a few surgeries on it. Look here." Jack held out his left arm with a grimace. "See these here scars? These are from the surgeries."

"Hmmm, looks like you had some external hardware. What happened to it?"

"It got crushed a couple years back. No big deal. It's nearly good as new. Just sometimes it hurts a little. That's all. Ain't nothing else. I got some little white pills I take when the pain's real bad. I just want one of those."

Jack tried to downplay it as much as he could while still trying to get pain medicine. He was afraid that if he told them just how bad the pain was, they would think it was the bends and send him to the chamber. That would take six hours, and he had no desire to stay that long.

"Well, Mr. Johnson, I can't give you anything that strong if the pain isn't that bad. It sounds like what you were prescribed was possibly oxycodone and I simply can't order that."

"Yeah, that's right! Oxy something or other. That's what I take."

"You'll have to wait until we discharge you and you get home to take whatever your pain doctor prescribed you. In the meantime, I would like to do a cardiac workup. Since it's only your left arm and none of your other joints, I don't think you're experiencing decompression sickness. But I am concerned that you might be having a heart attack, and I'd like to rule that out."

"I ain't havin' no heart attack, doc! I swear to it."

"Well, I still have to rule it out. I'm going to have them do another EKG and draw more blood."

"Can't you use the blood y'all already drawd?"

"Unfortunately, that blood was used for other tests. We'll need more. It'll be a small poke. Shouldn't take more than an hour or so to get the results. If everything checks out, I'll discharge you tonight."

The doctor turned on his heel and walked out of the room while the nurse started preparing to draw blood. Jack laid there frustrated at the situation.

"Mr. Johnson, in case we do end up discharging you, do you have anyone that can come pick you up?"

"Pick me up? Where am I?"

"You're in Pensacola, sir."

"Pensacola?? Aww, hell!"

If Jack hadn't already been frustrated enough, that really set him off. He didn't have anyone that would drive three hours to pick him up and bring him back to his truck in Marianna. Jack suddenly realized he wasn't wearing his drysuit anymore. He looked under his hospital gown and all he had on were his boxers.

"What happened to my drysuit and my undergarments?"

"Excuse me?"

"The clothes I was wearin'. My dive suit."

"Oh, I'm sure they cut that off of you before they loaded you into the helicopter."

"Cut it off a me! What the hell? Do you know how much that suit cost? That's a two-thousand-dollar suit. And the undergarments were a couple hundred. Did they get my clothes from my truck, at least?"

"I didn't see them bring any clothing in with you, Mr. Johnson. We have some paper scrubs we can give you when we discharge you, though."

"Paper?"

Just as Jack said that the nurse stuck a needled in his arm.

"Aww, shit! That hurt! Warn a guy first!"

"I'm almost done. Hold steady for a minute."

The nurse finished taking Jack's blood and left him in the room alone. Jack pulled the tubing with the little prongs that stuck up inside his nose off of his face. The nurse had insisted he keep it on, but she wasn't around, and it was annoying. The oxygen was blasting up his nose and bugging the crap out of him. He didn't know how people could stand that. He'd rather have a mask over his face than those prongs up his nose. He didn't think he needed either one. The last he remembered he only had a decompression obligation of nine minutes. He could swear he had cleared his decompression obligation before that damned current blew him out of the cave. He couldn't figure out what had happened.

It suddenly came to Jack. He remembered that Simmons kid flipping him over and pulling on his arm. Had he been pulling on his left arm or right arm? Maybe that was why his left arm hurt so much. Sonofabitch! That Simmons kid pulled him out, just like he and his girlfriend did two years earlier. It wasn't bad enough it had happened once. Now everyone was going to be hearing that Jack Johnson had to be rescued by Simmons again. What in the hell kind of horse shit was that? What higher power had it out for him to do this to him again?

"I've gotta get outta here. I've gotta get this shit under control quick." Jack whispered to himself.

"Nurse! Nurse!"

"Mr. Johnson! Please don't yell like that. If you need me for anything, press the call button that's sitting on your lap."

Jack looked at the device on his lap.

"Sorry ma'am. I just need a phone. I need to find me a ride, and then it's gonna take a while for someone to get here. I wanna get them on the way as soon as possible."

"I'll bring you a phone shortly. Hmphm! Mr. Johnson, did you take the nasal cannula out of your nose?" The nurse grabbed the clear tubing with the prongs and started wrapping it around Jack's face and ears. "You need to leave this on. It's very important to have extra oxygen for someone in your condition. Whether it's decompression sickness or a heart attack, you need supplemental oxygen."

"I don't have either of those. I just need a phone."

"I already said I'll get you a phone, but you must leave that in your nose."

"Alright, alright! I'll leave it."

The nurse left the room. Jack thought about pulling the prongs out of his nose again, but he didn't want to piss off the nurse and have her not bring him a phone. He wasn't sure who he was going to call. He didn't have many numbers memorized. Most of them were in his phone which was sitting in his truck in Marianna. Maybe he'd ask the nurse if the helicopter was still there and could give him a ride back to his truck.

"Here's a phone for you, Mr. Johnson. Can I do anything else for you before I attend to my other patients?" The nurse's tone sounded like she was being put out by his requests.

"Actually, I don't know any phone numbers. They're all in my phone and I'm assumin' that's back in my truck in Marianna. Is the helicopter still here? Can they bring me back?"

"No, they aren't here. They left a long time ago. They wouldn't be able to bring you back anyway."

Jack had an idea who he could call.

"Can you get me the number to Cave Masters in Marianna? What time is it by the way?"

"It's almost seven."

"You'll have to hurry up with that number. They's about to close."

The nurse pulled her cell phone out of her pocket and looked up the number.

"It's 850-555-CAVE. Looks like that's 2283."

Jack dialed the number as the nurse spoke it. It rang twice.

"Cave Masters. This is Danny. Hope you're having a great day! How can I help you?"

"Danny, m'boy. This is Jack Johnson."

"Oh Jack! I heard they airlifted you from Jackson Blue earlier. How are you doing? Are you okay? What happened to you? How far back in the cave did you go that you got bent?"

"Whoa, kid! I'll tell you what. I'll answer all your questions and more, but I need a big favor first."

"Oh sure Jack! Boy, are they going to be happy to know you're okay. That's crazy how Joey rescued you again! You were real lucky he was there!"

Fuck me…

52

Lindsey

Joey didn't answer his phone this time. I wondered if he was pissed at me or if he was busy with Kelly. No. I had to stop thinking that way. I would try again later.

"C'mon, Kona! Let's go!"

The sun didn't set for another hour. We had time for a walk around the park. Kona moved to the heel position on my right, and I started walking with her at my side. When I first got her, she naturally heeled on the right. I tried to train her to heel to the left. She preferred the right side for some reason, so there she stayed. I headed toward the pond to the west of the soccer field, being careful not to get too close. I tried to keep a respectable distance from the water because I didn't want a 'gator or crocodile to jump out and attack my sweet girl. I hadn't personally seen any there, but we were in Florida and bodies of water always increased the chances of there being 'gators around.

Kona knew the route well and walked slowly at my side, stopping to sniff interesting smells along the way. No matter how many times we came to this park and walked the same route, there always seemed to be new smells that grabbed her attention.

I continued to think about the situation I was in. On the one hand, I wasn't sure I wanted a baby at the moment. It was a lot of responsibility and would change my life drastically. I'd have to take time off from the dive shop. That was the big issue. I might have to resign. I was the only full-time employee that Joanne had. There was a part-timer that filled in on my days off and when I had to teach on the weekends. Joanne filled in when the part-timer wasn't available, which wasn't often. But Joanne had no desire to be in the shop full-time. She would have to hire someone to replace me. I knew Joanne depended on me and really liked me, but would she be willing to hire me back after my maternity leave? Would I even be able to return?

Kona and I continued around the pond, slowly making our way around the perimeter as I continued to ponder my predicament.

Daycare was going to be an issue. I worked an odd schedule, not the typical Monday through Friday banker's hours. I doubted any of the regular daycares would be able to accommodate it. Mom would help, but how much? She had her own job and her own life. She might be okay with picking up the baby after work, but would she be willing to watch the baby every other weekend when I had to teach? I also wouldn't be able to cave dive anymore. How could I expect mom to babysit every single weekend? Or even three weekends a month? That would be too much.

I could give up some of my teaching weekends. I had been teaching every other weekend to increase my certification numbers so I could continue to rise in the ranks and eventually become a course director. I supposed that could be pushed back. But I was so close. I was already a PADI Master Instructor. It would only be another year or two before I could test to be a PADI Course Director. That would help so much, especially if I was going to buy the shop from Joanne one day.

Kona and I made it around the pond and walked across the empty soccer field toward the baseball field and the playground. I could see a few kids on the slides. It would be so nice to bring a child here and watch her or him having fun with other children. To hang out with the other moms and dads. To plan play dates and birthday parties. As we got closer to the playground, I heard one of the moms call out to her daughter.

"It's time to go, Britney. Say goodbye to your friends."

"Nooooooooooooooo!!!!!" Britney let out a high-pitched sscreech. "I don't want to go yet! I want to stay here with my friends and keep playing!"

"Britney! You do as I say right now, or we'll never come back to this park again!"

"I don't wanna! I don't wanna! I! DON'T! WANNA!!!"

I watched Britney throw herself onto the ground. Once in a prone position, she hit and kicked the ground with all her might. The mom walked over with an angry look on her face. When she was standing right next to Britney, she reached down, grabbed her around the waist, and pulled her up. Britney continued to flail her arms and legs and screamed her head off.

"Eeeeeeeeeeeeeeeeeeeeeeeeeeeeeeeee!!!!!!!"

We crossed the baseball field, and I steered Kona to the left toward the swings so we could avoid the playground where the scene was unfolding. I was trying to make it to the splashpad on the chance that there were no kids playing in it. Kona loved to run through the jets of water coming out of the ground. It was one of her favorite things about the park. We cleared the trees and made it to the splashpad, which happened to be free and clear of kids. Just as we got there, I saw Britney being dragged toward the parking lot by her mom, still kicking and screaming.

Maybe I wasn't ready for a child.

53

Joey

"No shilly. Why would I be in Marietta?" Kelly's answer came out heavily slurred.

"It's Marianna, not Marietta. Marietta is in Georgia. Are you positive you weren't there? I'm pretty sure I saw your car earlier today. This was around five or so."

"Lesh forget that. I don' wanna talk. I wanna kish."

Kelly threw herself at me. I quickly moved back farther, but the arm of the couch stopped me from moving far enough. Kelly missed making her mark of putting her lips on mine, and instead, fell over with her head landing on my lap.

"Ooooo… Whatta we have here?"

I pushed Kelly off of me and stood up. As repulsed as I was by her drunken state, I was also strangely a little turned on. I didn't understand why I would be aroused. I didn't like Kelly. She was tolerable enough at times, mostly when she was sober. I especially didn't like her in the current state of mind that she was in. And I didn't like her throwing herself all over me. But at the same time, a part of me seemed to like it. A part of me wanted to give in to her advances.

I thought about Lindsey and everything that had gone on over the past week. She moved out without talking to me. I had no idea what was going on. We were supposed to meet the next day, but she backed out of that. I wasn't sure if Lindsey and I had a future together anymore. As far as I knew, we were broken up and had no commitment to each other. So why did I feel like I was doing something wrong by being in Kelly's apartment with her trying to throw herself all over me? Why did I feel guilty when I hadn't done anything?

Maybe I *should* hook up with Kelly. She did say she didn't want a commitment. All she wanted was an occasional fling. What was wrong with that if I wasn't in a relationship anymore?

As I was lost in my thoughts, Kelly stood up and rushed me. When she was a couple of steps away, she tripped over her own feet and came flying toward me. I reached out and grabbed her, accidentally getting hold of one of her breasts. I directed her to the couch so I could get her into a sitting position and hopefully prevent her from falling and hitting her head on the coffee table. As I got her down on the couch, I felt Kelly reach around my waist. She pulled me down toward her. I was off balance and came down directly on top of her. I felt her lips on my lips. I felt her tongue forcing my mouth open. She pulled me in closer so that my body was flush against hers. I wanted to pull away. I wanted to stand up and leave.

I didn't. Instead, I kissed her back. I pushed her tongue back into her mouth with my tongue and kissed her hard. I felt Kelly's hands sneak beneath my shirt and move up my back. I felt her fingernails claw their way down my back. Then I realized that the hand that had unintentionally grabbed her breast was still holding it. I questioned whether it was really unintentional. Was it an accident? Or did I mean to grab her there? I moved my hand down to her waist and back up beneath her shirt, cupping her breast as we continued to kiss.

I felt Kelly's hands move from my back to the front of my waist. She undid the button on my shorts amazingly quick. A lot of guys pride themselves on being able to unsnap a bra quickly. Most wouldn't come close to the adeptness demonstrated by Kelly in undoing my shorts. She could barely stand up, but she had no problem unbuttoning my shorts. I felt her hand reaching inside. She didn't have to go very far. I was aroused.

Was I really doing this? Was I really going to sleep with someone I could barely tolerate? Was I going to cheat on Lindsey? Was it cheating considering the current state of our relationship, or whatever it was that we had?

All of these thoughts flew through my head as Kelly and I continued to make out on her couch. I had to make up my mind within the next few seconds. We were that close to reaching the point of no return. Kelly already had my shorts undone. I could feel her trying to tug her own shorts down. I didn't know what to do. I knew it wouldn't mean anything to me. I didn't know if Kelly really meant it to be just a one-time thing or an occasional fling. Besides, she was drunk, very drunk.

I felt my shorts and briefs sliding down my legs. Somehow, during all of this, our shirts had come off. I didn't know if we pulled each other's shirts off or took them off ourselves. I was so caught up in the moment, I couldn't remember. I was lying on top of her and we were kissing. In another second or two, we would both be completely naked, and it would be difficult to turn back.

I had to make a decision before that happened.

54

Lindsey

I put Kona on a twenty-foot-long leash and let her play in the splashpad. As she was having fun darting through the streams of water, I watched Britney get pushed into the backseat of a gray minivan. Her mom leaned in, strapped the crying child into her car seat, and hit the button to close the door. I could hear Britney screaming from inside the minivan as the poor mom backed out of her parking space and drove away from the park. The kid had some lungs on her.

Maybe I wasn't ready to have a child. What if my child behaved the way that Britney just did? Could I deal with that? Would I have the patience to put up with it? I wondered if that was a daily occurrence for Britney or a rare one. Did she throw fits like that every time she was told to do something that she didn't want to do? If so, why would her mom bring her to the park?

Just when I thought I was ready to keep this baby, I found myself with doubts again. Would my child be like Elsa or like Britney? Were Elsa and Britney the way they were because of their parents? Or was their behavior just who they were? Could that be nurtured out of them?

I had so many questions. The problem was that I didn't know where to begin to get the answers to those questions. I didn't even know if it was worth looking into. After what I had seen with Britney, I no longer knew if I wanted to keep the baby. I wasn't ready to be a mom to a kid like Britney. If I had a guarantee that my kid would be like Elsa, I would do it.

Then again, would I? I only saw Elsa for a few minutes. Did she throw her own tantrums? Were there things that her mom made her do that she didn't like? Did she react to those things the same way that Britney had? Why was this so difficult?

A car pulled into the parking lot and I watched a dad and his kids, a boy and a girl that looked like they were about a year apart in age, get out. The kids were close in age to Elsa and Britney. As soon as they exited the car, they ran toward the splashpad. I pulled Kona back in close to me. She wouldn't do anything to hurt the kids, but some parents were funny about dogs being around their kids. When I had Kona by my side, I swapped out leashes and put her on the six-foot lead I had around my neck. I started walking away from the splashpad so I could roll up the long lead and put it into my bag when the dad called out to me.

"Y'all don't have to leave. Linus and Lucy love dogs."

Linus and Lucy! Who names their kids Lucy and Linus? They were probably too young to be made fun of for their names yet, but it was coming. Kids could be cruel when it came to things like that.

"Oh, it's okay, we were just finishing up."

"That's a shame. I don't get to pick up the Peanuts' gang until later in the day and we always get here after all of the other parents are gone. That leaves me stuck here watching them play while I have no one to talk to. I'm Mark, by the way."

"Hi Mark. I'm Lindsey and this is Kona. So, Lucy and Linus, huh?"

"Yeah, that's what happens when you have kids so young. My ex and I were only eighteen when Lucy was conceived. Linus came a year later. She liked the Peanuts gang a lot. She even has a tattoo of Woodstock. She also has a dog named Snoopy. I was too young to care one way or another and agreed to it. I guess it could have been worse. They could be named Peppermint Patty and Pig-pen."

I laughed hysterically at Mark's joke. It felt good to laugh. To truly laugh at something. I looked at Mark a little more closely than I had when he first walked up and noticed he probably wasn't much older than I was. Lucy looked like she was seven years old so that would make Mark twenty-five or twenty-six. He had become a parent much younger than what I would be if I went through with the pregnancy.

I turned to watch Lucy and Linus running across the splashpad, trying their hardest to avoid the waterspouts while still getting wet. They were laughing with each other and having a great time.

"Are they always this happy and well-behaved?"

"Not always. According to my ex, they misbehave after they've been with me. She calls me the fun parent and complains about having to always be the disciplinarian. What can I say? They never act up when they're with me. I will admit that because I only have them for a limited amount of time, I always have fun activities planned for them."

"What about when it's time to leave here? I just saw a little girl throw a fit when her mom told her it was time to go home."

"Oh, you must be talking about Britney."

"Yes! That was her name. I guess this wasn't her first tantrum."

"Definitely not her first. Britney has done that before. I've managed to get here a few times right before they left and witnessed the tantrum. It's not pretty. I don't know how Melissa's eardrums haven't ruptured yet."

"Britney was loud."

"Lucy and Linus have never done that. At least not with me. But like I said, I'm the fun parent. After we leave the park, I take them to McDonald's for Happy Meals. They look forward to that almost as much as the park. Actually, they might look forward to it even more than the park."

"That's smart. Maybe Melissa should do something similar."

"I suggested it once. You would have thought I had suggested she take her kids to the Grand Canyon and push them over the edge. She glared at me and told me to mind my own business, except not in such nice terms. I would venture to guess that Britney is the way she is because her mom is that way as well."

I laughed again. Mark was funny. He was also easy to talk to.

"So what happened with you and your ex?"

"Oh, the usual thing. We were young. The kids didn't make life easy for us. Neither of us had a chance to grow up ourselves before Lucy came along. And we hadn't learned from the surprise pregnancy with Lucy. Before we knew it, Linus was on the way. That only made things more difficult. It was too much for us to handle as such a young couple with kids that demanded most of our time. Anyway, I'm sorry. I'm rambling about this. I didn't mean to."

"No, it's okay. I asked. I'm sorry for prying. It's just..."

I burst into tears again. How embarrassing! I just met Mark, and I was bawling in front of him.

"Hey, sorry. Was it something I said?"

"No, not at all, Mark." I laughed at his sweetness in thinking he caused my tears. "It's just that I found out I'm pregnant and I've been on an emotional roller coaster. I'm not quite as young as you and your ex were, but I'm still younger than I intended to be for my first pregnancy. It's been a tough day."

"Well, don't let my experience influence you in any way. I'm certainly not a good example." I watched Mark glance down at my left hand. "What does your husband or boyfriend think about all of this?"

I held back the tears and braced myself to speak.

"Boyfriend. Actually, ex. I haven't told him yet. I just found out myself last night. We kind of broke up at the beginning of the week. Well, actually, I moved out and kind of broke up with him."

"Hmmm, that's a tough one."

"Yeah, now I'm wondering if I did the right thing or if it was the pregnancy hormones that had me all messed up."

"You should definitely tell him and let him be a part of the decision. My ex didn't tell me right away and that's part of the reason we're not together anymore. I don't think we would have not had Lucy, but I felt like she slighted me by not including me in the decision. I think that was a big reason for the distance between us."

"You know what, Mark, you're right. I've been wracking my brain trying to figure everything out on my own before talking to Joey, but

I need to include him. This isn't just my baby. It's our baby. Thank you so much for talking with me. You've been a big help."

"No problem, Lindsey. And if you think you need another counseling session, I'm here every Thursday evening about the same time." Mark flashed me a big smile.

He was cute. If things were different, I might consider dating him, kids and all. But things weren't different. I needed to get a hold of Joey so we could start working out our issues.

55

Jack

It took the damn kid long enough to get to Pensacola, Jack thought as he watched Danny pull up into the drop off bay in front of the hospital. The doctor discharged Jack almost two hours earlier. Since that time, Jack had been stuck in the hospital lobby waiting for Danny to show up. Jack knew it would take Danny a couple of hours to get to Pensacola, but it still annoyed him that it actually took that long.

He didn't know why they had to send him to a hospital in Pensacola anyway. There was a hospital right there in Marianna. It didn't have a hyperbaric chamber, but it was still a hospital. There was also the hospital in Panama City, which did have a hyperbaric chamber. Except those asshats in their infinite wisdom decided to shut it down to divers. They only used it for wound care. That pissed Jack off.

Jack sauntered out of the lobby toward Danny's car. He saw his reflection in the glass. He looked ridiculous in the paper pants and shirt they gave him. He didn't even have shoes on. Just those stupid hospital socks with the rubber grips on the bottom. He couldn't wait to get out of them and into his clothes.

Danny's car was a little Toyota Corolla, one of the older models. Not five or ten years old. More like twenty years old, before they began making them the size of the Camry and making the Camry bigger. Jack steeled himself for the long drive back to Marianna cramped into the small Corolla and having to listen to the non-stop chatter of the kid. It was bad enough having to listen to him go on and on about his cave diving aspirations whenever Jack stopped in to get his scuba tanks filled.

Jack didn't have a choice, though. He didn't have anyone else he could call that would drop everything to drive the two and a half hours from Marianna to Pensacola to pick him up and drive him back to his truck. He couldn't be too sore at the kid. He was doing Jack a huge favor. Jack would even give the kid gas money for his troubles. The problem was that the price was going to be much higher than just gas money. He was going to have to listen to the kid ramble on and on and on the whole way back.

"Hi Jack! Wow! I'm glad you're okay! Everyone was real worried about you for a while there. I let everyone know you're okay and that I was coming to pick you up. They were all pretty surprised that you called me for that. I guess you just like me, though, huh? Anyway, so what happened on your dive? How did you get bent? How far back in the cave did you go? How…"

"Whoa kid! Enough already. Take a breath, will ya? Let's get outta here. You didn't happen to bring me my clothes, did ya?"

"Sorry, Jack. Sometimes I just can't help myself. A deputy stopped by and said his sergeant would drop off your tanks and scooter in the morning. He didn't mention your dry suit or undergarments. I don't know about your clothes, either. How are you feeling? Were you really bent?"

"Dammit! Well, at least my stuff isn't setting on the ground at the park for someone to steal. No, kid, I wasn't bent. The docs don't know what happened. They checked me out and everything is alright. I don't know why they sent me all the way to Pensacola. This all could've been done right there in Marianna."

"You mean you didn't get a ride in the chamber? Aww, man! I had all these questions for you about that. How it felt. What it was like. Were you in one of those small monoplace chambers, or do they have a big chamber where the nurse sits in it with you? I wonder what it's like for the nurse to have to be in the chamber every day. I imagine it can't be that great for them. Even divers don't do deep decompression dives day after day. It's usually just on the weekends. I…"

"Kid! Take a breath!"

"I did it again, didn't I?"

"Look, you just pay attention to keeping us in the lane on the road and I'll tell you all about it. Alright?"

"Yessir!" Danny responded with a huge smile.

Jack almost felt bad for the kid. He didn't mean any harm. He was just excited about cave diving. Jack could remember when he got that excited about cave diving. That was a long time ago. Jack had been cave diving for more than twenty years. He still remembered his first time in a cave with his instructor and then his first time in a cave without his instructor. He also remembered the first time he found unexplored cave passage. Those memories were distant but fresh in his mind as if they happened a week ago. Something had changed over the years. The excitement was no longer as strong. Jack still liked being in underwater caves. It still got the adrenaline flowing. But it wasn't the same. Something was different.

"Jack? Jack? Are you okay?"

"Huh? What's that kid?"

"You zoned out for a minute there. You were gonna tell me what happened, but then you got quiet and were staring off into space."

"Oh, yeah, I'm alright. I was just thinking about things. Anyway, here's what happened kid. I was scootering into Jackson Blue. I was about three thousand feet back. No wait, more like four thousand feet. Yeah, I was four thousand feet back when suddenly I started to get woozy. I don't know what caused it. I wasn't doing nothin' out of the ordinary. Maybe I got some bad gas. Do y'all check your banks to make sure the gas is good? When's the last time the filters were changed?"

Jack was making things up on the fly. He knew it was the little white pill that had affected him, but he couldn't let anyone else know that. Especially the kid. That kid had a big mouth, and everyone would know it before the weekend came around.

"Uh, yessir, we analyze the gas every day, and the filters are changed regularly. I changed them myself just last week. No problem there."

"Well, I don't know then. Maybe it was somethin' else. Anyway, as soon as I started feelin' strange, I turned around to head out. Weird thing was every time I had to go a little deeper, the feelin' got worse. It took me a lot longer to get out than it had to get back to five thousand feet."

"Wow! That must have been freaky! Did you feel like you were gonna pass out? Did you think you were gonna die? Did you…"

"No, never felt any of that." Jack cut him off. "I maintained total control all the way out from six thousand feet in. I got to the Deco Room and did my decompression stop. When that was done, I swam outta the cave. Just as I was gettin' to the surface, that Simmons kid grabs me and pulls me toward the shore. He took me completely by surprise. Next thing I know, they're shoving me in a chopper and taking off to Pensacola talking about me being bent. I don't know what gave 'em that idea. Certainly wasn't anything I said or did."

"Wow! That's crazy! I've been around for a few divers getting bent at Jackson Blue, but I've never heard of someone being hauled off like that. I guess maybe they were being extra cautious cause it's you and all."

"Yeah, maybe kid. Anyway, let's just keep this between you and me. Don't go tellin' anyone 'bout this. I'd just as soon a whole bunch of people don't know my business."

Jack said this last part to Danny knowing full well that the kid would not keep his mouth shut. He would *secretly* tell everyone that would listen everything Jack had just told him. That was exactly what Jack wanted him to do. Maybe with the kid telling everyone the story Jack told him the rumor mill wouldn't get so out of control like it usually did in cave country.

There would still be some who didn't believe the kid. There would be some who would listen to Simmons' version of events, but this would hopefully be enough to put doubts in their minds. That was what Jack was hoping for, anyway.

Jack changed subjects and started telling the kid about his cave exploration ventures. He was hoping to keep the kid quiet during the ride back to Marianna. It also wouldn't hurt his own reputation because the kid would repeat everything he heard to everyone who would listen. Jack was killing two birds with one stone, as they say.

Two and a half hours after Danny picked Jack up, they pulled into the Blue Spring Recreation Area. The kid pulled up to the gate, put the Corolla in park, and jumped out to enter the code and push the gate open. Jack unfolded himself and stepped out of the car. He needed to stretch his legs after sitting in the cramped space of the Corolla for so long.

"I got it, Jack. You don't have to get out."

"Oh, yes, I do. I need to stretch out my legs and my back. No offense intended, kid, but you ought to get yourself a truck. It's a lot more comfortable to sit in for so long, and you'll have a lot more room in the back for all a your dive equipment."

"I'd love to get a truck. I can't afford it right now. I'm saving up to buy the rest of my dive equipment to use for cave diving."

The kid opened the gate and ran back to the car to pull it through.

"I'll get the gate."

Jack walked over and closed the gate. Anything to keep the kid in the car and to keep him from talking.

As Jack walked past the kid's car, he felt every small pebble he stepped on penetrating through the hospital socks. He continued anyway.

"I'll meet you down the hill. I need to walk and stretch my legs."

Once at the bottom of the hill, Jack saw a dark pile on one of the tables under the pavilion closest to the water. It was already too dark to make out exactly what it was. He walked over to the light switch on the center pole and flipped it up. The bright fluorescent lights under the pavilion flickered on and broke through the darkness.

Jack looked at the pile he had seen. It was his drysuit and undergarments. He picked up the undergarments. They were torn to shreds. Not only was the body of the suit slit up the middle, right next to the zipper, mind you, but the arms and legs were slit up the length of them. They hadn't even tried to salvage the undergarments. That was two hundred dollars cut to shreds.

Jack tossed the undergarments aside and picked up his drysuit. It was in the same condition. A slit was cut diagonally across the torso, right below the zipper. The arms and legs were also cut the entire length of them. The worst part of it was that the drysuit cost ten times what the undergarments had. Two thousand dollars! Jack felt sick to his stomach. He had just spent four hundred dollars replacing the neck and wrist seals because they had started to dry rot from Jack not using the suit for more than two years. Those had been cut as well. That brought the total loss to twenty-six hundred dollars. If he could replace the suit and undergarments for twenty-two hundred dollars. Jack sat down on the bench, leaned over, and put his head in his hands.

"Are you okay, Jack? Are you feeling sick again? Should I take you to the hospital?"

"Nah, kid, no hospital. I'm feelin' sick, but it's not that kind of sick. I'm feelin' sick about my drysuit and undergarments bein' destroyed."

"Maybe I can help you with that. You can use my discount at Cave Masters to get them replaced."

"Kid, everyone gets that discount. Haven't you figured that out yet?"

Danny's shoulders dropped and he hung his head down. Jack looked at the kid and felt sorry for him. Either he was oblivious to it, or he never put two and two together. Jack was surprised that he hadn't known. He felt a little bad about being the one to break it to him. Someone had to do it, though.

"Don't get all bummed about it, kid. You're not the only one being taken advantage of. You weren't the first and won't be the last. I'll tell ya what. You did me a huge favor by coming out to pick me up tonight and driving me back to Marianna. I'll see what I can do to help you get your cave classes scheduled."

"Really? You would do that for me?"

"Yeah, kid. Now you better get yourself home. It's already past one in the morning and I know you have to be at work by eight."

"Oh, I'm good. I'm usually up this late playing video games. I'll get the gate for you. Then I'll go."

"I 'preciate that, kid."

Jack tossed his destroyed drysuit and undergarments into his truck bed and turned to Danny.

"Hey, kid, can you do me a favor? What you said earlier when I called you from Pensacola. That thing about the Simmons kid rescuing me."

"Yessir?"

"You know that ain't true, doncha?"

"It sure doesn't sound like the story you told me."

"I didn't tell you no story, kid. I told you the truth. I need to make sure everyone knows that. I need to make sure everyone knows I wasn't rescued. Simmons has had it out for me ever since I rescued him a couple years back. I think this is his way of gettin' back at me. That ain't right. We have to make sure the truth is known, not some cockamamy story that some asshole made up to get back at me for his own screwup. You understand me, kid?"

"Yessir, I think so."

"Good. I'll see what I can do to get you into a cave diving class with a buddy of mine. You just do your thing."

"Yessir, I will." Danny responded with a big smile on his face.

Jack would keep his reputation intact after all. Simmons wasn't going to take him down again.

56

Joey

I pushed myself off of Kelly. I couldn't do this. I couldn't have sex, or hookup, or whatever she wanted to call it. I wasn't ready to give up on Lindsey. I wanted to work things out between us. I wanted whatever it was that had set Lindsey off to go away and for everything that happened this past week to be put behind us. I couldn't do that if I had sex with Kelly. I would feel guilty. Even if it was just a one-night stand and didn't mean anything to either of us. It would mean something to me. It would mean me being unfaithful to Lindsey. I didn't care if she had moved out and broken up with me. I hadn't agreed to it. I didn't even know why it had happened!

"What are you doing? Get back down here on top of me, big boy. Oooo, you are a big boy."

I suddenly realized that I was standing naked at full attention in front of Kelly. My hands moved to cover things up while I looked for my clothes.

"Don't be embarrashed. I like what I shee. Do you wanna move thish onto the bed? Is that why you shtopped?"

"What? No! I don't want to move this anywhere!"

"Then get back down here."

Kelly reached up, grabbed my arms, and pulled me toward her. I had to admit, from the neck down, she wasn't bad. I was looking at her curvy body and feeling movement in my groin. No! I couldn't do this to Lindsey. I especially couldn't do it with someone she knew and had come to trust. Although, I was wondering why Kelly was trusted.

If she was such a good friend, she wouldn't be doing this.

I felt Kelly's hands trying to pull my hands away from my crotch. Her head was only inches from it. I pushed her back down onto the couch and stepped away from her. I saw my clothes on the floor where I had been standing. I extended my right foot forward and snagged my shorts with my toes, pulling them toward me. Kelly was trying to sit up again, but she was too drunk to be effective. I took another step back, dragging my shorts with me. Once I felt like I was a safe distance from her, I reached down and grabbed them.

Just as I stood, Kelly tackled me to the floor and straddled me. I rushed to block her with my hands. She pushed them out of the way and began rubbing herself against me. I tried to push her off, but she pinned my arms down above my head. She pushed down and put most of her weight on my arms so that I couldn't raise them up. I thrashed my hips side to side to try to knock her off of me.

"Oh, you like it rough. I can deal with that."

I thrashed even more. She couldn't get me inside of her without removing one of her hands from my arms. And if she removed one of her hands, I would get my leverage back and be able to throw her off. We were in a standoff. Kelly kept trying to rub herself on me while I thrashed my hips. I was no longer turned on by what was going on. I was scared. I didn't like not having control. Especially not with Kelly being the one in control. Lindsey and I had played around with things in the bedroom, but it wasn't our thing. At least, not to this extent.

"You know you want me. Shomething told on you."

Kelly winked at me as she said that. She really thought I wanted her. She thought this was a big game. I had an idea.

"You know, you're right. I don't know why I'm fighting it. I'm going to need you to help me get inside of you, though. It's not working in this position."

I watched Kelly's eyes light up at the idea of her finally getting her way. She let go of my left arm to bring her hand down and help me slide inside of her. That's when I made my move. I reached across with my hand, grabbed her left arm, and rolled to my right, pushing her onto the floor below me.

"Oh! You want to be in control. I'm game for that."

Except that wasn't exactly what I wanted. I pushed myself off of Kelly, grabbing my clothes as I stood, and ran toward the door. I glanced back and watched Kelly drunkenly trying to get up from the floor. She was having a lot of difficulty. I pulled her door open and ran out of her apartment, searching for my keys in the pockets of my shorts. I hoped they hadn't fallen out inside of Kelly's apartment. I finally felt the hard metal of the keys and pulled them out while holding the shorts in front of my midsection.

I ran toward my apartment door, looking around, hoping no one was outside. I fumbled with the key, finally getting it into the lock and turning it. The door swung open and I glanced around one last time before slipping inside. The last thing I saw before I got all the way through the door jamb was Kelly running out of her apartment stark naked and Roger coming down the steps from the third floor. The look on his face told me he saw that we were both unclothed.

Fuck!

57

Lindsey

Kona and I headed back to my parent's house. I had been on an emotional rollercoaster since the park. So many things happened with the kids there that made me consider keeping the child, then doubt rose up, then I was considering it again. It was too much. Truth be told, this entire week felt like an emotional rollercoaster. Was this how pregnancy was? The nausea and vomiting in the mornings weren't enough? Would I have to endure these wild mood swings for nine months?

I didn't know if I could do that. It already seemed overwhelming, and it had only been a week. I needed to get in touch with Joey. I needed to talk to him and get everything out in the open. Maybe I was misinterpreting things. Maybe nothing was going on and it didn't even amount to a hill of beans.

Joey was also stressed. The project we were working on at the far end of Jackson Blue was important to him. It meant a lot to him. He had devoted so much time and effort toward that project. And a lot of money. It wasn't cheap to drive two hours each way both Saturday and Sunday every weekend. I enjoyed going with him when I wasn't teaching for the dive shop, but it was more his thing. It was his baby. I brought my hand to my belly and rubbed it. This was his baby.

I had to talk to Joey and get everything back in perspective and right between us. I didn't know if I'd be able to control my emotions and my mood swings, but hopefully Joey would understand and be willing to have patience with me through the next nine months. Or eight months, or however much longer I had. If he wasn't able to do that, did I really want to be in a relationship with him?

I arrived at my parent's house and walked in the back door. My parents were in the living room watching the news. Some things never changed with them. With all of the sources we had for news, they still sat in front of the television set every night to get what the local station felt was important enough to squeeze into its forty minutes of broadcasting hidden between all of the commercials. I stopped in the kitchen so Kona could drink some water and I gave her a couple of small treats. When she was done with both, I called her to follow me to my bedroom.

As soon as I shut the door, I hit the speed dial on my phone for Joey. It rang three times before he answered.

"Hu-hu-hello."

He sounded out of breath. That was strange. Joey didn't do anything physically demanding other than scuba diving. And that didn't require enough effort to cause someone to get out of breath.

"Joe? Are you okay?"

No response. I could hear Joey trying to catch his breath. I began to regret my decision to call him. I shouldn't have done that.

"H-Hey, s-s-sorry about that. I-I just got out of the shower and was running around the ap-p-partment looking for my phone."

Why was Joey stuttering? He hadn't done that in a long time. The stuttering had been evident when we first met. I thought it was cute and endearing. As his confidence grew over the past couple of years, the stuttering diminished. He could go several days in a row without stuttering at all. The only time I recalled hearing him stutter in recent months was when he was nervous about something. He would occasionally stutter when he spoke with his mom, but she intimidated him and made him feel less confident about himself. She wanted things a certain way and Joey wasn't always agreeable to doing them her way, but he had a difficult time telling her so. His stuttering also got bad when he was waiting on grades from a hard class he was taking at the local community college. I wondered what was making him so nervous now. Was he with someone else? Was something going on?

"Sorry, this was a mistake. Never mind. I shouldn't have called."

I pulled the phone away from my ear just as I heard Joey yell.

"No! Wait! Lindsey! Please!"

Another mood swing. I had to get those under control.

"Okay, sorry, things haven't been right in my head this past week. I'm ready to talk though. I know I postponed the meeting we were supposed to have tomorrow, but I've changed my mind again. If you haven't already made other plans, I'd still like to talk tomorrow."

"No, I haven't made other plans. I can even meet you tonight."

"Tonight's no good. We both have to work in the morning, and this might take some time to get through. Let's just plan on meeting tomorrow after I close the dive shop. I can head straight to the apartment from there."

"Ummm… How about we meet at the beach? You know, the usual spot. We could go for a walk and talk."

That was strange. Why didn't Joey want me at the apartment? No. I pushed that thought out of my head. I didn't want to read too much into it. Joey and I went to the beach to talk regularly. We had good memories there. We had our first kiss there. Maybe he was trying to create that mood.

"Okay, the beach is fine. I'll see you about quarter after seven."

"I love you, Linds."

I disconnected the call without responding. It was probably mean to leave him hanging like that. I wasn't ready to say it, though. We needed to talk first. I tossed the phone onto the other side of the bed and pulled Kona into my arms. I lay there holding her while she made the cutest little high-pitched grunts. Then an idea came to me.

"Stay here, Kona. Mommy will be right back."

I burst into tears as I stood up. I always referred to myself as mommy when talking to or about Kona. But saying it with a baby growing inside of me made it all that more meaningful. I was no longer going to just be a fur mom. I was going to be a real mom. I sat back down and held Kona a little longer. Once the emotional outburst passed, I wiped my face and got up, careful not to say or think of anything that might set me off again.

I stepped out of my bedroom with Kona at my heals and headed into the bathroom to wash my face. I glanced at myself in the mirror. I looked terrible. I had been crying way too much. I had to make an appointment with my OB/GYN and see if there was anything I could do to control the mood swings. I doubted it, but it was worth asking. I couldn't be the first woman to go through this.

I dried my face and thought about applying makeup to improve my appearance. I decided against it. I rarely wore it. There was no point in putting some on for what I had planned for the next hour. I wasn't looking to impress anyone. I walked out of the bathroom and told Kona to go into my bedroom. She jumped on the bed and curled up near the pillows. I left her there and walked into the living room.

"I'm heading out for about an hour. Kona is curled up on my bed. Don't wait up for me."

My father grunted. My mother turned her head toward me with a worried look on her face but didn't say anything. I stepped out of the back door and headed to my car. When I got settled into the driver's seat and started the car, I looked at the clock on the dash. It was after ten. Kelly should still be awake. She worked nights and usually stayed up on her nights off. I hoped it wasn't a work night for her. I had some questions to ask her.

58

Joey

I was happy to hear from Lindsey and know we were going to talk about this mess the next evening. I was also a little worried. She caught me off guard. I was out of breath from fighting off Kelly and running to my apartment naked. It made me stutter. I had worked so hard to make that stop. I hated that it still popped up. It was hard for me to even tell a white lie without the stuttering giving me away. Especially when it came to Lindsey. She knew my tells.

I placed my phone on the counter and threw my clothes in the hamper. I laughed at myself for doing that. I usually threw them on the floor, causing Lindsey to get upset with me for being a slob. I walked into the bathroom and stepped into the shower. I turned the hot water on. I needed to scrub Kelly off of me. Not just off of my body but off of my mind. I didn't know why my body responded the way it had. It shouldn't have done that. I should have had more control. I had no feelings for Kelly. I loved Lindsey and only wanted to be with her.

I don't know what possessed me to go to Kelly's. I should never have gone there to question her. That couldn't have been Kelly in Marianna. She didn't even know how to pronounce the name of the town. It was stupid of me to think that was her at Jackson Blue. What business would she have there?

I soaped and scrubbed myself several times, rinsing with hot water in between. I wished they had the water heater set higher. My parents kept the water heater in their house set really high. The hot water was scalding. The apartment complex didn't do that. It was hot but tolerable. It would have to do. I stood in the shower until there was no hot water left. My skin was beet red and my fingers pruned. I couldn't get the memory of Kelly holding me down out of my head. I would never have expected that kind of behavior from her. She didn't seem like the type. I guess I had her figured all wrong.

I turned the faucet off before the water got too cold. I grabbed my towel and patted myself dry rather than rubbing the towel all over like I normally did. My skin felt raw. I combed my hair and cleaned my ear with Q tips. My mother always chastised me for sticking them in so far. But it felt so good to rub the inside of my ears with those tiny cotton covered sticks. I was careful to not push them in too far and hit my eardrums…most of the time. I'd get overzealous every now and then and poke an eardrum accidentally. That happened with my mom standing in front of me once and she knew by my expression what I had done. She took the opportunity to reprimand me for using the Q tips the way I did.

I stepped out of the bathroom toward the dresser to grab a pair of house shorts and an old t shirt. I had no plans to go anywhere else tonight. I pulled the shorts and shirt on, grabbed a beer from the fridge, went out to the living room, and dropped onto the couch to see what I could stream. As I was flipping through my options on Netflix, I thought about the things I had to do the next day. I would deal with Kelly tomorrow after work when she was hopefully sober. As much as I would have liked to ignore it, I couldn't. She lived a few doors down from us. It would be awkward not to address it. Kelly had to be told that what she did was unacceptable and being drunk was no excuse. I still couldn't believe what had happened in her apartment earlier.

A knock on the door interrupted my Netflix browsing and my thoughts. Who the hell was that? It couldn't be Kelly. That was a lot of nerve if she came over here after that. Then I remembered seeing Roger. *Dammit!* I set the remote on the coffee table and walked to the door. I didn't feel like explaining myself to anyone, especially Roger. I looked through the peep hole. It wasn't Roger. It was Kelly. She was standing, or rather swaying, on the other side waiting for me to open the door. Her shirt was disheveled and one of her breasts was almost hanging out of it.

282

59

Lindsey

Ten minutes earlier

I pulled into the apartment building complex and parked in my usual spot. I smiled at the thought that even after being gone for several days, no one was parking in it. I shut off the car and sat in the dark for a moment. Did I want to do this? Did I really want to confront Kelly? I didn't think anything was going on between her and Joey, but it was strange that they went to breakfast together on Monday.

Monday. That was only three days ago. It seemed like a lifetime. So much had happened over the previous three days. Most of it was probably my own emotional responses. Yes, I needed to talk to Kelly. I needed to clear things up with her before I spoke with Joey. I didn't want anything hanging over me.

I opened the door and stepped out of the car. As I walked toward the apartment building, I thought I heard Kelly's voice coming through the breezeway. She sounded like she was yelling. I picked up my pace and started jogging across the parking lot. I heard Kelly calling out Joey's name. It sounded as if she was desperate. It sounded like she was drunk. As I ran through the breezeway, I encountered Roger standing in the shadows.

"Hi Lindsey." Roger said with a huge smile on his face. "What are you up to? I thought you moved out a few days ago?"

I didn't have time to deal with Roger, not at this hour. He was a nice enough guy in the shop, but I didn't want his advances. I didn't need this to happen right now.

"We're working on things, Rog. Everything will hopefully be back to normal tomorrow evening."

"You better listen to what I have to tell you before you decide."

* * *

I stopped hearing Kelly calling out to Joey a few seconds after I saw Roger. Then Roger began to tell me what he had seen. I couldn't believe Joey would do something like that to me. He had been in the dive shop just this afternoon begging me to talk to him. Did he go straight to Kelly's from there so he could fuck her? Was that how little our relationship had mattered to him? Had I interrupted them when I called him earlier?

I thanked Roger and he walked off toward the parking lot. I thought I saw a smirk on his face. The bastard. It was strange for him to be going somewhere after ten on a Thursday night. I'd known Roger for several years and knew he worked early Monday through Friday. It didn't matter. I didn't know why I was thinking about that. Actually, I did. I was trying to avoid the immediate issue facing me.

I was tempted to run up the steps and confront Joey about what Roger told me. I wanted to see the look on his face when he found out I knew what was going on. I wanted to see him squirm. The sooner, the better. It would be better to get it out in the open so soon after it had happened. Or would it?

What if this had been happening for several weeks? What if they hooked up soon after Kelly moved into the apartment complex? Joey and I didn't work the same hours. He didn't always stop by the dive shop after leaving work. When he didn't, he would text and say he had a long, rough day and wanted to go home to shower and relax. What if he was meeting up with Kelly?

Should I confront him tonight? Or should I walk away from it all? Should I forget about him and decide what I wanted to do about this baby growing inside of me on my own? Oh God! Did I really want to raise a child as a single mom? Or would it be best to…

I couldn't think about those things right now. I had to decide whether I wanted to talk to Joe or not. I had to make up my mind. It was almost eleven. If I didn't go up there right this minute, he'd be asleep by the time I did. Or was Kelly over there right now lying on my side of the bed?

I decided to confront Joey tonight. If Kelly was with him, it would be even better. I pushed myself off of the breezeway wall where I had been leaning when Roger dropped the bomb about seeing Joey running from Kelly's apartment with no clothes on. I walked the rest of the way through the breezeway toward the courtyard. A couple of minutes later, I stood in front of the door to the apartment where I had lived only three days earlier. I made a fist and brought it up in front of me. The thought of knocking on the door to the apartment I had lived in for more than a year felt strange. I held my hand a few inches from the door, hesitating, still questioning whether I wanted to do this tonight.

Just as I started to move my fist toward the door, I heard a door opening to my left. I looked over and saw Kelly stumbling out of her apartment. Her clothes were disheveled, what little clothing she had on. She was not wearing a bra. One of her breasts was practically hanging out of her low-cut blouse. Her hair was a mess. I moved and ducked into the shadows around the corner. She stumbled as she made her way in my direction, stopping in the exact spot where I had just been standing. It appeared that she hadn't noticed me when she exited her apartment. She took a moment to try to straighten out her hair and clothes. It only made them worse. The breast that had been almost hanging out fell out completely. Kelly didn't seem to notice. She finished whatever she had been trying to do with her hair and clothes and knocked loudly on the door.

60

Joey

What the hell!?! Was that Kelly again? I hadn't opened the door earlier. I hoped she would get tired of knocking and go away. Thankfully, she had. About five minutes after the knocking had started, it stopped. Either she gave up and went back to her apartment, or she passed out in front of the door. I wasn't going to check. It looked like she had at least had the decency to put some clothes on before coming over to knock on the door, partially on anyway. I still didn't want to talk to her. The clothes had come off far too easily earlier.

I didn't want to see or talk to Kelly ever again. I couldn't believe she had the nerve to come over and knock on my door after what she did. I didn't care if she was drunk. It wasn't appropriate. It was unacceptable. She shouldn't have done it. What made it worse was that she knew Lindsey. I thought she and Lindsey were friends. Lindsey liked her enough to invite her over to our place a couple of times a week. She liked her enough to let her drink our beer and eat our food. She liked her enough to think of her as a friend. How could Kelly betray that friendship? How could she betray that trust?

The knocking came again, only louder this time. I knew it had to be Kelly coming back to try once more. She had probably gone to the parking lot to see if my car was there and came back to try to get me to open the door. I didn't want to talk to her, but I didn't want her out there knocking on my door all night and disturbing the neighbors. It was bad enough Roger saw us. Besides, I had to go to bed soon. I wasn't going to be able to sleep if I didn't put a stop to her knocking right this minute.

I turned the television off and went to the door. I looked through the peep hole again and saw Kelly swaying in front of the door. I unlocked the deadbolt and doorknob and cracked the door open.

"What do you want, Kelly?"

"I jus' wan'ed to 'pologise. I wan'ed to shay I'm shorry."

She was really slurring her words. The collar of her blouse had dropped even lower and her left breast was exposed.

"Fine, now leave me alone."

"But…"

"Look, Kelly…"

Just then she started to fall toward me. I pushed the door out of the way and caught her in my arms, her bare breast resting against my right bicep. As soon as I had my arms around her torso, I felt Kelly's arms come up around my waist and she pushed me into the apartment, kicking the door closed behind her. The backs of my legs hit the arm of the couch, and I fell backward onto the cushions with Kelly coming down on top of me. She was laughing as she fell. She had fooled me into thinking she was passing out and I had fallen for it.

I pushed Kelly off of me onto the floor between the couch and the coffee table, knocking the half full beer that had been sitting on the table onto its side. I watched the beer spill onto the carpet and start to foam up. Lindsey would not have been happy with my clumsiness.

I pushed myself up and over the arm of the couch so that I was standing at the end. I turned to look down at Kelly struggling to get up, both breasts now exposed. I wasn't going to fight her this time. I jumped over her legs, over the spilled beer, and ran toward the bedroom. I heard a commotion behind me as I slammed the door shut and locked it. Yes, I was being a coward, but my chances were better that way.

Kelly banged loudly on my bedroom door.

"C'mon, Joe, open the door. Don' hi'e from me."

The banging got louder and more forceful. I could see the door shaking against her strikes. I got on the other side of the dresser and tried to push it against the door. It was too heavy and wouldn't slide along the carpeting. I got on the other side, opened a top drawer, and lifted that end to pull the dresser. It moved a few inches before I had to put it down. I was exhausted from all of the activities since confronting Kelly. I pulled the drawers out and put them on the bed to make the dresser lighter. With the drawers out, I was able to move the dresser against the door. I put the drawers back in to give it more weight. Kelly continued to slam her fists on the door.

"Joe, Joe, Joe, Joe, Joe. Open the door. Open the door. Open the door. Open the door."

I didn't know how long Kelly would last doing that before she passed out. I had a feeling she would pass out in front of the door, so I'd still be stuck in my bedroom. It didn't look like I would be getting much sleep. I'd probably have to call out from work a second time. I looked for my phone and realized I didn't have it on me. It must have fallen out of my pocket when Kelly grabbed me and pushed me onto the couch. Dammit! I couldn't even call anyone to come and help. I couldn't call work in the morning unless Kelly left.

The knocking and yelling continued.

I scanned the bedroom, not sure what I was looking for. My laptop was also out in the living room, as was my tablet. I had no way of communicating with anyone outside of the room. Then I noticed the windows. Maybe I could climb out. I ran over, unlocked the latch, and slid the window open. I stuck my head outside. *Dammit!*

The windows opened out toward the parking lot, but there was nothing to grab onto. I could try to drop to the ground, but that was a good twelve feet from the bottom of the window. I could easily break an ankle or leg doing that. And then what would I do? I didn't have my car keys on me. I'd be stuck outside of my apartment while Kelly continued to bang on the bedroom door. I wouldn't be able to get back into the apartment once she passed out. If she passed out.

I stood at the window with my head sticking out of it trying to figure out the best way to escape. I thought about the hell I had created for myself by going over to Kelly's apartment to confront her about my stupid suspicion.

How could I have thought that was Kelly's car at Jackson Blue earlier? What would she be doing there? I had gotten so wrapped up in this ordeal of being scooped that I wasn't thinking straight and now look what was happening. I had a knack for getting myself into these situations. I thought back to incident at Eddy Spring more than four years ago with Earl Hewitt.

"Joeeeeeeeeeey! Ohpehn the dooooooor!"

As I was standing there with all of these thoughts going through my mind, I heard someone's footsteps coming from the breezeway to my left. It sounded like someone running with flip flops. I got ready to yell for help as soon as I saw the person come out of the breezeway. I held my breath and waited, ready to call the person over. A shadow popped out of the breezeway and just as I was about to yell, the person came into the light. It was Lindsey. What was she doing here? Why was she running toward the parking lot? What had she seen and heard?

61

Lindsey

I couldn't believe what I saw. It confirmed what Roger had told me. Joey was involved with Kelly. Joey was fucking Kelly. As soon as Kelly disappeared into the apartment and the door slammed shut, I ran past the door and down the steps. I had to get out of there. I wanted to get as far away from them as possible. By the time I got to the bottom of the steps, I could barely see. I was crying so hard that everything was blurry. It reminded me of the last dive I did in that cave in Cozumel, Mexico six months earlier. Not only had the halocline blurred my vision, but my tears made it worse it. I ran blindly through the breezeway back toward the parking lot. I wanted to get into my car and hold myself until this feeling passed.

"Lindsey!"

I heard Joey's voice to my right. He was yelling. Actually, it wasn't exactly yelling. It was more of a whispered yell.

"Lindsey! Please stop!"

More whisper yelling. I stopped running. I wiped my eyes with my sleeve, trying to dry my face of the tears. I turned to look for Joey. He was hanging out of our bedroom window waving his arms over his head. I walked in that direction until I was standing below the window looking up at him.

"What do you want?" I snarled at him.

"I need your help! Kelly is the drunkest I've ever seen her, and she threw herself at me earlier. Now she's in our apartment outside of our bedroom door trying to get in. I'm trapped!"

He was no longer whisper yelling. It was more of a whisper talking. I didn't know why he wasn't just talking. The loud whispering wasn't that quiet.

"Joeeeeeeeeeeey!" I heard Kelly yelling in the background.

"Likely story, Mister! I don't believe a word you're saying. Roger saw you coming out of Kelly's apartment without any clothes on. He saw Kelly hanging out of her apartment door without any clothes on. Is that what you call throwing herself at you? You hated it so much you took your clothes off?"

"No! That's not how it happened! Please…"

"Then I saw her throw herself at you practically naked just a few minutes ago. You're not fooling anyone but yourself."

"Lindsey! I swear! I didn't do anything with Kelly. I thought I saw her at Jackson Blue earlier and I went to her apartment to question her about it. She threw herself at me and pulled my clothes off. I got out of there as soon as I could get away from her and ran. That's why Roger saw me naked. I didn't have time to get dressed because she would have thrown me down and pinned me to the floor again. You have to believe me." He was talking so fast his words were running together.

Was he telling me the truth? Joey had a few inches on Kelly. He wasn't a weakling. I wasn't buying it. I didn't believe that she could throw him down and hold him on the floor.

"Joeeeeeeeey! Lemme in! C'mon! You know you want some more of this!"

"How can I believe anything you say, Joseph? Listen to that girl. It doesn't sound like nothing happened between the two of you. Is that what you were doing at breakfast with her? How long has this been going on? How long have you been fucking her?"

I turned to walk away.

"Lindsey, please stop! Okay, she caught me off guard and kissed me and I kissed her back. She pulled my shirt off and I didn't stop her. But then she started to pull my shorts off and when I tried to stop her, she pushed me back and got on top of me. She took me by surprise and pinned me down. She held my arms down over my head and had leverage on me. I finally fooled her into thinking I was willing to do something, and she lowered her guard. That's when I pushed her off, grabbed my clothes, and ran out of her apartment naked. That's it! That's the truth. Now please help me! She has me trapped in the bedroom. My phone, my laptop, my keys. Everything is out in the living room. I'm ready to jump out of this window, but then I'll just be trapped out here and unable to get back into the apartment. I swear nothing more happened. I swear I never intended anything to happen. She caught me off guard tonight. You know I can barely stand her."

I stopped and stood there, not looking at Joey, but not walking away either.

"Please Lindsey."

He sounded pitiful. I could hear the desperation in his voice. He also wasn't stuttering. Maybe he was telling the truth. Maybe Kelly did throw herself at him. She did look really drunk a few minutes earlier.

"Okay, I'm going to come up there and get her out of the apartment. I'll do that much for you. But then I'm leaving. I don't know if I can do this with you anymore, Joe. I don't know what I want."

"Thank you so much! That's all I'm asking right now. She stopped knocking a couple of minutes ago. I don't trust her, though. She's probably waiting to see if I'll come out. I'm afraid of what she might try to do again."

"Okay, I'll be right up."

I hoped I didn't end up regretting this. I wanted to believe Joey. I wanted to trust him. Things were just so messed up in my head. I didn't know if it was justified or if it was my hormones affecting my emotions.

I walked through the breezeway to the courtyard. A couple of minutes later I was standing on the second-floor landing in front of the apartment door again. This time I had my keys out. I listened carefully to see if I could hear Kelly inside. All was silent. Either she had passed out, or she was waiting for Joey to come out of the bedroom. I slowly and quietly inserted the key into the lock and turned it, turning the knob at the same time and pushing the door open. I stuck my head inside of the apartment. It smelled like a bar on a Saturday night. The odor of alcohol was so strong I was afraid I might get a buzz.

I saw Joey's phone on the floor in front of the couch. There was a beer bottle laying on its side on the coffee table. The contents were puddled on the table next to the bottle and dripping onto the carpet. Kelly was nowhere to be seen. I saw her throw herself into the apartment only minutes earlier. Maybe she was in the bathroom. Or maybe she was hiding and waiting for Joey to come out. I walked in and slowly walked toward the bedroom. The odor of alcohol got stronger. When I got closer to the alcove leading to the bedroom and bathroom, I saw Kelly splayed out on the floor between the doors. She had passed out.

"Joe." I whispered, hoping to not wake Kelly. "She's passed out. Open the door."

I heard Joey struggling with something behind the door. After about a minute, I watched the door open slowly and saw Joey's head stick out. He looked down at Kelly, shook his head, and pushed the door completely open. Our dresser was behind him against the foot of the bed. Joey carefully stepped over Kelly, and I moved into the living room to give him space. He came toward me and tried to put his arms around me. I held my hands in front of me.

"I'm not ready for that, Joe," I whispered.

He put his hands up as if I was pointing a gun at him.

"Sorry. I'm just so relieved to see you. I'm so relieved you stopped to help me."

"Well, now that you're not trapped anymore, I'm leaving."

"Wait! You can't leave me here with her lying there on the floor. Please help me get her out of here and back to her apartment. I'm afraid if I try it myself, she'll wake up and throw herself at me again. I don't want her to spend the night here."

I hadn't planned on doing any of this. I wasn't even sure why I had come over here at this point. It was a bad idea.

"Wait. Why were you here tonight, anyway? We weren't supposed to talk until tomorrow. Not that I'm upset that you are here! I'm just surprised to see you."

"Truth be told, Joe, I was coming over to talk to Kelly. When I got here, I decided I would talk to you instead. I didn't want to wait until tomorrow night. Now I don't know if I want to talk to you at all."

Joey's head dropped with his chin on his chest. Maybe he was telling the truth about all of this.

"Look, let's just get Kelly up and to her apartment. Then we'll both try to get some rest tonight and I'll call you tomorrow to let you know what I've decided. Fair enough?"

"Sure. I guess."

I walked over to Kelly and pulled her shirt up over her breasts. I pulled her shorts up so that part of her was also covered. It looked like she had started undressing herself.

"C'mon, you take the right arm, and I'll take the left. We'll lift her up and get her onto the couch so we can reposition and figure out how we're going to get her to her apartment. Hopefully, her door is unlocked because I don't see anywhere that she could be carrying keys."

Joey and I each grabbed an arm and hoisted Kelly up into a sitting position. She remained passed out. We adjusted ourselves so that our arms were under hers and lifted her into an awkward standing position. We pulled her across the room to the couch, her feet dragging behind, turned her around, and sat her down. Just as we were getting her to the couch, she opened her eyes.

"Heeeeeyyyyyy," she slurred. "I didn't know you two were into threeshums. I'm game."

Kelly grabbed us both around our waists and pulled us down on top of her. She was incredibly strong. Stronger than I would have believed. My right hand closed into a fist, and I punched her in the chin. I believe it was something called an uppercut. Kelly's head snapped back and she passed out again, or maybe for the first time. I grabbed my fist with my other hand and rubbed it. I had never hit anyone before, and I didn't think it would hurt like it did. Joey pushed himself up off of the couch and ran into the kitchen. He returned a few seconds later with an ice pack.

"Here. You'll need this."

I started to apply the ice pack on Kelly's chin.

"No, not for her. For your fist."

Duh! I placed the ice pack on my fist.

"I'll grab her from behind and get her to her apartment if you open the doors for me. I think she'll be passed out for a while now."

Joey lifted Kelly's deadweight and dragged her across the living room. I opened the door for him and he started to drag her out.

"Wait! She doesn't have shoes on. You'll tear up her heals if you keep dragging her like that. Let me grab her legs."

I tossed the ice pack onto the couch and lifted Kelly's legs. We got her out of our apartment and to hers a few doors down. Fortunately, her door was unlocked. Joey set her down on the couch while I got a blanket from her bed. I tossed it over her. We locked the door and left. Hopefully, I hadn't hit her so hard that I had caused permanent damage. I didn't care too much about it at this point. At least not enough to stay and keep an eye on her overnight.

"Look, can we talk for just a few minutes? Can I tell you what happened tonight? I don't want you going off thinking the worst about me. I'm only asking for a chance to explain while I'm not hanging out of a window."

I stood there looking at Joey trying to figure out if he was being honest or if he was just trying to cover his tracks. He hadn't stuttered once since I had arrived there. He might be telling the truth.

"Okay, I'll give you thirty minutes. That's it. Then I have to go home and get some sleep. I still have to go to work tomorrow. And so do you."

"Thirty minutes is fine. I won't even need that long."

62

Joey

Forty-five minutes later I had Lindsey caught up on everything that had happened since Monday morning when I played hooky and went to Jackson Blue without telling her. She sat silently at the opposite end of the couch as far from me as possible. I waited. I let her think about it.

I tried to read her expression. I tried to read her body language. She gave nothing away. I had no idea whether I had pushed her farther away or if I had managed to convince her to consider forgiving me for lying to her about playing hooky. That was where it all started. That was the catalyst for all of our problems that week. At least, that's what I thought.

"It's not all your fault, Joe."

"But it is! I lied through omission."

"Let me finish."

"Okay, sorry." I stood and began to pace around the room.

"Please sit down. You're making me nervous. Besides, you're going to want to be sitting for what I'm about to tell you."

That didn't sound good. I thought about taking a seat closer to Lindsey on the couch, but I didn't know if she would be open to that, especially after what she just said. Instead, I sat down at the opposite end where I had been. I sat at an angle so I could face her and leaned forward with my elbows on my knees. I waited for her to continue.

"Like I was starting to say, it's not all your fault. I've been going through some things this week. When I woke up Monday and saw everything you had done for me before leaving for work, or rather to go diving…"

That last part was said in a snarky tone. She hadn't quite forgiven me.

"…I was filled with happiness. I couldn't believe how thoughtful you were that morning."

I sat up straight and smiled at my thoughtfulness. I had hit that one out of the park.

"But then I got suspicious. I mean, why would you do all of those things out of the blue unless you were trying to cover up for something you did or were about to do?"

The smile immediately left my face and I felt my shoulders slump. I hadn't thought about that aspect of things. I shouldn't have done any of it. I should have treated it as a normal morning. I gave myself away with my *thoughtful* acts.

"Then I got sick. Nauseated. I threw up. I didn't know what was going on. I figured it was a stomach bug. I wasn't feeling hungover or anything like that. Just sick to my stomach. That passed and I went to walk Kona and then to work. Shortly after I opened the dive shop, Jack showed up wanting to buy a mask."

So Jack had gone to see Lindsey. Dammit!

"But you know what? Jack being there pissed me off more than him telling me about seeing you and a girl at breakfast. I suspected it might have been Kelly. I know how she is. I just couldn't figure out why you would agree to go to breakfast with her."

Lindsey paused for a moment. I wondered if she was waiting for me to give her an explanation. When the silence became a little uncomfortable, I decided to offer one.

"Well, I didn't want to go to breakfast with her. But she insisted and I was afraid that she would knock on our door and wake you up if I didn't. She saw me carrying my dive equipment to the car. She even helped me by carrying my oxygen tank. When I declined her invitation to breakfast, she asked if you were awake. I was afraid she would wake you up and you would find out before I had a chance to tell you. So I kind of had to agree to go to breakfast with her to keep her from blowing my plans."

Lindsey stared at me.

"I know it was wrong. I shouldn't have done that. I shouldn't have kept anything from you."

"But you did. And it had me worked up all day Monday. I tried to call you several times throughout the day, both before and after Jack showed up at the dive shop. I finally decided to call Kelly, using the excuse that I was checking on her because of how drunk she had been the night before. That's when I confirmed it was her you went to breakfast with. She blurted it out like she wanted to rub my face in it. Like she was trying to make me jealous."

"What?!? But there was nothing to get jealous of. You know I can hardly stand being in the same room as her!"

"Yeah, well, my emotions were doing me in on that. I thought it was an act to throw me off. I thought both of you were playing it up so I wouldn't get suspicious of anything. As much as you claim to not like her, you always get so animated when she asks about your exploration project. You didn't seem to mind telling her about that."

"That's because of how much that project means to me. And I haven't been able to tell anyone else about it with Gary and Jim being out of town. I felt safe telling her because she's not a cave diver. I was finally able to talk about it and tell *someone* about it."

"I get that now. But a few days ago I had all sorts of thoughts going through my head. I started seeing that as how you really were with her. You only acted like you didn't like her when I was there. What I couldn't understand was why you didn't just break up with me. I couldn't understand why you continued staying with me if you were seeing Kelly."

"But I wasn't!"

"I know that now. I didn't know it then, Joe. My emotions have been all over the place this week."

I dropped my head. I had to try to look at this from Lindsey's perspective. I had to see it with the limited information that she had at the time. When I considered it that way, I understood why she had reacted the way she had. Sort of. What I didn't understand was why she didn't bother to talk to me about it.

"Why didn't you ask me? Why move out without talking to me first, Linds?"

"I'll get to that. Just hear me out. After Kelly told me she went to breakfast with you, I had to leave work. I couldn't do it anymore. I even broke down in tears in front of Roger when he came in to return the scuba tanks he had rented over the weekend."

"You cried in front of Roger?"

"Yes, I couldn't help myself."

"Did you tell him anything?"

Lindsey paused before responding.

"Yes. I told him I thought you were cheating on me."

My shoulders sunk even more and my head dropped to my chest. I knew Roger had a crush on Lindsey. It was pretty bad. Until now, I hadn't let it bother me. Roger knew we had been together for more than four years. He knew he had to admire her from afar. But now things were different.

"Don't worry about him. I ran into him again and he tried to ask me out, but I shot him down."

I was happy to hear that. I was especially happy to hear Lindsey talking like we were still together by telling me not to worry about Roger.

"Anyway, I called Joanne and asked her if she could come in to relieve me. I was too emotional to finish my day. I left work early and went to the apartment to pack an overnight bag. I already knew I needed time away from you to sort things out in my head and my heart. I didn't know what I wanted to do. I needed distance. That's when I ran into Kelly in the parking lot. She didn't say anything else about the two of you but seeing her made things even worse. I left quickly. I got a hotel room that night and ended up getting sick. I was throwing up. I think I had a fever. I didn't know what was going on. I didn't know why I was sick. You know I never get sick."

"I'm so sorry, Linds. I'm sorry I put you through all of that."

"Well, it's not all your fault. Partly your fault, but not all. So, fast forward a couple of days. I spent those days on the beach reflecting on things and feeling sorry for myself. I finally checked out of the hotel this morning and went to work. You know what happened when you came into the dive shop this afternoon."

"I'm sorry about that, too. I didn't know what to do. I didn't know how else to get you to talk to me."

"I know. I'll admit that's my fault. I should have talked to you sooner. There was just so much going on. There were so many emotions rolling through me. I wasn't thinking straight. You'll understand why in a few minutes. I'm about to get to that part."

I sat there patiently, or not so patiently, but trying to give the appearance that I was being patient. I waited to hear the end of Lindsey's story.

"I left work and went to my parents. I had already spoken to my mom and told her I was moving back in."

My jaw dropped. I wanted to say something but closed my mouth and bit my tongue. I didn't want to interrupt Lindsey again.

"Mom kicked dad out of the house so we could have a heart-to-heart talk about things. I told her about my week. I told her about everything that had been going on. I told her I thought you were cheating on me and why. She stuck up for you. She didn't think you were doing anything. She alluded to something about her going through the same thing with my dad. But that was all after she suspected something else was going on. And dammit if she wasn't right!"

"What's going on? What are you talking about, Lindsey?"

Lindsey began to cry.

"Oh, Joey! I'm pregnant!"

63

Jack

Jack was finally home. It had been an unbearably long day. The effects of the little white pill wore off hours earlier. The doctor in Pensacola refused to give him anything to deal with his pain other than ibuprofen. He needed something stronger. He dug out his pill bottle, looked into it, and counted the little white pills on the bottom. There were only five. That wasn't good. Those would be gone in a couple of days. Three if he could stretch it out. He'd have to get more.

He had managed to get the prescription renewed a couple of times. But his primary doctor told him he wouldn't renew it again. He told him the pain shouldn't be so bad that he required something that strong. He said they were addictive and the government monitored those prescriptions carefully.

"Gotdam gubmint!" Jack said out loud as he dropped one of the pills into his palm and popped it into his mouth, dry swallowing it. Four pills left. He wondered where he could go on the street to get more.

Jack had the pills he had only because he had learned his primary doctor was away on a two-week vacation. He went to the clinic the very first day he was gone and got squeezed in to see one of the other doctors. That doctor agreed to prescribe a small amount to get him through until his primary doctor returned. It was a one-time thing. It gave him another few months. He was out of options now.

Jack brought his dive equipment into the house, what he had of it. Most of it was at Cave Masters. He still had his tools and back up equipment, though. It took twice as long as usual because the pain in his left arm had flared. He could only use his right arm to carry things. That was why he needed the pansy-ass hand truck. It grated on his nerves every time he thought about it.

Once everything was inside, Jack grabbed an ice pack from the freezer and applied it to his arm. He needed to calm it down while he waited for the pill to kick in. It amazed him that such a tiny little pill could make him feel so good, yet a pill like Tylenol, almost ten times as big, did nothing for him. It didn't make sense.

While Jack was icing his arm, he looked at his drysuit and undergarment. Such a shame. He wished they had taken the time to pull the suits off of his body rather than cut them up. Didn't they know how expensive they were? Jack wondered if his dive insurance would cover the cost of replacement. He had his doubts. It would probably only cover the cost of the helicopter ride and the hospital visit. He dropped his suits into a pile on the floor.

It was almost two in the morning, but Jack was in too much pain to sleep. He walked to his desk and fired up his computer. He would shop for a new drysuit and undergarment while he waited for the pill to kick in. He had a backup drysuit that he could use in the meantime, but it had a few leaks. He could last a couple of hours in the water before he got too wet and cold to remain any longer. The undergarments were older, thinner, and didn't provide as much insulation as they used to. He hoped whatever he ordered wouldn't take long to arrive. Until he had new suits, he wouldn't be able to spend as much time in Jackson Blue as he wanted to. As he needed to.

Half an hour later, Jack's arm was still screaming. The little white pill wasn't working. The ice was only slightly numbing his arm. It took the edge off, but didn't dull the pain as much as he needed it to. He thought about taking another pill. He had done that a few times in the past when the pain got really bad. But taking another pill would leave him with only three remaining. That made him feel nervous for some reason. It made him anxious.

Jack didn't understand the way he had been feeling lately. He had never been an anxious person. The feeling was foreign. When he first felt different, he looked up the symptoms. The internet said it was a panic attack. Jack didn't feel panicked. He didn't feel like it was as out of control as the internet described it. The other possibility was an anxiety episode. That sounded more like what he was experiencing. It still wasn't right. Jack Johnson did not have anxiety.

Except at the moment, he was feeling very anxious. Jack looked around the room to make sure he was alone and not being watched. He turned back to the computer and pulled up a search engine. He looked around the room again. Then he typed *where can i get oxycodone on the street*. He scrolled through the results. Just a bunch of medical articles about the effects of the little white pill. Nothing telling him where he could buy it. It figured.

Jack thought about the town he lived in. He knew where the worst parts of it were. He wondered if it was too late to find something that night. He was too anxious to take one more of the four little white pills sitting in the bottle that he held tightly in his hand. At the same time, the pain in his arm was getting worse. Jack stood up, grabbed his keys from the counter, and headed out to his truck. He wouldn't know unless he tried.

64

Lindsey

I couldn't believe I had just told Joey I was pregnant. I hadn't planned on saying anything today, or maybe ever, especially after hearing what Roger had witnessed. But Joey seemed so sincere. He seemed truly sorry for everything that had happened. I was beginning to believe that my emotions were more to blame for how bad things had spiraled out of control than Joey's initial omission of the truth.

After I told him I was pregnant, I noticed that the corners of Joey's mouth turned up slightly, giving me a glimpse of a smile. Then he moved toward me but stopped himself when he was about a foot away. I knew he wanted to take me into his arms but wasn't sure if he was allowed to. Lord! I had put him through so much this week. I had put us both through so much. I hoped it wouldn't be like this for the next nine months. I would drive both of us crazy!

I closed the gap between us, grabbed Joey's hands in mine, and pulled him toward me. He immediately scooted over and took me into his arms. I burst into tears, but this time they were tears of happiness. We sat on the couch holding each other tightly for a couple of minutes. It was exactly what I needed. It was what I wanted.

"Oh Joey, I'm so sorry!"

"No, no, babe, you have nothing to be sorry about. I'm the asshole. I'm the one who screwed things up. I let the whole thing about being scooped by someone take over my…my…my whole being. It consumed me. That isn't an excuse. I'm just trying to explain my actions. I shouldn't have let it affect me that way."

"Well, it didn't help that I'm one big raging hormone right now. I burst into tears at the smallest little thing. I can't control it. I don't know if I can do this for nine months, or eight months, or however long."

Joey pulled back from me but kept his hands on my waist.

"So, you want to keep it? You want to go through with the pregnancy?"

I saw another hint of a smile. He wasn't asking because he didn't want the baby. He was asking because he did want it. I was surprised. We hadn't talked about it before, and I didn't know how Joey felt about having kids. We hadn't even talked about getting married that many times. It had been months since that subject had come up.

It was a big step for us to move in together a little more than a year earlier. We were still getting used to that. Bringing a baby into our lives would complicate matters. I didn't know if Joey would be willing to go through this with me or if he would want to bail. Even after being together for more than four years. I felt stupid for thinking that way. It seemed that I wasn't thinking about anything logically lately.

"Yes, of course I want to keep it! I think it would be amazing to raise a little Lindsey together!"

"Or a little Joey. It could be a boy, you know."

"Well, let's hope whatever it is, it takes after you!"

I pulled Joey closer and hugged him fiercely. I melted into his arms. This was where I wanted to be. This was where I belonged. What had I been thinking all week?

"What now? Are you…are you…going to move back into the apartment?"

"Of course! I should never have moved out. I shouldn't have left you like that, without even giving you a chance to explain yourself. You have to promise me something, though, Joe. Promise me you won't do anything like you did a few days ago ever again. Talk to me next time. I know you were stressed about what we found in the back of Jackson Blue on Sunday. I know it was eating away at you. I also know I downplayed it. I shouldn't have done that. You're passionate about what you do, and I should have acknowledged that. I shouldn't have made you feel like you had to hide it from me."

"It was my fault. I shouldn't have snuck around behind your back. I should have told you my plans, but I thought you would try to talk me out of it. I didn't want to deal with that. It wasn't worth the hell I've gone through this past week not having any idea what was going on and what was going to happen with us."

"We'll both have to work on things. And I'm going to apologize if I don't completely stick to it. With the way my hormones are right now, I can't be held accountable."

We both laughed. It felt good to laugh with Joey again.

"What are we going to do about Kelly? I don't feel comfortable walking around here alone anymore. Not with what she did to me tonight. I know she thought we were having problems. Hell, we were! But to do that to me only four days after hanging out with us in our apartment and drinking our beer."

"The good thing is she's only here on a travel contract. Maybe once her contract is over, she'll leave and go somewhere else. She's been here, what, five weeks now? I think she said something about a thirteen-week contract. That means we only have eight more weeks before she moves on. We can figure something out and work around that."

I picked up my phone and looked at the time.

"Holy crap, hon! It's after three! You have to get up in less than four hours to get ready for work."

"I'll be fine. I haven't been getting much sleep this week and kind of running on autopilot anyway. What's one more day?"

"I'm worried about you, Joe."

"I'll be fine. Let's go to bed and get a little bit of sleep. With you by my side I'm sure I'll sleep a lot better, even if it's only for a few hours."

* * *

I woke up briefly when Joey's alarm went off but fell back asleep almost instantly. Then I woke up with a start a little before eight. The nausea was horrible. The morning sickness was the worst it had been. I ran into the bathroom, getting there just in time. Was this ever going to end? I just started having morning sickness five days earlier. How long was it supposed to last?

Once the nausea passed, I grabbed my phone to do some research. I had to know what I was facing. I had to know how long this was going to be happening. According to Google, morning sickness didn't usually start until a woman was about four weeks pregnant. My jaw dropped. Could I really have been pregnant for a month?

I thought back to all of the dives I had done in the past month. I was in the water every weekend and not just teaching dives with open water scuba diving students. I had also done several long dives with long decompression stops over the past month. Four of those to be exact. Every other weekend I was at Jackson Blue with Joey, and we headed back to his exploration area. That put us doing one to one and a half hours' worth of decompression stops. That couldn't be good for the fetus.

I no longer cared about the nausea. I looked up decompression diving and pregnancy next. I found nothing good on the topic. There was nothing about it other than warnings to not do it. I guess it was difficult to get data without actually putting pregnant women through decompression dives and mandatory stops at depth. No one was willing to put their baby at risk in the name of science. Not that I blamed them.

Experts warned that the baby could die. They also warned that there could be developmental abnormalities if it didn't die. That brought me down another rabbit hole. The abnormalities that could happen included neurological issues with the brain, malformed limbs, abnormal heart development, blindness…

I slammed my laptop shut. I couldn't read anymore. I couldn't think about it any longer. What had I done? What if our baby wasn't born healthy? Would we be able to deal with that? Could Joey and I raise a special needs child? Would we have the patience to do that? We had almost broken up over a stupid cave diving project. What would happen to us if we had a child that wasn't healthy?

65

Jack

Jack woke up the next morning feeling groggy. He rolled over and looked at the clock on his bedside table. It wasn't morning after all. He slept past noon. It was almost one. He rubbed the sleep out of his eyes and ran his dry tongue over his cracked lips. It felt like he was rubbing two pieces of sandpaper against each other.

Jack swung his legs over the side of the bed and pushed himself up into a seated position. His left arm hurt, but not nearly as much as it had been hurting the night before. He shook his head and tried to piece together what had happened before he passed out.

He remembered going out to look for some more of those little white pills. He got lucky and found a guy who knew another guy who could hook him up. The first guy was hanging out in front of a twenty-four-hour convenience store located in the shady part of town. He told Jack to wait fifteen minutes and he would be back. It ended up being closer to twenty minutes, but the guy returned with exactly what Jack wanted.

Jack had done some research while he was waiting for the dealers to come back and found that the going price was about a dollar a milligram. He looked at the bottle he had. The pills were five milligrams each. That would be five dollars for each of those little white pills. Things were going to add up fast. Jack wished his doctor would prescribe more for him, but the doctor told him unequivocally no during his last appointment. So Jack stretched out the supply of pills he had until his doctor went on vacation. He'd been stretching out his last supply as well. It was rough.

He tried alternatives. None of the over-the-counter stuff worked so he turned to CBD, Kratom, and a few other products that he could legally find. Some of it helped, but none of it did what the pills did. He was forced to ration. There were times he had to talk himself down to keep from taking one of the pills. He was finally about to run out and had to buy his own. He could feel the anxiety taking control of his entire body.

Running out of pills couldn't have come at a worse time. With having to buy a new drysuit and undergarments, things were getting expensive. It had to be done. Jack pulled his wallet out and counted the money in it. Five hundred and fifteen dollars. He did the math in his head and figured he could buy one hundred pills. That should last him a while. Hopefully.

The guy he found returned with the guy he knew. The new guy showed Jack a sample of five pills in a little baggy. Jack held the bag up to the light but had his hand immediately swatted down.

"Keep it low, caveman! Don't wanna advertise to the poh-leese what we doin' here." Emphasis on the po. "Here, use this."

The guy made a chopping motion with his mobile phone and the light came on. He held the light out so it was aimed at the baggy. Jack got a good look at one of the pills and compared it to the last of the pills that he had in his medicine bottle. The markings looked the same – K 18 with a line between the letter and the numbers.

"How do you know I'm a cave diver?"

The guy nodded at Jack's truck. Jack turned and saw the cave diving bumper stickers stuck to his rear bumper. He might have to scrape those off if he was going to keep doing this.

"How much?"

"Seven fitty a piece."

Jack flinched. That wasn't what he found on the internet. These guys were trying to rip him off.

"You can do better than that. I know the goin' price and it ain't no seven fifty."

"Seven fitty. That's my price. You wan'em or not?"

"You have a quantity discount?"

Seven-fitty smiled at Jack.

"How many you want?"

"I want a hundred."

Seven-fitty's smile got even bigger. He pulled out a large bag full of a bunch of smaller baggies and began counting them out.

"I gots fifteen baggies. That's seventy-five. I can get you the rest tomorra."

"That's alright. I'll take what you have if we can come to a more agreeable price. I'm thinking more like five each."

"Seven."

"Five. That's for everything you have and for a steady customer. You'll be seeing me regularly."

Seven-fitty tried to look like he was thinking about it.

"A'ight. I'll giv'em to ya for five, but this is a one-time thing cuz you buying all my inventory. Can't guarantee they'll be five next time. Ya know, 'flation and all."

"That'll work."

Jack ran the numbers in his head and counted off three hundred and seventy-five dollars from his stack of bills. He handed the money over and took the large bag full of smaller baggies.

"Payment in full, bro."

"That is the full payment."

"Nah, caveman, I mean for all hundred."

"That's not the way it works. I pay you for pills I don't get tonight and I'll never see you again. You'll get the rest tomorrow when you bring the other twenty-five."

Seven-fitty leaned back and squinted his eyes at Jack.

"You slick. A'ight."

"You alright with me countin' these?"

"You do whateva you want, caveman."

Jack counted the baggies, making sure he saw five pills in each one. He checked at least one pill in each baggy to make sure the K 18 marking was on it.

"Looks good. You have a number I can use to get in touch with you when I need more?"

"Yeah, here's my card. Just text the quantity and K18. Then meet me here in the same place at midnight the day you text. I'll be here with yo stash. And I'll be here with another five bags at midnight."

"Sounds good sev…compadre."

Jack returned home, took a couple of the pills, and passed out.

That was why Jack felt the way he did this morning. He had taken two pills instead of his usual one. No, make that three pills. He felt like he had a hangover. Maybe it hadn't been a good idea to take that many. He had never taken more than one. The pain had been really bad, though. The anxiety was also worse than usual.

Jack grabbed a baggy from his bedside table and looked at the pills. That line in between the K and the 18 probably meant he could cut the pills in half. He would try that next time. He'd see how one and a half worked for him now that he had a steady supply.

Jack stood up and walked to the bathroom to splash some water on his face. He wanted to go to Jackson Blue and finish the dive that he had started the day before. He remembered the doctor telling him not to dive for two weeks but fuck him. Jack Johnson wasn't staying out of the water for two weeks. Not when he was just getting back into it after being away for two years.

With an empty bladder and cold water splashed on his face, Jack headed into his scuba room to look for his backup drysuit. Maybe he could do something about the leak. He couldn't wait for a new drysuit to arrive before he went diving. He would be diving that day.

He found the drysuit in a storage tub on the shelves against the wall and pulled it out to inspect it. The seals were in good shape. He turned it inside out and looked at the feet. That's where it was leaking before Jack replaced it with the suit that the medics cut up. Maybe he could put some duct tape on it and slow down the leak long enough for him to do the dive he wanted to do without getting too wet and cold. He grabbed the duct tape off of his workbench and lined the foot pocket with several strips. He inspected his work. He knew it wouldn't be watertight, but it should slow the leak down a good bit.

Jack tossed the drysuit aside and dug around for his old undergarments. He found those in another tub and pulled them out. They smelled like mothballs. He brought the undergarments to the back patio and hung them under the porch to air out. He tossed the drysuit on the couch.

Some coffee, a little breakfast, and a shower and Jack would be ready to leave. It would be another dive late in the day, but he planned on finishing this one. He planned on making it back to the area he wanted to check out.

He looked at the time. It was close to two. He tossed some grounds into his coffee maker, filled it with water, and hit the brew button. The coffee would be ready by the time he was out of the shower. He would drink it on the way. If he got on the road by three, he could make it to Cave Masters with plenty of time to get his scuba tanks filled and begin his dive at a somewhat reasonable hour. More importantly, he would be done with his dive in time to meet Seven-fitty at midnight.

66

Meanwhile at Jackson Blue

Brad and Steve were getting ready to do another dive in Jackson Blue. It had been a couple of days since they were there. It's not that they didn't want to dive it. It was that there had been a lot of activity and they were trying to keep a low profile. They decided to spend the past couple of days diving Hole in the Wall and Twin caves. Both were on Merritt's Mill Pond and decent caves to dive. They just didn't have the exploration potential that Jackson Blue had. At least, not that Brad and Steve were aware.

They had heard what happened the day before to Jack Johnson. News like that traveled fast. Someone posted about it, probably before Jack had even been put in the helicopter. There was already a lot of speculation on the internet about what caused Jack to have a problem on his dive.

Brad and Steve had no idea what was true, if any of it. They didn't care. All they cared about was that Jack would probably not be diving again for a while, so they were free to head into Jackson Blue to do as they pleased. The Simmons kid was probably at work. They hadn't seen him since Monday and didn't expect to see him until the weekend. This was their last opportunity to get back into the cave without having any eyes on them.

The park was empty except for them. They had replenished the line on their explorer reels and were ready to go. They finished setting up their equipment and placed it along the top of the retaining wall. All they had to do was suit up and get into the water. Then they would head into the cave and continue to work on what they had begun.

With their drysuits on and their truck locked, the two divers jumped into the water. They clipped their scuba tanks onto their harnesses and grabbed their scooters, checking everything one last time before submerging themselves in the cool, clear spring water. It was three in the afternoon. They didn't plan on surfacing before seven that evening. Steve was already thinking about the beer and Mexican food he would be eating after the dive. Brad was thinking about the dive they were about to do. Nothing else mattered to him at the moment.

The divers dropped below the water, got horizontal. and let their scuba tanks settle into position. They looked at each other and exchanged the okay hand signal. Brad hit the trigger on his scooter and took off into the cave opening with Steve following closely behind. They would be on the triggers for more than a mile.

67

Jack

Jack left his house a little after three. He hoped it wasn't busy at Cave Masters. He wanted to get in and out of there fast. He wasn't in the mood to take any shit from anyone for going diving the day after he was air lifted after a dive. Fuck 'em if they did. Who were they to tell Jack how to live his life?

A short time later, Jack arrived at Cave Masters and backed his truck into the parking lot. There was no one else at the shop. Hopefully Danny had already filled his tanks. He just wanted to load them and his equipment into the bed of the truck and head to the spring. After spending two and a half hours in the car with Danny the night before, he had enough of his ears being talked off.

"Oh, hey, Jack! What are you doing here today? Shouldn't you be home resting? I mean, you got hauled off in the chopper last night. I would imagine they would want you to stay out of the water for a while. Are you…"

"Enough already! Nah, kid! I'm good. Ain't no little issue gonna keep Jack Johnson outta the water. Dijya get a chance to fill my tanks? Can ya load 'em and my equipment in the truck? I gotta use the head."

Jack escaped into the dive shop. He didn't have to relieve himself. He just wanted to escape Danny's incessant chatter. He didn't want to have to make excuses for going diving. He just wanted his tanks and equipment and to get the hell out of there.

About ten minutes later, Jack walked back out of the dive shop just as Danny was loading the last of his stuff into the truck bed. Jack had wasted just enough time. He spent it looking over a bunch of social media posts in which everyone was speculating about what had happened to him the day before. It was already out, and the vultures were moving in. They even knew that it was the Simmons kid who pulled him out of the water. *Goddammit!* He couldn't catch a break.

"Here's somethin' for ya, kid." Jack handed him a twenty. "Put the fills on my tab. Sign me into Jackson Blue. Oh, and I'd wait a while before goin' into the shitter."

Jack climbed into his truck and started it, gunning the engine and drowning out anything that Danny was saying. He wanted to get out of there and get into the water. A few minutes later, he turned off of Blue Spring Road and stopped in front of the gate to Blue Spring Recreation Area. He jumped out, unlocked the gate, pulled through, and resecured it. It was a pain in the ass, but it was better than the way it used to be when the key had to be signed out at the sheriff's office. They only had two keys and on busy days both were signed out if you didn't get there early enough. That meant once you arrived at Jackson Blue, someone had to be on the surface to let you in.

Jack turned to drive down the hill to the parking area and saw another truck already there. *Dammit!* That was Brad and Steve's truck. He thought he was late enough that no one else would be in the park. Well, it was Friday evening. Hopefully he could get in the water before they surfaced.

Jack had read Brad's two cents on the forums on what he thought happened to Jack the day before. It wasn't favorable. Jack backed in next to the truck, making sure to leave Brad very little room to open his door. He jumped out, immediately got his equipment assembled and ready to go. He was in a rush to get in the water. No little white pills this time. Just Jack and the cave.

68

Joey

Work seemed like it would never end. It didn't help that I hadn't slept much the night before. After Lindsey and I went to bed, we spent another hour talking. We were both amped up about everything that had happened the past several days. I think we were both happy to be back together, even though it was only a brief breakup. We also had a baby to look forward to raising together. I thought about it all day. I was ready to go out and buy Lindsey an engagement ring and make it official.

Lindsey and I had discussed it a few times, especially over the previous year since we moved in together. It was the obvious next step in our relationship. We hadn't been too serious about it. We didn't have enough money to do anything special but were saving a little every payday. Lindsey thought we were saving for another Mexico cave diving trip. Although I really wanted to return to Cozumel, I had other things in mind. I wanted to give her the wedding of her dreams. Now it looked like that might not happen. I wanted to get married before the baby was born. There was no way I could save enough for a dream wedding for Lindsey in the next couple of months.

Her parents were comfortable but by no means wealthy. They couldn't pay for an extravagant wedding, and I wouldn't expect them to. I didn't even know if that was a thing anymore. I didn't know if the parents of the bride were still expected to pay for the wedding. Maybe we could finance it. I'd have to check into loans.

I wondered if my parents would lend us some of the money. At least one thing was good. I already had more than enough for an engagement ring. The extra was going to be for the cave diving trip but was now for the wedding.

Things eventually slowed down at work. People were getting ready for the weekend and weren't going to come to the vet. I wasn't disappointed. I sat in a corner of the clinic and leaned against the wall. I dozed off a couple of times. My manager finally told me to take off and go home to get some sleep. I gladly followed orders.

Instead of going home, I stopped at a jewelry store to look at rings. I found one I liked and that I thought Lindsey would like. We had looked at some designs online and I knew her tastes. I put a deposit on it and told the store associate that I would be back on Monday with the rest of the money.

I thought about going diving, but I was way too tired. Besides, with Lindsey and me back together, I wanted to spend the evening with her. I wasn't sure I was ready to leave her side to go diving. My exploration project no longer meant as much. I wanted to bring Gary and Jim to the area I had been exploring, but I wanted to spend more time with Lindsey. It had been a difficult week, and we needed to make up for it. I'd see how I felt later. Maybe Lindsey would want to come with us and hang out on the surface while we went diving. She was supposed to teach a scuba class anyway, and since that was no longer possible...

After the jewelry store, I headed to the dive shop. I was exhausted but wanted to see Lindsey. I missed her even though I had seen and talked to her briefly that morning before leaving for work. I had to make up for lost time this past week.

I pulled into the parking lot and parked in the open space next to her car. I sat in the car exhausted. I had flashbacks to that time a few years earlier when I fell asleep in the car after Earl Hewitt had kept me up most of the night pulling a dead body out of Eddy Spring. I shuddered at the memory.

I climbed out of the car and walked across the parking lot to the dive shop feeling every bit of exhaustion in my body. Maybe taking a day off from diving would be good in more ways than one. I reached the glass door and saw Lindsey inside sitting behind the counter, a worried look on her face. I pushed the door open and rushed in.

"What's wrong? You look like someone died!"

"Oh babe!"

Lindsey came rushing around the counter and into my arms. I pulled her in and held her tightly. A minute later, she released her grip on me and stepped back.

"What's going on?"

"Oh Joey! I've been researching it all day. All of those decompression dives we did in Jackson Blue over the past month. I could have hurt the baby! It could come out with some serious health issues! Or worse, it could die!"

"Wait! Hold on! What are you talking about? You don't even know how long you've been pregnant. You just started getting morning sickness this week. None of those dives should matter."

"Joe, the morning sickness doesn't usually start until a woman is four weeks pregnant. I've been pregnant for at least a month!"

It hit me like a ton of bricks. We had put our baby at risk. I was sure there were plenty of moms that went scuba diving before finding out they were pregnant. There were plenty that drank alcohol and smoked, but how many of them were doing decompression dives? This could be a bad thing.

Not only that, but it also meant we had one month less to plan a wedding if we wanted to do this before the baby was born. Before going to sleep, we had talked about trying to get married before Lindsey was showing. Instead of four or five months, we had three or four. With this hanging over our heads, would we really be into planning a wedding? Would we be excited about it? Or would we be too worried about our baby being born with a defect of some kind?

What kind of memory would this be for Lindsey? Would a big wedding matter to her? For all I cared, we could elope to Las Vegas and get married there, but this seemed to mean a lot to Lindsey. She seemed to want a nice wedding with family and friends present. Not a huge wedding, but definitely not a trip to Vegas wedding.

"Look, we'll get through this. I'm sure there are tests they can do to determine if there's anything wrong with the baby. We need to get you in to see a doctor so we can figure out our options."

"I already have an appointment Tuesday afternoon."

"Okay, good. I'll make sure I take the afternoon off from work to meet you there."

"Really? You want to go to the appointment with me?"

"Of course! Why wouldn't I?"

Lindsey fell into my arms and hugged me tightly again. We stood like that for a while. I almost fell asleep with my face resting on her head. Then suddenly, the door chime went off.

"You two kids stop that! I guess y'all are back together."

I turned to see Roger walking into the dive shop. The thought of going over to him and punching his lights out flashed through my mind, but then I saw the hurt look on his face. I saw the realization that his crush would never come to fruition. That was enough to satisfy me. For now.

"Oh hey, Rog! I have your tanks right there." Lindsey said as she wiped her eyes dry. I didn't know she had been crying.

"Thanks, Lindsey."

Roger grabbed his tanks and quietly exited the dive shop. He was usually talkative, but I guess knowing his dreams were shattered so soon after he thought they might become real was too much for him to handle.

"Why don't you go home and get a nap? You look exhausted. I only have a couple more hours here then I'll be home and wake you up. I want you well rested so I don't have to worry about you tomorrow while you're in Jackson Blue diving with your buds."

"I don't know, Linds. I was thinking about taking a day off tomorrow to spend it with you. And now, especially after what you just told me…"

"Ridiculous. Listen. I'll go with you and hang out on shore while you're diving. I might even go over to Cave Masters for a little bit to keep Danny company."

"Oh, you're brave!" I paused for a moment. "I don't know. I hate to make you wait for me for four hours, possibly longer."

"I don't mind. But we'll talk about it later after you've had a nap. Now get out of here."

I hugged Lindsey and kissed her on the forehead.

"Okay, I'll see you in a couple of hours."

A few minutes later, I was driving east on Highway 98 toward home. I was anxious about running into Kelly alone, but I was exhausted and needed to get some sleep so I could spend time with Lindsey.

Fifteen minutes later I pulled into the parking lot of the apartment complex. I saw Kelly's car parked in its usual spot. I parked in my spot, got out of the car, and ran across the parking lot to the breezeway. Then I thought better of it. I veered off so I could head into the courtyard from a different breezeway. I didn't want to risk running into Kelly in case she was preparing to leave for work. I ran around the building to the other side and entered from there, watching the door to Kelly's apartment, ready to duck and hide if it opened.

I made it up the steps and into my apartment just in time. It wasn't Kelly I saw coming out, but Roger coming in with his scuba tank rentals. If I had seen him in the parking lot, I might have punched him. I guess the look on his face wasn't enough. I made sure he didn't see me. I didn't want him to go back to the dive shop to bother Lindsey. She could take care of herself. I witnessed that when I saw her punch Kelly in the face. But she didn't need Roger hitting on her after everything that happened this week.

I kicked my shoes off, fell onto the couch, and closed my eyes. I didn't have a chance to grab the remote to put on some background noise before falling asleep.

69

Somewhere in the Florida panhandle

It had been four days since the last dive at Jackson Blue. A lot could happen in four days. There were too many divers poking around in the cave. Too many divers looking for the area that Simmons had found. It was always like this. Someone found a new section, and everyone swarmed to the area to try to get in on the action. They were like a bunch of flies attracted to a pile of steaming dog shit.

It was time to get back there. Who knew how many other divers were there in the past four days? The day before, there were a few vehicles at Jackson Blue. Too many to be able to get in there discretely. What a waste of time. Hours of driving only to have to drive back home with nothing to show for it. A quick stop at a Tom Thumb for a case of beer helped, especially with three bottles drained during the remainder of the drive home. The numbness that came with it helped.

Simmons had been at the park. So had Jack Johnson, or at least his truck had been there. There were a few other guys. A total of four vehicles. There had also been an ambulance and a sheriff's car. Too many people. No clue as to what had happened.

Had Johnson gotten hurt? It wasn't Simmons. He had been standing next to two other guys. For some reason, he was standing there practically naked wearing nothing but a pair of tighty-whiteys. Johnson was the only one unaccounted for. It had to be him. That was ironic. He was the one that got his arm crushed during a cave collapse a couple of years earlier. Could there have been another collapse?

The dive equipment remained in the car overnight. After four hours of driving with nothing but a case of beer to show for it, three bottles already consumed, unloading heavy dive equipment from the car was not happening. Instead, the case of beer minus the empties laying on the floorboard of the backseat, was the only thing brought inside. Drinking on the way home wasn't the smartest thing to do, but seeing all of the activity and having to abort the plan made it a necessary distraction.

Back home in the living room with a fourth beer open, this time as a chaser for the shot of scotch. The television was on. The plan was to get so drunk the night would pass quickly. The next day would be spent sleeping all day in preparation for another attempt at diving Jackson Blue later that night.

* * *

It was Friday night. There was no hangover to contend with from the drinking binge. Hangovers were rare. Grandma was to thank for that. Grandma always came to the bedroom with a tall cup of ice water in the middle of the night after those teenage benders. She always seemed to know. The water was gratefully accepted and greedily drunk, every last drop from the twenty-four-ounce cup. Hydration was the key to avoiding a hangover. Grandma probably didn't know what she was doing. She wasn't a drinker. Never had a single drop. But she knew about hydration.

Déjà vu came as the car turned onto Blue Spring Road a little more than twenty-seven hours since the last time. Three and a half miles to Blue Spring Recreation Area. Hopefully no one was at the park this time. It was late. Everyone should be gone. It had been a bad idea to go so early the day before. Lesson learned. Tonight was going to be different. Tonight would bring new results. Too much time had passed since the last dive.

Three days of some other cave diver going there every day. Some cave diver who managed to find the new section that Simmons had found. Three days of opportunity to find the real continuation of the cave passage. There was evidence that someone else was exploring the area. There were lines that didn't belong to Simmons. Lines without Simmons' line arrows claiming the discovery. It didn't appear that they had found the other section. That seemed to remain unknown to anyone else. At least three days earlier it was unknown.

Johnson had been there regularly. Could he be the one back there? It seemed unlikely. Johnson was too cocky to leave lines in the cave without putting one of his own line markers on the line to claim it. He would want anyone who found his lines to know that he had been the one to put them there.

Johnson wouldn't care what Simmons thought about being scooped. He probably didn't care if Simmons claimed he got scooped by Johnson. Johnson would deny it and turn the table, claiming Simmons scooped him. Who would know the truth? It wasn't like Simmons was bragging about his discovery on social media, or anywhere else for that matter.

The driver left the park gate open and pulled to the top of the hill to scope out the situation. No point in closing it if a quick getaway was necessary. The night before someone had left the gate open so it was easy to get in and out. That was a good thing since Simmons gave chase up the hill. In his skivvies! That had been close.

There was a truck parked in the lot near the pavilion. It looked like Johnson's. It wasn't easy to tell from a distance. There was only a sliver of moon out, so the lighting wasn't the greatest. There were no lights around the lot. There was no one to be seen. The risk would have to be taken again. Leaving wasn't an option. Not a second time.

Once the gate was secured, rather than parking in the lot next to the truck, the car was parked behind the pavilion on the other side of the spring basin. If Johnson surfaced from his dive in the next half hour, he wouldn't see it and wouldn't know anyone else was there.

With the car hidden from the view of the spring basin, a small battery-operated camping lantern was used to provide lighting. The pavilion had lights, but they were too bright. If Johnson surfaced while they were turned on, he might walk over to investigate.

The trunk was unloaded under the dim glow of the camping lantern. Once the equipment was set up, it was carried down the hill and placed near the edge of the water out of view on the other side of the diving platform. It would have been much more convenient if Johnson wasn't at the park. That hill was a killer on the knees.

It was time to suit up. A quick glance around the area to make sure nothing was left on the ground or table, then the dim light was turned off and tossed into the trunk. It felt good to ease into the cool water a few seconds later.

There was still no sign of Johnson. No bubbles were coming out of the cave opening. That was good. It would be necessary to keep an eye up ahead once in the cave, ready to scoot off to the side and hide from Johnson to avoid detection. That would be easy. Everything was falling into place. The diver began to relax.

With tanks secured in place and the scooter clipped on, the diver turned on a small mask mounted backup light to begin the journey into the cave. The primary dive light would be used later, either after passing Johnson, or once it was confirmed that Johnson wasn't in the new section. That should be easy enough to determine. Johnson would have jump lines in place.

The main passage was straightforward, and familiarity with it was sufficient to not have to use a more powerful light. The backup light was dim and would make it easier to spot Johnson's much brighter primary light as he was on his way out. It was also quicker to turn off in the event of a Johnson sighting. The diver laughed at the inuendo.

Surprisingly, there was no Johnson encounter all the way back to the thirty-three-hundred-foot line marker where it was necessary to transition from the gold line of the main passage to the maze of passages lined with thinner white cave line that led to the section being explored. There was a jump spool already in place bridging the gap between the gold line and the line in the offshoot tunnel. The initials *JJ* were painted on the side of the spool.

The diver hesitated, not sure what to do. This was one scenario that hadn't been considered. Placing a second jump spool between the lines would tip Johnson...*Johnson tip*...another chuckle...that someone else was in the cave. Not just in the cave, but in the same area of the cave. What was the point of all of the stealth if that one thing would give it away?

Johnson would most certainly retrieve his jump spool on the way out. That would leave a gap between the lines. This was a silty area of the cave. The water flow was minimal. A silt out could eliminate the visibility for hours.

A decision had to be made. Continue forward or turn around and return another day. Two foiled days would be no good. The risk would have to be taken. It was too soon to let anyone know that someone else was exploring the area. Another jump spool line would be a sure giveaway. The intersection of tunnels was a decent size. The chance of it being silted out was minimal. In all of the dives that had been done back there so far, it had never silted out.

With a squeeze of the trigger, the scooter came to life. The gold line was left behind with a chance it wouldn't be connected to the white line on the return. That elicited a feeling of anxiety, but it was necessary. It would be fine.

70

Lindsey

"Hey babe! Time to wake up! It's time to get going."

"Huh? What? What's going on?"

"It's Saturday morning. We have to get going if you're going to meet Gary and Jim on time. I've been texting them."

I bolted up into a seated position, throwing the blanket that had been draped over me to the floor.

"Saturday morning?!? What the hell? You were supposed to wake me up when you got home from work!"

"I tried, Joe. You weren't having it. You wouldn't wake up for anything. I was up for a couple of hours making myself something to eat. I even had the TV blasting, but you didn't stir one bit. You must have been exhausted."

"Holy crap! I can't believe I slept that long. I wanted to spend time with you last night."

"Babe, you were exhausted. It's fine. I was just happy to be back home with you. Even if you were snoring so loud the neighbors were complaining."

"Ha ha. Very funny."

"Seriously, you were snoring loud. I'm not making that up."

I pulled a video up on my phone and played it for him. Joey playfully shoved the phone aside, jumped up, and headed into the bathroom.

"You want me to fix you breakfast?"

"Nah, I'll just have a couple of pop-tarts." He yelled out from the bathroom.

"You can't eat a couple of pop-tarts before a four-hour long dive, Joe. You need something more substantial."

The bathroom door opened, and Joey stepped out.

"I don't know if I want to go diving today without you. I think I'd rather stay home and spend time with you."

"Aww, that's sweet, but Gary and Jim are up and ready to leave once we text them that we're on the way. They really want to see your new section of cave, babe. You don't want to let them down, do you?"

"They'll live."

"C'mon, Joe. I'm coming with you and hanging out while you're diving. I might head to Cave Masters for a couple of hours to hang with Danny. That'll make his day. We'll still have the drive there and back and we'll have tonight to be together. Besides, I know how much you've been wanting to get back into the cave to see what's going on with the additional lines. You'll get a lot more ground covered with the boys. You should go. We should go."

"That's a long time for you to wait for us. It'll probably be four hours."

"Do you not want to go diving?"

"Well, I do. I just don't want to upset you."

"Joe, that's behind us. I think my reaction was due to my pregnancy hormones. Let's go."

I felt a wave of nausea overcome me. That would be the second time this morning. I woke up nauseous and had to run to the bathroom. I barely made it in time. I pushed Joey aside and ran to the bathroom again.

"Linds! What's wrong? Are you okay?"

After I finished throwing up my breakfast, I splashed cold water on my face and gargled some mouthwash.

"I'm fine. It's just morning sickness. It's been happening all week. This should be it. It usually only happens a couple of times each morning and this was number two."

Joey stood there staring at me. I'm sure he didn't know what to make of it. That was okay. This was new to both of us.

"I'll be fine. I promise. I'm getting used to it. You better fix your own breakfast. I don't think I'm ready to face food again for a little while."

"You sure? I mean it. We don't have to do this."

"I've already done enough to screw up the week for both of us. I want to do this."

Half an hour later we were in the car on the way to Marianna. I sent a text to Gary to let him know so he and Jim could get ready to leave in about thirty minutes. That would get us all there at about the same time.

I hadn't seen Kelly's car the night before when I got home from work. She must have been scheduled at the hospital. I had intended on going over and talking to her. I wanted to set her straight on things. What she did to us, what she did to Joey, wasn't acceptable and I wanted her to know it. I was hoping she had just gotten so drunk that she didn't know what she was doing. I didn't like it that drinking so much made her lose her inhibitions. She had been at our place drinking plenty of times. How close had we been to her trying that before? I also didn't like that she had those feelings for Joey, and maybe even for me.

Kelly's usual parking space was still empty when we left for Marianna. I looked for her car but didn't see it anywhere else in the parking lot. She must have had a late morning at work. I planned on talking to her later in the day after we got back. It had to be done. If she worked last night, she should be home tonight. Hopefully she wouldn't be on another drinking binge because this needed to be done with her sober.

"What's the plan for today? You never told me about your dive on Monday. What did you find that day?"

"That's right. I never got a chance to tell you about it."

Joey paused for a moment. I wasn't sure if he was trying to organize his thoughts or going for the dramatic effect. I waited for him to continue.

"I think there's more than one group back there scooping my project. That intersection that we saw. I checked both lines. The line that went straight ended in a large room. I didn't see where the passage might continue, but I might have missed something. I didn't stay there too long looking because I wanted to check out the other line at the intersection."

"It just ended? Was there a line arrow on the end of the line?"

"Yes. At first, I thought it was my initials. The more I thought about it, it could have been JJ instead. I wish I had grabbed it and brought it out with me. I didn't survey or count knots, but the line was probably about fifteen hundred feet long. I couldn't believe how far back it went. This was based on the time it took me to get there."

"Fifteen hundred feet?!? How long were you in the cave?"

"No longer than usual. I scootered the entire distance. The passage was big, and I was able to go full speed. It only took me nine minutes to get to the end of the line. That's about how long it takes me to get to the Hall of the Mountain King."

"Were there other leads along the way? Any other line intersections?"

"No, just that one that we saw and then fifteen hundred feet of line. I'd be willing to bet whoever put that there didn't survey the line."

"So what was down the other line?"

"That was more interesting than going straight. It was a maze over there. I don't think I saw half of the lines that were placed in that area. There were lines everywhere going into offshoot tunnels on both sides of the passage. I couldn't believe how complex it was. It was so confusing that I clipped my scooter off and swam. I was concerned that if I kept scootering, I would miss a line intersection and get lost. There were very few line markers back there. They all had *JS* or *JJ* on them. It was hard to tell which one. I don't know if they ran out or just didn't bother."

"What makes you think there's more than one diver?"

"I don't know. It could be only one, I suppose. But there are a lot of lines back there. I don't see how only one diver would have gotten all that in there in only one week's time. It has to be two or three guys."

"Does it keep going?"

"Probably. I have no idea. I found one area that looped back to the main line. I never got to the end of the other line, though. I checked out a few of the offshoot tunnels. Most of them didn't go very far. I swam about fifteen minutes from the intersection before I had to turn around. I never saw the end of the line. I'd like to take Gary and Jim back to that area so we can join forces and try to get a better idea of what was done there. For all I know, someone has been in there all week and put in more line since I was there on Monday."

"Wow! That's crazy! It does sound like there's more than one diver. It can't be Jack then. I don't see him sharing an exploration project with anyone. Besides, he would have left his markers all over the place to stake his claim. He's not the type to care what you would think if you saw his line arrows. He's like a dog pissing on every tree he passes."

"You have a point."

"Who do you think is doing this? Do you have any idea?"

"I saw a truck pull in on Monday and then take off. I've seen that truck there before, too. But I've never seen who's in it. They've been behaving strange enough that I think they might be the ones doing this. There's another guy I saw. I nicknamed him Maniac Manny. He had a road rage moment in his truck behind me on Monday. I was daydreaming at the light and missed it turning green. He got pissed and started shaking his fists at me while he was laying on the horn. I was able to leave him stuck at the light when it turned red. Then I saw him in Destin. I stopped by the shop to talk to you, but you weren't there. He followed me into the parking lot. I don't know if he followed me all the way from Marianna or if we just happened to cross paths again. He had another road rage moment in the parking lot, though, because I was stopped in front of the shop trying to see if you were in there. He jumped out of his truck and ran toward my car. I got out of the parking lot fast and lost him in traffic. Maybe he's been back there, too.”

"I don't know, Joe. I don't think someone with that kind of personality disorder would have the focus to do dives like that.”

"Maybe not. Either way, he was nuts. I hope I never see him again.”

We remained silent for the rest of the drive. I called Cave Masters when we exited the interstate.

"Cave Masters! This is Danny. How can I help you on this fine Saturday morning?”

"Hey Danny, it's Lindsey Carter.”

"Oh hey, Lindsey. How are you? Are you back already this weekend? Didn't you have a class to teach?”

"Yeah, there was a change of plans. I got another instructor to cover for me. Anyway, can you sign me and Joey in at Jackson Blue?”

"Sure thing! Are y'all diving with Gary and Jim? They just called to sign in, too.”

"Yes, we are. They're finally back from south Florida.”

"Yeah, I saw them on Thursday. They were here to see Joey and stopped in to drop off their tanks. How long will y'all be diving today? How far back do ya plan on going?”

"The dive should be about four hours long, so you shouldn't expect to hear from us for six or seven hours.”

"Wow! Four hours! That's a long time! Seems everyone's been doing long dives in there lately.”

"Who's everyone, Danny?”

"Oh, maybe I shouldn't have said anything.”

"It's okay. You can tell me. I won't say anything.” I said in my most seductive voice knowing it would melt Danny right where he stood. He started giggling.

"Oh, I guess it's okay to tell you. Ummm, Jack Johnson has been doing long dives. Well, except a couple of days ago when he had to be airlifted to Pensacola. But he's alright and was already back in the water yesterday. There were also these guys named Brad and Steve. They've been doing long dives. And this other guy named Mark. That's pretty much it besides you and Joey.”

"Hmmmm… Interesting. Thanks, Danny! We'll stop by on our way out to top off our tanks."

"Alright, see you later!"

I ended the call and turned toward Joey.

"So Jack was diving yesterday. That's interesting. You'd think after having an issue in the cave that you had to rescue him from, he'd take a few days off. He must be one of the divers going back there."

"I don't know. Like you said, he's not one to go incognito. He would want everyone to know he was exploring new passage."

"He would have two years ago. Maybe he's changed since the ceiling fell on him."

"Could be."

"Danny also mentioned a couple of guys named Brad and Steve. Ring any bells?"

"None at all. Never heard of them. They might be the ones in the truck that's been doing strange things."

"He also mentioned a diver named Mark."

"That could be Maniac Manny. I guess I'll have to start calling him Maniac Mark… Nah! I like Manny better." Joey laughed.

A minute later we turned off of Blue Spring Road and Joey stopped the car in front of the gate. I opened my door to unlock the gate and felt Joey's hand on my arm.

"I'll get it. You don't need to overexert yourself."

"Don't start that, Mister! I'm barely pregnant. I can still do things. When and if the doctor tells me I need to slow down, then you can wait on me hand and foot. Until then, I WILL still do things."

I stepped out of the car and walked to the gate to open it. Joey pulled the car through just as Gary and Jim pulled up. I waved them through.

"Why thank you ma'am! I didn't know we were going to have first-class service this morning. I would have brought some money to tip you." Jim laughed.

"Yeah, yeah, smart ass! Just pull through so I can close the gate before anyone else pulls up. I'm not staying here to let everyone in.

It's great to see you guys again!"

"It's great to see you, Lindsey! You owe me a Coke!" Gary and Jim both laughed.

"Y'all haven't changed a bit!"

"It's only been a month! You owe me a Coke!"

I rolled my eyes and laughed at them. Some things never changed. After the week I'd had, it felt good to be with my people again. It felt good to laugh.

I closed the gate once they were on the other side of it and got back into the car with Joey. He drove toward the turn off down to the pavilions near the water. I noticed a car partially hidden from view behind the pavilion on the other side of the spring basin. I couldn't tell what kind of car it was. It was strange that someone would park up there, though. The only person I knew to park on the other side of the spring basin was Doron Nof. He was a Florida State University professor that studied oceanography and pretty much anything to do with water. He was diving at Jackson Blue almost every weekend. He had polio when he was younger so he would park his little silver Toyota Celica right next to the water on the other side of the basin. It was interesting watching him drive his car along the stepped landscape down to the water. He got it done. He was a really nice guy. I enjoyed talking to him and looked forward to catching up with him later while he got ready for his dive.

There were a couple of trucks where we usually parked. One of them was Jack Johnson's. He was here early. Danny said he was diving last night. He didn't mention Jack being back again this morning. He must have stayed in the area overnight and gotten here before the shop opened. I didn't recognize the other truck.

"Is that truck next to Jack's one that you've seen here before? Maybe Brad and Steve's? Or Maniac Mark's?"

"No, that truck belongs to a cave diver from Alabama. He's this tall, goofy guy with a heavy Alabama accent. I've seen him here a few times. He was diving with some German cave diver a few times. They usually lay a blue tarp out on the ground to change on. It's interesting that Jack is here so early, though. He's been diving in the afternoons or evenings."

"Danny mentioned he was diving yesterday evening. Holy shit! Do you think something happened to him on his dive last night? Do you think he's still in the cave?"

71

Joey

I didn't know what to think. After seeing the way Jack was on Thursday afternoon, I didn't think he would be diving for a long while. If Danny hadn't said Jack was diving last night, I would have thought he hadn't picked up his truck since his incident two days earlier. What the hell was he doing back in the water so soon?

"I hope he's not. Should we call Danny and ask him if Jack signed out last night?"

"I doubt he signed out. The shop would have been closed by then."

"Then maybe he signed in this morning."

"Maybe. I'll call Danny and ask."

I got out of the car to say hi to Gary and Jim while Lindsey stayed and called Danny.

"Hey guys! How was your drive? You ready for this? You think you'll remember how to cave dive? It's been a while since you've been in the water. You might need a refresher course."

Gary and Jim both laughed.

"Ha ha. A month isn't that long. I think we'll pick it back up pretty quickly." Jim answered.

"You know, though, I think this has been the longest we've been out of the water since we finished our cave diving training. Can you believe that?"

"We were out here almost every weekend. I really missed it. I can't wait to get back in the cave and see those beautiful wet rocks!"

"Well, just in case, y'all better follow me. I wouldn't want either of you to get lost."

"You're a riot." Jim laughed.

It felt good to be back with the guys getting ready to go for a dive. With the stress of the past week, this was exactly what I needed.

Lindsey stepped out of the car and walked toward us, a worried expression on her face.

"Hey Joe, Danny said Jack didn't sign in this morning."

"Oh crap! That's not good."

"No, it isn't."

"I guess we're going to have to look for him. Are we still allowed to dive or are they shutting it down?"

"Danny didn't say. He said he was going to make a few calls. He seemed really nervous, like he knew more than he was saying, which isn't like Danny. I've never known him to keep any secrets, especially when it comes to cave diving."

"Maybe I was wrong about Jack not being one of the divers scooping my project. I thought for sure he would never go incognito on something like that. Maybe he was."

"I think you're right. I have a bad feeling about this. He shouldn't have gone diving so soon after being airlifted from here.

"Yeah, well, it looks like he did. We better set up our equipment and get in there." I turned toward Gary and Jim. "Y'all will probably still get a chance to see my exploration area. I have a feeling that's where we'll find Jack."

I opened the trunk, pulled my scuba tanks out, and placed them on one of the picnic tables. Then I grabbed the scooters from the back seat. Even though I was diving with Gary and Jim, I was bringing Lindsey's scooter as a backup. Better to have it and not need it than to have to tow each other out if one of the scooters had an issue during the dive. I started setting up my equipment.

"Hey, where are your tanks, Linds? Aren't you diving with us?"

"Well, Gary, you see, I'm dry docked for a while."

"Dry docked? What happened? Did you get bent while we were gone."

Lindsey laughed.

"Funny, Jim. You know if anyone is going to get bent it will be Joey, not me! No, I can't dive for the next nine months."

Gary and Jim stopped what they were doing as they processed what Lindsey told them. Then they both rushed her and grabbed her into a bear hug between the two of them.

"Holy shit! Congratulations! That's amazing!"

"Yep, you're both going to be uncles." I said from behind them.

Gary and Jim reached out and grabbed me and pulled me into their hug. We stood there and held each other for several seconds.

"Alright, that's enough of this. Let me out of here before you suffocate me and the baby. And I'm not talking about Joey this time."

Everyone laughed. I was the youngest of the group.

We turned back to our equipment and finished setting it up. Once the scuba tanks and scooters were on the retaining wall, we pulled on our undergarments and drysuits. We were silent the entire time while we thought about the dive we were about to undertake.

"You sure you want to do this, Joe? You have some new things to consider now. You can't put yourself at risk willy-nilly anymore."

"Yeah, I'm good, G. I'm not going to do anything stupid. Besides, y'all don't even know how to get where we're going. Even if I told you, it's confusing."

"Alright, but if you change your mind at any point, even when we're in the cave, just say so."

"I will."

We became silent again as we continued to suit up. Once we had our drysuits on, we walked to the water and jumped in. We did this from the retaining wall. No diving board antics for us this morning. I wasn't looking forward to this dive. It was all too reminiscent of my dive in Eddy Spring more than four years ago. I just wanted to do a nice leisurely dive with my friends and show them the cave passages I had found. I didn't want to be looking for another dead body in a cave. Especially not someone I knew, even if it was Jack.

We clipped our tanks onto our harnesses while Lindsey called Cave

Masters to update Danny on the situation.

"Danny called his boss and they're trying to figure out what to do. He said that if you find a body to bring it out and then we'll call the sheriff's office. If you don't find it, they'll start contacting other cave divers to head over and begin a search."

"That's gonna be like looking for a needle in a haystack. This cave is huge. There are so many tunnels he could have gone into. And if he did make it back to my area, that's going to make it even more difficult. I don't know how we'll get his body through the restrictions in the Freiway."

"Don't put yourself at risk, Joe. You boys either. It's not worth it. If you find Jack, remember that he's dead. There's no urgency in getting his body out. It's not worth putting yourselves in danger."

"Yes ma'am." The three of us replied. The boys didn't even respond to saying the same thing at the same time in the usual fashion. Our normal antics were behind us. The thought of Jack being dead in the cave was looming over our heads. He was an ass, but he didn't deserve to die that way. No one did. There was nothing in that cave worth dying for.

"I expect to see bubbles coming out of the opening within three hours."

"Better make it three and a half. It might take us a little longer to make our way out."

"Okay, three and a half. At least one of you needs to be back in the Deco Room blowing bubbles out of the cave."

Normally, one of us would have made some juvenile comment about blowing bubbles, but we all remained silent. The mood was somber.

"Be careful; all of you! I love you all. Especially you, Joe. You better come back to me! You have a baby to think about now."

"I love you, too, Linds. Don't worry. I'll be back."

"Love ya, girl," the boys said in unison.

We descended below the surface of the water, got horizontal, and situated our scuba tanks. I looked at Gary and Jim. I could see the seriousness in their eyes. It wasn't a look I was used to seeing. This was not the way to resume diving after a month-long hiatus.

I turned toward the opening of the cave and hit the trigger on my scooter. The propellor began spinning. I steered into the opening and into the darkness beyond.

72

Lindsey

I watched the boys disappear into the cave. I checked the time. It was twelve past ten. I should see bubbles from their exhalations no later than one forty-two. I set an alarm on my phone. I looked back at the surface of the water. Bubbles continued to escape the cave for about a minute after they entered the opening. Then the bubbles stopped. They were gone. The boys must be heading down the chimney fissure by now.

I was worried. They were all capable divers and could do this. I knew Joey could. He pulled the body of that dead diver out of Eddy Spring years ago not long after he got certified. The difference between then and now was that he didn't know the diver back then. He had no clue who he was. He had never met him.

Joey knew Jack, though. Even if we didn't like Jack, it was different when you knew a person. Gary and Jim had never had to deal with this. This would be their first time encountering a dead body in a cave. I didn't know how they would respond to it. They seemed to be okay with what they were about to do. But things changed when you were faced with them head on.

I hoped none of them pushed themselves too hard. I knew they were competitive with each other. None of them would want to be the first to call the dive. None of them would want to seem like the weak link. I hoped they could put their egos aside for safety's sake. Just this one time.

I walked back to the parking lot and looked inside Jack's truck.

What if he had left the truck parked here for some reason? What if he wasn't in the cave? I wish I had thought to look before the boys began their dive. I looked in through the front passenger door window. There was nothing in the front seat. When I tried to look through the back door window, I couldn't see into the back seat. The tint was too dark. I looked in the bed of the truck and didn't see anything in there either. If he was out of the cave, his scuba tanks would be there. Jack had to be in the cave.

I had three and a half hours to kill. Maybe not the best way to put it. Three and a half hours to endure while the boys did their thing. I had planned on lying out in the sun and finishing the book I had been reading, but my mind wasn't up for that. I didn't think I could focus on it. I was too worried about the boys. I shouldn't have let them go in there. I should have insisted they let someone else go into the cave to look for Jack.

The problem was that no one knew about this new section. Well, not many people knew about it. It was just Joey and possibly Jack. Or was it? Could there be others going back there? What about the guys Danny mentioned? Brad, Steve, and Mark. The more I considered it, the more it seemed like there could be others scooping Joe's leads. Joe knew it best, though. He found it and he could get there faster than most anyone. I hoped he kept his mind focused. I wished I could be in there with him.

I grabbed my phone and called Cave Masters again. "Hey Danny, the boys just started their dive. I don't expect them back until after one thirty."

"Wow! That's gonna be a long dive!"

"That's just to get back to the Deco Room. They're going to have an hour or more of decompression stops before they can surface after that. Can you get in touch with someone to be here and ready to get into the water so they can pass the body out and not have to stare at it during their decompression?"

"Yeah, I'll make a few calls and track someone down." Danny paused for a few seconds. "Hey, wait! Why aren't you diving with them? Or why can't you go in to get the body from them?"

I didn't know how to respond to that. I wasn't ready for the world to know I was pregnant. Gary and Jim were one thing. They were like brothers to me. Danny was a good kid, but I couldn't call him a friend. He was more of an acquaintance. Besides, he talked a lot. If I told him I was pregnant, every cave diver in a five-hundred-mile radius would know by this afternoon.

"Oh, I, um, I injured myself this past week. Twisted my ankle. I was supposed to be teaching a class this weekend and had to find someone to substitute for me. I would probably be okay just going into the cavern, but it wouldn't look very good for me to be diving after passing my class off to another instructor. Besides, I don't have my scuba equipment or my drysuit."

"Aw, man! Sorry to hear that! That really sucks! Dontchoo worry, though! I'll find someone."

"Thanks, Danny." I looked around the park and noticed the car on the other side of the basin behind the pavilion. "Oh, hey Danny, who else signed in to dive this morning. Besides Jack's truck, I see another truck and a car parked here."

"That's strange. Only one other person signed in this morning besides y'all and the Tally boys. Just a fellow from Alabama named Eric."

"Okay, well maybe the car belongs to someone who works for the county parks department. It's not parked down where we all usually park."

"Yeah, that's probably it. They might be doing some maintenance or something."

"Let me know who you find to come help, Danny. I'll talk to you later."

"Bye, Lindsey."

I ended the call and walked to the pavilion. I sat at one of the tables and scrolled through my social media accounts. Nothing exciting there. It was Saturday so most of the people I had connections with would be diving and not online. I continued to scroll, looking at posts that were made during the week. I hadn't spent a lot of time on social media during my hotel stay. It was too depressing. I saw that I hadn't missed much.

As I was scrolling, it occurred to me that it was Saturday. What would someone from county parks be doing here on a weekend? I got up and ran around the spring basin, up the hill, and toward the pavilion with the car parked behind it. As I got closer and saw more of the car, I got a sense of familiarity. When I reached the top of the hill and was able to see the entire car, it hit me. I knew that car. I knew who that car belonged to.

Fuck!

73

Joey

We cruised at top speed on our scooters through the main passage of Jackson Blue. We were moving close to two hundred feet per minute. That was a fast pace to be moving through a cave, especially one that had some smaller sections. We were all experienced and skilled and could easily handle it. At the moment, it seemed like we weren't moving fast enough.

It would take us about fifty minutes to get to the new cave passages. Then we'd have to begin the search. It was possible Jack hadn't gone back there. It was possible he went somewhere else and got himself in trouble in a different area of the cave. I didn't think it was likely though. At least we hadn't come across his body in the main passage yet. We were already in the Trash Room and there hadn't been any signs of him.

Two days earlier, Jack had a nine-minute decompression stop according to his dive computer. He couldn't have gone very far into the cave. I doubted he had gotten as far as the Trash Room. I wondered if he made it this far last night.

We arrived at Stage Rock and stopped to drop off the stage tanks we had been breathing from. I saw a stage tank already secured to the line. It had to be Jack's. It was our first confirmation that he was not only in the cave, but beyond this point. We secured our stage tanks to the line next to Jack's and continued our progression through the cave to our next stop eight hundred feet farther in.

Four minutes later, I was placing a jump line from the gold line in the main passage to the white cave line in the offshoot tunnel we had to take to get to the area of the cave I had been exploring. There was no other jump line in place. That didn't mean anything, though. Jack was known for doing visual jumps, jumps in which a line wasn't used to close the gaps between two other lines. It was a dangerous practice. If the silt was disturbed and visibility was diminished, it would be very difficult to find the other line, especially with a lengthy gap. This gap was about forty feet long.

When I finished closing the gap, I pulled my scooter around and hit the trigger again. The boys followed close behind. There were no more gaps, but there were plenty of line intersections ahead. I steered with my left hand as I retrieved my line markers from my pocket and clipped the holder to one of the D rings on my chest. I saw the first intersection appear in the distance and got a non-directional line marker ready to place on the exit side. That would allow me to know which way was out if the visibility was disturbed.

I had flashbacks to pulling the body out of Eddy Spring a couple of months after I was scuba certified. I hadn't been able to see a thing. I also didn't have a guideline to lead me out of the cave. There was a large pipe, but that didn't help when I lost control of my buoyancy and popped up to the ceiling. I was a much newer diver back then. I didn't have good buoyancy control and didn't know how to fin properly so that I wouldn't stir up the sediment on the floor. There were so many things I didn't know back then. It was a miracle I didn't die.

I shifted my speed down so I could place a marker on the guideline. I followed the line heading off to the right. I prepared another marker for the next intersection which was less than a minute away.

Ten minutes and six line intersections later, we were at the restriction leading into the Freiway. This would be Gary and Jim's first time going through it. I released the trigger on my scooter and coasted to a stop. I placed another marker on the line and turned to swim toward the restriction. I moved as slowly as I could, trying to minimize the amount of sediment I stirred up. It was impossible to pass through the restriction without disturbing it at all. It was too small.

The good thing was that there was a lot of sand on the floor in the area. The bad thing was that there was also mud mixed in. It would be hazy for a while. The current coming out of the Freiway was strong enough that by the time we got back, it would be clear. At least we had that going for us.

I got to the restriction and unclipped my scooter from the D ring on my waist. I clipped the scooter to my second stage tank and pushed it through the small space in front of me. My stage tank followed. I had been breathing from the tank, so the pressure had decreased enough to make it neutrally buoyant.

The floor in the restriction was mostly comprised of sand granules and happened to be located in a bend in the passage. The strong current pushed the granules that were stirred up by my stage tank past me to the side of the passage. This helped maintain good visibility behind me for Gary and Jim.

With the scooter and stage tank through the restriction, I followed behind. I had to turn my head sideways to prevent the regulator in my mouth from digging into the sandy bottom and getting clogged. Fortunately, the restriction was bigger than it had been the first time I encountered it. Going through it so many times over the past month had caused some of the sand to be displaced and gave me more clearance. Some of it fell back toward the middle during the week, but it got a little bigger every weekend. Over the past few weekends, it seemed to be growing in size exponentially. That was clear evidence that other divers were going through it.

When I had completely passed through the restriction, I looked back and saw Jim pushing his scooter and stage tank toward me. He hadn't hesitated. I was more concerned about him than I was about Gary. Gary and I had been in small passages during our trip to Cozumel earlier in the year and I knew what he was comfortable with. This was the smallest restriction I had witnessed Jim going through, but he was also the smallest of the three of us. This wasn't as much of a restriction for him as it was for me. I moved forward to make room for Jim. Once he was through, I started swimming forward to give Gary room.

The next eight hundred feet was a combination of swimming and scootering. The passage got big enough in some areas to scooter, but then the ceiling and walls squeezed in requiring us to release the scooter triggers and swim. It took us about ten minutes to get to a passage that was big enough for all three of us to face each other. A couple of hundred feet later, we were at the Firehose Restriction. Our second stage tanks were secured to the guideline about thirty feet before it. Another one of Jack's stage tanks was also clipped to the line.

The current coming through the Firehose Restriction was so strong that my scooter couldn't overpower it. With the scooter at full speed, the current still pushed me backwards. I had to kick my fins and pull myself through to get to the other side of it. Fortunately, it was only about thirty feet long. On the other side of the restriction was a large room where the current was barely discernable. This was where the real search began.

We hit the triggers and made our way through the passage, looking for signs of Jack. Twenty minutes later, we hadn't found any evidence Jack had been there. I didn't go to the end of the line that terminated in a dead end. I didn't think Jack would bother with that. Instead, I focused on the maze of lines I had found on Monday. That was the area being actively searched. That had to be the area where Jack was going.

Except he wasn't there. There were no signs that he had been. Then again, we didn't know how much area we hadn't covered. There could be passages that we didn't know about. There could be a passage with a line that wasn't connected to the lines we found.

With that in mind, we turned around and began a slow exit. We were going to focus our attention on the walls. Maybe Jack had done another jump without installing a line to close the gap. Another possibility was that something happened to Jack in the main passage and the current pushed his body toward the side of the tunnel and into a nook. I remembered the stage tank before the Firehose restriction. Jack had to be back here. I checked my pressure gauges. I had sufficient air in my scuba tanks, even with enough in reserve in case we found Jack's body. I was certain Gary and Jim had about the same pressure in theirs.

I signaled Jim to stay near the line while Gary and I searched along the walls. We had done that in Cozumel with Lindsey on the line. It made it easier to check beyond the shadows along the walls. Maybe we would find Jack's body hidden in the darkness beyond where our light beams reached.

The line was positioned close to the wall on the right, often touching it, so Gary and I moved along the wall on the left side. Jim remained above the line and searched that wall in case we had missed something. We tried to stay no more than twenty feet away from him. I swam along, poking my head into every hole I found.

In one of the alcoves, I came across cave line tied to a protrusion. It wasn't just an alcove. It was a restriction leading to a larger tunnel. I wondered if it was connected to the maze of lines we had just come from. Was it the end of one of the lines? Or did this lead to a different area of the cave?

I signaled Gary and Jim to hold their positions. I swam back to the main guideline, clipped my scooter to it, and placed one of my line markers next to the clip. I grabbed a jump spool, secured one end of the line to the marker, and turned, spooling line out as I swam toward the line I had just found. I went to one alcove but didn't see any line when I poked my head inside. I moved back from the wall and reassessed it. I had gone to the wrong location. There was another alcove to the right. I swam to that one and found the line around the corner.

I wondered if Jack would have gone into this restriction without closing the gap. He had already left one gap open. He probably also left this one open. It made no sense because there was no way to move through this restriction without disturbing the sediment on the floor. I knew Jack thought he was the best of the best, but even he wouldn't think he could get through this restriction without disturbing the sediment. Or would he?

I secured the spool to the line I found and pushed myself through. I popped out into another passage that was almost as big as the one I came from. It was amazing. It was the most beautiful part of this area of the cave. The ceiling was at least thirty feet above my head and the walls had to be forty feet apart. The rock formations were incredible. There were striations of colors running the length of the walls as far as my light beam penetrated.

As I hovered at the entrance to this room frozen in awe, I saw a light appear from behind. I almost jumped out of my drysuit. It was Gary. He had followed me and was coming out of the silt cloud I created. I tried to regain control of my breathing and to slow my heart rate down. Looking for a dead body was creeping me out.

I swam forward into the new passage. I felt anger build up inside of me. I was angry at Jack for coming back here and finding this before I did. I was angry at him for stealing the glory from me. I was angry at him for being the first person to see what I should have seen first. This was my project. He should have stayed out. He should have respected it. Even if I wasn't saying anything about my exploration in here, my line markers with my initials were all over the place. It was obvious that I was the one exploring the area. It was obvious that it was ongoing exploration.

I tried to push my feelings of anger aside. It wouldn't do me any good. Jack was dead. I needed to find his body and get it out of here. Or at least get it back to the main passage of Jackson Blue so someone else could bring it the rest of the way out of the cave.

I slowly followed the line. Jim popped out of the restriction and joined us. I wished I had brought one of the scooters. Swimming was going slow. We might not make it to the body before we had to turn to exit. We went around the next corner, and that's when I saw it. A scooter secured to the guideline. The current pushing it so that it was pointing directly at me.

A few feet after the scooter was another stage tank secured to the line. We had found the area where Jack had gone. As I got closer, I noticed something strange about the scuba tank. It wasn't an aluminum eighty scuba tank like we usually used for stage tanks. This tank had a rounded bottom. It was a steel tank. It appeared to be a sidemount tank. It was rigged like a sidemount tank. That was strange. I wondered what would make Jack remove one of his sidemount tanks and leave it behind.

I swam past the tank. Something else felt off about it, but I couldn't put my finger on it. About ten feet later the line ended. It was secured to a protrusion coming out of the wall. A few feet beyond the end of the line I saw a set of black fins sticking out from a restriction in the wall on the left.

74

Joey

I signaled the boys and focused my light on Jack's fin tips. We stopped and took a moment to let the situation sink in before doing anything. It looked like Jack was tightly wedged into the restriction. The real work was about to begin. It was not going to be an easy task.

I swam toward the fins and grabbed one of Jack's ankles. I had more flashbacks to the dead diver in Eddy Spring. I pushed them aside. Now wasn't the time to get squeamish. Gary swam up next to me and grabbed the other ankle. Jim hung back and provided light for us to see what we were doing. I counted off to three with my fingers and we slowly pulled back. Jack didn't budge. Not even an inch. It appeared he had done a good job of getting himself stuck. I held my hand up to signal Gary and Jim to wait. I wanted to try something.

I pushed my hand in above Jack's legs. More flashbacks to my dive in Eddy Spring came to mind. This time I couldn't push them aside as easily. Having to reach into an area that I couldn't see was having an effect on me. I was a little freaked out about touching a dead body. Jack's dead body. It wasn't as disturbing as it had been four years earlier touching that body I found beyond the grate, but it wasn't something I wanted to be doing.

At Eddy Spring, I was a new diver. What Earl made me do had messed with my head, and I didn't even know the dead guy I had found. For some reason, trying to recover Jack's body wasn't bothering me as much. I didn't know if it was because it was someone I knew, even though he was an asshole, or if I had matured and become more tolerant of these things over the years.

It wasn't that I was tolerant of touching dead bodies. This was only the second dead human body I had touched. I had lots of experience touching dead pets, though. Maybe that had hardened me. Touching dead pets continued to bother me, even after having done it more than a hundred times. It still made me feel sad when furry creatures died. I didn't have any of those feelings in this situation.

I tried to squeeze my hand between Jack's body and the ceiling of the restriction. I was attempting to reach the exhaust valve on his buoyancy compensator. I didn't know if it would make a difference. Jack should have let all of the air out of it before he tried to go into the restriction. I tried anyway. I pushed my arm in as far as it would go, but I couldn't reach the valve. The dive computer on my wrist was preventing my arm from moving farther.

I pulled my hand back and pushed the dive computer up my arm so it was closer to my elbow. I started to put my hand back into the restriction but thought better of it. The dive computer would still prevent me from reaching far enough. With my hand back out, I slid the dive computer completely off of my arm and handed it to Jim. I slid my arm back into the restriction.

This time I got my hand far enough in to feel Jack's BC. I moved my hand back and forth trying to find the cord to the exhaust valve. After several seconds, I found it and grabbed it between my index and middle fingers. I pulled it toward me. I didn't feel any change. I don't know if I would have. I wasn't sure if I had made a difference. I pulled my arm out so Gary and I could try to pull Jack out again.

We grabbed his ankles and pulled even harder this time. We weren't going to hurt Jack. He was already dead. We tried to remain respectful, but we had to get his body out. I thought I felt the body move. I couldn't be sure. If it had, it wasn't very far. I reached in again to feel around and see if Jack was caught on anything. This time I noticed that his drysuit seemed to have a lot of air in it. That was strange. He should have exhausted the air from his drysuit before going into the restriction. Unless…

I signaled Gary to move aside so I could get on Jack's left side. Drysuit inflators are located on the chest. I remembered one time when I was going through a restriction, I had been squeezed between the floor and ceiling tightly enough that the button on my drysuit inflator was depressed. My drysuit filled with air. Had I not stopped and pushed myself back, I would have gotten wedged in the restriction.

My guess was that Jack had done the same thing, only he didn't try to back out. He kept pushing forward and wedged himself even worse. He probably couldn't reach across to open the exhaust valve on his left shoulder to let the air out. Maybe I could squeeze beside him in the restriction and open the exhaust valve. My other option was cutting his drysuit, but that would allow water into the suit and make it difficult to bring him out of the cave. That would be a last resort.

I assessed the space to Jack's left. It was small. I wasn't sure I would fit, even if I took a scuba tank off and left it behind like Jack had. I couldn't understand why he would attempt to do something like that. What had he been thinking? It was one thing to plan on doing a single tank no mount penetration into a restriction, but it was another thing to do an impromptu no mount penetration using a scuba tank set up for sidemount diving. What did Jack think he would do once he got to the other side of the restriction? Was he going to continue without his second tank? I had so many questions. None of which would ever be answered.

I thought about the layout of the cave. The picture in my head indicated that the restriction was heading toward the maze of lines we just came from. We couldn't be far from that area. Did Jack know about that other area? Had he been to it? Was he aware of the proximity? Or was he trying to find a shortcut?

I didn't see the point in any of it. If this restriction was supposed to be a shortcut, it wasn't much of one. It wouldn't do divers any good if they had to remove a scuba tank to get through. The situation was strange. It seemed out of character for Jack. Sure, he was an ass, but he wasn't stupid. Or was he?

There was no way I would fit into the space beside Jack. I was too big. But Jim might fit. When it came to cave diving, being small was advantageous. I faced Jim and signaled toward the space to the left of the body. I twisted the exhaust valve on my own left shoulder and pointed at Jack. Jim understood what I was asking him to do. He moved toward the restriction, unclipped one of his sidemount tanks, and pushed it in front of him. There wasn't enough room in the restriction next to Jack to go in with both tanks at his sides. Gary and I watched nervously as Jim wiggled his way in, clouds of sediment pouring out from around him.

When Jim's torso was swallowed by the restriction, he stopped moving. All we could see of him were his fins. I held my breath as I waited. I began to doubt myself for asking Jim to go into the restriction. It was a mistake. Jim was going to get stuck and we'd have to get him out before he breathed through all of his air. At least he had both of his tanks accessible. But we were more than a mile from the opening.

Jim's fins began moving slowly as he tried to reach the drysuit exhaust valve. I watched bubbles escape from the silt cloud as he exhaled. About a minute after he stopped his forward movement, Jim crossed his fins. That was the scuba signal for being stuck. My shoulders sank.

Gary bolted forward and grabbed Jim's left ankle. I moved with him and grabbed the right one. We pulled back. He wasn't moving. Jim was stuck in the restriction next to Jack's body. I got creeped out thinking about it. Gary and I pulled harder. We tugged on Jim's legs while trying not to hurt him. I could feel Jim trying to wiggle his upper body. A few seconds later, whatever had a hold of Jim released its grip on him and he came flying out. A giant cloud of sediment followed. I exhaled the breath I was holding, relieved.

When Jim was back among us and had his scuba tanks situated, he gave us the okay signal, a circle formed with his thumb and index finger. He seemed to be unfazed by having been stuck. I was thankful for that, but I was chastising myself for asking him to put himself in danger like that. We could have lost him. I would never have forgiven myself.

Jim aimed his light beam at Jack's feet. They were barely visible in the silt cloud that was still hanging in the water. Gary and I each grabbed an ankle and pulled. Jack's body didn't move. I braced myself on the wall above the restriction not caring about creating more disturbance in the visibility. It was already down to five feet. I pulled harder. Gary did the same on his side. The body broke loose and began coming toward us. Gary and I continued pulling. About half a minute later, we had extracted Jack's body from the restriction.

Jack's feet floated toward the ceiling. He was almost upside down. The silt cloud continued to grow and enveloped Jack's torso and head. All we saw were his legs protruding from the top of the cloud. All of the weight he had was distributed around his torso. The scuba tanks that he normally had attached to his harness accounted for some of the weight that made him neutrally buoyant. With only one tank, he was positively buoyant. And that tank had been unclipped from the harness at the waist and pushed in front of him. It was also empty.

The sediment continued to pour out of the restriction. We had to get Jack situated and away from the area before the entire room was engulfed in silt. I reached through the cloud around Jack's torso and found his scuba tank. It was hanging below his body.

I pulled the tank back as Gary and Jim pushed down on Jack's legs. I clipped the bottom of the tank to the harness. The redistribution of weight brought Jack's legs down and put his body into a sideways orientation with the scuba tank lying on the floor of the cave.

Jim swam to retrieve Jack's other sidemount tank and brought it to us. We would need it to balance Jack's body. While Jim clipped the top of the tank to the left side D ring on Jack's chest, Gary clipped the bottom of the tank to a D ring on Jack's waist. With both tanks secured, Jack's body settled onto the floor face down. We pulled it away from the silt cloud so we could prepare to bring it out. I looked at it and thought about how small Jack looked in this state. He looked like only a fraction of the man he had been.

I turned to Gary and Jim. It was time to decide how we were going to get Jack out of the cave. Jim was writing something in his wetnotes. A few seconds later, he handed them to me. He had come up with a plan.

75

Joey

I took the lead position while Gary and Jim were at opposite sides of Jack's body, each holding one of his arms. We retrieved Jack's scooter from the line and secured it to the D ring on his waist. I clipped the tow line on the front of the scooter to the same D ring I clipped my scooter to. I towed the scooter which, in turn, towed the body. Gary and Jim assisted from behind. When the walls got narrow, they took turns to make sure the body remained on a good plane behind me.

Once we were back through the restriction, we retrieved our own scooters. We used the low speeds on them and pitched the propellers down so we weren't flying through the cave at two hundred feet per minute. Even with the slower pace, the three of us working together made good progress. We had open passage until the Firehose Restriction.

Getting through the Firehose Restriction was no easy undertaking. We unclipped the scooter to get through. I went first, stopped on the other side, and turned around to face the restriction. Gary and Jim then let go of Jack's body and the current pushed it toward me. I put my hands out and caught Jack's shoulders. He seemed so diminutive in this state. Lindsey and I had helped him out of Jackson Blue after the ceiling fell on him, and I had pulled him out of the water only two days earlier. He wasn't a small man. But here, in the cave, lifeless, he seemed small.

We made it through the Firehose Restriction and into the Freiway where our stage tanks were waiting for us. We left them behind. It would be too difficult to bring them along with the scooters and Jack's body. We checked the air pressure in our tanks and decided we had plenty of air to get to the Deco Room. Besides, Lindsey and I had safety tanks that could be retrieved and used, if necessary.

On the other side of the Firehose Restriction, we reattached the scooter to Jack's harness. I held the tow line in my hand as Gary moved behind Jack. Jim was behind Gary. About a hundred feet later, we moved into the Freiway which was too narrow for us to move through in anything but a linear formation.

The current in the Freiway was strong. It would be both a help and a hindrance. It would help us move along quickly, but there were a few twists and turns that would be difficult to negotiate and would slow us down. It didn't help that we also had our scooters with us. We couldn't leave those behind. We needed them to expedite our exit once we were in the main passage.

We had eight hundred feet to traverse before we could use the scooters again. I pushed my scooter in front of me while towing Jack's scooter and his body. Gary followed behind Jack, controlling his legs. Jim pushed Lindsey's scooter in front of him. Gary and Jim towed their own scooters behind them. That's how we moved through the Freiway. One long train. I thought about leaving Jack's scooter behind but decided against that. We were using it to tow him out. We might need it if one of our scooters stopped working. The additional drag of Jack's body would suck up the batteries fast.

We continued through the Freiway. There were a couple of areas where Jack's body was pushed into alcoves, and we had to pull it back and redirect it. Other than that, the traverse went smoothly. Until we arrived at the final restriction. This one was going to be a tough one. It was the smallest restriction we had to pass through. I stopped before we got into the part of the tunnel where there was no turning back.

I motioned for Jim to hand me the scooters he had and move ahead. I took Gary's scooter from him. I clipped the five scooters in line and directed Jim toward the restriction. I signaled him to go first and turn around once he was on the other side. I would push the first scooter into the restriction toward him. Jim would pull the scooter train through while I maintained tension so they wouldn't bunch up before getting across to the other side. I would follow the scooters and turn around to help Gary get Jack's body through. It would have been easier if we could cut Jack's body into little pieces, but that wasn't going to happen.

My plan worked. It took about fifteen minutes, but we got through the restriction with minimal issues. We only had to reposition the scooters twice and Jack's body once. It was time to implement part two of Jim's plan.

We took back our scooters. I clipped Jack's to his harness with the tow rope clipped to my harness. We would scooter out the same way we had before we got to the Firehose Restriction. I was going to tow Jack while Gary and Jim kept Jack's body streamlined by maneuvering his legs. It had worked for the short distance before the Freiway. I was hoping it would continue to work over the next four thousand feet of passage. Once we were in position, I crossed my fingers and hit the trigger.

We made it back to the main passage in fifteen minutes. It took us five minutes longer than usual. That was without stopping to retrieve our line markers. There was no time for that. Without our stage tanks, there wasn't enough air. I was beginning to regret the decision to leave them behind. I checked the air pressure in my sidemount tanks. I was still okay. I tried to run the math in my head accounting for a fifty percent increase in time to exit. It would be close. We might have to use the safety tanks. I prepared myself mentally for the possibility of leaving Jack's body in the cave for someone else to recover.

Once we were in the main passage and had the current pushing us out, things went much easier. We moved faster. It wasn't as fast as we normally exited, but it wasn't going to take us fifty percent longer either. I did more calculations in my head as we zoomed through the cave. It was only going to take us about a quarter longer than normal. We could work with that. We wouldn't need the safety tanks. We also wouldn't have to leave Jack's body clipped to the line in the cave.

We stopped to retrieve the stage tanks we had left at Stage Rock. Jim held onto the body while Gary and I secured our stage tanks to our harnesses. As soon as we were set, Gary and I continued to make our way out while Jim retrieved his stage tank. We moved slowly enough that Jim would be able to catch up.

The only area that I thought might slow us down was between the Trash Room and the Rabbit Hole. That passage was low, and the current was fast. There was also a sharp left turn where Jack's body would be pushed to the right as I went around the corner. I decided to swim that section to allow Gary or Jim better maneuverability behind me.

Even though we laid off the triggers and swam through the smaller area, we had difficulty. The current pushed Jack's body to the side and made it harder for me to get to the Rabbit Hole and through it. I hit the trigger on my scooter to assist. Either Gary or Jim was behind me struggling to keep Jack's body straight. It took a couple of minutes, but we got through the Rabbit Hole and on our way. Only nineteen hundred feet to go.

I looked at my dive computer display. We had more than an hour of decompression to do before surfacing. I hoped Lindsey had found someone to come into the Deco Room so we could pass the body and not have to hold onto it the entire time. That would be miserable.

Fortunately, the rest of the exit from the cave was uneventful. We had to slow down in a few spots where we encountered restrictions, but they were nothing like the ones we had already passed through. We stopped at the bottom of the chimney fissure and reconfigured things so Jack's body was no longer attached to me. We were less than three hundred feet from the Deco Room. We would ascend up the chimney fissure with Jack between two of us and swim him out through the Rock Garden and into the Deco Room, like Lindsey and I had done after the ceiling collapse.

We had a few mandatory decompression stops in the Rock Garden, but most of it would be spent in the Deco Room. That was the worst part. I wasn't looking forward to spending another hour in the water decompressing. All I wanted to do was surface and collapse into Lindsey's arms.

76

Lindsey

It was getting close to the time when the boys should be arriving in the Deco Room. They had half an hour left, but I was starting to get worried. If there was a body in the cave and it was who I thought it was, this could be stressful for Joey. It wasn't the first time he'd be pulling a body out of a cave, but did it ever get easier? I doubted it.

I heard a car driving over the gravel road at the top of the hill. I looked in the direction of the sound and saw Danny's Corolla turning to drive down to the parking lot behind me. I got up from the diving platform and walked toward it. I got there just as Danny was exiting his car.

"Hey, Lindsey! How are you? I thought you hurt your ankle. You're not limping or anything."

Fuck! I forgot about that little lie.

"I've been sitting out here soaking it in the basin and letting the cool spring water work its magic. You know they say these springs have healing powers."

"Wow! Really? That's so cool!"

I was relieved that he didn't question my lame excuse.

"Who did you find to come out and help the boys?"

"Ummm… I couldn't find anyone. Seems no one is answering their phones this weekend. Strange weekend because we haven't had anyone stop in to fill their tanks or sign in to dive. I don't know what's going on."

"That is strange."

"Yeah, well, since we didn't have nothing going on at the shop anyway, I decided to lock it up and come over to help y'all out. I'll go in and take Jack's body from Joey and them."

"Hold on, Danny! I don't think that's a good idea. You're not a fully trained cave diver. You shouldn't be doing this."

"I'm an intro cave diver. I've been in Jackson Blue a bunch of times. This is just in the cavern of the cave. In the Deco Room, right? I'm not going beyond that. Besides, there's no one else around to do it. What other options do we have?"

I hated to think about Danny going into the cave to bring a dead body out. I worried about the psychological scars it might leave on him. He was young and full of life. He was so optimistic. I didn't want him exposed to this. But he was right. What other options did we have? After everything I read about pregnancy and diving, I was too scared to even go into the cavern. I also didn't have my dive equipment or my drysuit with me. Either Danny would have to do it, or the boys would be stuck in the Deco Room for an hour with a dead body. Neither was ideal, but the boys had been through enough.

"Alright, you make a very good point. But I want you to just go in there and bring the body up to the surface. Don't dawdle. And don't take any unnecessary risks. If the body starts to get away from you, let it go. I'm going to get in the water and wait for you on the surface. I'll be there to take the body from you and get it onto the beach."

"Yes, ma'am."

That was strange. Danny had never called me ma'am before. I guess I did sound kind of bossy just then.

Danny set up his dive equipment and pulled his wetsuit on. I wondered if he was saving up for a drysuit. He was skin and bones and had to be cold diving in the sixty-nine-degree spring water. He was young, though, and still excited enough about diving that he had a lot of adrenaline going to keep him warm.

Just as Danny finished suiting up and was about to jump into the water, I saw bubbles breaking through the surface. I ran to the diving platform above the cave opening and watched the bubbles streaming out of the cave. They were finally back.

"They're in the Deco Room, Danny. Are you ready?"

"I am."

"Okay, remember what I said. Don't put yourself at risk. Take the body from them and bring it to the surface where you're standing if you can. If it's too much to handle, let go of the body. I don't want you getting hurt."

"I'll be fine. I can handle this. Don't worry."

I didn't know if the look on Danny's face was because he was hurt that I didn't think he could handle it or if he was trying to be macho for me. Either way, I worried that he would let ego get in the way of rational thought and end up hurting himself.

"I am worried, Danny. I would never forgive myself if you got hurt from doing something I asked of you."

"I won't do anything stupid. I promise. I won't let you down."

"Stay safe, sweetie."

I watched a big smile appear on Danny's face as he descended below the surface of the water. He put his body into a horizontal position and situated his scuba tanks on his harness. A shiver moved through my body as I watched him move toward the cave opening.

As Danny disappeared into the cave, I ran to the retaining wall and kicked off my flip-flops. I lowered myself into the cold water, chills running up my spine as the water hit my lower back. It was colder than I remembered it being. I walked as close to the cave opening as I could while still keeping my head above water. I wanted to be right there when Danny came out with the body. I wanted to take the body from him immediately.

A few minutes later, I saw a hooded head inside the cave. It was slowly moving toward the opening. A few seconds later, the body emerged with Danny behind it, pushing it out. He was positioned above the body and holding onto the legs. It looked like he was trying to steer the body toward me. I took a few steps back so I could get shallower and more firmly planted on the sandy bottom. I watched as Danny and the body continued to get closer.

When the body was just outside of the cave and about ten feet away from me, Danny fumbled with it. It looked like he was losing control to the strong current coming from the opening. He struggled to hold onto the body. I watched his head turn to face my direction. Danny let go of the body and the current carried it into the eel grass that was growing around the perimeter of the opening. Fortunately, it was also ascending to the surface.

I dove into the water and grabbed one of the arms, pulling it back toward me. Once I had a good grip on it, I forced my feet down toward the bottom and planted them in the sand. I felt the sliminess of the eel grass as it swayed back and forth around my legs. I fought the force of the current, pulling back on the body as hard as I could. I finally got control of it and began walking backwards, pulling it with me. My head was submerged throughout all of this. I needed to get shallow enough to get my face above the surface so I could take a breath.

A few seconds later, my head popped above the surface of the water.

"I'm so sorry, Lindsey! I lost control of it! Are you okay? Did you get hurt?"

"I'm alright, Danny. Just get over here and help me pull her over to the beach."

Danny moved beside me and grabbed the arm on the opposite side. We pulled the body out of the current and into the shallows that were clear of eel grass.

"Let's get these tanks unclipped and some of the weight off."

"Sure thing."

Danny worked on the tank on his side while I worked on the tank on my side. I reached underneath to release the hoses from the power inflators and pulled the regulator hoses from around the back of the neck. Both tanks dropped to the bottom of the basin at the same time.

"Get over by the feet and push while I pull. Alright, Danny?"

"Sure thing."

Danny moved to the feet. He wasn't acting his usual happy self. I was afraid this was going to happen.

"Okay, let's flip her over facing up before we get too shallow. I don't want to drag her face through the sand."

"Sure thing."

We rolled the body over so it was face up. I looked at the face and confirmed my suspicions.

"Umm… Lindsey?"

"What's up, Danny?"

"Why is the water around your legs so dark?"

I looked down and saw the water was not just dark; it was red. Then I noticed a warmth between my legs. I was bleeding.

Epilogue

Joey

The boys and I surfaced more than an hour later. Danny was sitting on the diving platform waiting. A sheriff's deputy stood next to him. I guessed that the body had already been taken to the morgue. I looked around the park for Lindsey. She was nowhere to be seen.

"Danny! Where's Lindsey? Did they already take Jack's body away?"

"Ummm… Let me help you with your scooters, Joey."

I lifted one of the scooters up to Danny.

"Where's Lindsey?"

"Uh… She…she went to the hospital in an ambulance."

"What? What happened? Why did she go to the hospital?"

"She, um, she started bleeding?"

"What do you mean?"

"I don't know. She just started bleeding. I'm sorry."

"Bleeding? Bleeding from where?"

Danny looked away embarrassed.

"Ummm… Down there." He nodded his head down.

"Down there? You mean between her legs???"

"Uh, yeah."

"When did that happen? What was she doing when that happened?"

I handed Danny the other scooter and hurried to get my scuba tanks unclipped from my harness. I had to get out of the water. I had to get to the hospital to check on Lindsey.

"She was in the water waiting to help me with the body. It got away from me as I was ascending. The current was too strong for me to hold onto it. Lindsey dove in to grab the body and pull it back. She got it, and we were moving it toward the beach and Lindsey said to roll her over so we wouldn't drag her face on the bottom. That's when the bleeding started."

"Was she okay? Was there anything else going on? Danny! Tell me what happened!"

"She was fine, Joey. She just started bleeding when she was in the water. By the time they put her in the ambulance, the bleeding had stopped. She told me to tell you not to worry. She said these things happened sometimes. She just wanted to make sure you were okay after bringing the body all that way and having to do such a long deco after handing her over to me."

"Her? What do you mean her? Who are you talking about? That was Jack Johnson!"

"Ummm… No it wasn't. It was some girl. Lindsey said she knew her. Said her name was Kelly. I never met her. Apparently, she was sneaking in here at night. She never signed in at the shop."

I felt like I had been punched in the gut. That was Kelly? She was the one sneaking back there and putting so much line in the cave? I didn't believe Danny. It couldn't have been Kelly. She was clueless when it came to cave diving.

I thought about it. It all started to make sense. All of the questions she asked about what we were doing. All of the interest in the project and pretending to not know anything about cave diving. She was always willing to listen to every detail I told her about my exploration. It was the only thing that made her visits to our apartment tolerable. I had someone I could talk to about the project without worrying about getting scooped.

Except she was a cave diver. She was the one who scooped me. She was the one who had gone beyond the end of my line. She put on a good act. She asked the dumbest questions. It never occurred to me that it was fake. It was a ploy to get information from Lindsey and me.

I even showed her the map I had made. I showed her exactly how to get to the area.

I wondered if the day on day off schedule was really because Kelly had a bitch of a supervisor or if she requested it so she could drive to Marianna every other night to sneak into the park and dive Jackson Blue.

The car! That *was* her car that pulled into the park on Thursday. She lied about that, too. And then threw herself at me. I glanced at the car parked behind the pavilion to my right. It was Kelly's car. How had I missed it? How had I not figured it out?

I looked toward the lot where my car and Jim's truck were parked. Besides Danny's car and the police cruiser, those were the only vehicles parked there. Jack's truck was gone.

"Where was Jack? His truck was here when we arrived this morning."

"He just left a few minutes before you surfaced. When he surfaced last night, he wasn't feeling too good. Said he wasn't feeling well enough to drive. So he called someone he knew and got a ride. He came back a little bit ago to get his truck."

I couldn't believe it. All this time I thought it was Jack or those other guys. It was Kelly all along. That bi…! I stopped my thought. It wasn't cool to think ugly thoughts about the deceased, but I couldn't help myself. She had played me. I wondered if she was really drunk all of those times at our apartment. She always seemed to go to the bathroom with a full bottle and return with an empty one. I wondered if she was drunk Thursday night when she threw herself at me or if that was an act.

I put the last of my scuba tanks on the grass just beyond the retaining wall. Danny had grabbed Gary and Jim's scooters, and they had removed their tanks. I jumped up out of the water and ran to my car. I needed to get to the hospital. I needed to find out what had happened to Lindsey.

A terrible feeling came over me. What if she lost the baby? What if she had a miscarriage? All because Kelly went and got herself killed doing something stupid. If it wasn't for Kelly, Lindsey would never have been in the water and exerting herself physically.

I changed out of my drysuit and undergarments and into my clothes.

"Hey guys, do you mind loading my stuff into your truck and meeting me at the hospital? I have to get to Lindsey. I have to make sure she's okay."

"Yeah, of course. Go on. We'll meet you there in about half an hour." Jim replied.

"Go do what you have to do." Gary added.

"Sir, I'm going to need to get a statement from you before you leave."

"Deputy, can you please follow these guys to the hospital. That was my girlfriend that left in an ambulance earlier. I'm really worried about her."

It was the same deputy that was here Thursday evening when Jack got hurt. He looked at his watch.

"Sure. I'll talk to your friends and then head over there. Just make sure you don't leave the hospital until I talk to you."

"No sir, I won't. Thank you so much!"

I ran to my car and jumped in. I tore out of the parking lot so fast I kicked up gravel and dirt behind me. I didn't care. I had to get to Lindsey. The gate was open so I didn't have to stop. Ten minutes later I pulled into the hospital parking lot. It was full and I had to park on the street. I got out and ran across the grass toward the entrance to the emergency room. I burst through the doors and ran to the check-in desk.

"My girlfriend was brought in here about an hour ago. Lindsey Carter. Can I go in to see her?"

The nurse slowly pecked away at the keyboard with two fingers. I was able to see that she was typing Lindsey's name. It took every bit of self-control to not reach over, grab the keyboard, and type it in myself.

"She's here. I'll call back and let them know you're here. Someone will be out to talk to you soon.”

“Can’t I just go back to her room? Can’t you let me in? She’s pregnant with my baby and she came in bleeding!”

“I’m sorry, sir. Someone will have to bring you back. It shouldn’t be long.”

I wanted to shove the computer monitor off of the desk. I was so frustrated. Instead, I turned around and found an empty seat close to the door with an emergency department sign on it. Maybe I could sneak in the next time the door opened.

I was still waiting for someone to come get me fifteen minutes later when Gary and Jim arrived. The deputy followed shortly after them.

“Have you heard anything yet? Is Lindsey okay? What’s going on?”

“They know I’m here, but I haven’t heard anything. I’m waiting for someone to bring me back to see her.”

“Your friends told me what happened. I’m going to need your driver’s license to add you to my records as a witness.”

“Witness to what? I didn’t witness anything.”

“It’s okay, Joe. He means a witness to finding the body and bringing it out. We already told him the whole story about how we were in there diving and came across the body.”

“Oh.”

I pulled out my license and handed it to the deputy.

“I’ll be right back. I’m gonna walk out to my car to scan this into the computer.”

I had a déjà vu moment back to the time I was driving away from Eddy Spring. Why was this kind of stuff always happening to me? Just then the door to the emergency room opened and a woman wearing scrubs stepped out.

“Joey Simmons.”

I stood up and turned to Gary.

“Get my license back from the deputy. I’m going to go be with Linds.”

“Sure thing. We’ll be here waiting for you.” Gary gave me a hug. Jim stepped in behind him and hugged me too.

"Is Lindsey okay? Did she lose the baby?"

"Follow me and we can discuss it inside.

Thanks for reading *Beyond the End of the Line*!

Please take a moment to leave a review on Amazon. Reviews help provide more exposure to books. The more reviews a book has, the more likely Amazon will be to show it in search results. A simple statement is all that's needed to help boost exposure. But if you're so inclined, a more thorough review is always appreciated. Rob does read the reviews and uses suggestions to help improve his writing. You can find a link to the Amazon listing on the List of Works page at www.RobNeto.com/list-of-works. If for some reason, Amazon rejects your review (they've been doing that lately), please at least leave a star rating.

If you liked this book and want to see more by Rob Neto, please visit www.RobNeto.com for a list of his other books. Rob has drafts of several more books, including four other books beyond this one. Be sure to check out Rob's other award-winning adventure series, *Beneath the Jungle of Cozumel*. The first book, *Connecting the Crowns*, is already available for purchase. In this series, Rob gives a factual account of the cave exploration he has done in Cozumel. You might even recognize some of the scenes from *Beyond Hope* in it. Rob will also be publishing his next adventure series, *The Hidden Rivers of Florida*, based on his explorations in the underwater caves of Florida, soon after this one.

Once you're on the website, make sure to subscribe to the monthly newsletter. Email addresses are not sold or distributed, and you will only receive one email a month to update you on Rob's books and alert you to any exclusive price specials he may have going on. You'll be the first to hear about new series, new books, and to see cover reveals.

See you in the next book!

ABOUT THE AUTHOR

Rob Neto is a cave diver who lives in the Florida panhandle just minutes away from some of his favorite caves, including Jackson Blue. He is a cave explorer and retired cave and technical diving instructor. He spent more than 10 years teaching scuba diving in Arizona and Florida. He is also the author of the book Sidemount Diving The *Almost* Comprehensive Guide, the first comprehensive book about sidemount diving. With almost 300 pages of information and photos, Sidemount Diving is on its 2nd edition and has been translated into Dutch, German and Spanish, and is currently being translated into more languages. Rob published his first novel, *Beyond the Grate,* in July 2023. *Beyond the Grate* was awarded a Silver Award in Suspense Thrillers by the Global Book Awards in September 2023 and has received numerous reviews on Amazon, GoodReads, and Facebook. Rob is already working on the fifth book in the Joey Simmons series, *Beyond the Shadows,* as well as a couple of other books.

Rob is married to his wonderful, supportive wife of 22 years and has a household of furry family members. At the time of this publication his family consisted of four dogs, one inside cat, and several outside cats.

Coming Soon!

Beyond the Shadows

Joey is suffering from post-traumatic stress disorder. Who wouldn't after pulling two dead bodies out from underwater caves. It's so bad that he can't find it in himself to return to the cave where he last encountered a dead body. Then Gary and Jim found a GoPro video camera among the refuse in the Trash Room. They retrieved the camera and headed home eager to see what was on it. They were shocked by the video that was saved on the memory card. What they saw would change their lives forever.

Join Joey and his friends as they push the limits of their underwater cave diving adventures even further when they try to uncover the truth behind the video from the GoPro camera. Will they be successful? Will they find out what really happened? Or will the truth remain forever hidden *Beyond the Shadows*?

1

Joey

I snapped my head around, moving my hand almost as quickly to direct the beam of my dive light toward the corner of the room. Gary and Jim stopped and faced me. They were no longer startled by my sudden movements. They had gotten used to it. I did it at least three times during every dive, usually more. I couldn't help myself.

Finding a dead body inside of an underwater cave can have that effect on someone. I hadn't found just one body. I had found two. The nightmares that began after the second one were even worse than the nightmares after the first. Every time I swam around a corner, I had this overwhelming feeling that I would find another motionless body, devoid of life. And the next time it would be someone I cared about.

After the first body, I didn't think it would happen again. What were the chances of finding a second dead diver in a cave? Yet, it did. I did. Both times I had been the one that had to recover the body and bring it back to the surface. The first time, I was barely two months out of my initial scuba diver training. I hadn't even completed twenty dives. And there I was in an underwater cave, pushing a dead body out to the surface.

I had no choice. I was forced to do it. The person I told threatened me. He said I would be dead next to that body if I didn't do it and keep my mouth shut. I was nineteen years old and didn't know any better. I was afraid to tell anyone else because I was afraid he would make sure to carry out his threat. I had nightmares about that. They lasted a couple of years, maybe three. They were beginning to subside. I was getting over it when I found the second body.

Unlike the first body I found, I expected to find the second body. In fact, I went into the cave looking for it. It was my obligation. I knew the person I was looking for. At least I thought I did. It turned out to be someone else. It was someone I knew, but the circumstances were not what I had anticipated. The nightmares returned, and a year later, they persisted. These were much worse than the ones I had after finding and recovering the first body. I didn't have much hope that these would end.

It wasn't just the nightmares. My dives were affected. I was seeing things. I saw dead bodies beyond the shadows of every dark recess in the cave. There were times that the feeling was so overwhelming I had to signal Gary and Jim, my regular dive buddies, that I was done. It was time to turn around and exit the cave. I couldn't remain there any longer. The feeling was too intense. Sometimes it happened an hour into the dive. Sometimes it happened ten minutes in. Thankfully they understood. They had been with me during the second body recovery.

Even if Gary and Jim hadn't been on that dive, they would have turned the dive on my signal. The first rule of cave diving was that any diver could call any dive at any time for any reason. No questions asked. I was invoking that rule a lot lately. Gary and Jim obliged me every time. They had to be getting tired of it, though. I had no idea how much longer they would tolerate it. They had their own nightmares after our last experience except theirs weren't as bad. I was waiting for the day that the boys no longer wanted to dive with me. I wouldn't blame them. When only about a fourth of the dives we did went as planned, how could I?

I was trying not to let it happen. I was trying to work through my demons. Gary, Jim, and I had a good thing going. I didn't want to lose them as dive buddies or as friends. We met several years earlier outside of Jackson Blue, the head spring to Merritt's Mill Pond in Marianna,

Florida. It was in Jackson County, thus the name Jackson Blue. This was also the cave where we found the second body. The boys and I found we had a lot more in common than cave diving. We were all victims of Jack Johnson's ego. Jack claimed to have rescued all three of us from the bowels of Jackson Blue. Not at the same time. Gary and Jim's incident occurred a few months before mine while they were doing their cave diving training. My incident occurred during a solo dive when I almost ended up dead more than two thousand feet from the cave opening.

Gary and Jim didn't know they were having an incident until Jack showed up. They thought their instructor was putting them through a training drill. I rescued myself and was almost out of the cave when Jack showed up. I could see the daylight penetrating through the cave opening. During both incidents, Jack accompanied us out to the surface and took credit for rescuing us. He fabricated tales about what had happened. He told everyone if it hadn't been for him, we would have all died in the cave. At the time, Jack had been revered by the cave diving community and Gary, Jim, and I were new to cave diving. The cave diving community believed Jack. For a while, anyway.

This common thread bonded us on the day we met. With the exception of one month, Gary, Jim, and I had been cave diving with each other almost every weekend since. The month we didn't dive together happened after Jim's dad had a heart attack followed by emergency open heart surgery. Gary and Jim had been in south Florida visiting Jim's parents after returning from a cruise to the Bahamas. The boys stayed with them to help with Jim's father's recovery.

During that month, I found a previously unexplored area of cave passages in Jackson Blue. I spent half of my time exploring it by myself and the other half exploring it with Lindsey, my girlfriend at the time. Gary and Jim returned home just in time to join me on a dive that scarred us emotionally and psychologically. It was the dive that started the renewed nightmares.

We hadn't been back in that area of the cave since. None of us was ready to go there after what we had seen and what we were forced to do. The exit from that dive was horrible. We didn't realize it during the dive, but after everything had settled, it hit us like a ton of bricks. The nightmares returned. They came at least three times a week. Gary and Jim tried to convince me to return to the area. They said we needed to face our fears. I wasn't ready.

Lindsey had been with me during half of the exploration dives, but she wasn't with us during the dive when we recovered the body. She had just found out that she was pregnant with our child and was no longer able to scuba dive. It would have put the fetus in danger. Lindsey tried to help as much as she could and ended up hurt. She shouldn't have been physically straining herself. She shouldn't have been doing anything. I pushed those thoughts aside. Everything about that day was an emotional roller coaster. I still wasn't over it.

Gary and Jim convinced me to do a simple dive in Jackson Blue a few weeks after the incident. I gave in and met them at the park. It was my first dive since the body recovery. We kept it nice and easy, penetrating the cave eleven hundred feet. Danny, the tank monkey at Cave Masters, was disappointed when we told him. He always wanted to know how far back everyone went. The farther the better in his opinion. Danny wasn't a fully certified cave diver yet. He was working on it. He had just completed his decompression diving training and only had the last step to go. He was beyond excited about it.

Despite Danny's disappointment with our lack of a lengthy penetration, the dive went well. I didn't get as stressed as I thought I would. That was when it started, though. That was when I began thinking I was going to find another body around every corner. After pulling two dead bodies out of two underwater caves, what could I expect?

Gary and Jim convinced me to do a second dive with them the following day. We scootered sixteen hundred feet in and swam the rest of the way to King's Canyon, one of my favorite places in Jackson Blue. The Canyon extended three hundred feet with the opposite end coming out onto the main passage at the nineteen-hundred-foot line marker. I thought it would be okay until we stopped to visit the memorial plaques. We shouldn't have done that.

The three plaques were placed on a shelf in the cave to memorialize three cave divers. One of the divers died near the location of the plaques. A second diver died in Eddy Spring while looking for the body that I had been forced to pull out without telling anyone. I felt guilty about that, which might have been part of the reason for the anxiety. I didn't know who the third plaque was for. I hadn't heard of that diver.

We had always made it a point to stop at the memorial plaques to pay our respects at some point during our dives in Jackson Blue. I didn't think anything of it when Jim shined his light at the shelf. We swam toward them. As we got closer, I saw the top of one of the plaques appear in our light beams. That's when all hell broke loose. Seeing the plaques released the dam of emotions I had been desperately trying to hold back. Seeing the plaques made the memories of the dead bodies I had found in the caves come flooding into my mind. I immediately turned around and raced out of the cave. I didn't signal Gary and Jim. I just left. I haven't been back to Jackson Blue since. I didn't know if I'd ever be able to dive that cave again.

After that dive, Gary expressed his concern about me leaving them without communicating my intentions. I told him I didn't have any control over it. My body just took over. He suggested I take a break from cave diving. He thought it would be good for me to focus on a different activity until the PTSD resolved itself. Jim suggested I see a counselor and talk things out. I couldn't argue with them. I took a short break. It didn't last long.

I couldn't stay away. All I thought about during those few weekends away from the caves were the caves. The nightmares hadn't gotten any less frequent. but I knew I couldn't stop cave diving. I looked into counseling. I couldn't afford it. Even with the money saved from my short cave diving sabbatical, it was too costly. The hourly rates were a lot more than I was spending diving on the weekends. My health insurance didn't cover counseling sessions.

I called Gary and Jim after a few weeks and arranged to meet them the following weekend. I promised I wouldn't leave them in the cave. We went diving. I still saw things beyond the shadows, but I was able to control myself better. We hadn't returned to Jackson Blue, though. We continued to meet every week. Every weekend, Gary and Jim suggested it. Every weekend, I declined. Every weekend, there was at least one dive in which I signaled to turn around before our planned time.

I had to do something about my condition. I was pushing the limits of my friendship with Gary and Jim. I thought it was only a matter of time before they refused to dive with me. They wouldn't stop being my friends, but if we weren't diving together every week, our friendship would suffer. It had suffered during those few short weeks that they were in South Florida.

I didn't want to hold them back any longer, but I didn't know what to do. I was keeping them from doing the dives they wanted to do. I had enough awareness to realize that. I wasn't ready to dive alone, though. I told myself I had to keep cave diving to get through it. I told myself it would eventually get better. I hoped that Gary and Jim would be able to tolerate me long enough for that to happen.

As time passed and we did more dives together, my condition wasn't getting any better. It was actually getting worse. The nightmares were more frequent. I was having more episodes during the dives. I was not only fearful of finding another dead body in the cave. I began to feel like someone was lurking beyond the shadows watching us. Maybe it was the spirit of one of the divers I had found. Maybe it was the spirit of some other cave diver whose life had been lost in the cave we were exploring. Whatever it was, it was freaking me out.

I explained this to Gary and Jim after every dive. They thought I was being paranoid. They didn't see or sense anything. They insisted there was nothing there. It was all in my head. They didn't understand. How could they? They weren't as personally vested in it as I was. During the last body recovery, we went into the cave knowing we were looking for a dead body. We were also going into the cave to look for the body of someone who had wronged me. We were looking for the body of someone who had betrayed my trust and violated all of the unspoken rules of underwater cave exploration. I had discovered the betrayal a week earlier. During that week, it grew and festered and consumed my life. It almost destroyed my relationship with Lindsey. It had done worse than that. I couldn't think about that day.

This was a big part of why Gary and Jim didn't have the post-traumatic stress that I was experiencing. It was their first time encountering a dead body in a cave and there was no personal connection. They didn't know the person and they hadn't been betrayed. They hadn't lost anything. That had to be why they didn't feel the same way. That had to be why they were processing it so differently.

* * *

I held my hand out to the boys, signaling them to hold their positions while I slowly moved my light beam around the area and squinted my eyes to try to see better. Nothing was there. At least nothing that I could see. I peered into the shadows looking for a spot that was darker, a spot where the light wouldn't penetrate. A spot where a body might have been trapped. Still nothing.

I placed my right hand over the beam and blocked the light. Gary and Jim followed suit. They knew the drill. They knew better than to argue with me when I got into this mode. The criticism would come after the dive. They would express their understanding. Then they would try to convince me I was being paranoid. Maybe I was.

I waited for my eyes to adjust to the darkness that enveloped us. A soft glow emanated from the displays of our dive computers. This wasn't the first time I wished we had the option to turn the displays off. I always forgot to rotate the dive computers on my forearms so that they faced away from my face and directed the illumination behind me.

I tried to push the dive computers around, but I couldn't reach the one on my right forearm with my left hand and my right hand was occupied covering my primary dive light. I closed my eyes so I wouldn't blind myself with the sudden burst of light and moved my palm away. I could sense the brightening of my surroundings as the beam attempted to penetrate my eyelids. I squeezed my eyes shut tighter and the darkness took over again, replaced with phosphenes, flashing stars across my visual field. After a few seconds, the stars burned out and I was in total darkness.

I rotated the dive computers so that they were facing away. I knew Gary and Jim were doing the same. They had become accustomed to the routine. I was hoping that rotating the displays would be enough to keep the brightness of the numbers and letters providing data about my current dive from disturbing the darkness in the cave. The displays used LCD rather than LED technology, so they didn't produce much illumination. Unfortunately, in a room devoid of all light, it didn't take much to penetrate the darkness.

I covered the light head again and relaxed my eyelids. I didn't see any light trying to penetrate through. Gary and Jim had already covered their own lights. I opened my eyes and looked around. It was much better with the computer displays facing away. I didn't see anything in the shadows, or rather where the shadows had been. There were no stray emissions of light coming from someone else's dive computers. Someone meaning not Gary or Jim. Those would have been the only possible sources of light. A dive light would have drained its battery after four hours of use. If someone had died in this cave the night before, the battery would have been drained long ago.

I must have imagined it again. My paranoia was getting the best of me. My mind was creating things that weren't there.

I unshielded my dive light again, this time leaving my eyes open, and returned my focus to the passage ahead of us. We were almost at our turning pressure. I had pushed myself during this dive for the sake of my friendship with Gary and Jim. This was the longest I had managed to make it before becoming too freaked out to continue. Maybe it was getting better. Maybe I wouldn't need counseling.

9 781961 612150